HIGHLAND BRIDE

"Are you saying you want a marriage in name only?" Makenna asked.

"I am not a monk, Makenna, nor do I intend to live like one. I am a man who wants sons, and this will be a marriage in every sense of the word," he vowed before claiming her mouth for his own.

The second his lips touched hers, Makenna felt herself responding. His mouth was warm and soft, silently urging her to comply. Half her mind waited for the feeling of wrongness to take over and end this insanity. But it didn't feel wrong. It didn't feel like she was kissing the man who made her curse more in the past twelve months than in all her painful years of training. Colin was teaching her what it was like to be a woman, to kiss like a woman, to feel like a woman. It was incredible, unexpected, and powerful. And Makenna wanted more.

As if they had a will of their own, her arms stole around his neck as her lips parted in a silent plea for him to deepen the kiss. Colin needed no further encouragement. He moved to cradle her head between his hands and urged her to her tiptoes. She complied and he kissed her long and soft and deep, capturing her tongue and drawing it into his own mouth.

Never had a kiss been so satisfying. . . .

Books by Michele Sinclair

THE HIGHLANDER'S BRIDE

TO WED A HIGHLANDER

Published by Zebra Books

To Wed a Highlander

Michele Sinclair

ZEBRA BOOKS
Kensington Publishing Corp.
www.kensingtonbooks.com

ZEBRA BOOKS are published by

Kensington Publishing Corp.
850 Third Avenue
New York, NY 10022

All Kensington titles, imprints, and distributed lines are available at special quantity discounts for bulk purchases for sales promotion, premiums, fund-raising, educational, or institutional use.

Special book excerpts or customized printings can also be created to fit specific needs. For details, write or phone the office of the Kensington Special Sales Manager: Attn. Special Sales Department. Kensington Publishing Corp., 850 Third Avenue, New York, NY 10022. Phone: 1-800-221-2647.

ISBN-13: 978-1-4201-0014-3
ISBN-10: 1-4201-0014-9

First Zebra Mass Market Printing: July 2008

10 9 8 7 6 5 4 3 2 1

Printed in the United States of America

To my mother, Lynda,
who inspired me my whole life.
I owe her much more than this book.
I love and thank you.

Chapter One

Lochlen Castle, Scottish Borders, 1309

"Enough!" bellowed the old laird as he rose stiffly from his chair. His commanding voice belied the weakness of his slow-moving body, as did his brightly lit green eyes. His thick hair, which had once been a dark red, was now a beautiful silver gray barely reaching his shoulders.

Emerald shards of frustration and aggravation lashed out at the two seething figures in his dayroom. Both remained unaffected by his looks of fury. They were too obstinate to realize that his toleration of their mutual detestation had vanished. No longer could they avoid the inevitable.

Alexander clamped his jaws together as a shot of fire coursed through his chest. The pains were becoming more frequent—and more powerful. His time left was limited, and before he died, he vowed his clan would be in the hands of the one man who could ensure its survival.

He glared at the powerful highlander towering motionless near the hearth, and then slid his gaze toward the obstinate redhead across the room. Her jaw was clenched and her hands were clasped behind her back as she paced furiously back and forth across the planked floor. Neither of them was any closer to conceding.

In two strides, Alexander was in front of the hearth and met the fierce gaze of two bright cobalt eyes intense with controlled emotion. Alexander Dunstan knew he was considered a large man by his Lowland peers and had often used his height to intimidate those who had raised his ire. However, the idea of his imposing figure affecting Colin McTiernay was ludicrous. The man was a giant even among Highlanders. And while Alexander would never admit it aloud to anyone, he usually avoided being in situations in which he had to look up at his son-in-law. However, right now, the anger, fear, and frustration boiling in his blood made him oblivious of Colin's towering stature.

"Pride!" Alexander growled. "Aye, your damned, maddening, and unreasonable pride! It prevents you both from accepting what must be." Refusing to wince as the burning pressure in his chest strengthened, he returned to the comfortable, oversized chair situated in the middle of the room.

He sank into the well-worn leather cushions hoping the man he had learned to trust above all others would now trust him. Alexander knew his people disliked outsiders, but he also knew that given time, they would follow and respect the Highlander. Colin was one of those rare men a laird was lucky enough to meet, let alone welcome as family. He was a highly skilled soldier, but even more important, Colin's ability to train and create unbreakable bonds with his men made him an exceptional leader. Loyal, strong, and fair, the Highlander was Alexander's undeniable choice to lead his proud people. But, more than that, Colin was the only one who could save them.

Alexander shifted his gaze to the slim athletic woman with the fiery red mane and flashing clover-green eyes. There was no doubt she was his daughter. Her long, wild, slightly curly hair matched the color of his youth. Her eyes were both proud and compelling, and her unconventional demeanor reflected more of himself than any son he might have had. But, right now, his youngest daughter's willfulness was going to destroy not only her future happiness but also that of everyone and everything she loved.

Makenna Dunstan was not exactly ignoring her father, but whenever the Highlander was in sight, her heart raced and her blood boiled. She stopped pacing, crossed her arms, and stared defiantly at her fate looming over the hearth. She then looked at her father and shook her head firmly no, hoping to exhibit the inflexibility of her decision.

Alexander closed his eyes and after a few moments reopened them. "I love you, *Áille*, but your pride will give you no lasting joy," he cautioned her solemnly.

Makenna increased the grip she had on her arms. Her father's special epithet for her—*most beautiful*—had not masked the seriousness of his comment. He fully expected her to be at the chapel tomorrow, in front of everyone, and do the impossible. She would not bend. She could not bend . . . not on this.

She marched over and knelt by her father's chair. "Your affections will not dissuade me, Father. I openly admit to my pride. It has given me self-respect and a sense of value. And with my *pride*, I can promise you I will never marry *that* overbearing bully of a giant," Makenna huffed, locking eyes with her oversized nemesis. She rose slowly.

"He might have convinced my sister to marry him, but he will *never* convince me."

Colin clutched the timber portion of the hearth's mantel so tightly he could feel the wood begin to give beneath his fingertips. Makenna Dunstan was by far the most infuriating woman in all of Scotland, and despite her impassioned claim, it was *he* who was refusing to marry *her*. "I also have my pride, woman, and it does not include latching myself to a female who refuses to know her place. I want a wife who can maintain a keep, not see it go to ruin as she rides wild on her horse trying to be a man she can never be." Colin's voice was level and soft, but its impact was just as strong as if he roared the words aloud.

He watched as a slim hand calmly smoothed back loose wisps of curly red hair. The action revealed insolent jade pools framed by long dark lashes. The woman was like unrestrained fire, constantly challenging him on everything. It mattered little to her what her father wanted or what her four older sisters encouraged. She had been allowed to indulge in her peculiar interests for too long. She had never learned how to be a woman, let alone a wife.

Makenna refused to turn away from his cold gaze. She would not give him the satisfaction.

Colin was unmistakably a Highlander, and definitely a McTiernay with his giant build, dark brown hair, bright blue eyes, and stubborn jawline. When Colin married her sister, he had entered the Dunstan home and consequently Makenna's life. Within weeks, he had started banning her from the few activities that gave her confidence. Even though she was better at them than most men and had been doing them for years, *he* deemed them unsafe for a woman. Now, for almost two years, she had been forbidden to hunt wild boar or any other beast he deemed to be dangerous. She was never to ride alone, and he had prohibited her from training with his soldiers. One by one, Colin McTiernay had stripped away her favorite pastimes, and all with the blessing of the one person who had previously championed her unusual diversions—her father. She would never marry the dictatorial colossus, tomorrow or any other day.

Makenna released the back of the leather chair, swung around, and begun pacing again. Her father had had enough? Well, she was also done with this conversation. For weeks, she had felt like a caged animal being pressured into a binding agreement that would eventually steal her sanity. Despite her stream of vocal refusals, her father had moved forward inducing her older sisters, Ula and Rona, to plan the wedding. Every local laird had been invited, and most had come. Tomorrow they would all be disappointed.

Makenna took several intakes of breath, determined to maintain her composure. "I cannot do as you ask, Father. I am not ready to pledge myself to any man, but I *especially* won't to this one. Deirdre might have loved him, and I have never fathomed why. I don't disagree that he can lead men and rebuild our battle strength. I will even admit that he should continue to train our soldiers, but I just cannot marry him. I will only make us both miserable, and that cannot be good for anyone, including our clan."

Shocked by her flattering admission of his abilities, Colin was too stunned to do anything more than stare at her. Never before had Makenna acknowledged his skills or supported his efforts to reestablish the Dunstan army. Outside of his soldiers and Alexander, no one had verbally recognized what he had accomplished. He was about to say as much when Alexander indicated with a flicker of his fingers for him to remain silent.

Alexander understood his youngest daughter's reluctance. Marrying a Highlander would be difficult, and promising oneself to a McTiernay would be even harder. Their enormous size, dark looks, and cool blue eyes made even the most composed of men sweat. But marrying the husband of her dead sister? It was a near impossible thing to ask. *Near.*

"I have heard your pleas, Makenna. I have catered to your rebellious ways for too long and now that I require you to act not only for yourself, but for others, you refuse me."

Makenna winced. "Father, it is not for me, but for this clan that I refuse."

Alexander's eyes narrowed and he attacked her declaration. "It is for you. And even your sister, who watches you from above, knows it. Do not pretend otherwise. Accept for once that I know what is best and lean on my judgment. For if you do not, it will be my cousin who decides this clan's fate—as well as your own."

Alexander shifted his focus to Colin. "I have heard your excuses as well." He saw the swift turn of his son-in-law's head and the burning fire smoldering in the cobalt depths of his eyes. The man had complete control of his actions, and though Colin outwardly appeared calm and collected, Alexander knew he was suppressing his instinct to draw blood. Alexander also knew his words had to strike hard to achieve his goal. He had no more time to wait. "Aye, I said excuses, Colin. Deirdre died nine months ago, and she loved you, son, but she would not have wanted you to live this way—constantly driving yourself and the men. You have a decision to make. Keep your pride and return to your Highlands or finish what you started here. Make your choice. You're out of time."

Alexander rotated in his seat and leveled his eyes on his youngest daughter. She stared back undaunted. He had often felt enormous pride in her ability to remain staunch in her convictions. Too many times his delight with her willful behavior had resulted in him giving way to her unorthodox desires. Now she was the only one of his five daughters unmarried. "And you, my *Áille*, keep your pride as well, but learn to be lonely. For one day, possibly very soon, you will no longer have me to applaud your unusual accomplishments. And whom will you have then? You claim you desire no man, but I put forth that what you have always wanted was for someone to accept you, be proud of you, and love you. I have given you this, but still you want more. Someday you will realize that what you seek needs to be offered by a man, a real man, not one of the malleable *ògans* who follow you about professing their awe at your skills. Go and prepare yourself for a sad and solitary life, daughter."

Alexander watched a visibly shaken Makenna absorb his words. More softly, he added, "Colin is right, Makenna. You have little knowledge about being a proper wife, but you could learn." He paused and waited until she looked at him. "What a man seeks most in a wife you have to give in abundance. That I promise. You just must first learn to trust in him and in yourself."

He leaned back against the cushions. "And, Colin, despite your year with my Deirdre, you learned very little about being a good husband. Aye, I know the truth. Remember, she was my firstborn, and I knew her for almost six and twenty years before she finally chose you for a husband. Do you know how many she had turned down before you asked for her hand? Do you know *why* she desired you above all others? Aye, it might have been love, for indeed, she did love you, but she knew even before I did that you could save our people. She waited to marry until she found someone who could do just that. If you choose to leave, her desires for her clan will have been for naught." Alexander watched the deep blue of the Highlander's eyes grow darker.

Colin stood silent for several moments before moving toward the large dark walnut door and pushing it open. He stopped his exit halfway into the passage's outer stone corridor. Gravely, he pivoted and declared quietly, "This isn't what I wanted, Alexander."

Green eyes weakened by pain and loss captured the blue ones of the man Alexander had learned to trust and lean upon. "I know," Alexander replied, "but it has to be. Either you and Makenna marry tomorrow or you leave. Both of you, go now and make peace with your decision."

Alexander closed his eyes and listened to his daughter's light retreating footsteps followed by Colin's heavier ones. Two years ago, when his eldest daughter had announced her decision to marry the second eldest of the famous McTiernays, he never dreamed he would select Colin to be the next laird of his clan. Yet soon after their marriage vows, Alexander knew Colin was the one man who could ensure that his Dunstan lineage continued to grow and be prosperous.

His clan was not ready for another war, and yet despite Edward I's celebrated death, a fight was coming in the shape of his son, England's new king. Located on the Scottish Borders, the Dunstan clan was especially vulnerable. It needed a brilliant leader like Colin, who possessed the rare ability to train raw men into skilled warriors ready for combat.

Makenna, with her unorthodox habits of training with the soldiers, was the only one of his offspring who understood just how depleted the Dunstan forces had become while supporting Wallace's cause. Without McTiernay's leadership and legendary ability to train and build a loyal force, his people would be enveloped by another branch of Dunstans, and his bloodline would fade as if it never was. Makenna would most likely be forced to wed the man designated to run Lochlen Castle, and Colin would be obliged to return north, causing his soldiers to either go with him or disperse. Some would join Robert the Bruce's campaign, but very few would remain loyal to the Dunstans. Most had joined to follow McTiernay, and the majority of them would follow him to the Highlands if he left. Eventually the Dunstans would be no more.

There would be a marriage tomorrow.

There had to be.

Colin marched out of the dayroom and descended the tower's stone spiral staircase. Rounding the last turn, he exited into Lochlen Castle's inner ward and proceeded along the southern curtain wall leading to the inner gate. Named for Malcolm Canmore III, the Canmore and Forfar Towers were two of the castle's most prominent structures.

After the Viking raids, Malcolm III was one of Scotland's first rulers to defy the Norman kings of England reluctant to accept Scottish independence. Malcolm's leadership inspired the construction of many keeps, including Lochlen, named after the small lake located southwest of the castle's town wall. Continually fortified for over two hundred years, Lochlen had been transformed into a small, well-fortified castle nestled between the Lammermuir Hills and the River Dye Water. Seven towers unevenly spaced to fit the rolling contours of the land formed the castle's odd-shaped inner ring. Surrounding the main castle was a thick outer curtain wall connected by intermittent round drum towers situated to protect the two main outer gates.

Colin had intended to continue expanding and securing Lochlen by completing the town wall surrounding the local village. While it would only protect clansmen who made their home behind the stone barrier, the wall would create a place for Dunstans and allies to come and seek refuge when under attack.

With Alexander's decree that he leave, the wall would be completed without him.

Colin's mood darkened with each step. He had been walking among Dunstan clansmen for almost two years and still the men and women scampered like frightened children out of his path. Today was no different as one by one they ceased their occupation and dashed out of view. He knew his black mood was clearly etched on his face, but Colin doubted his expression was the cause behind their fast disappearance. The Lowlanders darted out of sight because of who he was—an unwanted outsider, an undesired future clan leader, and worst of all—a Highlander.

Only one man in sight was brave enough to approach Colin rather than flee. With one brief glance, Dunlop discerned his commander's ill temper and the conversation that had caused it. Wide-shouldered and muscular with thinning brown hair, Dunlop deluded many to believe he was older than a man of five and twenty years. Even Colin had been surprised to learn Dunlop's age when he was first conscripted into the Highlander's burgeoning cluster of men. Soon, though, Dunlop and his best friend, Drake, were true converts, learning much from the Highlander, including how to trust and follow an outsider. Colin in turn had made them both his commanders. In time, Dunlop and Drake learned how to train and then strengthen raw, inexperienced men with the necessary skills to become warriors. It was now their responsibility to observe the ranks and ensure that the skills of every man grew steadily each day.

In order to hide their multiplying numbers, Colin had split his men into two groups. Those ready for combat honed their abilities behind the Lammermuir Hills under Drake's command. A lack of natural passes and the hills' steep gradients, though not especially high, formed a formidable barrier. Consequently, travelers circumvented the area, unaware of the nearby force being trained discreetly. Dunlop worked with the second group, consisting of new and inexperienced recruits, in the Dunstan training fields located east of the town wall in an isolated spot to discourage casual observation.

Colin was well aware that many believed his army consisted of only those men spotted training in the fields. They thought his training slow, his numbers few, and the soldiers unprepared. He did not intend to convince them or anyone else otherwise.

Soon after his arrival, when the army's growth started becoming noticeable, Colin and Alexander decided to keep its true size a secret known only to them and his commanders, Dunlop and Drake. Makenna was the one person Colin suspected might be able to discover the truth. Despite ending her eccentric habit of training and sparring with his men, the willful woman wanted to watch. Very quickly, she would have noticed skilled soldiers disappearing from the training grounds and would have sought him out for answers. Colin had no intentions of giving explanations, especially to where his more advanced soldiers had gone. Consequently, he had forbidden her to come near the grounds, a decision he had paid for many times with loud curses and verbal attacks.

Dunlop turned and fell into step alongside his commander. Walking beneath five raised iron portcullises, they traversed the large inner gatehouse. Entering into the wide outer yard created between the inner and outer curtain walls, they passed the armory. Dunlop took his cue from Colin and only gave a perfunctory nod to the older gentleman standing in the doorway. The action conveyed that Colin's conversation with Laird Dunstan and his daughter had ended even worse than Dunlop had originally surmised. For it was rare that his commander did not stop and greet Camus, a sword smith Colin both respected and called friend.

Colin headed straight toward the stables located against the southwest corner of the outer curtain wall. Dunlop followed but stopped just inside the stable doors. A cold expression filled his commander's face, and he could not discern whether he should leave or stay. Not able to choose, Dunlop waited patiently for instructions as he watched Colin prepare and then mount the monstrous black horse. Despite the beast's size, the animal was quick and nimble and responded to Colin's slightest commands.

Dunlop leaned against the wide door frame and gestured for the stable master to leave. Colin rarely exposed his anger, but in his present mood, it would take very little to antagonize him.

The source of Colin's frustration was not in question, but Dunlop wondered at the exact cause of its current intensity. For the past month, both Colin and Makenna had been steadfast in their convictions not to marry, and the laird had been equally clear about his disappointment. Then again, the pressure to marry was steadily increasing as the stream of visitors continued to arrive at Lochlen for a ceremony that was supposed to happen on the morrow.

Colin sat bareback for a moment staring at the black mane of his horse. Pulling the reins to depart, he realized Dunlop was still calmly standing at the entrance. Lines of frustration deepened along Colin's brows and along his forehead. "Ride with me, Dunlop, but I warn you, I am not prepared to speak of my exchange with Alexander."

Dunlop gave a light shrug in agreement. "Aye. Where do we ride?" he inquired, moving to jump onto his preferred brown stallion.

"We'll follow the river," Colin replied as he urged his black out of the stables and toward the town gate. Once outside, he drove his horse over the green and gold grassy knolls and headed south toward the River Dye Water.

Dunlop assumed Colin would ease the force at which he rode once they reached the river's rocky banks, but Colin just turned east and continued hard beside the water's strong current. Dunlop had begun to wonder if Colin was planning to ride all the way to the North Sea before he finally reduced his speed.

Slowing to a stop, Colin slid off the animal's wet back and stared into the setting sun. The ride had done nothing to end the war raging in his head. Two incompatible options loomed before him, both with unacceptable consequences.

Instinct said to return to the land that spiraled into the sky with frigid cold lochs and men and customs he understood.

Pride required he stay and complete what he had started. Honor was forcing him into doing the unthinkable.

He needed to keep the promise he had made to his lovely wife, Deirdre.

She had been so weak for most of their marriage, but in her last hour, she had suddenly become strong in her desire to have him understand what he needed to do. "My dearest Colin, you have taken such good care of me. I fell in love with you when I first saw you. I will never regret one moment of the time we have shared."

Her voice had been soft, but unusually firm. It scared him. "Don't speak, my *bean sì*. Just conserve your strength and get better," he whispered, clasping her pale, cool fingers as he knelt by her bedside. Fear gripped him. He was going to lose her.

Her hazel eyes smiled at him. "I have been so unfair to you, my Colin, so incredibly unfair, and yet you never wavered."

He kissed her lips lightly and smoothed back the pale gold strands of her hair, fingering their softness. "You have never been unfair to me, Deirdre. I never wanted to marry until I met you, and never once have I had a single regret."

Deirdre reached up and caressed his cheek. "No, I have been selfish, Colin. I was never the wife you needed me to be. I was just lucky to be the one you loved."

"I was lucky to have found you."

She lowered her hand and smiled, shaking her head. "Ah, Colin, you deserve someone who can match your passions, stand by your side when needed, and be a true friend. Until now, I could not be that for you."

"You have always been more than enough for me."

"It is kind of you to say, Colin. You may even believe that, but I know the truth." Deirdre put a finger against his lips, preventing him from arguing. "I needed you, Colin, and you were there for me, but when did you ever need me? I mean *need* me. I know you don't understand, but I pray that someday you will and that you will *need* your wife as much as she needs you."

Colin placed a warm, tender kiss against her palm. "Shhh. You are speaking nonsense. There will be no one else. I want only you, *bean sì*."

Deirdre sighed at his pet name for her. *Fairy woman.*

"For everything that you have given me, I want to give something to you in return." Deirdre took his strong fingers into her own and squeezed them. "Colin, I want you to marry Makenna."

Instinctively, Colin retreated several inches. "Marry Makenna! Are you mad?"

Her eyes danced. "I thought you said I was the sanest of the Dunstan daughters, and Makenna was the crazy one," she chided him softly.

He released her fingers and sat back, running his hand roughly through his hair. "She is! She's wild and crazy and completely without control. She does nothing but argue and fight against everything I do. The woman . . ."

"Makes you come alive. Listen to you. Even now you show more life at the mention of her name than anything I have ever done."

Colin was about to argue that he preferred her quiet nature when Deirdre began to cough. She was failing fast and the last thing he wanted to do was argue with her. He silently vowed to agree with whatever she said.

Deirdre fought to suppress her coughing attack and said firmly, "A marriage to Makenna will protect the clan, and despite what you think, she will make you a *good* wife. And, Colin, when you find yourself falling in love with her, I want you to know that it is a good thing, a wonderful thing, to find love twice. And when you find yourself happy—happier than you ever were with me— know that I am looking down with joy. That it's what I wanted. That above all other things, yours and Makenna's happiness is my last wish."

All these months later, he could still see the look of peace on Deirdre's face after he agreed to consider her request. Even today, he could not fathom why his lovely, gentle wife had thought he could be contented with such an irrepressible creature as her sister.

Colin had buried Deirdre on a cool foggy October morning truly believing her to be his first and last wife. Never did he imagine that nine months later he would be forced into the one thing he vowed never to do again—marry. And in truth, his oath had very little to do with Makenna.

He had been in Ayrshire fighting alongside Robert the Bruce at the Battle of Loudoun Hill when he met Deirdre, who was visiting her sister to celebrate the English's defeat. He thought he had finally found a woman with whom he could enjoy a marriage similar to his parents'. Beautiful as she was, petite, and with a smile that could warm the coldest of nights, Colin believed he and Deirdre would eventually create the unique bond only soul mates shared. Instead, he had watched Deirdre become ill again and again, becoming weaker each time, never able to do anything about it.

"Dunlop?" Colin asked abruptly. The sudden noise startled both his guard and horse.

"Aye, Colin," Dunlop responded after recovering.

"Do you know the laird's cousin? Is Alexander correct in his belief that his cousin would challenge me as laird if I remained unwed to a Dunstan?"

Dunlop took a deep breath and exhaled. So that was where Colin's mind was at . . . the possibilities of continuing his work here without having to marry. "I wish it were not so, but the man would undoubtedly oppose your being laird. Robert Dunstan swore an oath, as did Alexander, that only descendents of their blood would inherit Lochlen. He respects you and the McTiernays, but only if you were to marry and have children with a Dunstan would he support your claim."

Colin recognized the truth of his words. "Who would Robert name?"

Dunlop played with the hair on his chin, the one place it grew in abundance. "I assume you mean who besides Cedric would Robert name as laird," he stated, receiving affirmation by Colin's nod. "Aye, that is the struggle. I doubt there is anyone else. And while Cedric is likeable, he is no leader and definitely no warrior. Another reason why Robert would not interfere if you were married to Alexander's heir."

Colin flexed his fists. Cedric was an agreeable lad, but young and inexperienced. Despite his good intentions, Alexander's clan would collapse at the first sign of any battle—whether with neighboring Lowlanders or the English. Most Dunstan allies were at least a two-days' ride away, and it took time to muster forces and move them. For Alexander's lineage to survive, the Dunstan clan had to be capable of repelling an unexpected attack for several days, if not weeks. Even then, it was risky, as current allies were pledged to Alexander, not Cedric. Only since Colin had taken over the training and continued the fortification of the town wall was the idea of a safe and growing Dunstan clan becoming feasible.

Colin flexed his hands again. He needed more time, the one thing he did not have.

Dunlop grimaced and voiced the dreaded option of marriage. "Colin, I do not envy you or your decision. Makenna is a wild beauty and would be difficult to tame."

Colin felt his jaw clench. "Damn near impossible. And she is no beauty. There is defiance in everything about her, from her unruly red hair to her insolent green eyes."

"Aye, I've seen them, and it's not insolence, but fear you see," Dunlop disagreed, his tone hesitant.

Colin fought from snorting aloud. "Fear? Dunlop, are

you crazed? That woman fears nothing, no one. Even when she should."

Dunlop shook his head. It was dangerous to counter Colin, but it was important that his friend understood Makenna—especially if they were to wed. "Nay, she fears anything she cannot do well, including marriage. And she definitely *is* a beauty. Unconventional maybe, but unquestionably bonnie, especially when she leaves her hair unbraided. Many men think so, including Laird MacCuaig. It is rumored that he has more than once tried to convince her to marry him. She is probably the only person in the world more against the concept of matrimony than you."

Colin looked at the departing sun and twisted the dark mane of his horse in his fingers and easily swung onto its back. "She will have to get over it, then."

Dunlop moved toward his own mount. "You have made your decision?"

"I have. Ride and inform Laird Dunstan to find his daughter. We wed tomorrow."

"Aye," Dunlop answered, swinging onto the brown stallion. "Are you riding on?"

Colin nodded woodenly, still digesting his decision. "I'll tell the men later. Right now, I need to think." And thinking meant a long, cold swim.

Makenna took a step toward the edge of the small loch her home was named after and dipped her bare foot beneath the surface to test the temperature of its hidden depths. Despite the early summer's warmth, the water was still cool.

It was late and the dark night sky would blanket her path home, but at least she was finally alone. It had been difficult to elude the two guards Colin had ordered to watch her whenever she ventured outside Lochlen. At first, it had been easy to sneak by them, but they had learned her tricks faster than she could devise new ones. She had to be especially clever upon her return or yet another pathway to freedom would be stymied.

She yanked her red and green bliaut over her head and threw it on a nearby tree branch. Her off-white chainse immediately followed. "It's unfair!" she yelled at no one. "Of all the people in this world forced to marry, it should not be me. Father could have no doubts that I would make the worst wife. Colin certainly has none. Then what do I care what that man thinks? The only thing more intolerable than Colin McTiernay is being Lady McTiernay," Makenna said, shuddering at the idea.

Her older sisters had chided her for years about her tendency of talking out loud to herself, but like most of their criticisms, it had fallen on deaf ears. Makenna had told them it was an unbreakable habit. It was other people's burden, not hers. But, in truth, she hated being an annoyance or a millstone to anyone, almost as much as she hated to fail.

Makenna stripped off her last piece of clothing and without hesitation, dove into the cold waters. She held her breath and waited for her body to adapt to the icy sensation against her bare skin. When her lungs could stand no more, she broke through the surface and took in a deep breath. The cold was near unbearable, but the silence and the lack of company were worth the self-inflicted torture. Tonight, however, the numbing benefits of the loch could not remove the sting of her failure.

Lochlen Castle was slowly falling apart. During the first few months after Deirdre's death, life had progressed normally. Chores were done, linens were cleaned, and baths were drawn. Then for some inexplicable reason, random everyday activities had ceased. From the critical steward's constant looks of expectation and disappointment, she knew it was because of her. So many times she wanted to ask him what to do, but refrained at the last moment as memories of her failing even the most mundane female disciplines filled her head.

"And that is why I just cannot marry anyone. I don't know *how* to be a wife, let alone a *laird's wife*. Why, Lord? Why wasn't I born a boy?" she cried out in anguish.

Makenna stroked the water, focusing on the feel of the rippling water against her nude frame now moderately acclimated to the cool temperature. Since she was a child, she had deliberately avoiding any domestic endeavor, instead focusing on exciting activities such as hunting, riding, and swordplay. Those times she had been cornered by one of her four sisters into some keep endeavor, she had failed miserably. "Why is it that everyone wants what I cannot give and forbids what I can?" she sighed aloud and maneuvered to the large rock that jutted out from the water's surface almost forty feet from the shoreline.

Deirdre had been the one to show her this small secluded spot and had taken her here as a child to go swimming. Deirdre would never go in, but she would watch as Makenna frolicked in the water. Later, it became a place for them to talk, just them—no one else.

People, especially her father and later Colin, were so careful around Deirdre. They never raised their voice or challenged her on anything. Deirdre said she hated it, but Makenna, who did not feel inhibited by her sister's frailty, challenged the avowal. "You love it, Deirdre. You know you do. Everyone caters to your whims. Think how much it would bother you if someone actually challenged or refused one of your requests. If you were honest, you would not deny this."

"If I did make such a confession, then I would only do

so to you. You keep me grounded, Makenna. Without your honesty, I should be lost."

"Then I shall supply it forever. Besides, without you, I would be doomed for perpetual sorrow. For I know it is you who ran interference with that hulking husband of yours and got his permission for me to ride and hunt again."

"I am sorry Colin would not also let you train with his men. It was your most favorite of loves."

"I'll take what I can get. I just wish you would ride with me."

Deirdre shook her head daintily. "Not for me. I'll leave that lively activity for you. I'm perfectly happy running Lochlen."

"Thank the Lord," Makenna murmured aloud.

"You should be thanking your luck that Father Renoir decided to return to France. If he heard your language of late, you would spend all your hours in repentance."

Makenna headed for the shore. "I'm glad he's gone. If it weren't your husband nagging me on this and the other, it was Father Renoir. Both men are completely impossible to please."

"If you knew Colin better, I think you would like him . . . a lot. He's a great deal like you. All fire and passion. I often think he would be happier married to someone with your zest and energy."

"Ha! He's your husband, not mine," Makenna said, rising from the waters. "I choose never to marry."

Deirdre threw Makenna a cloth. "Not even to Laird Mac-Cuaig?" Deirdre asked mischievously. "I understand that he has been after Father for your hand for some time."

Makenna faked a shudder and continued drying her legs. "Especially not to him. He's . . . I don't know, but he is . . . something. I don't trust him."

Deirdre hopped off the low-lying limb. "Then neither

do I. I trust your instincts, Makenna. I wish you would trust mine about Colin. He really is a wonderful man. No woman could ask for a better husband."

The memories of her sister were so strong Makenna could still feel Deirdre's presence, even all these months later.

Makenna squeezed her eyes tightly together. If she did marry Colin, they would both be miserable regardless of her sister's fervent deathbed pleas otherwise. Deirdre had been graceful, petite, fair, soft-spoken, and mild-mannered. *She* was what Colin desired for a spouse, not her.

Makenna opened her eyes and peered over the semislick rock to study the other side of the slim oval-shaped loch. The opposite shoreline was a good distance away, but she knew instantly she was alone.

More than once, she had seen Colin use the grassy banks across from her secluded rocks as an entrance to the peace and cold the loch provided. She was positive he had never been aware of her presence. He was too focused when he swam, vigorously stroking the cool water as if he were trying to drive out a demon. She had watched in secret fascination.

He was big and powerful and proud. There was no mistaking him for a Lowlander. Everything about Colin, from his stance, to his walk, to his all-around demeanor exposed his Highlander origins. He was arrogant and overbearing, but he moved beautifully. She had never seen a man with such control over everything he did. Though she would never admit it, even to Deirdre if she were still alive, Makenna had often wished to find someone with Colin's self-discipline, muscular body, and ability to lead.

Never, however, did she wish it to be Colin McTiernay. "No, I want someone who will love me, not dominate me. I want someone I can trust, who will trust me in return. Forgive me, Lord, but, *damn you, Colin McTier-nay!*" she shouted before dropping down into the water and swimming underneath its surface to the shore.

Colin came to an immediate halt. He had debated on jumping into the cold retreat, but at the last moment, he had changed his mind. Instead, he had dismounted his horse and led it around the small loch knowing each step brought him closer to Lochlen . . . and his fate. He had no doubt Makenna's reaction had been explosive when Dunlop relayed his decision. She was most likely pacing in front of the outer gate preparing to spring a stream of arguments upon him.

Colin swallowed heavily. If he dreaded returning home now, how could he bear living with her . . . being married to her? The question was still ringing in his head when he heard the splashing and unintelligible mutterings of a female.

Colin moved into the shadows, welcoming the diversion, curious to discover who was foolish enough to swim alone and in the dark. A second later, he knew the identity of the fool. The familiar hiss followed by a "Damn you, Colin McTiernay!" left no doubt as to who the night swimmer was—Makenna.

Shaking his head in exasperation, Colin tied his horse to a nearby branch and turned to reprimand her for once again ditching her guards. Before he could utter a word, he was struck dumb and immobile.

Unaware of Colin's presence, Makenna rose out of the water completely nude. She threw her head back to wring out her hair. The action thrust her pale breasts upward. Colin watched unable to breathe as the droplets of water slid down the curvature of each full swell to her navel and then lower.

The cresting moon provided just enough light to reveal a level of female perfection he had not realized was possible until now. Colin knew he should move, say something to let Makenna know he was there, but he was finding it difficult to breathe, let alone speak. Instead, he stared transfixed and became, for the first time since he could remember, unmistakably—and worse— *uncontrollably* aroused.

The concept was inconceivable. He had always been able to contain his passions. He could blame the unexpected reaction on his empty bed. He could claim that seeing any naked woman would make him hard with need, but it would not be the truth. Makenna Dunstan was incredibly beautiful.

Her face, no longer hidden by her mass of fiery hair, revealed delicate facial bones and a full mouth. Her skin was the color of pale cream mixed with a bare pink tint. Long, wet tendrils fell behind her shoulders down to the middle of her back, softening her athletic appearance. For the first time, Colin could see both her strength and her femininity. Makenna was not a fragile, ethereal fairy creature, but a woman made for a man.

Makenna reached for her chainse and pulled it on. The worn cloth clung to her wet skin. Knowing now what secrets it hid, Colin wanted to reach out and rip the gown off her. He wanted to touch her skin and discover if it was as soft as it looked from the shadows.

Colin leaned back against the tree trunk and forced himself to take a deep breath. He had no idea what was happening, but he had to stop it. There was one sure way to end this violent need coursing through him and that was just to talk to her. Makenna could drive a man to the brink of insanity faster than anyone. Surely, three words from her and the world would be righted again. He opened his eyes and moved out from the shadows.

Makenna was wrapping the gold belt of her bliaut around her waist when she heard the crack of a twig break beneath someone's foot. "Who goes there?"

"It is I, Makenna," Colin said softly, emerging halfway out of the trees. He was waiting for his body to calm, but the fire in his loins seemed to grow only hotter when her eyes found his. Independence, strength, and passion shimmered in the bright emerald depths.

Makenna was startled by Colin's sudden appearance and low voice. He was half in the shadows, but she could still see his muscles rippling beneath his leine. The very way he stood was unlike any other man. She had never met anyone who was so at ease with himself as Colin McTiernay. Still, she always sensed he felt alone. He had the unswerving loyalty of his men, yet he never seemed to be one of them. Colin remained emotionally distant—even with his commanders.

She doubted anyone saw or even cared how isolated he was. Colin towered over everyone. He was undoubtedly the most skilled warrior his men had ever met. He exuded unbelievable strength just by his sheer size. Yet his blue eyes reflected a kind of lonesomeness she expected few saw.

Makenna suddenly realized she was staring at him. Pride immediately lashed out before he would realize the nature of her thoughts. "Decided to follow me yourself tonight, did you, McTiernay?"

Colin had thought for one moment they were going to have a real conversation, or at least a civil one. Her eyes had revealed concern and a longing for something right before they turned bright with indignation. The woman was a mixture of emotions, most of them incredibly exasperating. "No, it was by sheer accident I stumbled upon you still dripping from the loch," he contended, pointing at her wet tresses. "Where are Gorten and Brodie?"

"Where do you think?" she retorted, jutting out her chin and placing her fists on her hips.

Colin rolled his eyes at her childish stance and waved his finger at her pose. "I think you find enjoyment in doing whatever I ask you not to do."

"Not everything, McTiernay. But I admit to a wee amount of pleasure when I can rid myself of the two overseers you charged to ruin my life."

"I did not realize that keeping you safe and well was contrary to your future plans."

She took a step forward and replied through stiff lips, "My safety was never an issue before you arrived."

Colin took a step even closer. "The Dunstans were never a threat to anyone till I arrived."

"I've seen your army, Colin. We're still no threat."

Colin felt a muscle in his jaw flicker angrily. "If you knew me before I . . ." He paused and took three deep breaths. The woman was baiting him, and he was reacting to her gibes. "You should realize the folly of such assumptions. If you did, you would have made damn sure Gorten and Brodie were with you tonight."

He had stopped himself, but Makenna knew exactly what Colin had been about to say. "*Before I married your sister.*" It only proved once again that she was right to refuse her father and remain unwed. A marriage was between two people, not three. And Deirdre would always be there. She was Colin's first wife, her best friend, and their only commonality.

"I doubt your men wanted to go swimming with me."

Makenna Dunstan could try a saint. Before Colin realized it, he was shouting at her. "If you want to swim, tell me, and I'll take you."

"*Never*, McTiernay," she hissed. "I'll not have you or your men hanging about while I'm unclothed. I'll ride with your men, I'll even hunt with them, but I'll be damned if I *swim with them*!"

"*Mo Chreach*! My commands are not requests that you can choose to follow or disregard. Gorten and Brodie are to be with you each and every time you venture outside the town wall, and if I hear of you leaving again without them as escorts, *amaid*, you won't be leaving at all."

Makenna's eyes flashed with fury. She could not choose which angered her the most, his command that she be followed about, his threat to confine her if she disobeyed, or that he had just called her a foolish woman. But, foolish or not, she recognized the seriousness of Colin's threats. He meant them. He truly thought her to be unsafe alone in the lands and waters she had known her entire life. Even worse, if he believed her to be unsafe, so would her father. There would be no reprieve.

"Fine. They will be aware of whenever I leave, but they will have to keep up. I refuse to slow for your men."

Colin closed the distance between them with one last stride and clutched her arm before she could retreat. "I want your word, Makenna. You will tell Gorten *and* Brodie each and every time you leave the town walls."

His grip was strong, but not painful. It was meant to secure, not harm. Only by struggling would she hurt herself. The concept that he could both render her helpless and be in control of her fate was maddening. Makenna was tempted to stand silent and wait him out, but one look into his deep blue depths, she knew that despite her stubbornness, he would win the battle. "You have it," she whispered.

Colin immediately let go, knowing her pride would bind her to the promise more than any threat he could make. With Alexander's failing health, there was great debate over the fate of Lochlen and its people. Many neighboring lairds were here to witness a marriage and decide if the Highlander was to be called friend or enemy. They came with small armies, poised not only to protect but also to attack.

If Makenna Dunstan were captured, a battle for her release would follow, and Colin would lose a critical advantage. He needed to keep the size of his army a secret until he knew whom he would call ally and foe as the new Dunstan laird. As such, he would protect anything, or anyone, who could be used as leverage against him. And if that meant caging the exotic wild creature, he would.

Colin had chosen Gorten and Brodie to be Makenna's escorts with extreme care. Both were masters in all of her fields of comfort. Expert horsemen, they could ride, hunt, and if necessary disarm her if she decided to draw her sword against them. He doubted she would. Makenna was foolish, but not unintelligent.

"I assume by making me swear this oath it means you've decided to stay," Makenna said, her voice fading into hushed stillness.

Colin answered with a single nod.

"It's a mistake, McTiernay. You and I will never work. Hasn't the last few minutes proven that? I know you don't like the Lowlands. How could you? My people treat you horribly. They don't deserve you or what you could bring them. I don't understand why you don't leave. No one would think less of you."

Colin was taken aback by her statement. Not one person, including Alexander and Deirdre, had ever acknowledged the poor behavior of the Dunstans. "I would think less of me, Makenna. Honor demands that I stay."

"Nay, it is your pride that makes you resist what you know you should do. You hate it here. You have to," she said softly, pleading for him to agree. Instead, he shook his head.

"Actually, I love Scotland—all of it. And these Lowlands protect my Highland mountains. I stay because I want to, Makenna," he gently countered, watching her wring her hands in frustration . . . or maybe it was panic.

Stripped as she was of her haughty demeanor, Colin could see that Dunlop had been correct. Makenna was indeed afraid. Until now, Colin had not realized how much the idea of marriage frightened her. Gone was the snippy female who verbally attacked him whenever possible. In her place was a panic-filled woman who kept looking at him with large liquid-green eyes that begged him to change his mind.

Colin was about to pull her into his arms and whisper it would be all right, that she had nothing to fear, when Makenna tried one last plea for a reprieve. "If you marry me, you will grow to hate this land you now claim to love. I tell you the truth," she said, stepping backward until she bumped into a tree. "I would be a horrible wife for any man. I have no knowledge about running a home, let alone a keep the size of Lochlen. My knowledge of men is limited to what they can do with an axe and a broadsword, and no matter how hard I would try, I could never be the kind, gentle beauty Deirdre was." Makenna had barely spoken the last words when she found herself pinned between his two hands and the tree.

Hearing Makenna say that she would try and fail to be Deirdre caused a reaction in Colin he couldn't explain. It was incredibly important that she *not* be like his late wife. "Listen to me now, Makenna. I don't expect you to be, nor do I want you to *try* to be, Deirdre. She was my wife, and she is now dead."

Makenna gulped. His face was mere inches away from

hers. His blue eyes blazed with an intensity that reinforced his every word. Suddenly, her eyes popped open and became large with hope. "Are you saying you want a marriage in name only?"

Colin could feel the quick rise and fall of her handsized breasts. Just one more inch closer and he would feel her slim hips against his. She licked her full lips and Colin knew that he wanted to taste them, pull at them, devour them. No, this would not be a marriage in name only. "I am not a monk, Makenna, nor do I intend to live like one. I am a man who wants sons, and this will be a marriage in every sense of the word," he vowed before claiming her mouth for his own.

The second his lips touched hers Makenna felt herself responding. His mouth was warm and soft, silently urging her to comply. Half her mind waited for the feeling of wrongness to take over and end this insanity. But it didn't feel wrong. It didn't feel like she was kissing the man who made her curse more in the past twelve months than in all her painful years of training. Colin was teaching her what it was like to be a woman, to kiss like a woman, to feel like a woman. It was incredible, unexpected, and powerful. And Makenna wanted more.

As if they had a will of their own, her arms stole around his neck as her lips parted in a silent plea for him to deepen the kiss. Colin needed no further encouragement. He moved to cradle her head between his hands and urged her to her tiptoes. She complied, and he kissed her long and soft and deep, capturing her tongue and drawing it into his own mouth. Never had a kiss been so satisfying.

Makenna's untutored passion was unmatched by any woman he had ever touched. Her fiery nature made him desire her more than he dreamed possible. Was it because she was so different from Deirdre? His late wife had been too fragile for the passion and heat of desire. Whatever the reason, he no longer cared.

Makenna had been kissed, but never like this. Oh, Leon MacCuaig had tried often enough and every once in a while landed a lucky peck, but he had no idea how to touch a woman and cause her to burn up in flames. Colin was creating sensations and reactions she couldn't explain. Her body was quivering, and at any moment, her legs would give beneath her. She clutched his shoulders, afraid that if she fell, the spell would be gone.

Deep inside her, something had recognized and then responded to the masculine need in him. It wasn't just a physical need, but a connection. A commonality beyond that of her sister. It was two lonely souls finding one another in a storm of passion and need.

Colin nipped at her lips before plunging again into the warmth of her mouth, seeking her tongue. She welcomed every stroke, every caress with equally surprising passion. Makenna clung to him in confusion and desire. He could feel her tremble and pulled her close to keep her from falling. He was not ready to end this unexpected gift she was giving him.

Makenna was sharing a piece of herself she had shared with no man. Colin felt both satisfaction and fulfillment, knowing he was the first to discover the passions that lay beneath her prickly demeanor. It would be worth enduring a hundred verbal wars with her to experience this again.

Makenna moved closer, clinging to him as if her body knew there was more. Colin's heart was pounding so fast he thought it would explode. Every caress, every response she gave him was genuine, unrehearsed, *unforced*. She wanted him; he wanted her. Badly. So much that if he did not stop now, he wouldn't be able to.

When he finally forced his lips to release hers, his

chest was heaving with the effort it took to breathe. He gathered her close against him and thrust his fingers through her thick damp hair.

A deep sigh escaped her slightly swollen lips. She could feel his dark body hair beneath her cheek in the opening of his leine and decided she never wanted to move. He smelled so good, and it felt strangely right to be this close to him. Tomorrow she would wonder why she had been drawn to his embrace, and if she had only imagined the powerful emotions hidden beneath Colin's cool exterior. But for right now, she just wanted to relish his strength and control and the intoxicating effect of his kisses.

Colin held her for several minutes waiting for his body to calm. Instead, every muscle remained alive with need. She had to leave and quickly, before he lost the control he took such pride in having. "Be at the chapel an hour before the sun sets. Tomorrow we will be wed," he ordered gruffly, moving her away from him.

Colin quickly turned around lest she see his burgeoning manhood. Cold water was his only hope in dampening the fires she had ignited with her honest response to his embrace. Even with his back to her, he could still see the memory of her naked flesh as she emerged dripping with lucky droplets of water that touched every morsel of her body.

He dove into the cold waters thankful for their magical cure, but he knew it was only temporary. Later, as he sought sleep, he would remember her taste on his tongue—hot, wet, and sweet. Thank God, he only had to wait one night. Makenna would be his wife on the morrow and as soon as possible afterward, he was going to make love to her until all the needs pulsing through him were satisfied.

Makenna stood puzzled and hurt, staring at his retreating back for several minutes. After all his talk about running around unescorted, the man was actually going to leave her to ride back to Lochlen alone while he took a *swim*. The kiss was just a way for him to manipulate her into abiding his will.

She found her brown chestnut tied beside his large black mount and jumped on its back. She looked at the vacant spot from which Colin disappeared and uttered aloud, "You may be able to kiss, Colin McTiernay, but you're still an overgrown giant. And you may be getting a wife tomorrow, but that doesn't mean I will suddenly submit to you or your archaic rules. I *will* ride, and I *will* hunt, and I *will* keep training with a sword. And you can find someone else to run your keep and warm your bed."

Makenna turned her horse and began riding hard back to the noise and firelight of Lochlen. Tears flowed down her cheeks. "What were you thinking, Deirdre?"

Chapter Two

Makenna felt like her mind had temporarily dislodged from her body. From the moment she had woken up, the noise in her chambers had only grown in volume. Her sisters, Rona and Ula, had ordered everyone to report to them, and they had claimed the bride's room as their base of operations. Nonstop orders were issued to a constant stream of people shuffling in and out of her room. After years of watching her sisters orchestrate every clan event whether large or small, Makenna knew the role she was expected to play—silent and unseen. It seemed her wedding day was to be no different.

"There," Rona announced with a dramatic sigh, rising to close the door. "I believe everyone is ready but you, Makenna. I am not sure how you would have managed if Ula and I had not been so willing to sacrifice our time away from our own homes."

With her tall, elegant frame and enviable blond hair, Rona epitomized the Dunstan daughters and she had never let Makenna forget how incredibly different she was from the rest of them.

Makenna glanced at her sister before turning away to

roll her eyes. "It's the least you could do after barging into my room," Makenna mumbled to herself. "The sun had barely risen before I had to deal with you and Ula's never-ending chatter about every little thing from my hair to my dress."

Makenna knew she should have expected her sisters' early morning greeting. In an effort to gain their father's favor—and some of his riches—Ula and Rona had arrived at Lochlen over a month ago to ensure that the wedding went off as planned. Brimming with never-ending criticism about the feast, the ceremony, her dress, and even the priest presiding over the nuptials, they had been nearly intolerable. Throughout it all, Makenna had remained firm. There was going to be no wedding, so it was not necessary for anyone to make plans.

Until last night.

As usual during warm summer days, Makenna had opened the window's shutters and let in the cool night breeze. Normally, such conditions lulled her quickly to sleep, but after Colin's unexpected kiss and her bewildering response, rest had eluded her. Every sound, every whisper seemed to float up and into her room. She had not realized she had been waiting for Colin until she heard the fateful signs of his return.

The soldiers were just beginning to leave the lower hall for their beds when she heard the fleeing of clansmen feet outside her window. She sat up and listened intently for Colin's footsteps to follow. She could hear nothing. The man walked with a purpose and with complete control. He probably hadn't even shuffled his feet as a child.

Snuggling back under the covers, Makenna heard a jubilant roar coming from the lower hall. Colin had announced his decision.

"Those *tolla-thons* think it's all him. Well, somebody

should thank me as well. It's not just their commander sacrificing himself for them. I believe I, too, will be at that altar pledging my life away," she muttered out loud, ripping the light woolen throw off her legs.

Makenna grabbed the Dunstan plaid off the bed and wrapped it around her. The bold red material with bright stripes of yellow, green, and blue clashed terribly with her dark red hair, but it represented all that she loved.

She tiptoed to the heavy wooden door and lifted the latch quietly in case a servant was sleeping outside her door. It was unlikely. She hadn't had help for months. One day the girl had simply vanished. Left to fend for herself, Makenna soon discovered how much the chambermaids had assisted her with everyday things. Pride kept her from asking the old steward why they had suddenly left. No doubt he would just point a long, crooked finger directly back at her. The man was an expert at assigning responsibility, accountability, and then blame, but he never managed a word of encouragement.

Makenna crept down the hallway to the tower stairwell illuminated with torches at each floor. Her sisters were just below, but she did not intend to sneak past their chambers. She was going up.

Since Forfar Tower's erection, the laird's sons and daughters resided in its walls. Its counterpart, Canmore, housed the laird's solar and his connecting dayroom. Standing on either end of the fortified gatehouse, the towers secured the interior castle ward. Makenna's great-grandfather decided Lochlen's inner yard was not large enough to handle the clan's growing numbers and had ordered a second curtain wall to be built. The resulting enormous outer gatehouse towers provided the sleeping accommodations for most of the soldiers when assigned to Lochlen. This left the upper floors of the inner gatehouse for visitors and other people of importance, and the lower floors for storage, guards, and machinery to operate the portcullis.

Makenna entered the spiraling stairwell just as another euphoric burst erupted. Loud indiscernible shouts were now coming from both halls. Makenna wondered if there was anyone still protecting Lochlen. It sounded as if every soldier had joined the merriment below.

Holding on to the rope suspended down the center of the stairwell, she climbed the two stories from her third-floor chambers to the tower battlements. Lochlen's spacious fighting platforms provided good vantage points to launch arrows at attackers, but they were also superb spots for watching people undetected.

As soon as Makenna took a step out into the night air, she saw the hulking figure of her guard. Through the crenels, she could see the shadows of other soldiers still at their posts. The number of men on duty might be slightly lower than normal, but every tower and section of the inner and outer curtain walls was manned.

Brodie had heard someone coming up the stairwell and moved to intercept. Never did he dream it would be Makenna. Just minutes ago, Colin had cornered him and Gorten, ordering them to the towers. He was furious with them. Brodie didn't want to discover what levels his commander's anger would grow to if he found him with Makenna wrapped in a blanket and dressed only in her chemise. "Milady," he acknowledged hesitantly.

Makenna arched her eyebrows. Brodie had bright yellow hair many women considered quite attractive. He was of medium height, and so thick with muscles he appeared to be chubby from a distance. Normally, the good-natured guard was full of so much self-confidence it was nauseating. Right now he seemed perplexed . . . even nervous. "What bothers you, Brodie? My state of dress?"

Brodie's brown eyes widened in alarm. "If the commander knew you were here . . . with me . . . like that, milady, he would be very unhappy. And I would appreciate avoiding any more circumstances that might result in my being the target of his ire."

"*More* circumstances? Did Colin lecture you about my abandoning you for a brief swim?"

Brodie rolled his eyes and swallowed a snort. He looked over the wall at the drinking comrades he would have been with and snapped, "Why do you think I have night duty, milady? And will have it for the next fortnight."

"Good Lord, I assure you I had no intention of getting you or Gorten in trouble. Where is Gorten? Or did he escape the wrath of the almighty Colin?"

Brodie pointed to the top of Canmore Tower in the distance. The large shadow pacing the top was her second victim. Makenna felt instantly ashamed. "I'm so sorry. I will talk to Colin and end this ridiculous punishment."

Brodie shuddered. "Please do not do that, milady. You do not know our commander as we do. I'd like to keep what little pride I have left, and I'm sure Gorten feels the same."

Makenna yielded with a slight nod. It would only shame the large guard, and it would put Colin in an awkward position. Ego would keep him from rescinding the order, and possibly even increase the length of Brodie's and Gorten's sentences. A fate caused by her own self-interest. "I really had no idea Colin was so intent upon this . . . this protection. I don't want it, nor do I need it." She could see Brodie about to protest and put her hand up to stop him. "But I swore an oath to His High-handedness this evening that I will let you know when I am leaving the keep from now on."

"Gorten and I thank you enormously, milady."

Makenna pulled the blanket tighter around her. Brodie was not such a bad fellow. He still needed to gain the control and posture that made a man truly attractive, but he was kind, sweet, and in many ways very handsome. "Hmmm, well, it is not your fault to have such an awful duty. I know I can be quite a chore, and it must be miserable following someone about all day. I know I could never endure such an assignment."

Brodie laughed. "I must admit Gorten and I dreaded it when the order came. And while nights like these are not enjoyable, we have grown to take pleasure in joining you when you leave. You are truly unlike any woman we have ever known. Gorten says you are quite good with the sword."

Makenna's head whipped around. "He told you? That was supposed to be our secret. If Colin ever discovered that I have continued sparring with *anyone* . . . well, I have no idea what he would do, but I am sure Gorten and I would be the two most miserable creatures in all of Scotland when he was through."

"Truer words were never said, milady. However, you must be very good for Gorten to give you a compliment and continue risking potential misery for you. Still, having never seen you fight, I find it hard to believe *you* can wield a claymore with as much accuracy as Gorten professes."

Makenna leaned against one of the large stone crenations and looked out at the Dunstan village spreading outside the second curtain wall. "It's my Secret."

Brodie's eyebrows rose inquiringly. "Your secret, milady?"

"Aye, my Secret. A special blade Camus fashioned specifically for me. He's the one who convinced Father I could and even should learn the art of combat . . . that is, until someone unconvinced him," she bristled.

"You refer to the commander now."

"Indeed I do," she whispered, watching the late night activity of her clansmen and women. Body language alone told her that the euphoric voices she heard inside the walls did not match those of the shadows moving in the village. The few faces she could make out were mostly grim, and none were smiling. No, the soldiers might be overjoyed their commander was to remain with them and eventually become their laird, but her clan was not of the same mind.

"I should leave you before Colin wonders why there are two bodies up here and decides to abandon the party to investigate."

Brodie moved out of the way to give her access back down the stairwell. "Thank you, milady; however, the commander has already retired for the evening."

Makenna paused after descending one step. "He did? I thought Colin would be celebrating his grand decision with his men."

"No, milady. The commander announced you and he had decided it would be best for the clan and the men if you were to wed. I realize it was not of your choosing, milady, but I . . . all of us . . . appreciate the decision. We hope you both will find happiness and peace despite the reasons behind your union."

Makenna blinked a few times and stared up into the dark, clear sky. Colin had publicly declared that she, too, had made the decision and the sacrifice to wed. She could not recall anyone—especially a man—giving a woman credit in such a way. Not even her father whom she loved with all her heart. Her sisters' husbands exerted their control whenever possible, always seeking praise for efforts, decisions, and possessions that were not theirs.

Colin's generosity did not make sense. He had been so adamant against marrying her, implying she was inept and unsatisfactory as a woman. And without warning, he had changed his mind.

Then he had kissed her.

True, it had been her first serious kiss with any man, but she had not been prepared to experience such a rare, passionate connection. Even now she feared only Colin could create the powerful whirlwind of emotion it had awakened within her.

For a moment during their embrace, she believed Colin was experiencing the same tumult of desire, but she had been wrong. He could not have shared the same yearning, craving for her as she had for him and then turn cold and aloof so quickly. Within a blink of an eye, he acted as if the kiss had never happened. With the next blink, Colin made the decision to marry, and she was supposed to go back to the keep and abide by it. But if Brodie's revelation about Colin's announcement was true, she might have misinterpreted his reaction to their kiss. How was she going to live with a man who was such a mixture of contradictions and mystery?

"Mystery, Makenna?" Ula inquired, breaking Makenna's memories of the previous night.

"Did I say that out loud?" Makenna asked weakly.

"Aye, you did," answered Rona. "But you make no sense. What's a mixture of contradictions and mystery?"

Ula laughed condescendingly. "What else? Men! It's

about time little Makenna finally figured out why we women find them so fascinating."

Rona came up and draped a gold cross around Makenna's neck and clasped it. "Speak for yourself, Ula. My husband stopped being fascinating long ago. I tolerate him because he pampers me and stays out of my way. Though do not get me wrong. I am glad to be married to him. If I weren't, Father would be forcing *me* into marrying that hulking Highlander and not poor Makenna."

Ula faked a shiver. "You can say that again. Even our sister Edna escaped; though I think choosing the church is a little extreme."

Rona adjusted the gold strand and smiled in smug satisfaction. "Oooh, there. That's it. I must say, little sister, I never thought you could look this beautiful. Then again, you never would sit still long enough for any of us to see what was under that mass of red hair."

Ula nodded so enthusiastically Makenna thought her sister's head would snap off. "Aye, look for yourself, Makenna," Ula instructed, handing her a flat rectangular reflecting dish of highly polished silver.

Makenna was not fooled by her sisters' gaiety, nor did she believe their cheery disposition was indicative of her clan's feelings toward her pending nuptials. Still, they were telling the truth. She did look beautiful. For the first time in her life, she was glad not to possess the straight gold-blond tresses of her four sisters and her mother. She alone had received the Dunstan dark red hair and green eyes. And today, they did not appear to be wild or untidy, but captivating.

"I must say that while the Dunstan colors clash horribly with your hair, this McTiernay plaid does just the opposite," Ula commented as she finished pinning the pleats of the dark plaid so that it hung off one shoulder and flowed to the floor without disturbing the beauty of the blue bliaut that lay beneath. "When your husband—"

"He's not my husband yet," Makenna countered, hoping that by some miracle Colin never would be.

"Fine, when your *soon-to-be* husband handed me his plaid and instructed that you wear it today, I was concerned it would mar the overall look Rona and I spent hours trying to create. But it has done just the opposite. Don't you think, sister?"

Rona moved alongside Makenna plucking at phantom pieces of dust before agreeing with Ula's assessment via a long-winded speech, which spawned a rambling response from Ula and another from Rona.

Makenna tuned them out and again picked up the reflecting dish. She stared into it for several seconds before laying it down. The outward transformation was complete. The navy cloth Ula had used to create her bliaut represented purity and complemented the deep blue in the McTiernay plaid. The rich green of her chemise made the emerald color of her eyes come alive beneath her thick, dark lashes. She looked every bit like a woman about to be married. Her hair was right, her dress was right, her jewelry, even her plaid were just how they should be.

But she was not like any other woman.

Other women knew how to be around men, laugh and flirt with them, manipulating them to do their bidding. Other women would know how to make a man, especially one like Colin, happy. Makenna had never learned the craft. She had never even wanted to. Her sisters believed she desired to be a boy, based on her affinity toward "male-oriented" activities. They were wrong.

Born late and last, Makenna was burdened with four elder sisters. One ignored everybody and everything

that was not of the church, but the other three loved to
impart instruction whenever possible. Deirdre's coaching had not been laced with ridicule, but even she had
repeatedly reminded Makenna how she didn't excel at
even one domestic activity. By the time Makenna was
ten, the difference in their ages became even more apparent as her siblings began to enjoy men's company
and connived of ways to attain it.

Never had Makenna felt more uncomfortable and
out of place than when her sisters had entertained. Her
awkward, still-growing body never would do what she
wanted. Frustrated with her clumsiness, her sisters had
ordered her to stay away when guests arrived until she
could be in a man's company without sputtering or
knocking something over.

It had been Camus, the wonderful old sword smith,
who had come to her rescue. He showed her how to
wield a ballock knife. In doing so, Makenna learned
how to control her body and understand where she was
at all times relative to others and objects around her.
In time, she became confident in herself.

Witnessing Makenna's natural ability and how much
she liked the masculine activity, Camus had convinced
her father to allow Makenna to continue training. Soon
she was able to throw a halberd, and her confidence
grew even more as soldiers complimented her skills with
the Lochaber axe.

On the training field, Makenna was comfortable
around men, never feeling nervous, anxious, or out of
place. Only in the great hall did she secretly yearn for
her sisters' effortless ability to converse with men and
command their attention as a *female.*

After Ula and Rona married, Makenna decided she,
too, wanted someone to love. Trying to mimic her sis-

ters' tricks to gain male attention had been a humiliating disaster. As a result, Makenna decided to perfect those activities men respected and ignore the feminine ones she despised.

Makenna put the reflecting dish back on the table. Now the only way she knew how to be around a man and receive notice or admiration was not through physical looks and silly flirting games but through her skills in riding, hunting, and fighting. Fate was cruel, forcing her to marry the one man who admired neither her abilities nor her as a woman.

Makenna stood as everyone disappeared out the door and down the hallway. It was time. She nervously collected the small bouquet of flowers and herbs one of the servants had gathered that morning and debated one more time whether she was doing the right thing. She looked like someone she wasn't—someone beautiful, feminine, and fragile. If Colin believed her capable of becoming what she currently appeared to be, they were both doomed.

Makenna descended from the last tower step and exited Forfar's arched stone entrance. As she came into view, a deafening roar erupted from the crowd gathered in the inner ward. Practically every person shouting was a soldier Colin had recruited and trained.

Drake suddenly appeared on her right and escorted her through the throng to the Dunstan chapel located in the opposite corner of the inner yard. The average-size sanctuary had been unused for the past two years since Father Renoir had vacated his post for one in France after the death of England's king, Edward I. Deirdre had died soon afterward and neither Colin nor her father had searched for another priest. Consequently, Father Lanaghly, the McTiernay priest, had agreed to travel from the Highlands and preside over Colin's second wedding. When he arrived three days ago, Makenna had been surprised to find the older priest overflowing with kindness and possessing a mischievous twinkle in his deep brown eyes. She wondered whether he would have been so nice if he knew about the friction between her and Colin.

At the chapel tower's entrance, Drake bowed and left to go inside and join Colin and Dunlop. Makenna took several deep breaths and stepped through the carved stone archway. Immediately the pressure from eyes following her every move came crashing down.

Colin knew the moment Makenna had entered the chapel. Most of the morning he had spent alone and deep in thought. The confusion, the uncertainty he had been feeling about marrying Makenna had vanished the second she responded to his kiss. Never had he dreamed the undisciplined tigress would melt in his arms. But it wasn't her response that disturbed him the most . . . it was his. No woman had ever caused him to lose control, and while he had managed to refrain from bedding her yesterday, it had been close. His desire for her was so sudden and intense it had overruled all logic, all conscious awareness, all sanity. He had wanted to devour her and almost had.

He had been the first to truly taste Makenna's soft lips, and the experience had made him feel powerful and very much a man. It also terrified him.

All morning he had wondered whether he should once again refuse to marry Makenna, but this time for her sake. Deirdre had been terrified of mating because of his size and strength. The protectiveness he felt for his dear wife had overruled his need to make anything but tender love to her the few times they had joined. But with Makenna, he doubted he would have such control. His desire to take her, drive into her, possess her, and make her totally and completely his again and again frightened him. And he had no doubt that if he ever did lose control, it would terrify Makenna and end their inexplicable, passionate connection. Nevertheless, Colin sensed that their coming together was inevitable.

She was the exact opposite of Deirdre. Far from being fragile, Makenna was all fire and spirit, and yet he still wanted to protect her. Rather than quench her zeal for life, he wanted to guard it. And all morning he feared that meant guarding her from him.

As the hour drew nearer for him to marry for the second time, Colin resolved to see it through. He knew he would never love Makenna. He doubted he would ever again risk his heart to any woman. No, he would not vow love, but he would promise his protection and by doing so, it would stretch to the whole Dunstan clan.

Now, as he looked down the small chapel pathway as Makenna walked slowly toward him, all of the morning's doubts faded. Never before had he seen Makenna look so beautiful, soft, and feminine. She captivated him. She was not beautiful in a traditional sense like his wife or even his sister-in-laws, but in a very powerful way all the same. Her athleticism had given her a firm, thin frame and command over her movements. And though he never recognized it before, Makenna was incredibly graceful.

The colored light from the stained glass windows caught the rich highlights of her upswept hair. The small tiara made of hand-painted golden beads intermixed with blue and green gems completed the look. Normally hidden behind layers of red curls, the delicate nape of Makenna's neck was now visible, revealing a soft, vulnerable curve begging to be repeatedly kissed. The dark gown complemented Makenna's fiery features and highlighted the pale flawlessness of her skin. Unlike the typical V-necked bliauts of most women, Makenna wore an off-the-shoulder gown. Its cowl neck was adorned with gold embroidery that matched the stitching on the cuffs of her tight-fitting sleeves. A similarly embroidered band settled low on her hips, accentuating their swaying movement.

Dunlop fought to keep from staring. Makenna was stunning, mesmerizing everyone in the overly full chapel. He quickly scanned the crowd of interested onlookers. Though Colin and Makenna had only just agreed to Alexander's demand for their union, the ceremony had been scheduled for almost a month. Neighboring lairds interested in seeing the vows or meeting the much-talked-about Colin McTiernay transformed the planned small ceremony into an event that would be talked about for months to come. One very interested visitor was Leon MacCuaig.

"Do you see MacCuaig, Colin?" Dunlop murmured.

"Aye," Colin lied. He couldn't take his eyes off Makenna, who looked to be growing more nervous with each step.

"I do not like how he is openly staring at your bride," Dunlop said lowly through gritted teeth.

The comment got Colin's attention. He searched for the young southern neighbor. The man was considered extremely good looking by the fairer sex and had a reputation for being deadly when fighting one-on-one with a sword.

Dunlop was correct. The man wore an intense expression of anger and possession. Colin's eyes narrowed. He was about to order Drake to remove MacCuaig from the chapel when he heard Dunlop exhale a low "This can't be good. . . ."

Colin immediately transferred his attention back to Makenna, who had inexplicably halted halfway down the path. She was scanning the crowd, her eyes darting here and there, landing on no face longer than a fraction of a second. Then, unfathomably, she turned to him, as if she instinctively knew Colin could and would save her from this fated decision. Her green eyes were dark and large with terror. Colin had never seen Makenna look anything but confident; convinced she knew what she was doing. But every hesitant breath, each gulp she took, and the flickers of her tongue across her bottom lip, forecast what was about to happen. She was about to flee.

"Do not do or say anything," Colin ordered his commanders without removing his eyes off Makenna. He took a step off the small raised platform and moved toward her. For reasons he could not explain or fathom, last night had forged a bond between them. A bond that transcended their confrontational relationship into something he didn't yet comprehend, but it enabled him to understand exactly why Makenna stood frozen in terror.

Makenna watched as Colin advanced toward her. Moments ago, glancing side to side seeing the sea of faces, some familiar and some not, she could feel the pressure of all those present upon her. Her father needed a leader for their clan, her people expected her to run their castle, her neighbors questioned their alliances, but worst of all was Colin. He wanted a wife. A real wife in every sense of the word. In just a few steps, her ability to have any say in her life would be over. Panic filled her, causing her to stop, unable to flee in fear or find the courage to continue. Somehow, Colin understood, and he was coming to her rescue.

He stopped in front of her and fought an urge to stroke the softness of her cheek. Instead, he clutched the sword hooked to his belt and leaned closer so that only his lips touched her ear.

As he moved closer to whisper, Makenna had never felt so small, nor he so huge. Yet she didn't feel fear, or even his normal arrogance. Just understanding. He came close and his breath on her cheek was warm and reassuring. "Makenna, I will make you a good husband, but I will understand and support your decision if you do not want to do this. I'll never force you into something you don't want to do."

Makenna closed her eyes. The words were whispered low, only for her. An unexpected peace washed over her that she had not felt in a long time—perhaps ever. The rich tones of his baritone voice had rung with sincerity. Colin gave her a promise. It was not offered out of desperation or coercion, but from understanding.

He knew.

He knew how much freedom meant to her. How much she feared being caged, physically or spiritually. How terrified she was of being married.

Makenna raised her green eyes and watched his blue ones swirl with emotion. Colin had always seemed so remote, rigid, without emotion. Suddenly she knew his hardness was just a mask he wore. He, too, was filled with a myriad of questions, uncertainties, and doubts.

She wanted to tell him that she knew and understood his worries and his pains. That she understood that he was a strong, proud man who had been second all of his life. Second to his brother, the famed McTiernay laird. Second to her father. And now he had to live with his second choice in marriage.

He needed to be first to someone, somewhere. He

needed to know that his needs, dreams, and desires were important, and suddenly Makenna realized they were . . . to her. Silently, she vowed, "I may not be your first choice for marriage, Colin McTiernay, but you are mine."

Colin did not completely comprehend what had transpired between them in the few seconds they stood staring at each other in silence. Makenna, always so guarded in the presence of others, now stood unafraid, trusting him. She was a woman aching for passion and full of self-doubt. She needed a man not to tame her as Dunlop suggested, but to reassure her and ignite the fires smoldering within. A man who could do that would be richly rewarded.

Makenna reached out her hand, and Colin clasped it in his. He turned and together they approached the altar and stepped up to make their vows. Colin heard his voice ring out solidly, without doubt and then it was Makenna's turn. Her tone was softer, serene, and filled with sincerity.

Colin felt her slim, soft fingers unconsciously squeeze his, as if his nearness gave her a confidence that would otherwise not exist. Again he felt the surge of hope that with Makenna he would know a *real* marriage. Not an imprisonment as he earlier feared, but a second chance to find what he never did with Deirdre. It would not be what his parents had shared. He did not love Makenna, nor she him. But they had something. Passion, and now the beginnings of trust.

It was enough.

As soon as the ceremony ended, Colin was surrounded by interested parties who knew what such a marriage might mean. Feeling Colin's hand slip away from hers,

Makenna turned around and became engulfed as the crowd shuffled her outside for the breaking of bread.

Crumbs fell about her and the women immediately stooped to pick them up. She had stepped free of the semicrazed mob and felt the warm familiar fingers of her father close over her hand. He tugged gently, and she followed.

Alexander looked down at his youngest daughter with tears in his eyes. He had hoped that he had done the right thing by forcing this marriage. Colin and Makenna were so different, but so alike. Though neither had realized it, after Deirdre's death, they had both retreated into themselves. It was only when they were verbally sparring with each other that they came alive. His clan needed this marriage, but he truly believed Colin and Makenna needed each other as well.

His fears had disappeared the moment Makenna trusted Colin to help her in the chapel. Their vows were not made under protest, but were heartfelt. At that moment, Alexander felt true hope for his daughter and his clan. He could let go now. He just needed to say good-bye.

Makenna smiled at him, and Alexander hooked her arm in his, leading her away from the chaos. "I'm glad you are no longer still angry with me, *Áille.*"

"How could I stay angry with you, Father? You are the only man I will ever love."

He smiled at her innocence. "Ah, Makenna, you have so many changes ahead of you, but do not let your adventurous spirit be one of them."

"Don't worry, Father. I doubt I will be transformed into a dutiful, dull domesticate just by merely uttering the words."

"No, I doubt that anything in this world is powerful to fully tame your wild nature." Alexander maneuvered

Makenna out of view to a private spot just inside the base of the rear tower. "But what I want you to understand is that marriage will change you, but it will be for the better. If you let him, Colin will not take away, but *add* to your life. Learn to lean upon him for the hard times. If you do, you will never be alone again."

Makenna shook her head. "Father, you just don't understand how it is between Colin and me. You have no idea what he has said and done over the past few years. He thinks I am wild—"

"You are wild," Alexander responded, interrupting.

"—and impetuous. He thinks I care for no one but myself."

"Then you must show him differently. I have seen more than you realize, *Áille*, and you and I both know that he has only seen one side to you. I know it has been hard these past two years, especially after losing Deirdre. I went through the same after your mother passed. You were young, but I know the feeling of abandonment and how it changes a person. It makes one very defiant, not wanting to rely on anyone or anything."

"He has definitely seen my defiance," Makenna replied, looking down as she twisted the ties to her bliaut.

Alexander put a finger under her chin and lifted her gaze. "Does he know of your loyalty? Does he understand your perseverance to perfect what you are determined to learn? Has he seen that you have a heart more full of compassion than anyone—aye, anyone—I have ever known?"

"I'm telling you he has known me for almost two years and doesn't care about those things. Only you can see the good side of me."

Alexander dropped his hand. "I was there in the

chapel when fear overcame you. It was Colin, not I, that gave you the peace to continue."

Makenna stared at the ground, remembering. "He made me a promise."

"A promise?"

"To never make me do anything I didn't want to."

"Do you think he meant it?"

Makenna nodded, the movement barely detectable. "He meant it. Colin is arrogant and self-assured and loves to intimidate everyone near him. Probably why I enjoy showing him that he cannot with me. But he never does or says anything he doesn't mean."

"Do you trust him?"

Makenna rolled the question over in her mind, knowing the answer. Outside of her father, she trusted Colin more than any other man. With him, she might be aggravated, but she always knew where she stood. Yet she found it impossible to say as much aloud.

Makenna looked directly into her father's green eyes and nodded. "I do."

Alexander knew how difficult that had been to admit, but he knew Makenna was telling the truth. "Trust me, *Áille*, everything will be fine. Remember I love you, and I would never have asked you to commit yourself to Colin if I did not truly believe your life would be the better for it. He can make you happy . . . if you let him. And though you cannot imagine it to be true now, you have it within you to make Colin happy as well. Now, let us say good-bye before we go to the hall and the crowd takes you away from me."

Makenna hugged her father tightly and felt him return the firm embrace. She wondered if there was anyone who could ever make her feel as safe and as loved as he did.

Alexander held on to his youngest and most beloved

daughter, knowing that this would be the last time. He could finally let go. She was safe. She was Colin's now, and he would protect her. In doing so, the young Highlander would discover that he had received the greatest treasure a father could give, someone to love and be loved by.

"When?" Colin asked, only paying half attention to the discussion. Laird Crawford had joined him a few minutes ago, and based on the direction of their conversation, the Lowland laird intended to ally himself with Colin.

"Perhaps a week or two, maybe longer," a friendly, but solid voice replied. "My boys have talent but they need a firm hand, one away from the accolades of their mother. God bless her soul, she is the one person I cannot say no to. Any other man and I'd have been able to stop the nonsense hindering those two. I've seen your men, and how you train them. If you aren't too busy being a new groom, it would be a great relief and honor if you would agree to train my sons and a few of their friends."

Colin nodded in agreement. His real focus was across the room. Makenna. Just a few hours ago, they had said their vows, and instead of being distraught and angry, she appeared content and untroubled, even happily married.

He mulled over the idea. Was Makenna happily married? Did she consider him to be a good man?

Yesterday when he had unilaterally made the decision they should marry, he had not cared about her feelings for him. It mattered not if she considered him decent, trustworthy, or even honorable. He knew he was and that was all that mattered—then. Now, seeing Makenna relaxed, and happy, talking with Crawford's wife, he wanted her to be just as comfortable when she was with him.

Jaimie Crawford watched the large Highlander stare questioningly at his new wife. When he had met Colin two days ago, he witnessed the loyalty Colin generated from his men and the reasons why. Calm, steady, and self-assured, this commander would not only teach his sons how to wield a claymore with accuracy, but he would give them the wisdom needed to lead the Crawford army when Jaimie passed. Colin was a rare leader of men, possessing talent to guide and teach as well as command. But, watching him tonight, Jaimie wondered if Colin knew what it meant to be a good husband.

Laird Crawford was not tall, but wide and strong from hours in the training fields and the occasional good-natured fight. And since Colin was even bigger, it never occurred to him not to ram his elbow into the Highland giant to get his attention.

Shocked by the unexpected attack, Colin moved swiftly only to be stopped by the biggest grin he had ever seen.

"Now, hold on there, Highlander," Crawford cautioned with a chuckle. "You cannot be telling me I hurt you, for that would be an untruth. And how else is a man to get your attention when you're forever looking at your bride over there? I've been wondering why you aren't with her, and I've come to the conclusion that you are just like me on my wedding night. Now, I knew Trista was for me the first time I saw her. She had all that brown hair and the merriest hazel eyes a man could ever want. So I asked her to marry me. I needed some-one to take care of my keep, provide heirs, and keep my bed warm at night. But, in truth, I also wanted a friend. Probably won't shock you, but I love a good laugh, and my lively woman can keep a man laughing. It's nice to know that in my old age, there'll be someone at my side I'll enjoy being with. Now, I tell you this, because you look just as I did before my wedding night."

Colin waited patiently for Crawford to end his intentional pause and finally gave in. "And that was?"

Crawford smiled and slapped Colin on the back. "Now, in trade for your willingness to train my sons, I'm going to give you something more valuable than gold. Your bride, she reminds me of my Trista, bubbling with delight, enchanting all that see her. But she wasn't always thus."

"No?" Colin inquired, only slightly curious as to where the burly laird was going, for it was obvious he had a destination with this story.

"No, I'm ashamed to say. It wasn't until a few months into our marriage that it occurred to me I had only been focusing on what I wanted, needed, and liked in a wife. I never once had considered her desires in a husband."

Crawford downed a big swig of ale, and Colin sank into a nearby chair, stretching his feet in front of him. Colin assumed the man was done. "I thank you, but I am not sure how that piece of information is so golden or how it applies to me."

"Because . . ." Jaime waited until Colin cranked his head to look the Highlander straight in the eye. He was about to call Colin a fool and decided otherwise. A friendly punch to the ribs he could get away with, but assaulting the Highlander's pride? He would be leaving on his arse regardless of his title.

Crawford took another swig of ale. "It turns out that my Trista wanted the same thing I did. A friend to laugh and grow old with, to raise a family, and live a good life." Jaimie took a deep breath and exhaled for effect. "I'm just wondering why you married Makenna. We all know Alexander's reasons for wanting the union, but beyond that, what hopes do you have? What do you want? I'm guessing that whatever it is, Makenna desires the same. Give her that, and you'll be a happy man every night— even on the nights you fight. And though it may not seem like much now, if you heed my words, you will come to see their extraordinary worth. Now, I think it's time that I dance with my wife," Jaimie finished, rubbing his hands together in anticipation as he jigged over to a laughing and eager Trista.

Colin watched as the hefty laird swung his wife around and thought on his counsel. No one had ever really talked to him that way before. Especially someone who knew very little about him. People usually came to Colin for advice, and never did anyone have the nerve to give him unsolicited suggestions about anything. Most assumed that because Colin was previously married, he knew all about the subject. How did Crawford discern the truth? And did the older laird know what he was talking about?

For years, Colin wondered why his parents' marriage had worked so well. Was this the secret? If so, then what *did* he want in a marriage? With Deirdre, he had wanted someone to love who loved him. But he soon learned that it was not quite enough. They had love, but never once did they approach the closeness his mother and father had shared.

What, then, was the part of marriage that made the soul happy? What did he truly want?

And the answer struck him so deep down that Colin almost fell out of his chair. He wanted someone to trust and believe in him completely and without reservation. But, more than that, he wanted to be first in someone's heart, body, and soul.

Could Makenna truly want the same? Did Makenna

need someone who trusted and believed in her? Someone who placed her first above all others?

Colin knew a trust was growing between him and his new bride, and though he had never said so, he did believe in her. If Makenna decided to make something happen—or not happen—she persisted until she found a way.

But how could he make her first when he had already given Deirdre his heart?

Pretending to concentrate on the dancing and the music, Makenna peripherally watched as Colin approached her. She had been intensely aware of him all evening. If it had not been for Lady Crawford to anchor her thoughts and divert her attentions, she would be shaking so bad all would know of her fear and anxiety of what was to come.

Colin stopped in front of her and stuck out his hand. "Shall we join Laird Crawford and his wife and show them how the estampie is truly to be performed?"

Makenna sat shocked for a moment and then gave him a large smile that would have warmed anyone who was the recipient of it. Colin was glad to have been both its cause and its receiver. "Do you know *how* to do the estampie?" she asked, taking his hand. "I don't think I have ever seen you dance."

It was true. He had never danced with Deirdre. She had been too weary to perform the lively dances he preferred. "There is a lot about me you don't know, Makenna," he said, swinging her onto the floor. They quickly joined the crowd stomping their feet to the wailing music created by an assortment of skilled musicians.

Soon Makenna lost herself in the rhythm of the dance.

The music shifted and the room seemed to get louder as more and more men joined in and swords appeared on the floor. Makenna jumped into the crowd beside a grinning Trista and clapped loudly as she watched Colin's skill unfold. Very few practiced the form of dance Colin, Crawford, and a handful of other men were exhibiting. The dance was both celebratory and highly athletic as they jumped over swords and spiked shields with great accuracy and speed. Each time the tune repeated, the musicians would increase the tempo.

One time while sparring with Gorten, she had asked him how he had learned to be so quick on his feet. He had told her that it was hours of performing the sword dance. Colin made them all learn and practice the complex maneuvers. She had supposed Gorten to be teasing her, but now she realized he had been in earnest. The quick, intricate weaving in and out of the war dance would not only help develop a soldier's stamina, but it could build and test one's strength, accuracy, and agility.

The music continued to build and by now any man capable of performing the *Gillie Chalium* was on the floor. The room reverberated with stomping feet and shouts of triumph. Trista cried out to her husband, encouraging him in his desperate attempt to keep up with those around him. He was bested, and he knew it, but like many who had joined in, he did not care.

Makenna's smile grew even wider. An odd sense of pride surged through her, knowing that the man with the most superior skill was grinning back at her. The musicians finally ended the tune and began another. It was slower but still had a lively beat and Colin deftly glided over to entice Makenna back onto the floor. Others followed Colin's lead, and the crowded great hall became even more so as the room shook with laughter and the stamping of feet.

Alexander's green eyes were filled with peace as he watched the couple from the now almost empty table. All would be well. Makenna and Colin were both stubborn and prideful, but their passion and honor would see them through. And if they continued to lower their defenses, they might even find the rarest thing this world had to offer—love. The special love one discovers only with one's soul mate.

Colin had loved Deirdre and she him, but their love and marriage had been based on need and protection. Makenna would meet Colin as an equal. She would be able to share his burden, protect him in ways he never knew he needed, and he would do the same for her in return.

Alexander wished he could live long enough to witness this transformation, but it was not meant to be. The squeezing pains in his chest had been growing all afternoon. It was painful to breathe, and now the burning sensation in his upper abdomen was spreading to his arm, neck, and jaw.

His eyes roamed to his other daughters. Edna could not be here, but he knew that she had found happiness at the abbey. Ula and Rona would have to adjust somehow, for Colin would not be as susceptible to their ploys as he always had been.

Most everyone was on the floor. All except one. Alexander stole a glance to the man who had chosen to remain seated at the table.

Leon MacCuaig.

The young man had physically matured over the past few years. With light brown hair and deep-set black eyes in a rugged face, he was undeniably handsome. He was also pitiable.

Alexander had tried to guide the young laird after his father had died, but Leon enjoyed commanding others versus listening. He had grown to be a callous leader, ruling by fear rather than trust. Sitting quietly for most of the afternoon, he had not fooled Alexander or Colin for a moment. MacCuaig had remained at Lochlen to discover which and how many Lowland lairds would ally themselves with the Dunstans once a Highlander was in charge. Colin wanted to observe MacCuaig's reactions and agreed to let him stay.

Alexander gripped the arm of the chair and stood. He fought the dizziness and ordered his body to comply with one last command. He would walk to his chambers without assistance. Scottish pride demanded no less.

Chapter Three

Leon drummed his fingers idly against the wood table, oblivious of Alexander Dunstan's look of pity or his disappearance. His attention was solely on the Highlander flaunting his obvious attraction for the woman that should have been his wife. Blatant hatred filled him as he stared at the merry couple, and he cared little who saw it.

Today, Makenna Dunstan had unmasked her beauty to all. And though many had been surprised by her physical transformation, Leon had not been one of them. He had known for years what a unique and striking woman she was. That alone should have entitled him to her hand and not the arrogant Highlander.

Leon clenched his jaw as another Dunstan soldier called out. With each story praising Colin's leadership and skills, Leon loathed the Highlander a little more. For two years, he had been hearing about McTiernay and the fictitious tales that surrounded him. No one could be that good at discovering raw talent.

Twice, Leon tried to plant one of his own men within Colin's ranks to uncover the truth behind the Highlander's methods. Both times, the soldiers had disappeared, forcing Leon to rethink how he was going to outwit Colin McTiernay.

His next idea had been simple. Leon had never encountered anyone who could best him one-on-one with a sword. He would goad McTiernay until his pride demanded revenge, and then strip the Highlander of not only his arrogance, but also his life.

But before he could put his plan into effect, the news came.

The Highland creature was to marry Makenna Dunstan, the woman everyone knew Leon had claimed to be his. Leon had worked for too long toward a union between him and the red-haired beauty. So much had been overcome to be stripped away so easily by the hands of an outsider.

MacCuaig watched as the couple moved more slowly. The sexual tension between the two was palpable even halfway across the room. Leon clasped the quaich in front of him and tried to keep from shaking with rage.

That was supposed to be him.

He was the young, good-looking, powerful, Lowland laird. All women wanted him, desired him. They begged for chances to be near him. "Soon Makenna will as well," Leon promised himself.

McTiernay might think he had won, but he would soon learn differently. The clueless Highlander was ill prepared for his future. Leon MacCuaig settled back in the deep chair and forced himself to appear relaxed. Colin's army might be loyal, but they were few in number. Not nearly enough to stop Leon from taking everything McTiernay possessed.

"I shall pluck them from your fingertips, one by one. First the clan, then the castle, and finally . . . Makenna," he swore quietly to himself before downing the rest of his mead.

* * *

Colin whipped Makenna around in his arms, once again mesmerized by her beauty. Two years he had lived at Lochlen and never once had he heard Makenna laugh as she was doing tonight. Only once had Deirdre acquiesced to a big festival in the castle the winter before she died. They had celebrated Twelfth Night, the last day of the Epiphany. It had been a joyous evening for the clansmen, but Makenna and Colin had elected to watch rather than participate.

Deirdre was recovering from a bad cold she had been fighting for several months and didn't want any type of activity. She had only agreed to the festival because of Makenna, who knew how much the clan needed the release a celebratory gathering would bring. Makenna, in turn, had stayed by Deirdre's side tending to her needs so the lady's maids could participate in the festivities.

Looking at Makenna now, twirling with an easiness that made her eyes sparkle and dance in delight, Colin realized that he had not been Deirdre's only willing captive— Makenna had been ensnared as well. She had placed her life on hold and had put Deirdre's happiness ahead of her own. Not until tonight did Colin grasp how unfair it had been to the lively beauty.

Colin felt Makenna sashay by him to the beat of the pipes and then back again. He inhaled deeply. Instantly he was reminded of the previous night and the last time he had enjoyed the fresh clean scent of her skin and hair. Makenna moved toward him and out again, making innocent contact. The brief touches were driving him mad. Each time her small, firm breasts grazed his lower chest, Colin fought his need to gather her in his arms and march out of the hall uncaring of what the guests and his men would say.

Makenna drank in the feeling of being with Colin. She loved to dance, and Colin was an artist on the floor. Like everything else he did, Colin moved effortlessly to the rhythm regardless of its speed. He would bring her in and spin her with an intoxicating level of control.

When the men had thrown down their swords, Colin's face had alit with a delight she had not known him capable to possess. At first, she had watched the intricate quick movements of his feet with awe and admiration. Then he had laughed aloud, revealing two dimples as his face split into an infectious grin.

Makenna had seen him smile many times in the past, but until tonight, she could not recall it reaching his eyes.

Colin swung her about, pulling her closer each time. Her pulse raced and she knew Colin's did as well. No one would discern it by looking at him. Outwardly, he appeared happy and relaxed, but Makenna felt the growing tautness of his frame.

And she knew why.

Last night had not been a random incident of bizarre need erupting out of charged emotions. The desire to touch him and be touched by him was drowning out all other thoughts. She looked up into his bold blue eyes. They held a clear and unmistakable message. *I want you. I will have you. I will know you as no one ever has.* It was both intoxicating and terrifying at the same time. Makenna broke away from the dance.

Colin watched Makenna practically run to the table under the pretense of needing a drink. Only for a moment did he consider joining her. The instant deep attraction between them was inexplicably strong. Colin had struggled most of the night searching in vain for any reason that would rationalize his deep ache to carry her to his bed and make her his.

Colin's eyes roamed the hall and saw the empty chair Alexander had been sitting in. He also noticed the looks of heavy admiration several of his men were giving his new wife.

His nails bit into flesh as his fingers clenched into a fist. Something primitive and all-consuming roared through his veins. He was *jealous*. Never did he dream he could be jealous of anyone, especially over the wildest of the Dunstan daughters. But, seeing the open looks of desire for Makenna, thoughts about the circumstances causing their marriage vanished. She was his—or would be soon. And with every passing hour, it was getting harder to quash the rush of sexual anticipation stirring within him.

Father Lanaghly saw Colin's narrowing eyes and walked over to prevent the impending eruption. Unlike his excitable brother, Conor, Colin usually was in full control of his emotions. Tonight, however, if someone did not divert his attention and quickly, it would be Colin initiating the mayhem. "Ahem, I believe Laird Dunstan has retired for the evening. I saw him rise, nod approvingly at you, and your lovely new wife, and then leave."

Colin blinked at the interruption before comprehending what Father Lanaghly was talking about. "Did Alexander have assistance?" Colin inquired quietly.

Although Alexander had hidden it well, the old laird had been in severe pain for most of the night. More than once Colin had wanted to suggest that he retire, but each time he resisted the temptation. Laird Dunstan had earned the right to keep his pride, especially among his allies.

Father Lanaghly pointed to two empty chairs in front of the smaller hearth nestled near the less crowded end of the great hall. "As he left, no. However, Alexander was moving somewhat slow so I followed him to the inner yard in which I saw two men go to his aide when he thought no one was looking."

Colin visibly relaxed. "Alexander should have retired long before he did. Events such as these are hard on him these days. He should have rested more."

"Laird Dunstan is a wise man. His hours are numbered, and he wanted to spend them assuring himself of his daughter's well-being, his clan's future, and even *your* happiness."

Makenna observed through lowered lashes Father Lanaghly directing Colin to a chair. That was the closest she had ever seen Colin appear to be subservient to *anyone*. She placed her cup back on the table and casually sauntered over to the stone wall. Curiosity ate at her and she slowly edged her way toward the small hearth, stopping only when she came into earshot.

"You should not have journeyed so far, Father, but I will admit it is good to see someone from home." Colin sighed.

"Aye, I'm sure it is. I was privileged to marry your brother. . . ."

"What a surprise that was," Colin retorted as he stretched back in the chair, recalling his eldest brother's earnest declaration to never marry. When news arrived that Conor had taken a wife, Colin had not believed the herald. He could not imagine his brother married, and most especially to someone half English. The summer following the news he had traveled to see them expecting anything but what he had found.

Love. True love. The kind he had so desperately wanted with Deirdre, but never had.

Father Lanaghly lightly elbowed the large man he had known since he was a small boy. "Indeed, but what a good match Conor has made. I'm just as honored to have married you this time. And if the good Lord agrees, I shall be the one to see all you McTiernays joined with fine women."

"Keep praying, Father. You may eventually have a chance with Craig and Clyde, but Cole, Crevan, and especially Conan are unlikely to pin themselves down."

"Nay, I do not think so. Cole reminds me of you. He needs a woman of fire and substance, and needs to stop looking at the meek ones."

"What—" Colin tried to interrupt and get clarification, but Father Lanaghly just continued.

"Now, I know why you added Crevan to your list of permanent bachelors. At times, his speech can be slow, but he is a fine man and someday a smart woman will see what lies beyond his inability to speak quickly. And what a lucky woman she will be."

Father Lanaghly paused and linked his fingers together. Colin waited for him to explain how the contrary Conan was marriage material. Becoming impatient, Colin pressed, "And Conan?"

Father Lanaghly wrinkled his nose and then let out a sigh. "Conan will get married."

"You don't sound as convinced as you do with the others."

"In truth, I'm not. The man is far too intelligent, and he is most intolerant of anyone, especially women, who cannot match wits with him. The only one he dares not tangle with is Laurel. But that is not his biggest impediment to his finding a wife," Father Lanaghly revealed.

"And that is?" Colin prodded.

The priest shrugged his shoulders and let go a long sigh. "Your brother has no interest in one. And unlike yourself and Conor, his declaration seems quite heartfelt."

"Conan always was the smartest of us."

"There is still time. He is fifteen years of age now. It took Conor until he was thirty to find Laurel. I'm sure someone will capture Conan's attention. Just as Laurel did Conor's, and Makenna did with you."

Makenna stretched herself to hear Colin's response. She dared not lean any farther lest she lose her balance and fall.

Colin chuckled. "Ah, Father. I will spare you the details, but this marriage is not one of love."

"But your wife is lovely, and she has such life. Rarely does one see such sparkling energy from a young woman who has endured such sorrows."

"Makenna is all that."

"But she does not have your heart."

Colin shook his head. "I gave my heart to my first wife. I fear God did not make a woman who could claim my soul. At least not how my mother claimed my father's."

"That is not so, son. You just need time to learn that for yourself."

Colin was saved from responding. Dunlop and Drake were motioning for him to join a table of neighboring lairds that had convened near the main hearth. Now that Alexander had retired, alliance discussions were commencing. Colin knew that no declarations would be made tonight. These conversations were only to discern how Colin intended to lead the Dunstan clan after Alexander passed away.

Watching Colin retreat to the other side of the room, Makenna moved to a nearby wooden screen, trying to mask the emotional warfare waging inside her. She did not love Colin, nor he her. But what about her sister?

Makenna glanced behind the partition for any servants preparing food on the hidden table. There were none. She stepped behind the vertical planks, glad to be hidden from the crowd. Leaning against the small table, Makenna considered her sister's marriage.

Makenna could not remember seeing Colin and Deirdre engaged in one affectionate embrace. She had supposed it was because Colin was so reserved. Tonight he had proven otherwise. His normally stoic expression had been replaced with one much more relaxed, even happy when he was dancing. And then, to Father Lanaghly, he admitted that while he loved her sister, Deirdre had not claimed his soul.

Makenna rubbed her temples. Why did she care if Colin and Deirdre had not been *deeply* in love? "Because, Makenna, this is your greatest fear," she answered aloud. "Not only are you afraid that God did not make a man who could claim your heart, but that if he did, your chance of finding him is forever lost since you married Colin."

But she knew, even as she whispered the words, that her deepest fear was something far more terrifying. Colin would be the one to claim her soul . . . but she would never be able to claim his.

Makenna closed her eyes and gathered the strength to reenter the great hall. Just before she exited, two female voices came through the slats, stopping her cold.

"I cannot believe she did it," commented a higher-pitched voice full of astonishment.

"Aye, neither can I," replied a voice Makenna instantly recognized. The woman had married into the Dunstan clan and had been a troublemaker even before her husband had passed away. Lela constantly sought ways to rouse ire and angst in her fellow clansmen. Find a conflict and Lela Fraser was the probable instigator of it. Why people tolerated—and worse, listened to—her evil spirit, Makenna never could understand.

"Betraying her people to a *Highlander*. She should be ashamed. I cannot believe *she* will be the next lady of our clan," Lela added, baiting a response. When one didn't readily follow, she tried again. "Not only does she disgrace us with her inability to run Lochlen, but to force that . . . that heathen upon us is unforgivable. He might have been able to fool poor Deirdre and our laird, but the man is crazed if he thinks we will let an outsider tell us what to do."

The other woman clucked in agreement. "Never wanted his kind. I could forgive Deirdre. She didn't know what she was doing when she was deceived by his trickery. But Makenna . . ."

"Never doubt that she knew precisely what would happen," Lela concluded with satisfaction.

Unable to listen to any more, Makenna whipped round the wood partition. "And just what was I doing, Lela *Fraser*?" she demanded, loud enough to grab the attention of everyone in the hall. Makenna ignored the stares and locked gazes with the poisonous woman. Lela's almond-shaped black eyes were set deep and matched the midnight color of her waist-length hair. With a perfect figure and flawless complexion, Lela was a woman who used her beauty to gain power and influence however she could.

Lela raised a single eyebrow, pretending to be undaunted by Makenna's intentional reference to her own Highland background. Born a Fraser, Lela had been raised in the Grampian Highlands, and only met her husband by pure chance when he was in Aberdeen selling Dunstan hides and wool. Lela had thought him to be a rich merchant and maneuvered him quickly into marriage, never dreaming that he was really a farmer.

"What has stalled your vicious tongue?" Makenna asked, crossing her arms in a gesture of superiority. "Or did you forget that you, too, are a Highlander by birth and married a Dunstan Lowlander?"

"I may be a Highlander by birth, but I am a Lowlander by choice," Lela countered, rallying. "You cannot hold me responsible for where I was born, but I can and do hold *you* responsible for stripping away the last specks of our freedom. Your *husband* was leaving until you became a willing participant in this farce."

Makenna looked at the woman to Lela's left, who had joined the mocking and criticism. She was shocked to see it was someone she had once considered a friend. "And you, Joanna? Are you of like mind?"

Joanna narrowed her hazel eyes and nodded, refusing to cower in front of the crowd.

Makenna turned to the now very quiet and divided room. On one side stood the soldiers, and on the other was a small cluster of Dunstans. "And all of you? You, who eat in my father's castle, partake in his food and wine. Do you feel I have married foolishly? That I cost you your freedom? Can none of you see that I did it *for you*? Do you not realize how vulnerable we are and only *one man* can train our few men to defend us against attack?"

Lela sniggered. "We see him," she huffed, jutting her chin toward Colin, who was quietly sitting and watching the argument from across the room. "And when we do, all we can see is the reason our backs ache each night with his order to finish an unneeded wall."

"Unneeded?" Makenna gasped. "How can you say that? The English have barely departed our lands and even now there are rumbles that Edward II is plotting his revenge to retake our homes and property."

Lela would not back down. "You cannot scare us into supporting you. We know better. The Dunstan land is not strategic. We hold no great value. The English care nothing for us."

Makenna gaped at the recklessness of Lela's words. "You are foolish, Lela, and so are all who believe your nonsense."

The soldiers vacated a small path as Makenna headed straight toward Colin. "Say something. Explain. They need to know. They need to understand how much you have done to save them, that without your leadership this clan is doomed."

Often Colin had been tempted to do just what Makenna had asked and announce his worth, but he knew it would be a fruitless struggle that would gain him no loyalty. He needed to remain patient and think long-term. With a strong guard, he would be able to take and keep the position of laird of the clan, but it might be a long while before he would truly be a leader to these stubborn people.

Colin downed the last of the ale and considered the Lowland lairds waiting silently for him to speak. In one smooth movement, he rose from his chair and announced, "I believe, fellow Scots, that for me and my wife the party has just ended."

Pivoting, he swept a very astonished Makenna into his arms and exited the great hall.

Chapter Four

Colin ignored Makenna's impassioned pleas to put her down and continued his march across the inner yard. Anticipation filled him, but in ways he had not expected. The yearning consuming him since their vows had been enormous. He had forced himself to endure dinner and conversations when his primary thoughts centered on his wife, their bed, and the pleasures they would soon find in each other's arms. Tonight, Makenna would discover passion, and maybe, so would he.

Makenna suddenly felt Colin pivot and watched the distance begin to increase between her and her room in Forfar Tower. She began to struggle earnestly. She had assumed he was going to take her back to her room, drop her on the bed, reprimand her for a minute or two, and then return to the hall. She had been wrong. He was not heading toward her chambers . . . but to his.

The Black Tower was aptly named. Its unique onyx-colored stones formed the massive round anchor situated along the eastern wall between the Canmore and Pinnacle towers. Colin lived there alone.

Stopping his ascent on the third floor, Colin maneuvered down the narrow hallway until he came to a large arched door. He turned and pressed his back against the thick wooden planks until it gave under the pressure. Once inside the private bedchamber, Colin lowered Makenna until her feet rested on the soft rug extending across the room.

The dying embers in the hearth provided just enough light to illuminate the spacious area. Makenna guessed that even if the fire was ablaze, the dark walls would absorb the extra light and the chamber would still feel protected and set apart. Unlike the routine noise associated with the elite chambers of the towers where she and her father lived, Colin's room felt like a quiet enclave about which no one knew. She knew her sister had felt isolated in the silence, but Makenna enjoyed the peace it gave.

She walked over to the nearest of the three plain armchairs facing the fireplace and clutched its back while trying to look casually about the room. Before Colin, the steward had resided in these walls. Once, as a child she had tried sneaking into the tower but had been found and escorted back out.

Until tonight, she had only heard descriptions of the cavernous rooms the Black Tower held. Deirdre had visited only once and vowed never to enter the obsidian structure again. She claimed the dark stone walls were cold and menacing. Even her father said it lacked the cheeriness he preferred.

Makenna could understand their comments, but she did not agree with them. The room was not threatening. Instead, it was surprisingly warm, even welcoming. A woolen McTiernay plaid covered the four-poster bed. A simple table to its right held an unlit candle. Nestled underneath two of the room's four large windows was a long, sturdy bench with silk stuffed pillows at each end. The understated tapestry hanging above the bed was not ornate enough to be one of Deirdre's creations. The picture of a young Scotsman standing by a river offering his heart to a shy maiden evoked an atmosphere of tenderness, and hope, and vulnerability. It was not what she had expected to find adorning Colin's walls.

But even more surprising was the lack of anything feminine. Makenna could see not a single remnant of Colin's relationship with her sister. She silently wondered if there had ever been anything of Deirdre's to remove.

Besides the hearth chairs, the only other item in the room was a beautifully carved chest situated along the far wall. Instead of the slab legs of the typical six-board chest, the sizeable hutch had an elongated front and back and its stiles extended to the floor to make four legs. She didn't recognize the piece and it did not resemble the furniture in the rest of the room. "Colin, is that chest yours?"

Still standing by the door, Colin glanced at the chest his grandfather had made him when he was a young boy. That and his mother's tapestry were the two treasures he had brought with him from his childhood home, McTiernay Castle. "Aye," he replied.

Makenna moved closer to the unusual trunk and knelt down to finger the carving etched into its face. "Is this the McTiernay crest?" she asked. "It's beautiful."

"Aye. The eagle represents strength. It clutches a branch of our Highland mountain ash. Those drops you see off the talons are blood."

"Of your enemies?"

"Our comrades. To remember the fallen."

Makenna nodded in silence hearing him voice the McTiernay pledge. It was not a mere saying to him, but a true belief. Despite their squabbles, she knew Colin would never forget a single man he ever fought alongside. He would ensure that their deaths had meaning and purpose.

Makenna rose and gracefully waved her arm in front of her. "Your room is very similar to my own with the exception of your tapestry. It is captivating. I've never seen one that portrayed such a pure emotion before. If I were ever to weave, I would want to design a motif such as that," Makenna ended quietly, unaware that she had voiced her inner thoughts aloud.

Colin exhaled slowly. He was surprised to be relieved by her approval. Deirdre had always made it clear that he was to come to *her* chambers if he desired her company. Consequently, he had never cared if his room appealed to anyone else. He had not realized how much of himself was exposed in this simple sanctum.

A renewed surge of desire swept over Colin. He picked up a log from the stack of dried kindling he had replenished that morning and threw it into the hearth. Long after the fire sprang anew, he continued to stoke it, knowing that if he did not keep his eyes and hands occupied, his control would snap.

Makenna watched as Colin stabbed the burning logs, sensing his palpable frustration. The dying fire was just another example of her clan's refusal to support and honor an outsider. If he were a Lowlander and welcomed, all candles would have been lit, the bed turned, and the fire would have been blazing with warmth.

Not knowing what to say to counter such a display of disrespect, Makenna walked over and lightly touched Colin's forearm, marveling at the strength and tension held within the sinewy muscles.

At her touch, Colin flinched, but when Makenna tried to remove her hand, he instinctively reached out and kept it in place. If asked, he would not be able to explain why he wanted to prolong the gentle sensation.

He had reacted without thought. Her unexpected gesture was soft, warm, and so very giving. For the second time that day, he felt as if she understood and believed in him.

Makenna stood by his side for a long while and stared at the flickering flames, mystified at her desire to remain with Colin. But it was time to leave. Their ruse should now be complete. Everyone who witnessed their notable exit would trust they had consummated their marriage by now. Makenna released her light hold and headed toward the door.

"Where are you going?" Colin asked, his voice low and curious.

Makenna stopped and turned toward him. "I think it is safe to leave for my room now. I don't hear any movement outside. Don't worry, if anyone can roam about this castle unseen, it is I."

"Of that, I know all too well," Colin scoffed.

"Don't sound so churlish. Tonight my skills are going to benefit your deception. No one will be the wiser we spent the night alone."

"*My* benefit?" he asked, turning to look at her.

Makenna nodded. "Aye, yours, and mine, too, if you want to be particular. What does it matter?"

In three quick strides, Colin blocked her path, physically challenging any method she might try in order to exit. "Makenna, do not pretend with me that you do not recall what I said to you last night."

Makenna did remember. He had vowed their marriage would be real and not in name only. But never did she dream Colin would make good on his promise so soon. Certainly not tonight. Why, just yesterday they had each vehemently sworn the other to be the last person in the world they would want to spend time with, let alone marry.

But then he had kissed her.

It was amazing how a single embrace could change one's view so dramatically, but it had. Not only had it proved they were compatible physically, but that each held an innate understanding of the other's most private needs and fears. Still, Makenna could not accept that Colin intended to make good on his promise this very evening.

"But . . . but this is our wedding night!" she squeaked, not realizing how ridiculous the words sounded.

"Aye, and I have been thinking about you all day," Colin replied.

"About me?" Her voice was barely a whisper and laced with doubt.

He pushed back a lock of red hair that had become loose from its comb. "Aye, you. Every man in the hall was thinking of you . . . and they were wishing they were me."

Makenna blinked. Colin made her sound as if she were some siren able to induce men into desiring her. The concept was unreal. "Colin, be serious. . . ."

"Oh, but I am, Makenna." Her name was a soft growl as he bent his head to capture her lips with his own. He kissed her slowly, lingeringly, and with a deep, tender possessiveness.

Makenna shivered as a mysterious liquid warmth began to grow inside her. All doubts about whether she had imagined the intensity and pleasure of his touch were erased. For this, she had changed the fate of her life.

Makenna felt Colin strain against an unknown force as he moaned softly and drew her closer to him. The kiss differed from their last, but was no less powerful. Instead of hard and demanding, it was gentle and persuasive. She could feel his tongue move across her bottom lip, teasing it open. She complied, welcoming him.

It was a dream come true. To be touched and kissed and made to feel so very feminine. She didn't think feelings and cravings like the ones coursing through her veins were even possible until Colin had proved otherwise. He had shown her that she was capable of feeling desire, physical need, and passion. That she was not devoid of such emotions, but burning with them when he held her in his arms.

Colin parted her lips and tenderly explored her mouth with his tongue. Her body was in chaos. Makenna fought the instinct to wrap her arms round his neck and return the intimate caress. She almost lost the battle.

Almost.

With Colin, she was experiencing every dream she had ever wanted from a man. All except one. To be truly desired. No matter how good Colin made her feel now, it would not match the pain of discovering that she was just a surrogate, a live manifestation of what he once had. At the altar, she had thought passion would be enough. And it might be, if he needed *her* and not a substitute for Deirdre.

The second his lips touched hers, Colin knew Makenna wanted him. Her response was too pure, too genuine. Full of longing and innocence, it was more intoxicating than the strongest of ales. If she knew the intensity of his desire to touch and intimately know every inch of her body, she would be terrified. He forced himself to slow down and keep the kiss gentle, exploring the softness of her lips.

He inhaled her sweet scent of wildflowers. Never would he be able to ride through the fields again without thinking of her. He moved to deepen the kiss and immediately sensed a change. Makenna did not pull away, but a tautness filled her that wasn't there before.

Instantly Colin withdrew. Deirdre had never responded to his kisses the way Makenna had last night. Deirdre had pretended to enjoy them, but deep down he had always known it was toleration—not pleasure— she endured in his arms. Had he needed it to be different with Makenna so badly that he imagined her response?

Colin cupped Makenna's face and peered into green eyes swirling with doubt and emotion. His fears were immediately assuaged. Despite all their arguments and clashes over her unusual inclinations, he understood her and why she retreated. She was afraid—not of what he might do—but what he thought her to be. She feared being compared.

Colin closed his eyes but didn't let her go. His new bride had no way of knowing that whenever he touched her, spoke with her, kissed her, the last thing he thought of was his dead wife. It would be impossible to mistake the wild passionate creature in his arms for Deirdre.

Makenna watched him close his eyes and hoped in silence that he would release her and let her leave, but seconds later his deep blue eyes reopened and looked at *her*. He was not remembering his past. Colin was completely in the present, and his sole thoughts were about her. His gaze conveyed such glittering need Makenna felt herself tremble just before he leaned down and recaptured her lips with so much tenderness it seared her senses. She heard a moan escape, and knew it was her own body betraying her. Unable to fight the passionate assault any longer, her fingers clenched his shoulders as she leaned into him, kissing him with a hunger that belied her fears.

Colin felt a calm invade the deep place that had grown tense with apprehension. No longer was Makenna fighting their connection, their physical attraction. She wanted him, and she was admitting it with her actions.

His lips trailed a line of kisses to her ear and whispered, "I will never hurt you, Makenna, but I won't deny that I want you. Very much. And I believe you want me, too."

Before she could respond, Colin pulled her body fully against his and kissed her mouth hungrily, thrusting his tongue deep into her velvet warmth. An elemental, dangerous sexual desire was building within him. Never before had his physical need for a woman been so raw and powerful. His power to control it was fading rapidly.

Makenna moaned as he crushed her lips beneath his. The full force of his own hunger broke over her. She returned the kiss with sweet fervor. The inexplicable need to touch him, taste him everywhere was growing to irrepressible levels.

Their first kiss by the loch revealed a need and a connection neither had realized existed. Tonight's initial embrace had been one of gentle persuasion and soft exploration. This, however, was completely different.

It was two souls, full of feverish desire, which had been deprived of fulfillment for far too long. The result was more intoxicating, more demanding, and far more blatantly erotic.

A sense of urgency was growing beyond her understanding. Passion once buried deep inside her now roared wild and hot through her veins. Makenna instinctively pressed herself against Colin, seeking release from the unknown tension suffusing her body.

Colin was burning with desire. Makenna's unconstrained response ignited a fire within him that had been dormant too long. He was so hard he hurt, and his imagination was going wild, thinking of all the things he'd like to do to her. When she moved closer, he held her, letting her feel the long, hard length of his arousal.

Immediately Makenna became aware of Colin's physical need. She learned enough about mating from her sisters, but never did she dream a man could be so very hard, nor so large. The rigidity of his body completely contrasted the featherlight caresses of his fingers igniting a liquid fire in her veins. She waited for fear to rise and compel her to end the spell he was casting, but it never came. Instead, more than anything, she wanted to be with him, touch him, and know him in every way imaginable.

Makenna's small sighs and light shivers made Colin momentarily lose his composure. A considerable shudder of need racked him as a raging hunger challenged his defenses. He knew his size and strength frightened women. It had terrified Deirdre. He wouldn't, he vowed silently to himself, lose control and frighten his virgin wife away.

He released her lips and plucked the combs from her hair. Burying his face in the loose red curls, he reveled in the thick silky mass finally free of its constraints. His lips paused to nibble on the soft crevices of her neck before trailing to the base of her throat and below. His hand curved around her spine where the low back of her gown offered access to her silken skin. Slowly he unthreaded the ties to the bliaut until it gave way and slid onto the floor.

"So soft, so sweet." He heard himself moan his thoughts aloud. "God, I need you, Makenna. I want you like I've wanted no other woman," he purred against her ear.

Her mouth finally free, Makenna asked, "Colin, what's happening? I don't know what's wrong with me. My body feels to be on fire, and yet I crave more."

Colin cupped her cheek, his control almost shattered by her innocently whispered words. "Nothing's wrong. Nothing has ever been more right. God, Makenna, don't leave me. Please don't tell me to go," he begged, uttering his fears aloud.

His eyes met hers, and Makenna knew she never would. "Not now, not ever."

The simple vow was heartfelt and real. Makenna meant every word. And suddenly his future seemed a lot less lonely. This strong-willed woman would no doubt argue and fight with him to their graves, but she wouldn't ignore him. With Makenna, he would never be alone again.

The knowledge released a surge of need Colin could no longer suppress. He yanked impatiently at his clothing and then, before she became aware of his nude state, he pulled her back into his embrace and drank hungrily from her lips.

Makenna clutched at him, savoring the feel of his warm skin against her palms. Each kiss was deeper and more stirring than the last. She was barely aware of Colin removing the last of her clothing.

Last night seeing her naked from a distance, Colin had been tortured to know what it would be like to feel such wild beauty in his arms. Now that he was actually touching her, she was even more magnificent than he had imagined.

Unable to wait any longer, Colin scooped Makenna up in his arms and carried her to the bed. Settling her against the pillows, he lowered himself until he covered her body with his own.

"Makenna." He paused, waiting until her eyes focused on his. "Never wonder whom I am thinking of when we are together. For it will always be you. I know who I am with, and I make love to you because I want and desire *you*, not merely because you are my wife and I can. Trust me. Coupling is only fulfilling if each of us crave the other. If you tell me you do not want this, I will cease and let you return to your room. No one will be the wiser."

Makenna stared into his very blue eyes. His desire was unmistakable. The control he was exerting right now was tremendous and at the same time comforting. He was huge, but he would never hurt her physically. The danger of lying with Colin was the emotional havoc he could inflict on her heart. For two years, he had been at Lochlen and not once did she long for him as a man. Then yesterday all that changed. She was unprepared to be this attracted to him. It was more than just physical. And that's what made it so terrifying.

Nevertheless, she would not leave. If only for tonight, she would know what it was like to be loved, to be held in a man's arms, and made to feel complete. They didn't love each other, but they had something rare and maybe more important.

"I don't know why, Colin, or even how, but I trust you like no other. When you kiss me, I feel alive in ways I cannot explain. I'm both terrified and eager at the same time. More than anything, I want you to experience these same sensations. Teach me how to be a wife, Colin. I *need* you to want me," she finished, her voice filled with quiet desperation.

Colin squeezed his eyes shut. He wanted to weep and laugh and cry out with joy. He reopened his eyes and lightly caressed her cheek with his knuckles. "I already do, Makenna McTiernay. I never expected to need anyone ever again. I have been empty for so long. God, Makenna, you make me realize what I have been searching for." Cradling her face in his hands, he closed his mouth over hers. Slowly he devoured her lips as if he could consume the essence of her vibrant spirit.

The sheer kiss was overwhelming. It nearly choked her, but instead of release, Makenna sought more. Her fingers bit into the hard contours of Colin's muscled back as her body begged for something, but she knew not what. Makenna knew only that Colin was the sole man who could give it to her.

Colin felt her back arch and her hips shift back and forth against his thighs. The movement caused his already aroused body to tighten even more with fierce, compelling need. He had to slow down and prepare her, for he had no doubt that he would be Makenna's first lover. He wanted the experience to be perfect. Never would his young bride look outside their marriage for physical release.

He held her hips still and finished ravishing her mouth before moving to reexplore her neck. Nothing had ever been this good, this perfect. Everything about her was so right. Her eagerness only intensified his pleasure. Each caress, response, whimper she uttered made him feel whole, like a complete man. It began last night. They had sparred, but the verbal exchange had revealed something quite unexpected, an understanding that she was just as empty and alone as he. Never would she feel that way again.

Colin transferred his weight to his side, giving his fingers access to her soft round breasts. His mouth explored the contours of her shoulders as he cupped her pert little mounds and began to rub his callused thumbs against the hardened nipples. Makenna gasped, and Colin felt the shiver that went through her as if it had gone through himself.

"God, Makenna, how I need you. Just let me touch you, taste you." And then his mouth covered her breast, his tongue felt like hot velvet against her skin.

Her breath quickened as his teeth lightly tantalized her taut nipple. He suckled, teasing it, making her squirm with want of him while his free hand moved over her abdomen and then lower. Lightly his fingers stroked the smooth flesh of her inner thigh. He was making her frantic. So many sensations were coursing through her veins it was akin to pain. "Colin, it's too much!" Makenna cried out, inwardly hoping that he would refuse to stop.

"Aye, *bean cheile*, it is, but trust me," he answered as he turned his attention to the other breast.

He felt one of her hands slip down to his thigh and sink her fingers into his hard, muscled buttock. Colin caught his breath, his whole body incredibly tight and heavy with barely controlled need. All instincts urged him to surge forward and drive himself into her.

Makenna felt his manhood, hard and impatient against her thigh. The sensation triggered a heavy pulling in her lower body. She clung tightly to him, wanting so very much for his hand to touch the place throbbing with enormous need. She could feel the rapid staccato rhythm of Colin's heartbeat and knew that his need matched her own.

"Please, Colin, please," she begged for what she knew not.

Colin's mouth reclaimed hers as he drew his fingers through the gathering dew between her legs. Never had he known the glory of making a woman react so completely to him. He was so hard he feared he might burst, but her lusty moans and hesitant caresses were food for the soul. He needed more.

He played with the soft hairs of her apex, reveling in her honest reaction. He slowly introduced his finger between the velvety folds. Only when she arched her hips inviting him to know more did he invade the sweet, vulnerable warmth. She cried out, and Colin steadied her writhing body. His tongue mimicked his finger as he gradually eased it into the tight, hot channel. She was so wet and ready he couldn't wait to lose himself in her.

"My God, Makenna," Colin groaned, knowing his

control was about to snap. He slid one leg between hers, making more room to slide another finger in and back out of the snug passage. He explored her with exquisite care, finding all the secret, hidden places, and made them tingle with need. And with each touch, each discovery, his own need grew in return.

Incredibly, Makenna wanted even more of him inside her, deeper, and lifted her hips against his hand. Her fingers splayed against his chest and then moved lower to touch him as intimately as he was touching her. Finding his flesh, her hand cradled his sex. She held him tight, moving the velvety skin up and down over the inner, rock-hard shaft.

Colin had hoped to bring her to climax before he took her for the first time. He wished for her to know the thrill of explosion before the pain of knowing a man. But the second she touched him he knew he could wait no longer.

His hands shook as he lifted her slightly and parted her legs to settle between them. He looked down at the fiery passion kindled in her beautiful green eyes. Her gorgeous red hair fanned the white pillow. She was beautiful. And she was all his. Never before had he felt so incredibly lucky.

Slowly he forged inside, letting her stretch to accommodate his size. She was so incredibly hot. And all for him.

Makenna shifted, encouraging him to go faster. The movement gave him so much pleasure it nearly ended the matter right then and there. Makenna moved again, and Colin plunged deep, sinking recklessly, hungrily into the snug channel of her body.

Makenna gasped and then cried out when the sharp pain of his entry shot through her body. For a moment, she thought he was too big, that she was too small, and the pain was too much to continue. Then almost as fast, it faded and the longing for something more swelled within her.

Colin's heart stopped cold at her cry. The tear flowing down her cheek tore him in two. He bent down to kiss it away and started to move out of the slice of heaven he had only just found. "I'm sorry, Makenna. I'm so sorry. I swore never to hurt you—"

"And you didn't," Makenna interjected, holding him, refusing to let him leave her completely. "Make love to me, Colin. Please, don't stop."

That was all he needed to hear. Colin gently reburied himself in the warm softness of her. Heaven had not forsaken him. It was right here. Never could he explain the comfort of knowing she wanted him as much as he wanted her. Easing himself in and out of her wet passage, he urged her into a passionate rhythm.

Makenna arched as he moved inside her, her inner muscles clinging to him, drawing him deeper within her. She knew that her tears were causing him to be slow and gentle. In an effort to hasten the pace, she opened her thighs wider, forcing his male member to sink even deeper inside her with each stroke.

Colin had tried to control the depth and speed of his thrusts. His jaw was locked with the effort, his muscles straining. But she refused to let him be gentle, meeting each thrust with one of her own. Suddenly his control broke and he drove hard and deep, his hips echoing the earthy movement of hers.

He had been with women before, he had loved Deirdre, but nothing he had experienced prepared him for the powerful force building within, becoming more fervent, more intense as they strained together. His breath changed to short gasps.

Makenna felt him deep within her and discovered the connection of two souls suffused together through their bodies. With a soft, choked exclamation, she surrendered to the tumultuous storm of sensation sweeping over her. The world had erupted into an array of dazzling stars. Nothing could have prepared her for the emotions associated with such rapture.

A second later, she felt Colin's hands pull her buttocks to him with a powerful strength that only added to her ascent. She heard him call her name, and then a heavy shudder racked him as his body surged to climax. A final triumphant exclamation escaped Colin's lips as he sagged against her. He had been torn apart and put back together again, this time whole and complete.

Makenna felt her body float back to earth and held on tightly to the one solid thing in her universe. Colin was hers, she thought happily. For this moment in time, he belonged only to her just as she belonged to him. Tomorrow would come and remind them both of ghosts and current responsibilities, but tonight he was hers.

Colin rested silently and tried to catch his breath. For years, he had heard men talking about their women or wives. And during those long weeks when they were forced to be away from their loved ones, he had never understood their talk of anticipation and need.

Even Conor had alluded to such bedroom pleasures, unwittingly chiding him saying that it was a shame only two of the McTiernay men knew the unequaled satisfaction of a wedding night. Pride had kept him from divulging that he and Deirdre had slept separately on theirs. The few times they had shared a bed, it had not possessed any of the magic he had just shared with Makenna.

Makenna. The wildest and most aggravating of the Dunstans.

He should be shocked for feeling this way about a woman who enjoyed arguing with him publicly, defied his orders, and actively looked for ways to infuriate him.

At a minimum, he should feel guilty for finding such pleasure from a woman he didn't love when he couldn't find it with the one he had. He searched for the feelings of betrayal but found none. Only gratitude for the precious gift Makenna had given him. A surprisingly beautiful and spirited gift he hoped to be worthy of receiving.

Colin rolled to his side, and Makenna sucked in her breath, preparing herself to be told to leave. Instead, he pulled his plaid over them both and drew her into his arms. Makenna exhaled and snuggled closer, treasuring being the object of his strength and security. She felt a lock of her hair being brushed aside and looked up into blue eyes shimmering with the intensity of a passing storm. His lips were so close to hers she could feel his breath on her upper lip.

"You are so beautiful," he whispered.

Makenna suddenly felt like an awkward little girl again, unknowing what to do or say in the company of a man. "I thought you considered me aggravating," she countered, hoping that levity would ease her discomfort.

Colin shifted so he could hold her gaze steady with his own. He could see her fear, but knew that he had the power to make it go away. "Aye, you are impetuous, stubborn, and indeed aggravating. But you are also very beautiful and incredibly alluring."

Makenna never thought anyone would find her beautiful, and certainly not alluring. Colin thinking her both made her a little uneasy. She was about to make another jest when he laid a finger lightly across her lips. "I cannot explain what just happened between us, Makenna. But it was incredibly unique and special."

Then something primitive and utterly feminine deep inside her stirred under the impact of his possessive gaze. His eyes burrowed into her deepest subconscious. *I know you,* they said. *I know you as no one ever has. And I want you.* She reached up and buried her fingers in his dark hair to pull his mouth down to hers. *You have me,* she answered.

She closed her eyes as his teeth suckled her bottom lip and willingly parted her lips beneath his gentle, persuasive mouth. How could she ever have thought his mouth hard and without feeling?

Makenna had ridden him with the passion she applied to anything she loved—fierce, wild, and free. He needed to show her the beauty and enjoyment of slowing down the experience. To savor the precious moments of pleasure. He was going to teach her about life, and she would teach him about living. Tonight was only the beginning.

Colin moved his tongue across her lips. They were still warm and full from when he had ravaged them earlier. He knew he would never get enough of their taste. She trembled and moaned, urging for more. He smiled and played with her bottom lip before releasing it to scatter light kisses over cheek and forehead. This time, he would take his time with their lovemaking. He would craft a slow, sensual dance, and Makenna would learn how much fun it could be to ride slow.

Chapter Five

Makenna stirred and flipped onto her back, feeling incredibly relaxed and happy. Life with Colin was not going to be the miserable one she had feared, but an exciting and blissful adventure. Finally, all was right with the world.

Sitting up, Makenna stretched her arms high and realized she was alone. The sun coming in from the window was bright, indicating she had slept in. She gathered her knees close and hugged them tightly to her. She wondered how late in the morning it was when Colin had left. He must have moved very quietly to have kept from rousing her. "Understandable, you were incredibly tired," she said, defending her unusual fatigue with a smile on her face.

She remained seated, motionless for several moments enjoying the peace. Her family was probably looking all over for her. It was past time to rise and meet them. She knew she would be unable to hide her joy, especially from her father. As soon as he saw her, he would begin congratulating himself on his prophetic knowledge. This time she would allow him such pleasure. Compared to the gift she had received last night, it was very little in return.

Stepping onto the wood-planked floor, Makenna saw the evidence of her virginity on the bed. Throwing the blanket to cover the stains, she walked over and washed herself with the small basin of water on the table aside the bed. Turning to get dressed, Makenna remembered she had nothing but her wedding dress to put on.

She shrugged her shoulders. "It's not like anyone will be surprised after Colin's show of hauling me away." She sighed.

Donning the chemise, Makenna considered calling for a chambermaid to fetch her new clothes when a knock came at the door.

"Thank the Lord," Makenna mumbled to herself. Then a sudden thought of terror came to her. It might be a soldier looking for Colin. "Who is it?" she called out, hoping a woman's voice would answer and not a man's.

"It's Ula, Makenna."

Makenna grabbed her bliaut and tried to tie it quickly, but it was not cooperating. Of all people, why would Ula be coming to see her? "Obviously, it's later than you think, *amhlair*," Makenna said to herself.

"That better not have been me you were calling stupid," Ula hissed through the door. "Let me in."

"I'm coming. I'm sorry, but I was not prepared for visitors," Makenna called out, rushing across the room to open the heavy door. "Including family, Ula. It *was* my wedding night." She couldn't help but add the snide sound to her voice as she faced her older sister.

Ula, however, seemed unaffected. She was preoccupied with twisting her hands. Tears stained her cheeks. Something was wrong. Did she and her husband have a fight?

Makenna clutched her sister's fingers in her own and asked, "Ula, whatever is the matter? Where is Rona?"

Ula took the offered chair and stared down at her hands. Her shoulders began to shake and large teardrops fell onto her lap as sobs took over the woman.

Moving beside her, Makenna knelt down and gathered Ula's weeping frame into her arms, wondering what could have saddened her hard-edged sister to such a degree.

"All will be well, Ula. I promise."

"No," Ula replied, pulling back, shaking her head. "No, nothing will be well again."

"Have you told Father? You know our great laird would do anything for one of his daughters," Makenna said, trying to evoke a sense of hope and cheerfulness in her tone. It did not work.

Ula straightened her shoulders. Her eyes narrowed with hatred. "*Our* great laird is no more. The almighty Highlander now orders us Dunstans about."

Makenna stilled. "Father?" she asked, her voice barely a whisper.

"He is no longer with us." Ula stood. Anger consumed her once again. "He passed sometime this morning."

"Does Colin know?" Makenna's voice was suddenly hollow and foreign to her own ears.

"Aye, it was he who found him and alerted the staff. My chambermaid informed Rona and me, but when we rushed to his side, it was too late. *Your* husband then ordered me *here.*"

Suddenly, Ula softened and approached Makenna. "Oh, little sister, how wrong I was to partake in yesterday's atrocity. Rona and I should have convinced Father that it was a mistake for you to marry the horrid giant. Whatever are you to do? Finding you here in his chambers, and seeing your hair so untidy . . . I suspect it is too late to annul your marriage. The Dunstans are doomed," she wailed, flinging herself back into the chair.

Makenna felt her jaw clench as Ula's statement penetrated the stunned state of her mind. A sudden urge to slap her sister washed over her. Her sister did not grieve for her father, nor for the Dunstans; she grieved for her own future. The woman no longer lived at Lochlen, but every time she and Rona visited, they pressured their father for funds to support a standard of living neither of their husbands could afford. Ula's husband, Uilleam, was too greedy, and Rona's was too inept. Ula obviously knew Colin would not be so generous with the Dunstan fortune.

"Our clan will survive. My *husband* is now laird, just as our father wished it. It is our responsibility to respect Father's good judgment and support Colin's leadership so that we will prosper and be strong once again."

Ula sat up defiantly. "You can say that even though he told no one of Father's death? I was told by a servant, and here I am trying to spare you the same insult. Good judgment, you say? Poor husband is my reply."

Makenna didn't know why Colin had delayed notifying her, but she knew there had to be a reason. A reason she would understand once he explained. "I must go. Will you be all right?"

"You really don't know what you have done by marrying him, do you? What sentence you have cast onto Rona and me?"

One of moderation, perhaps? Makenna thought to herself as she rushed out the door.

She flew across the courtyard and up the Canmore Tower steps. Along the passageway to her father's room were several soldiers standing in stoic silence. She pushed past them and entered the cavernous solar. Her father was lying unnaturally still in his bed. Colin sat next to him on a cross-frame chair clutching the man's hand as if he were alive.

Makenna approached the bed hoping Ula had been wrong. The stillness in her father's face revealed the truth. Her champion lived no longer.

A void threatened to consume her. Her father had been her last supporting figure. He had loved her completely, never ridiculing her unorthodox passions and unusual habits. He had never admonished her lack of domestic skills, instead encouraging her whenever she had made the attempt. Now he was gone, and Makenna felt her entire world had suddenly been swept away.

Colin waved his hand, and Dunlop escorted the few in the room out and closed the door. Why had such sorrow happened so soon? They were just learning to accept each other and what the other had to give. They had not yet built the trust needed to withstand such loss.

His hand let go of Alexander's. His close friend had departed, and now Colin had to take his place. Colin knew Dunlop trusted him and would follow his lead, as did Drake and the rest of his men. He had an army, but no longer did he have his friend to question him, challenge his decisions, or just be a sounding board when needed. Alexander was gone.

Colin felt cool, soft fingertips clutch his own. It was a small gesture, but it said so much to him. He looked up. The grief etched on Makenna's face pained him more than he thought possible. He gave a gentle tug and caught her as she collapsed into his arms sobbing.

For a long time, Colin cradled her as she wept. Sometimes hard and other times soft cries, but never did she let go. She needed him and right now he longed to be needed. It reminded him that he wasn't alone. That he wasn't just desired for his skill with a sword, but that on a deeper level, he was connected to someone who needed him more than anyone else.

The storms of emotions came in what seemed to be

never-ending waves. Her cries would ease just before she was sucked down into another spiral of grief. Through it all, Colin held her, never once rushing the process. Again, he had understood what she needed most and gave it to her without question or demands.

After some time, Makenna lifted her head from his chest. Colin cupped her damp cheek with his hand and used his thumb to brush away her tears. "He loved you, Makenna, so very much. Remember that."

Makenna blinked and new tears fell. "I've heard you talk about your parents and how much you loved them. How did you learn to let go?"

"We each must do it in our own way and time. I'll not tell you how to grieve, just know that you can with me. Alexander was a treasured friend I never expected to receive when I came to Lochlen. His loss will affect many."

"The clan will want to know what to do next."

"I will take care of everything, Makenna. You have had to endure much these past days by marrying me. I will not add to your burdens by making you prepare your own father's funeral."

Makenna furrowed her brow. Marrying Colin had not been a burden, just the opposite. "Colin, you are not—"

He quieted her with a soft kiss. Still keeping his lips tenderly against hers, he stood up and placed her feet gently on the floor. He released her and called out, "Dunlop!"

Instantly the door opened and Dunlop and Drake entered the solar room. "Laird?"

"Is Brodie or Gorten in the tower?"

"Aye."

Seconds later Brodie's head popped in, his usually jovial face now sad with grief.

Colin waved him in. "Brodie, escort Her Ladyship back to Forfar. Fetch someone to make her a bath. She will be eating in her chambers this evening. Her sisters may visit if Makenna wishes."

Colin watched in silence as Makenna left. Just before she exited, she looked at him one last time. Tentative trust echoed in her shimmering green eyes.

Once she was gone, Colin turned to his commanders. "Dunlop, find Gorten and have him join Brodie. I want both guards standing watch over Makenna's room. No one other than her sisters is allowed in. With so many guests still in the castle, someone might use this opportunity to influence my wife when she is most vulnerable. I'd better not learn of that happening."

"Aye, Laird."

It was the second time Dunlop had referred to him as laird. With Alexander's body so close it felt odd and a little presumptuous. But he *was* laird now. And if he were to retain that title, Colin had to act like the Dunstan chieftain, beginning immediately.

"And, Dunlop, once you have finished with Gorten and Brodie, go find Father Lanaghly."

Dunlop nodded and left.

Colin turned to Drake. "I want you to oversee Alexander's preparations for burial. We will have the ceremony in three days. That should give all clansmen an opportunity to come and give their respects. If you have any questions, come to me. If you need something or someone, ask Ula or Rona. Do not, under any circumstances, seek Makenna for help. She has been through enough the past few days."

Makenna stepped out of the tower. A large crowd of Dunstan clansmen filled the inner yard. Brodie leaned over and verified the tension she could see lining her people's faces. "Word has spread of Alexander's death. People are already questioning your husband's right to be laird."

Makenna nodded, letting him know she had heard his warning, but as soon as the thick crowd saw her they pounced. Brodie was pulling her through the mass, but everywhere she turned, there were questions. Who did she think she was marrying, an outsider and forcing him upon them as laird? Why could she not have married MacCuaig, a Lowlander who knew and respected their customs and ways? Did she regret her decision? Could she get an annulment?

No! she wanted to scream. She had no regrets, that she would never get an annulment, and that Colin held more respect for each and every Dunstan in his small finger than MacCuaig ever held for a single man, woman, or child of his own clan.

But she didn't have to.

A piercing bellow blanketed the crowd. Caught off guard, they instinctively squashed their carping and listened. Colin's deep baritone voice was laced with command and promise.

"I am now laird of this clan and claim Lochlen as my home. Alexander charged me with ensuring your safety and well-being and I intend to keep my promise to him. Any Dunstan who wishes to challenge me, let him come forward."

The crowd squirmed with dissatisfaction, but no one moved to contest Colin publicly. Near the great hall, the faces of several neighboring lairds came into view. This was not how he had hoped to establish relations and alliances, but he had no choice. This was the way it had to be.

"My wife, Deirdre, wanted this to be," Colin continued. "Alexander wanted this to be, and Makenna Dunstan married me so this would be. I am laird, and I will defend my rights as laird to any who oppose me. In return, I will regard any attack against the Dunstans—

whether it be clan, army, or nation—as a personal strike against me."

Makenna watched as Colin moved through the self-parting mass toward the great hall. No doubt he would be spending the next several days in conference. Many alliances would now be gone with the passing of her father. Some, like MacCuaig, would refuse to support a Highland leader.

A familiar voice rang out, this time aimed at Drake. "Drake, you are one of us. *You* should be laird, not an outsider."

Drake halted his long, lean frame and glared at the old man, his ice-blue eyes unwavering and unsympathetic. "It is time to heal this clan, Gannon, and save it from itself. *I* cannot do that. I give my support and loyalty to the only one I know who can."

Hearing Drake's unswerving loyalty shook Makenna to her core. His voice was laced with the same devotion Colin had just used. *My wife, Deirdre*, he had said. Makenna *Dunstan*, he had said. The man had been kind to her, nothing more. Colin had what he wanted. He was now laird.

Makenna entered Forfar Tower in silent misery. The loss of two men was more than she could bear.

Makenna was rising from her bath when a knock on the door echoed in the chamber. Just as Colin had ordered, only her sisters had been allowed to visit. They had chosen not to.

She finished securing her gown and opened the door. It was Camus. Makenna shrieked and hugged her friend and mentor.

"Ah, *laochag*, this should be a time of joy and celebration for you. Instead, you must deal with your father's passing. Laird Dunstan was a good and just man. He will be missed."

Makenna wiped away a tear and pointed to one of the chairs by the hearth. Camus relaxed on the wide, padded teak stool and examined his friend. His little warrior was trying to be strong, but streaks of recent tears were evident on her face.

Makenna pasted on a fake smile and attempted light humor. "How did you ever get in? I thought Colin had barred the entire male species from my chambers."

Camus recognized the effort at levity. "Ah, your husband may now be chief of this clan, but we have a history."

"I saw the visiting lairds join Colin in the hall. Do you know how the talks were faring?"

He shook his head with genuine concern. "I don't truly know, but if they are like the crowd outside, not well."

Makenna got up and went to stand by the window. She pulled the tapestry aside and gazed at the great hall below. The crowd had diminished, but several clansmen were still standing about, obviously complaining. "My father would not be pleased to know his people were acting thus."

"Aye, but his last thoughts were of you. He was happy last night knowing you and Colin were married. It gave him great peace."

Makenna sighed. The time between last night and now seemed like an eternity. "I think he was. I'm glad he passed believing all was well."

"Colin will need you now more than ever, just as you need him."

Makenna shook her head. "Colin needed me to marry him. I've done that. I've even consummated the marriage ensuring that an annulment is not possible."

"Makenna! You cannot truly believe that. Colin is a

proud man. He would never use a woman so, just to be the Dunstan laird."

Makenna looked up at the rafters on the ceiling. "He did. Truly. That is all he wanted. I was a means to an end. You heard him today. He still considers Deirdre his wife and me a Dunstan."

When word had spread that Colin and Makenna had agreed to marry, Camus knew something had transpired between them. Something much greater than a need to protect a clan. Unfortunately, she and Colin were still trying to understand the nature of their new bond when Alexander died.

"I do recall what Colin said, and to whom he was talking. A crowd of Dunstans with fleeting memories who need to recall it was not *you* who first brought Colin into their lives, but Deirdre. He was trying to protect you. He has demanded that your sisters take on the responsibility of readying the ceremony. He knew the distress it would cause you, and he wished to shield you from further hurt. You misjudge him greatly, little warrior."

"Are Rona and Ula complying with Colin's request?"

"More like Colin's demand, and they have no choice. Either they comply or leave. And both are still hoping to receive a stipend they feel owed to them."

Makenna rubbed her arms. "Good Lord, their hatred of him must be limitless by now. Does the rest of the clan feel the same?"

"Aye, in some cases, but in others Colin is securing their trust. Already he has ordered soldiers to assist with the keep's help. And when Drake brought Colin your father's sword, he ordered it to be returned to your father's side, claiming that he may be laird, but that did not entitle him to take what belonged to Alexander and the Dunstans."

"He said that?"

"My oath. That sword is worth a mint with its gold and jeweled hilt."

"It has been in my family for almost three centuries. Malcolm Canmore gave it to the first laird of Lochlen."

"And your husband respects that."

"But if Colin does not take the sword, who will?"

"Well, for a while your sisters squabbled over who had more right to it. Ula thought she did because she was older. Both came off incredibly greedy and selfish, diminishing the ill effects Colin had caused by ordering their aid with the funeral preparations."

Makenna turned from the window and fell into the chair beside Camus. She gathered her feet underneath her and finally asked, "Who won? Ula or Rona?"

"Neither," Camus said with satisfaction. "Colin declared it to be buried with Alexander."

Makenna threw her head back and sighed in relief. She loved that sword and understood what it had meant to her father almost better than anyone—except Colin. "That is good. It is the way it should be."

"Many think so. The decision definitely got the attention of most clansmen. Several of which are no longer open to hearing the constant cry for the new laird's departure."

"Good. Colin needs their support."

"What he needs is *your* support."

Makenna shook her head. "No, he has Dunlop and Drake."

"It is not the same, and you know it. We have known each other a long time, *laochag*, and I love you like my own daughter. But when you needed someone, who was the first person you sought? Could I have been a suitable replacement?"

Makenna stared into the leaping flames flickering in the hearth and thought about his question. Camus was someone she trusted without any reservations. Could he have provided her the same feelings of safety and comfort Colin had given her last night and this morning? The answer was an undeniable no.

"You have Colin now," Camus continued. "I know you find it impossible to lean upon anyone, and I know he is just as stubborn and independent as you. But if I can advise you one last time, learn to lean upon him and teach him to lean upon you. It will make you both stronger."

Makenna blinked tears of sorrow. "I wish it were possible, but Colin wouldn't even lean upon Deirdre, and he loved her. And while we have called a truce, Colin doesn't love me. How can I be something he couldn't find with the woman he *wanted* to share his life with?"

"You are not Deirdre," Camus scolded. "Stop trying to be. Be yourself. *That* is the person Colin needs to know. I've known you both for a long time now. If you two tried hard enough, you would be surprised at what you would find."

"Be careful, Camus, or I will think you are talking about love. And you know, just as well as I, that love is not what this marriage is based upon."

"Not now, but it can be. Before you will be able to love anyone, *laochag*, you will have to remove all the walls you have built around your heart. It calls for immeasurable trust. It took me many years to trust my wife. I hope it does not take you and Colin so long."

Makenna sat straight up and looked at him, her eyes wide with shock. "You were married?"

Since she had known him, Camus had been a bachelor who enjoyed being friendly with widows.

"Aye, a long time ago. She died before you were born." He paused and gazed into the fire, remembering. "I met Miriam when I was young. She was bonnie and feisty and it was time that I married, so I did. We were much like you and Colin. She loved to argue and was fiercely independent. Each time I took it as an affront to my manhood. I never knew how much she meant to me until she became pregnant."

"Camus! I never knew that you were a father."

"We lost the baby, Makenna. No one knows why. For a long time the loss ate away at me. I was so focused on my own grief I didn't realize my Miriam was hurting, too. One night she finally exploded, and it suddenly occurred to me that she needed *me* to tell her it was going to be all right, that *we* were going to be all right. We learned that night how much our strength came from each other. And whether you like it or not, Makenna, you and Colin are tied together now. He needs your strength. Once he knows that it will always be there for him, he will lean upon it. He won't be able to stop himself."

Makenna bit her bottom lip. Tears sprang anew. For the first time in hours, she felt hope again. Colin *had* been there for her—at the altar, last night, as well as this morning. Even now he protected her from possible cruelty while she adjusted to the idea of her father's passing.

"I am so glad you came, Camus."

"Then I'm glad to have been here for you, my little Dunstan warrior."

Makenna rose and this time produced a genuine smile for her friend. "I'm Makenna McTiernay now, wife of Colin McTiernay, laird of the Lochlen Dunstans."

Makenna awoke the next morning with a start. Something was wrong. She wasn't where she was supposed to be. This was her room, but it felt *wrong*. Like something was missing. Then she remembered. Not something— someone was missing.

Colin.

She had only spent one night with him and already his bed felt more right to her than the chambers she had slept in all her life. She wondered whether Colin had been glad of her absence or if he, too, had missed her company.

Still groggy with a poor night's sleep, Makenna found her wrap and put it on. She opened the door hoping to see a chambermaid outside waiting to attend her. Instead, two familiar faces stared back.

"Brodie! Gorten! Lord, what a burden I am to you. Have you been on watch all night?"

Both stared for a second. The light behind Makenna highlighted her loose hair hanging down around her shoulders and waist. Her pale skin made her green eyes pop with even more clarity and appeal. The guards blinked several times before responding. It was not good to find the laird's wife attractive.

Gorten raked his ginger-colored hair, hoping the action would clear his mind. "We took turns. It was no bother."

Brodie beamed a smile at her. "In fact we were grateful, milady. Forfar Tower is a far better place to sleep than the battlements."

"Well, I promise you that I won't give Colin a reason to send you back up here."

Gorten could feel his jaw crack. "How did you know . . . never mind. Was there something you wanted, milady?" he asked, giving his counterpart a withering glance.

"Ah, aye . . . I mean no," Makenna replied, looking around the empty hall. A chambermaid was nowhere in sight. Once again, the staff was declining to help her. Pride kept her from admitting the dejection she felt by her own people. Makenna knew if she uttered one complaint, either Brodie or Gorten would immediately go and drag back a servant. Help was wanted, but only if freely given. She would continue on her own.

"Just give me a few minutes, and then I will be ready," Makenna said, closing the door.

Brodie refused to shrink under Gorten's harsh stare. "You were staring, too, Gorten. Do not think I was not aware of your appreciative appraisal of Her Ladyship. You best figure a way to disguise your attraction."

"Best you be taking your own advice," Gorten returned. "And I wasn't troubled by your obvious affection, but by Her Ladyship's knowledge of our punishment. How did that come about?"

"She came up and caught me pacing Forfar's battlements the night Colin raked us for being so easily duped by one of her tricks yet again."

"You told her?"

"I told her nothing . . . at first. She surmised as much. She is as keen with her mind as you claim she is with a sword," Brodie said, somewhat bridled.

"Aye, this is a mess. Part of me wishes never to have gotten this assignment. I'd rather face a hundred men in battle. The laird really cares for his new wife, more than he is willing to admit. And if anything should happen to her now, we will not live long, friend."

"She will not make our task easy," Brodie forewarned.

"Her Ladyship? Perhaps. She does have a way of yanking down your defenses and making you vulnerable to her wishes."

"It is getting harder and harder to please both."

Gorten shook his head. "No, what's getting harder is the *need* to make Her Ladyship smile while keeping our oath to our laird."

The door suddenly swung open, and Makenna stood ready to leave. "What oath?" she asked casually.

Gorten moved to block her path. "The one to keep you in your chambers and not allow visitors."

"But that was just yesterday. I must go down and assist Colin."

"He said until the funeral and that is at least another day, possibly two, away."

"Two more days! I will not be locked away as a child for two days. I know I promised not to get you in trouble, but I'll just have to beg for your forgiveness when I find a way to get out."

"Milady, the laird doesn't see you as a child—" Gorten began.

"No, quite the opposite. Of all the people right now, you are most important to him," Brodie finished.

Gorten nodded. "It is true. Said so himself this morning when he checked in on you."

"He was here?" Makenna frowned.

Gorten nodded. "Aye, for almost half an hour he stayed with you while you slept. The man is most concerned for you."

"I felt him there. After he left, I suddenly felt cold, empty," Makenna whispered, not realizing that she was talking aloud.

Brodie elbowed Gorten. "You see, milady? Staying in your chambers is not punishment, but a gift."

"Aye, a gift," Makenna acknowledged bitterly. "But a gift that I do not want or intend to take."

"Now, milady, the laird wants you to be able to grieve in peace. He wants to protect your privacy."

"It is a kind *gift*, as you put it, Gorten. Yesterday, it was needed. Today, however, it is not. My father's death will weigh upon me for some time. Shall I lock myself away from duties and responsibilities until I no longer feel like crying?" Her eyes locked on to Brodie's before moving to Gorten's. Both men began shifting their weight uncomfortably. "I thought not. Now, if you will tell me where Colin is, I'll explain this to him myself."

Brodie swallowed heavily. "He rode toward the training fields when he left this morning."

"The training fields?" Makenna barely kept her voice from shrieking. "The man *would* pick the one place I pledged not to go. How dare he use my own oath against me!"

"I don't think it was intentional, milady. He needed to see the men. Tell them personally what was happening and give them assurance about leading the Dunstans."

Makenna bit the inside of her cheek. She really must learn not to voice her thoughts out loud. She reached out and seized Gorten's arm. "Of course, you are right. But I cannot just stay in my room all day. I *have* to be active. You can understand that, can you not?"

Brodie saw Gorten fight his reaction to her touch and quickly answered for his friend. "We do, but until the laird says otherwise, you must stay here. As soon as he returns, one of us will fetch him."

Makenna's shoulders slumped in resignation. Even if she did escape, she had no idea what she would do. Ula and Rona would order her about, and in truth, she had no desire to prepare her father's funeral. She needed to remember him the way he was the last time she saw him. At her wedding reception, happy and at peace.

Silently, she turned and reentered her chambers. The only way she could help her clan and Colin was to remain out of the way. But just as she pushed the door closed, a thought occurred to her. There *was* something she could do for her clan as well as Colin. And it could be done in the secrecy of her chambers.

She swung the door open and grabbed Brodie's hand in hers, gaining Gorten's attention as well.

As soon as they saw her emerald pools beseeching

their help, they knew they were doomed for a lifetime of night watches. For whatever Makenna was about to ask for, they were going to go through heaven and hell to ensure that she received it.

"Please, if you would do me one favor, I will stay in my chambers until my father's funeral without trickery."

Gorten and Brodie looked at each other and then back at her. "What is it, milady?"

"I want to prepare my father's sword personally. I will be the one to polish it and wrap it in a Dunstan plaid and place it in his coffin. All I ask is for you to fetch it for me *and* stop anyone who might try and reclaim it before I am done. Will you?"

"Colin has ordered several guards to protect Alexander until he is laid in the ground. It might be difficult . . ." Gorten began. The truth was Colin put several men around Alexander's chamber to protect the *sword* that so many were clambering to possess.

Brodie cleared his throat. "I will bring you the sword, milady. However, it might be best to tell no one of its whereabouts except Colin."

"If you think that best, Brodie, then I will agree and hide it when anyone comes to call. But I need that sword. It will be my way of saying good-bye. Colin will understand."

Gorten nodded in agreement. Colin would do anything for his new wife. He knew that after this morning. If retrieving the sword would make Makenna happy, then it would be hers. He didn't know how Brodie planned to do it, but Makenna would hold her father's sword by nightfall.

For two days, Makenna remained in her room working vigilantly on the most precious of Dunstan symbols.

Once done, she polished the blade until it glittered without a single blight to hamper its reflection. Carefully she wrapped the hilt in a strip of Dunstan plaid.

Soon it would be time. Father Lanaghly was even now praying over the body of her father. Each time she had looked out the window, she could see activity in preparation for the feast to follow. If she had not been so focused on getting the sword done in time, she would have gone mad needing to go down and help. Each time she felt the urge to escape, she reminded herself that despite her desire to be otherwise, she would just be in the way. She knew nothing about preparing for such events.

Makenna smoothed back her rich velvet green bliaut and checked the *Luckenbooth* pin securing the pleats of her plaid. Both were symbols of her marriage to a McTiernay. Her clan would probably be upset by the gesture, but she knew her father would be proud of the support she was showing for her husband. The Dunstan plaid would be displayed with the sword.

She moved toward the window and looked outside hoping to see Colin come for her. She had not seen him once these past two days, but knew that he visited her in the early morning hours before anyone was awake. It was only when he left her side that she awakened, each time to a feeling of something missing.

Many times, Makenna had wanted to ask Brodie or Gorten to go and fetch him, to bring him to her if only for a few minutes, but she always refrained. Colin was busy. There was much to be done with so many at the castle, and this was not the time to indulge in personal, unnecessary wishes.

Colin leaped off his mount and gave the reins to the stable master. He had been gone longer than anticipated. With all his commanders assigned to more pressing tasks, Colin had left two promising junior commanders in charge of the training fields. Until this morning, they had maintained order. Then a talented but very young soldier decided a new recruit was being instructed incorrectly. The junior commander's pride kicked in and soon complete mayhem erupted as men took sides as to how their laird would have trained the newcomer.

As soon as Colin arrived at the scene, he quickly deduced the true cause behind the havoc. The men's nerves had been so taut with tension, the fight had been inevitable. He had seen similar outbreaks happen before a long-awaited battle. If men didn't discharge their pent-up energy in a controlled manner, it exploded in unexpected and often unruly ways.

"Battle drills. Two hours on. Quarter hour off. From now until dark. Again tomorrow and the next day," Colin ordered.

Drake's eyes popped open. That was a physical challenge most of the men might not be able to meet. "For whom?" Drake inquired, hoping that Colin just meant the few men at the core of the disturbance.

"Every last soldier in my regiment. Including those in the hills. Drake, you take command now. Dunlop, it will be your turn tomorrow. I want you both practicing with the men."

Drake knew better than to protest. Colin had been in a silent, hard mood for the past two days. Talks with the local lairds had stalled. MacCuaig had demanded promises limiting Colin's ability to lead and protect the clan. While the other lairds understood Colin's quiet refusal, they could not comprehend why he did not call the young laird out on any of his many attempts to insult him. The lack of response was akin to cowardice, and many had said so. Colin simply shrugged at such remarks and asked, "How many battles have you fought the past five years?"

They answered with silence. All knew Colin had fought and led more battles than practically all of them together. In addition, William Wallace had considered him a friend and Robert the Bruce publicly called him an ally. It was hard to blend the calm man who casually dismissed insults with the fierce warrior his reputation alleged him to be.

On his ride back to Lochlen, Colin considered having Brodie or Gorten escort Makenna to the burial site. It had been hell not seeing her these past few days. An unanticipated hell. Not once during his marriage to Deirdre had he yearned for her like he was craving Makenna. It made no sense. The woman had plagued him for two years, but in just the span of a few days had turned his world inside and out. Control that had come so easily to him was now harder and harder to find. If she had come near him even once, he would have caved to his burning need for her. He would not have been able to stop with one kiss. No one was going to take advantage of her weakened emotional state, including himself. Consequently, all he allowed himself were those few brief moments early in the morning watching her sleep.

Today, however, Colin needed Makenna beside him. He did not think he could take another round of accusations without her by his side. He would need her presence to control the rage these men had no idea he was capable of.

Makenna was still staring out the window when she heard a single knock followed by the sound of the door opening. There was only one person who would enter without her permission. Colin.

Makenna spun around. She watched the play of emotions on his face. He was studying her, unsure of what he might find. Makenna couldn't believe that at one time she found him impossible to read. Camus had been right. He did need her.

Colin drank her in. She was wearing his colors. Instead of the usual single braid down her back, she had let her hair remain loose. Dunlop was right. Makenna had always been beautiful; he had just been too blind to see it.

Makenna dashed across the floor and threw herself into his arms, gathering him close. All her fears vanished. He held her tight, not ever wanting to let her go.

For several minutes, they clung to each other, drinking in each other's presence as if the other were the only possible food for their starving souls. Finally, Colin kissed her hair and gradually released his hold.

Makenna eased her grasp but refused to let go completely. She placed her cheek on his chest, relishing the steady rhythm of his heart. For the first time in days, she felt safe, and secure, and not alone.

"I'm glad I make you feel that way," Colin replied in a low voice, soft and clear.

Makenna squeezed her eyes shut. Once again, she had expressed her private thoughts. "I meant . . ."

Colin raised her chin and tucked her hair behind her ears. "I know what you said, and I know what you meant. And in return for your confession, I will give you one of my own. I, too, have felt very alone these past few days."

"Oh, Colin, I have heard about the talks." She saw his head swivel to look at the closed door. "No, not Brodie or Gorten, they would plunge a knife into their chests before betraying you. It was one of the servants bringing my meals. They told me a great deal, so much of it I wanted not to believe."

He let her go and walked over to the poster bed and

stood in the same place he watched her each morning. He stared at the pillow. "Are you also ashamed that I have not called out MacCuaig or any of the others?" he asked quietly without inflection.

She moved beside him and placed a hand on his arm. "Nay, it is not shame I feel. It's pride. Pride in a man who only pulls arms against his fellow Scots when needed, not when goaded. Give them time, Colin. They will understand what you bring."

"And what do I bring, Makenna?"

"Honor. Guidance. Security. You bring the chance that our children will grow up not knowing strife. You bring the knowledge that if battle was to come, our men will be skilled and able to return safe. They don't understand your ways, but they will."

"If you agree with my ways so much, why did you fight me so hard for two years?"

She smiled at his lighthearted tease and replied, "Oh, I have always thought you to be a fine leader of men, I just thought you a terrible brother-in-law."

"And what about husband?" he asked, his voice full of entreaty.

Makenna intuitively knew her answer was very important. She looked at his chest and played with the string on his leine. "I am just beginning to learn what he is like. So far, he is the most kind, generous, and understanding man I have ever met. I only hope to someday be as good of a wife my sister was to him."

"Makenna, never doubt your worth to me. I loved Deirdre, but she is gone now. I am with you now, and you will never know how grateful I am that you married me."

Then, powered by a need to prove his sincerity, Colin caught Makenna's face between his hands and brought his mouth down to meet hers. He let his tongue probe her passionate and welcoming warmth as he slid his hands slowly up her spine. He felt her arms stole softly around his neck as she kissed him back with a low, inviting fervor that took his breath away.

A knock came at the door, followed by another. Colin knew he should break off the kiss. Yet each time he tried, there was an even greater urge to brush his mouth lightly, possessively across hers one more time.

The knocks became louder and of greater numbers. Somewhere in the distance, he could hear the female voices of Ula and Rona ordering Brodie and Gorten to open the door. When he finally released her, Makenna's vivid eyes were luminous with promise.

Tonight he would not sleep alone.

Chapter Six

Makenna sat in front of the hall's hearth and soaked up the heat from the fire and the hot wine. She stared at the hypnotic flames lapping up the stone wall, barely aware of the conversations taking place around her. The weather seemed to know a great man had been buried earlier that day. The light drizzle had been accompanied by a cool breeze, making it feel more like late fall than midsummer. Normally, Makenna enjoyed the brisk warning of the imminent change in seasons. Today, it had chilled her to the bone.

She had believed herself to be ready to see her father and say good-bye. But when she laid his bound sword next to his side, it took all her strength not to crumple on the ground. As if knowing the exact time she most needed his strength, Colin had reached out and held her hand tightly in his own.

Makenna took another sip of wine and glanced around for Colin. He was still seated at the main table located at the end of the hall. He was in deep discussion with many of the same men she had seen the night of her wedding. Several lairds, however, had elected to congregate at a different table. They were the same ones who had vehemently objected to Colin's insistence that Alexander be buried with the Highlander rite, "earth laid upon a corpse." They believed her father should have been buried only with the Dunstan sword.

Keeping with tradition, Colin held a wooden plate and placed dirt and salt in its center. The soil represented the body becoming one with the earth, while the salt represented Alexander's soul, which would never decay. Makenna thought the symbol fitting, but when Colin proceeded to the grave and placed the plate on her father's chest, inappropriate objections rang out from the crowd. All knew they originated with MacCuaig.

Makenna sensed the tension rise in Colin and knew he was near the end of his tolerance. Startling all those present, she moved to stand alongside Colin and proclaimed loudly, "Alexander Dunstan was my father. He chose Colin McTiernay to be my husband and your laird. My father will have his sword." She paused, lifting the sword high for all to see before placing it alongside the still body empty of life. "*And* he will be buried with the Highland rite of respect. He loved Colin like a son, and I know he would have appreciated the honor."

Her words silenced the crowd. Immediately those who objected to the custom yielded, allowing Colin to finish without further interruption. They might have acquiesced to her request, but anger and resentment still stirred in their hearts.

Makenna resumed her concentration on the flickering flames. They seemed to dance in time to "Ex Te Lux Oritur," one of her father's favorite *clarsach* tunes. The sounds of the lone harp echoing in the valley repeated in her head as did the images of her father being lowered into his grave.

Makenna was about to retire, when a loud bellow

came from across the room. Immediately all eyes swiveled to its source. Leon MacCuaig.

"And *if* the English return, will the Dunstan clan continue to cower, refusing once again to fight?"

Makenna jumped to her feet and marched to the center of the room. The challenge issued was not a mere slight, but a huge insult, not only to Colin but also to every Dunstan present. More than that, it was unfair.

Under Alexander's rule, the Dunstan clan had been loyal followers of William Wallace. When Wallace had defeated the English army at Stirling Bridge in 1297, almost every able-bodied Dunstan left to fight alongside him. Many of the men died at Falkirk, and those who didn't, did so later in the continuous hit-and-run raids against Edward's men. The few who had survived, including Dunlop and Drake, returned home only after Wallace's capture and execution in 1305. In the following two years, Robert the Bruce began his rally for freedom. Alexander Dunstan had less than a handful of men left to protect his keep and was unable to send any to support Bruce's campaign.

Everyone knew all that had been left of the Dunstan army were young men naïve to the horrors of battle, or worse, untrained farmers who had fought with Wallace and barely escaped with their lives. Colin had been working hard to rebuild the Dunstan army. Those who had spied on the training camps knew their numbers were now close to a hundred strong. Their force would continue to grow as more and more men flocked to Colin's training and leadership.

Colin's eyes locked on to hers. They gleamed the darkest of blues, and Makenna knew his anger had been ignited. He didn't say a word, but she knew he wanted her to remain silent.

Earlier that day, the proud hellion of the Dunstan

clan had managed to shake his core. During her father's funeral, she again made her loyalty clear. Deirdre had refused to be confrontational with anyone. He had accepted her choice, not realizing how much he longed for the woman he loved to stand alongside him, openly declaring her devotion. Twice Makenna had risen to support him publicly. Tonight, he would stand up for her and her people.

Severing the brief connection with Makenna, Colin turned his attention to MacCuaig. "*When* the English return, the Dunstan clan will be ready. You have a McTiernay's word on it."

Colin's cool, penetrating words sliced through the room. No one said a word. The time for discussions was over. These men either believed he was capable of his claim, or they didn't.

Everyone watched in silence as Colin and MacCuaig remained standing. Minutes passed. To Makenna, Colin seemed to be growing larger, even more commanding, while Leon was beginning to sweat profusely.

Then the scraping of a chair filled the room. It came from Laird Boyd. "My father, Duncan Boyd, died fighting for Robert. And your brother, Conor, saved my life at the Loudoun Hill. The Boyds will stand behind the Dunstan clan as long as a *McTiernay* leads them."

A second later, a wide, muscular laird stood. "As will the Crawfords. The English ready themselves even now to attack again." He paused and then shouted with force, "*Tutum te robore reddam!*" Then, with deliberate calculation, he forcefully smacked his quaich down so that its contents sloshed onto the wooden table. "I will give you safety by strength," he said, repeating his clan's motto. "*If* McTiernay remains the Dunstan laird," he added forcefully.

Crawford's echoes were still bouncing off the walls

when Laird Moncreiffe stood and added his vow of solidarity. One by one the men of the lead table pledged their support, each making it clear he supported Colin, not the Dunstans.

The few Dunstans present listened as each laird stood and spoke of the English's impending retaliation against Robert, the new Scottish king. They needed protection. And for the first time, many realized that whether they liked the Highlander or not—they needed him and his allies.

MacCuaig stared at Makenna still standing in the middle of the room. Tonight had not gone according to plan, but then again, it had not been entirely unsuccessful. Several clans might have pledged their support to the new Highland laird, but many did not. Feeling the unstated backing of those seated around him, MacCuaig felt a sudden surge of power. Makenna might be married, but she was not forever lost to him.

"Can you all be so blind? You"—MacCuaig pointed at those around Colin—"so easily forget the old alliances, the long-standing promises. Makenna was *supposed to be mine.* The MacCuaigs will never support this *Highlander,* despite who is allied to him."

Makenna watched as Leon turned to address the room with a semicrazed expression. "Did you not witness how he flouted our traditions with the burying of your laird? Today he pollutes our most sacred of rituals. What will he corrupt next? I tell you we can protect our own without the Highlander."

Hearing enough, Dunlop interjected, "We stand behind our new laird. Don't we, men?" Sounds from falling chairs and benches erupted and filled the hall as every Dunstan soldier present jumped to his feet. A deafening "Aye" was shouted from the crowd as each man leveled his attention upon the Lowlander who dared to insult their chief.

Makenna stood speechless, frozen as MacCuaig dissolved under their stares. Spinning around, he faced Colin and whispered something she could not hear. When done he headed toward the door, but stopped when he got to her side. His eyes slid down her thin frame. Then, loud enough for the room to hear, he said, "Take care, Makenna. The MacCuaigs will not help your clan in their hour of need." He pointed across the room, but his eyes never left her. "Crawford, Moncreiffe, Boyd, and the others may back your husband, but their support is many days' ride away. Only I will be able to save you."

Colin saw red as sheer fury poured through him. "Leave now, MacCuaig, while you still can. One more word and I will consider it a challenge to be met here and now."

For the first time since his arrival, MacCuaig felt satisfaction. Nothing had worked. He had challenged McTiernay's honor, his clan, his Highlands. Makenna was his weakness. Ah, the joy he would get when he stripped her from Colin's grasp and made Makenna his own.

Unfortunately, now was not the time. The Highlander was more skilled than most with a sword and currently surrounded by his newly established allies. Leon needed an edge, one that he didn't have now. Soon, though, he would have everything owed to him. He just needed to be patient.

Makenna stared in shocked silence as MacCuaig bowed his head toward her and then to his table of potential comrades. She held her breath as he stormed out of the hall and ordered his men to prepare for immediate departure.

Exhaling, she felt relieved, but the sensation only

lasted for a moment. Her eyes searched for Colin and widened the moment they locked with his. His gaze was blazing with fury and anger, and it was aimed not at the departed Leon MacCuaig, but at her.

Makenna had thought she had witnessed Colin's anger many times since his arrival at Lochlen. She had been wrong. Never had she seen Colin truly mad.

Immediately following MacCuaig's departure, Colin had ordered Brodie and Gorten to escort her to the Black Tower and wait for him in his chambers. Makenna had presumed Colin intended to make her stew for hours, but no more than ten minutes had passed when he charged through the door.

Makenna usually could disregard Colin's imposing stature, but the raw fury roaring through him made her wish she were anything but its target.

She felt herself swallow heavily and shrink in fear. But just as she was about to retreat a few steps away from the path of his furious pacing, her inner voice called her a coward. "I have no reason to cower to you, Colin Mc-Tiernay. I have done nothing wrong," she said to herself, this time making sure her mouth was closed.

Donning a mask of calm indifference, Makenna sauntered over to the basin and splashed some water on her face. The action was a deliberate show of ease, that she was not one of the Lowland lairds easily intimidated by his commanding presence. She patted her face dry and then faced him, arching a single brow.

Colin watched with incredulity as Makenna straightened her back, briefly assessed him, and then marched to the table acting as if he were not even there, let alone furious. He had no doubt that she was fully aware he was seething. Still, she offered no apologies, no requests for leniency, and no entreaties for forgiveness. The woman practically challenged his right to be angry.

"When were you going to tell me?" he roared.

"Colin, stop yelling at me."

"I am not yelling. Whenever I do yell, there will be no mistaking it." He had lowered his voice by several decibels, but it was definitely still loud.

Makenna watched as Colin resumed his pacing in front of the cold hearth. She had been about to light a fire when she had heard him order Brodie and Gorten and everyone else out of the tower just before he had stormed through the door.

Over the past few years, she had witnessed him in several moods, but never one like this. And all because of MacCuaig's distorted sense of their relationship. Makenna decided to treat this argument with the level of intensity it deserved. None.

She leaned casually against the table and gripped the sides loosely. "Fine, then stop growling. It is most upsetting."

Her relaxed demeanor both floored and inflamed him. "Your indifference to my anger shows that you have no regard to how I felt when MacCuaig told me of your trysts in the woods. Were you ever going to tell me?"

"So that's what he whispered to you," Makenna mused aloud. Hearing Colin grunt, she crossed her arms and shrugged nonchalantly. "Honestly? I don't think I ever was going to mention it. It meant nothing. Those meetings, if you can even call them that, occurred long ago, well before you came to Lochlen. Leon didn't care that I wasn't like all the other girls. Every once in a while, he would be in the woods at the same time as I and join me in my hunts. He would praise my skills. It was very flattering, but I never thought his proposal of marriage was serious. Then or now. I remember him laughing when I turned him down."

Colin stopped his pacing and stood between two of the hearth chairs. He clenched the back of each chair and leaned forward. "Trust me, Makenna. Leon Mac-Cuaig was not laughing. Then or now."

Makenna quashed a shiver caused by the dangerous softness in his voice. Rallying, she replied, "See, I knew you would not understand. It was just a few innocent kisses. Flirtations to pass the time."

"That man was at our wedding!"

Colin could still remember seeing the tense look in MacCuaig's eyes when Makenna entered the chapel. At the time, he had dismissed it, deciding instead to focus on the vision coming to accept his hand. He should have confronted MacCuaig that very night, at the celebration when the man openly displayed his jealousy and lust. Instead, he had fought his instincts to call the man out, thinking that he was being irrational, seeing something where there was nothing.

But his instincts had been completely accurate. Makenna and MacCuaig did have a past, and it was enough of one to make Leon believe that she somehow belonged to him. The idea of Makenna with another man shot through Colin's mind, and he felt a new bout of possessive fury building within him.

Makenna furrowed her eyebrows in confusion. For a fleeting moment, she wondered if Colin's anger stemmed from a type of jealousy. She dismissed the idea. Jealousy would imply a level of emotional attachment, and Makenna knew she was too vulnerable to hope Colin was developing a tenderness for her. It was best to remain indifferent. "So he was at our wedding. I promise you Leon MacCuaig has no interest in me, why would he? The only reason he said any of those things tonight was to goad you into a response. He tried all other tactics. He was just grasping at anything to get you to react to his taunts. What I find hard to believe is that you allowed him to do so."

Colin looked at her with appalled silence. Was the woman completely unaware of her own allure? Could she truly be that naïve of how powerful her unconventional beauty was? The question suddenly brought back the conversation he'd had with Dunlop less than a week ago. *He* had failed to see Makenna as a beautiful, desirable woman. Could she also be incapable of seeing herself as others did?

"The man wants you, but you belong to me, Makenna," Colin muttered darkly, walking toward her.

She raised her chin, her green eyes glittering with pride. "Belong to you? I belong to no one, Colin McTiernay."

He reached out and pulled her fiercely against him. "Wrong, Makenna, you belong to me."

Makenna felt her temper start to flare and wrenched free from his grasp, moving backward until she bumped into the stone barrier. "Deirdre might have belonged to you, but I never will."

Colin placed his two hands on either side of her head and pinned her between his body and the wall. "That is where you are wrong again. Deirdre never belonged to me the way you do."

Colin's mouth came down with a fierce possessiveness, cutting off any attempt at a rejoinder. His lips moved against hers hard and deliberately, letting her feel the frustration and temper she had aroused in him. "Ah, Makenna, what you do to me," he murmured against her lips before plunging inside her mouth once more, tasting, teasing, voraciously consuming her very essence.

Stunned by the near violence of his embrace, Makenna instinctively stiffened only to find herself weaken and melt moments later. Desperately she tried to find some scrap of will to push him away and argue that she was not his, that she was her own person whom no one laid claim to.

The sensation of being so powerless to anyone, especially Colin, frightened her. But even more frightening was her unfailing reaction to his touch. Even when angry, the man created an instantaneous effect on her senses.

Makenna relaxed, and Colin's body came ablaze with desire. No matter how much she challenged him or angered him, she still came alive with passion when she was in his arms. Her fingers dove into his hair, pulling him tighter, pleading with him to deepen the embrace. His heart jolted and a sense of urgency drove him to comply with her wishes. The world was closing in, and he realized he needed to breathe. Inhaling, her elusive, womanly scent aroused him even further.

Not daring to raise his mouth completely from hers for fear that he might somehow lose her, he quickly removed her bliaut and then her chemise. Not until he heard the sound of his own leine ripping did he realize she, too, was undressing him. The feel of her naked flesh pressing against his, the sensation of her light and numerous kisses all over his chest, the knowledge that she truly wanted him after all that had happened, caused his blood to boil, driving him beyond the edge of his control. In one motion, he swept her into his arms and then down on his bed.

Gone was the gentle man of her wedding night. Colin's mouth was everywhere, hot, and sensual—branding him on her skin. Never would she be able to look at a man without thinking of Colin. Makenna needed him to feel the same about her.

Sliding her palm down his chest, past his abdomen, she closed her fingers around his masculine appendage. Feeling him large and hard in her hands, she wondered how her body could accommodate, let alone enjoy, their love-making. Slowly she rubbed the loose flesh up and down while using her thumb to massage the moistened tip.

"God, Makenna . . ." he moaned and arched his back away from the sensitive contact.

Emboldened by his reaction, Makenna pulled him back down with her free hand and captured his earlobe lightly between her teeth. "Aye, Colin. Do you wish me to stop? Or perhaps I should leave?" she teased, knowing that regardless of his answer she would do neither.

"You're killing me, but never has death looked sweeter," came a breathy, tight reply.

Makenna smiled and then heard herself gasp as he gently caught one hard nipple between his lips, laving it with his tongue. Makenna shuddered and squeezed the flesh in her grasp.

"Easy, I still need that," Colin murmured, gently removing her hand. But, instead of moving it to his chest as he expected, Makenna moved her palm even lower.

Her fingertips found his warm sacks and began to knead them in a blissful and torturous way. All he could do was bury his face in her throat and fight for breath. As he'd never desired to bed loose women, only in his dreams had a woman touched him thus. Her fingers were creating a magical sensation he knew he could not endure for any length of time.

On the verge of losing his seed before ever entering her, Colin seized her torturous hand in his own. "Now it is my turn. I shall drive you mad with desire. I want to feel you writhing in my arms, needing me as much as I need you."

Makenna was about to say that she was already insane with want of him, that she did need him—more than she thought humanly possible—but she didn't have the chance. He cut off her words with another seductive, mind-numbing kiss.

Collecting both her hands in his left, he stretched them above her head. He wanted all her attention on his every touch, every caress. His right hand then started along the side of her thigh, gliding lightly over her silken skin. Just before he reached the heart of her own fire, he moved down the inside of her thigh. Bringing his hand up her leg again, he paused until he was inches from the hot, damp core of her. Lightly he moved his fingers through her already moist hair, refraining from actually touching her.

Makenna felt herself arch in search of his fingers. Colin used his lower body to keep hers still as he tormented her senses with his caresses. At the same time, he continued his exploration of her mouth with his tongue. No mortal being could withstand the whirlwind of sensations he was creating.

Finally, his mouth broke free of hers to nibble at her earlobe and then neck. She cried out, "Colin!"

"Aye, wife?" he replied, kissing the quick pulse at the base of her throat.

"Please, I can take no more."

"Please what?" he asked, knowing exactly what she craved.

"Please touch me. Please," she pleaded.

"I am," he assured her as he lowered his mouth to her breast.

A powerful shudder reverberated through her. He wanted to drive her mad, and he was succeeding. "Colin, I need you to be inside me."

Colin knew she was on the brink, but she had driven him even closer. He stopped his onslaught, balanced himself on his elbows, and peered into emerald pools swirling with passion. "Say it."

Makenna licked her lips. The sudden cessation of his caress was almost as torturous as his touch. "Say what?"

He moved his lips right next to her ear. "Say it," he whispered.

"You're arrogant, overbearing, and a bully."

He just stared at her with a small knowing grin. It mattered not that he was in agony with pent-up sexual tension. Colin would stay there forever waiting for her to admit that she was his. He knew it, and she knew it.

"I belong to you, Colin," she said softly, knowing that despite everything, it was the truth.

Her avowal was like balm to his soul. Not until the words washed over him did he understand exactly how much he needed her to say them aloud. No amount of sexual torment could have forced her to make such a declaration if she did not believe it.

"Aye, Makenna, you do. And while I may be arrogant, overbearing, and a bully, I am also selfish. I will never share you with another soul. You are mine."

Then he kissed her, this time slowly, taking his time, letting her feel the endless need for her he had inside him. Without removing his lips, he moved so that he lay on his side, giving his fingers access to the dark red curls that concealed her most intimate of secrets.

Makenna closed her eyes and forced herself to breathe. His hand seemed to take an eternity. When she felt Colin enter her softness, she felt the world begin to spin. Slowly he began to stroke her, parting her with his fingers, opening her to his caress. She heard someone cry out.

Feeling her writhe with need for even more, Colin began to draw a pattern along the sensitive flesh just below her soft, wet channel. The delicate design nearly drove Makenna over the edge. He edged two fingers deeper, exploring her with a deliberate possessiveness that caused Makenna to shriek in surprise as throes of climax consumed her.

Colin felt her honeyed flood dampen his hand and moved to straddle her hips. He stared down at her body. Her chest rose and fell with rapid breaths. Settling himself between her legs, he hesitated. "Makenna, you feel so good. I . . . I am afraid I might lose control and hurt you," he warned, his voice thick and unsteady.

"You won't, Colin. Let go. Let go and join me. I need you as I need air, and I want it all. Even the parts of you that you fear. I need them. Please." Then she lifted herself against him.

No longer in charge of his baser instincts, Colin plunged, driving deep, seeking his own release. Instantly he was transported to another plane of existence. No experience in the past or in the future could match the exquisite feeling of being inside her.

He eased himself partway out of her channel and then entered her again with a long, sure movement. Makenna felt herself stretch to encompass him as new, even stronger sensations swept through her body. She rocked against him, taking him deeper inside her with each thrust.

Just as she felt the heavens open up, Colin cried out as he surged forward into her one last time. Buried deep within her, he felt shudders overtaking his body as he burst into a million pieces. For several minutes, his body pulsated with erotic release.

Thinking he might be crushing her, Colin mustered just enough energy to shift off her and gather her in his arms. For a long time, they lay clinging to each other.

Makenna had never been with another man, and this was only the second night she had lain with Colin. Yet she knew without a doubt that what they shared was powerful and unique. They were forever bonded together.

Raising herself on an elbow, she looked down at him, her eyes serious. "Colin . . . you belong to me." It wasn't a challenge, or an ultimatum. Just a simple statement of fact.

Colin reached out and twirled his fingers through her hair. "Aye, that I do, Makenna. I will never want another."

She let him pull her cheek down so that it rested on his chest. He did not offer words of love, but what he did give, Makenna treasured. He wanted her, cared for her. Not the way he adored Deirdre, but it was enough.

Colin lay awake stroking Makenna's hair, listening to her deep repetitive breaths proving she was asleep. Her body molded perfectly to his as if God made her only for him. She would never know how much he relished the simple act of holding her while she slept. It was a gesture of trust, and it made him realize just how lonely his life had been.

His sexual desire for her was still present, but it no longer consumed him. Yet he still wanted . . . no, needed her by his side.

With the exception of his eldest brother, only Makenna seemed uniquely immune to his temper. He had been furious earlier and had done nothing to conceal the level of his anger. Yet never once did Makenna cower and retreat. Instead, she told him to stop yelling and was shockingly honest. And though he had loved Deirdre, their relationship had lacked something vital. They never learned how to be completely themselves around each other. Consequently, they never shared the true passion he was finding with Makenna. She was completely different from his soft-spoken, gentle, fragile Deirdre. Makenna was wild, and impetuous and aggravating.

And she was his wife.

Deirdre was dead, and it was time to say good-bye. He would always love her, but Makenna was his future. A future he looked forward to and would only jeopardize with continual thoughts of his late wife. He had a second chance with Makenna. She was vastly different than Deirdre and maybe that made all the difference.

Chapter Seven

Makenna rolled over and pulled Colin's heavy arm around her. The room was dark, but she could see the faint rays of sunlight beginning to emerge. Her first day of complete freedom had arrived. All the lairds had departed for their homes yesterday evening, and Rona would be leaving this morning—finally. Ula had left days ago shortly after announcing that she would no longer remain "in the presence of a Highlander destroying her childhood home."

She and her husband, Uilleam, ran a small keep in South Ayrshire near the Crossraguel Abbey. It was a nice home and well built, but too small to be of notable significance. Uilleam had intended to remove and use the stone from the abandoned church to expand his estate until the Black Monks announced that they intended to rebuild. Supporters of the monks chased Uilleam away, making it clear they would attack if they caught him thieving again.

He and Ula then turned their greedy eyes to Lochlen hoping to convince Alexander it was they who should succeed him and lead the Dunstans. Alexander had not agreed. Next, Ula had hoped her father would repay her efforts to see Makenna married by funding Uilleam's ambitions to extend their home. Alexander died before she could ask, and Colin stated that he had no interest in providing any family member continuous financial support. Anger and spite drove Ula and her husband to support MacCuaig.

Mortified that Ula was publicly opposing her own father's wishes, Makenna had launched into a verbal tirade with her in front of everyone the morning following MacCuaig's hasty exit. Her fury had quickly transferred to Colin, who proceeded to drag her away from the hall, cutting off her final and most scathing remarks.

Colin normally would have found Makenna's escapade infuriating. He needed to be spending time building alliances, but then it isn't every day a husband learns the secret to mollifying his wife.

All the way to the loch, Colin had either watched Makenna fume or listened to her spew words about his bullying nature and high-handed ways. Apparently, no one before had ever dared to embarrass her in such a manner. It was then he realized that Makenna was totally unaware of how inappropriate and unladylike her behavior appeared to those around her.

Arriving at her favorite spot, Makenna huffed and gave Colin an icy look. The walk had done little to diminish her anger. She leaned against one of the waist-high rocks by the shore and boiled in silence.

Colin found himself at a loss for what to do or say. Part of him was actually pleased her anger stemmed from her loyalty to him. However, a larger part wished Makenna would restrain her sudden antagonistic urges.

He needed to return to the gathering, but subjecting Gorten and Brodie to her current mood would be a cruel order. Colin deliberated about bringing up her conduct but quickly dismissed the idea. Last year while visiting his brother, he had witnessed Conor come very close to losing some very precious body parts when he had tried to advise his wife on her behavior when she was still angry. Women can be the most sensible and logical beings in the universe, but drag them into a discussion when they are not in the mood, and watch irrationality explode.

And Makenna was clearly not in the mood.

Colin's only hope was to induce Makenna into thinking about something else. "You know I also wonder about your sister Ula," he started conversationally.

Makenna kept her arms crossed and looked at him from the corner of her eye. The man made absolutely no sense sometimes.

Colin saw her reaction and took it as a good sign. "Many think my mother's idea about naming her sons with the letter C rather odd. I must admit that I am one of them. Now, don't mention this to my brother Conor, and especially not to his wife, but they've actually decided to continue the tradition. And if you have hopes of doing the same, prepare yourself to be disappointed. Our children will have their *own* names."

Makenna squinted and shook her head in confusion. "Colin, whatever are you going on about?" she asked, not realizing that for the first time in an hour she was thinking about something other than Ula's betrayal and Colin's rude interruption.

Colin picked up some rocks and moved to rest beside her on the boulder. He took one pebble and threw it toward the water, watching it skip along the reflective surface. "Just this, my name was not my *choice*. I could not influence the way my mother chose to name her sons. Ula, however, *chose* to marry Uilleam. No wonder they are unhappy and take it out on others. Can you imagine if your name was Colina or if mine were Makenzie?"

Makenna felt her jaw drop. "I would never have married you."

"Nor I you," Colin replied, throwing another stone. Then a devilishly attractive grin flashed across his face. "But Ula *did* choose to marry Uilleam."

Maybe it was the way he said their names. It could have been that they were the butt of his joke. Regardless of what it was, Makenna felt her fury subside. She grabbed the last rock out of his hand and flung it so that it hopped several times before sinking to the bottom. "We can go back now, Colin. I promise to yell no more at Ula—if she is even still here."

"Glad you are feeling better."

Makenna moved to stand in front of him. "But you do agree that Ula deserved everything I said, maybe even more."

"And do you agree that I was right to haul you away?" he asked, pulling her between his legs.

Makenna shrugged her shoulders and played with the laces on his leine. "I guess. It matters so little to her. My father's wishes, her betrayal, Uilleam's greed . . . all of it. The only reason she was passably agreeable the day of our wedding was to influence my father."

"Alexander may have been soft when it came to his daughter, but he was not going to fund the expansion of her keep."

"You heard about that?"

"Aye. Uilleam actually approached me before the funeral. You can imagine my answer."

"That explains why he and Ula didn't hesitate to support MacCuaig. Revenge." Makenna paused and released a long sigh. "She is so blind. She cannot be reasoned with or even shamed into doing what is right. It was a waste of my breath and emotion."

Colin tugged her gently against him. "Let me give you

something you can invest your emotions into." He breathed before lowering his lips to hers. Makenna instantly melted and reached out for support. He kissed her slowly, letting her feel the endless need inside him. It was a long time before Colin ended the tender embrace.

That was nearly two weeks ago.

Makenna flipped over on the bed and began to play with the dark hair on Colin's chest. Ula was gone, and today Rona and her husband would return to their home. Rona's constant nit-picking had grown each day her husband remained and participated in talks of alliances. Discussions had ended late yesterday evening, and Rona's husband was among the many who had not yet pledged his support to Colin.

"Leave, Rona, life will be much more peaceful with you gone." Makenna sighed to herself. Her fingers danced in the soft curls that covered his upper body before tapering to a line down his abdomen.

Colin stirred, and Makenna knew she had once again spoken aloud. "Well, what do you expect when you have cultivated a habit for so many years?" she asked herself, making sure her lips were firmly pressed together.

Her hair moved, and she knew Colin was awake. Every morning began this way, regardless of the night before. They could come back to his chambers quiet, aroused, or angry, but they always ended in bed, sometimes with frenzied need, and other times with slow deliberation.

Makenna felt free to be totally herself when inside these walls. Lack of fear brought a sense of security and with that an unbridled passion Makenna was unaware she possessed until these past few weeks.

Colin was just about to attend to Makenna's playful hand when someone unexpectedly banged on the door.

No one would summon him at this early hour unless they carried important, and most likely bad, news.

"Stay here," Colin gently ordered before throwing on his leine and belt. Grabbing his sword, he headed toward the door. Before she could see who was in the hall, the heavy wooden barrier closed behind him.

The wood slats muffled their voices, but did not completely block their words. Makenna swung out of bed and threw on her chemise. She moved by the door and recognized Dunlop's voice.

"There were several fires set against outlying Dunstan families during the night. One boy was burned, but will live."

"Raiders?"

"No one saw or heard anyone."

"Select a small group of men to accompany me. I ride in an hour," Colin ordered, his voice disappearing as he descended the tower stairs.

Makenna swallowed. *Small group of men*, Colin had said. She wanted to find him, hold him tight, and make him promise to be careful. Pride kept her feet planted and her hands by her sides.

Suddenly feeling chilled, Makenna walked over to the hearth and added a log to the fire. She stoked it until the flames grew large again, heating the ambient air. Pulling the McTiernay plaid off the bed, she wrapped it around her shoulders and sank into the oversized padded chair she knew Colin preferred. Colin would return and explain what was happening before he left. She just needed to be patient.

"If I were to count all the minutes I spend studying the flames of a fire, I would no doubt learn that I have lost a year of my life," she mumbled, moving to rest her head in a more comfortable position.

Several piercing shouts from the courtyard below jarred

her back awake. Makenna blinked and saw that the light entering the room was significantly brighter than before. She had fallen asleep. At least an hour had passed.

Makenna stretched her deadened limbs and waited for the painful tingling sensation to fade so that she could go and see what was happening.

"Did you fall asleep in the chair?"

Makenna swung around to see Colin enter the room. "Aye," she replied softly as he pulled out a plaid from the chest. His manner was casual, but she could see the tension in his muscles. "What happened?"

"Nothing you need be aware of. I will take care of it."

His reply was short and terse. Makenna took a deep breath. He was treating her as if she were a child who needed blanket reassurance that all was well. She rose to her feet. "I do not doubt that you will resolve whatever is wrong, Colin. I am just asking what happened."

Colin closed his eyes seeking patience and finding none. "And once I tell you, you will want to know where I am going, how long I will be gone, and if it will be dangerous."

Makenna straightened her shoulders and eyed him closely. "Aye, those are considered basic questions a wife asks her husband when she sees him prepare to leave and not just for the day's work."

"I will not be explaining myself to you or anyone else. I am laird now, and I decide who receives what information and when," he instructed, his voice harsh.

Her hands flew to her hips. "You best *decide* to include me and *before* you leave, Colin McTiernay. I am quite knowledgeable about fighting, and I can recognize preparations to enter one."

Colin felt his insides clench and focused his attention on securing his belt around his pleated plaid. "Aye, I have heard about your alleged skill with a blade."

"*Alleged?* I'll have you know I am d—"

"And like so many of my young, ignorant recruits, you do not understand the great difference between wielding a sword with someone who won't kill you and with someone who will. And if I have anything to say about it, you never will."

Makenna's jaw dropped. "You are serious about leaving and telling me nothing. *Nothing about my own clan.* If we are in danger . . ." Her eyes were wide with heated awareness.

Colin stifled an oath. "If you were in danger, I would not leave, Makenna. You know that," he stated bluntly, wishing he could end this conversation by taking her to bed again. Unfortunately, there was not time to make her see reason, and by the look of her stubborn jawline and flashing emerald eyes, Makenna did not have the slightest inclination to be sidetracked.

"And just why should I know that?" Makenna asked, knowing the insinuation would prick his pride.

It worked.

Colin moved so quickly Makenna never saw him coming. One second she was fuming by the hearth chair and in the next Colin's hand was around her wrist dragging her across his chest. His blue eyes glinted and pierced her soul. "Because you know me."

He was right, and suddenly Makenna didn't want to fight with him just as he was about to leave, heading into possible danger. The fact was, whether he knew it or not, she *did* know what happened and where he was going. Their fight was about two souls and their pride. And somehow, keeping her pride with Colin was not nearly as important as it once was.

"Aye, Colin, I do know you. You are proud and stubborn, but you would never consciously leave Lochlen, my people, or me in danger. But you should also know that I am not dense. I know something has happened, and it requires you to leave. But what has not occurred to you is that this terrible news will eventually make its way back here. The more you trust me, the better I can prepare our people."

Colin stifled a groan, knowing their argument had not been terminated but merely postponed. Makenna understood that he needed to leave, just not his need to shield her. Colin dropped a soft kiss into her hair and threaded his fingers through her thick mane. It was gloriously soft, and he knew not being able to touch her for days, possibly weeks would be torture.

He pulled her head back and peered down into bright green pools glimmering with unshed tears. Makenna's eyes were keyholes to her thoughts, and right now they were full of apprehension. He leaned down and brushed his lips lightly across hers. "Take care of the keep while I'm gone. Drake's going with me. Dunlop will be with the men at the training fields if you need him. Brodie and Gorten are to remain here with you."

"I won't miss you," she promised softly as he walked to the door.

He turned back and replied, "Aye, you will." His answer was filled with both arrogance and fear. Colin looked at her for one last moment. And then he was gone.

Makenna stood transfixed for several moments. Their argument had been completely overshadowed by his last request. *Take care of the keep*. The words kept repeating themselves. Makenna felt the dark walls of the tower begin to close in on her. Ula had been right. The day when her lack of domestic skill would ruin her life had arrived.

"Damn you, Ula!" Makenna muttered as panic invaded her limbs, causing the need to move.

As she paced back and forth, every half-learned lesson about weaving, candle making, running the household, and preparing meals flashed in her head. In her youth, such activities seemed so simple and boring. Now they loomed in front of her as the most complex of chores. How could she take of the keep when she had no idea what to do?

"Stop, Makenna, and think. You can do this. You mastered the battle-axe and the claymore. You learned to hunt and ride. Each seemed impossible at first. You *can* do this; it's just a decision. You're smart, and probably know much more than you think. And what you don't know, someone can teach you. You're the Lady of Lochlen Castle."

Finishing her self-directed pep talk, Makenna felt enormously better. She poured some water into her hands and rinsed off her face. Deciding to forgo the bliaut today, she created an *arisaid* from the McTiernay plaid and marched out of Colin's room and toward the stairwell.

Clutching the thick rope attached to the center, Makenna moved to descend when a conversation drifted up the narrow cylindrical structure. Prepared to ignore the two women and go by them, Makenna stopped cold upon hearing her sisters' names followed by her own.

"Glad I found you," whispered the first voice. "We can talk now that the Highlander has departed."

"But what about . . . ?" asked a second woman. Makenna could not make out the rest of the question and assumed the woman was gesturing.

"Do not concern yourself so," the first voice replied. Makenna recognized its owner. Lela. "No doubt our *mistress* is still sleeping while we work."

"If you are so bitter, why did you elect to come back to Lochlen for work? Rumor has it you have a new suitor."

The second woman sounded familiar, but Makenna could not put a name or face with the voice. If only she had heeded her father's advice to learn all those who worked at the castle. "There will be times when recognizing the faces and voices of the castle will be more important to you than knowing how to wield a sword," he had warned. She had truly not believed him at the time, unable to envision a situation when domestic responsibilities would overlap with her life.

Ask her about horses, the stables, or even the stable masters. Ask her about weapons, their use, or her skill. These topics could hold her interest for hours. But the women who supported Lochlen were bizarre creatures with whom she had nothing in common. She had never spent one minute longer than she had to in their company.

"I do have a new man," Lela haughtily replied. "It was he who convinced me to stay and assist Lady Ula and Lady Rona while they were visiting."

"Didn't I just see Lady Rona leave?"

"Aye, she cannot stand to be at Lochlen without her older sister. And you-know-who has never been one for keeping a woman company."

Makenna bit her bottom lip and wondered if they were referring to her. She shrugged her shoulders and decided it did not matter. Restarting her descent, she had not totally lifted her foot when again their conversation stopped her.

"Too bad Lady Rona's husband did not show the same spine of Uilleam."

"I don't know, Lela. I doubt Ula will be allowed to visit again with her husband backing MacCuaig so publicly."

"It will not matter when Lochlen falls into MacCuaig's grasp. He may even have Uilleam manage Lochlen under his rule."

The second voice sighed. "I think Laird MacCuaig is somewhat delusional if they think the Highlander is going to so easily give up his clan and ranking. Uilleam is a fool, and Ula even more so for marrying him. He may have a pretty face, but weak knees. Same for Rona's husband. To tell you the truth, I'd rather have the Highlander."

Makenna smiled to herself, feeling a rush of pride that Colin was the preferred choice among some women. But just as hope was emerging in, a wave of reality washed it away.

"Never!" Lela hissed. "I would rather die the way of Wallace than submit to an outsider."

"Were you not an outsider coming from the Highlands yourself, Lela?"

Makenna mentally cheered the woman with her lips pressed together to ensure that her comments did not accidentally escape.

"The land, its people, and its customs *never* laid claim to my soul. Those mountains are miserable, and the men who claim them are barbarians. And now that one of them heads the clan of my dead husband's, the only peace I have is knowing that his home will soon be in complete disorder under the supervision of his new wife."

"'Tis true, what you say. Our new lady has not a notion of who comes and leaves. And it is certainly not my responsibility to know or care. The laird must be ashamed that his wife is so ill-equipped to help him run and protect his home."

Makenna took a step back and leaned against the cold stones of the staircase wall. What did they mean ill-equipped to protect his home? Wasn't it *Colin's* duty to see the keep was safe?

Lela tapped her fingers loudly along the small windowsill and looked out through the dirt coating the glass. It had not been cleaned for months. Her hostility was distancing Doreen. A new direction was needed. "I would wager a new luckenbooth our *lady* doesn't care. She doesn't care about her clan, her keep, or even her appearance."

"Aye, and what a shame. Who knew Lady Makenna could be such a bonnie lass? She caused quite a stir among the men at her wedding, even my boy Rufus went on about it. It's a pity she doesn't continue to at least try and make herself presentable."

"I predict the Highlander's eye will soon rove if she continues to be unsightly and conduct herself with such rebellious behavior," Lela prompted.

A light laughter tinkled up the stairs. "Your new beau's eye maybe, Lela, but not that Highlander's—even if she gives him reason. You may have your harsh opinion of the Highlands, but that man stayed true to Lady Deirdre despite her being ill nearly their entire marriage. I know; I attended her."

"Still, Doreen—"

"Still nothing, Lela. I was there when Laird Crawford told all who could hear that when the McTiernays make a promise, it is for life. And I believe him. I've seen it."

"Hmph," Lela muttered. Doreen was obviously not going to disavow their new laird . . . yet. "Well, regardless of how you feel about McTiernay's 'noble heart', he now is with a woman who would rather play all day than tend to her home."

Makenna's jaw tightened. *Playing! These people think I am having nothing but fun training and hunting! Aye, it's what I enjoy, but those things are hard.* "I'd like to see you hunt for the food I place in your mouth, Lela Fraser," Makenna whispered aloud.

Balling her fist, Makenna painfully banged the stone barrier. It mattered little what these two women thought.

Doreen clucked her tongue. "Now, that, Lela, is a topic we do agree on. Indeed, wouldn't we all want to be riding in the breeze or doing only what we enjoyed? You know, I think the lass actually believes we like cleaning, cooking, and taking care of this place."

Doreen's condemning words stunned Makenna. She felt as if the iciest loch waters had struck her while sleeping.

Lela, sensing Doreen was now ripe for suggestion, whispered surreptitiously, "That brings me to what I came to tell you. Some of us are leaving."

"Leaving? Where will you go?"

Lela scoffed. "Not the clan, Doreen . . . *Lochlen*. I'd rather assist in the fields or build that horrid wall than work in the disorganized nightmare this place is soon to be."

Doreen gasped. "But what will Lady Makenna do?"

"What do we care?"

"Don't you find that cruel to do to one of our own? Lady Makenna is not mean. In fact, I have always thought of her as quite kind."

"And unappreciative."

"True, but—"

"And no one wants to stay where there is no one overseeing things, no steward, and no cook."

"Oh Lord . . . the cook is leaving, too?"

"Left this morning after she made Lady Rona her morning meal and a traveling pack to go. This place will soon be a disaster. What help does stay will grow angry, and then . . ." Lela hinted, her voice trailing with a significant amount of malice. The woman was not merely unhappy about Colin, Makenna realized, but sought to punish her as well.

"Then *everyone* will leave," Doreen finished softly.

"You may want to consider avoiding the inevitable bitterness and depart immediately like me."

"I don't know. I don't want to work in such conditions, but I don't want to see Lochlen fall apart either."

Unable to hear any more, Makenna turned and reentered Colin's chambers. Closing the door silently behind her, she leaned against the dark planks and felt the first of many tears begin to fall.

How could she have been so naïve to think she could retain the title of Lady of Lochlen Castle without actually being one? How could she have so vastly underrated the importance of what everyone had tried to teach her?

She could easily dismiss Lela's remarks. They were malicious and spiteful. For some mysterious reason, the woman hated Colin and now hated her for marrying him. But the other woman—Doreen—she had agreed with too many of Lela's observations.

Makenna could barely remember the women who had supported her sister in her last days. But, from her comments, Doreen did not seek revenge. Her statements were her true feelings.

Forcing her wooden legs to move, Makenna staggered to the bed and collapsed on its unmade surface, crying into the pillow housing Colin's scent. Last night, he had told her she was beautiful, and she had believed him.

For years, her blond, blue-eyed sisters harped that she could be pretty if she would only try. And she had tried. What she discovered was that her hair was too thick to manage, her skin too golden from the sun, and her green eyes too shrewd to be considered sweet. So she stopped all attempts to do the impossible. Even if she wanted to recreate what her sisters' had done with her hair on her wedding day, she had no idea where to begin. She only knew how to leave it loose and unrestrained, which in the summer was far too hot to consider, or plait it down her back.

Makenna flipped over and stared at the beams supporting the above battlements. The remarks about her looks had stung, and they were indeed painful, but she had heard them before. The main reason behind her tears was fear that Doreen was right. *The laird must be ashamed that his wife is so ill-equipped to help him run and protect his home.* The comment haunted her.

People were leaving, and Colin would return humiliated and disappointed. Three weeks ago, she wouldn't have cared what he thought. Now it mattered a great deal. The task of running Lochlen Castle was enormous, practically impossible for one whose aptitude for such things was nonexistent.

Makenna suddenly realized she was indulging in what Camus used to call "destructive thinking." It was unlike her to wallow in self-pity. Colin did not believe her helpless domestically. He would not have asked her to take care of Lochlen while he was gone if he didn't believe her capable. She could be this castle's lady in all ways, not just name only. She just needed to make the decision. More than once someone had told her she was incapable of accomplishing a task, and each time she had proven them otherwise.

Makenna sat up in bed and wiped her eyes dry with her sleeve. This would be no different. She just needed to find someone capable of teaching her what she didn't know. And she knew just whom to ask.

A half hour later, Makenna felt much more herself. She brushed her hair until it shone and replaited the unruly locks, but only halfway so that a mass of curls spiraled down her back. "There, that is about all I can do for now," she told her reflection.

Rising, she went to the door and took three deep breaths before leaving. She rounded the last step, and instead of exiting, she turned inward and entered the cavernous room situated on the first floor.

It had been years since she had been in this room. There were no windows or even arrow slits through the fifteen-foot-thick walls. Its sole source of light came from the enormous hearth situated across from the entrance. The overall structure was the same, but its use had altered greatly.

A few years ago, the Dunstan steward had resided and worked within the Black Tower. Gannon stored specialty goods on the first floor, conducted business from the second, and slept in the chamber Colin currently used. Now the tower basement was divided by a wooden partition. On the left was a storage area housing a mix of items from perishable goods to supplementary weapons. The other side appeared to be a makeshift sleeping quarters for several servants.

"Who goes there?" a female voice snapped. Makenna turned around immediately and matched the face to the unknown voice she had overheard. A round-faced woman, Doreen was somewhere in her late thirties, perhaps even forty whose straw-colored hair was wrapped in a precariously listing topknot.

"Oh . . . oh . . . milady. My apologies. I never expected to find you here."

"No, no, don't apologize. I didn't realize what . . . Are these *your* quarters?"

"Ah, no. I stay with my husband and my son. Our cottage is just outside the outer wall."

"Your son, his name is Rufus, right?"

Doreen's eyebrows shot up in surprise. "Aye, it is. I wasn't aware that you knew my son."

"I have not had the privilege, but I hope to, soon."

Doreen shifted her weight from one foot to the next and back again. Never had Makenna taken the time to talk or converse with anyone not associated with horses or weaponry. Her knowing about Rufus, a simple farm lad, was unexpected and very disconcerting. "May I inquire to your needs, milady?"

Hearing the confusion in the woman's voice, Makenna walked over and clutched Doreen's fingertips with her own. It was a personal gesture, she knew, but it also felt natural. "I . . . I want to make a request."

Doreen felt her uneasiness lessen. Her Ladyship was just as nervous and unsure. Feeling the sides of her mouth rise, Doreen chuckled quietly. Who would believe, she, a lady's maid, would feel more at ease and confident than the actual lady of the castle? She patted Makenna's quivering hand and asked, "What is that, milady? You need me to fetch the stable master, or Camus perhaps?"

It was natural for Doreen to assume she would want to visit the horses or the sword smith. "No, I need to gather everyone who works at Lochlen just outside the great hall."

"In the inner yard? Everyone?" Doreen gasped, not even trying to hide her shock.

"Aye, in the yard, and as soon as possible. And no, I don't need everyone. The armorers, the soldiers on watch, and the stable workers are not required, but anyone else who supports this castle or is paid by the steward must attend. Oh, and Gannon, too, of course."

Doreen stood frozen in stunned silence. "I . . . there is going to be some resistance."

Makenna took a deep breath and exhaled. No turning back now. "Tell them it is . . . the Lady of Lochlen's request."

An hour later, Makenna stood in the inner yard looking out at the small group of two dozen women and a handful of men. There might be a lot she didn't know about running a keep, but she was reasonably certain the number of people in the yard was far below what was needed to run a castle of Lochlen's size.

Makenna's eyes searched the crowd and found Doreen. She motioned for her to come close and whispered, "Is this everybody? I was hoping to talk with *everyone* at Lochlen, not just those available."

"Aye, milady, this is everyone, except those you excluded."

"I thought . . . well, I thought there would be more people working here."

Doreen wanted to be anywhere rather than where she was. Wishing she had left when Lela suggested, she nodded. "There are, I mean . . . were."

Makenna frowned, feelings of frustration and panic rising within her. "I see."

A man moved to the front of the small crowd, his mouth thin with displeasure. "No, milady, I don't think you do see. If you did, you wouldn't be asking us to come to ye like this." His eyes were small, deep-set, and firmly positioned upon her.

"And why should I not want to see my staff?" Makenna asked, genuinely curious as to what his objetions could be.

One long finger pointed out at the crowd, as the other pushed back his wispy gray hair. "I have looked, but my eyes cannot seem to find the stable master or his lads. I also do not see the armorers or your friend, the sword smith."

Makenna felt her face redden and replied defensively,

"Well, no—they are not here. I did not want to take them away from their duties."

"But you have no remorse about pulling me away from my bread. The loaves I was kneading are now ruined and those in the ovens are probably burnt. Now do you see, milady? That's why so many of us have left. You support the soldiers, but they are not the only ones who work hard and ensure the safety of Lochlen. But you don't care about us, now, do you?"

The back of Makenna's hand flew to her mouth as she surveyed the crowd. Several heads were nodding up and down in agreement. She had just made another huge mistake. "Oh Lord, and for those who have stayed, I have just made your work all that much harder."

His black eyes relaxed as he saw understanding seep its way into his mistress's expression. "And now, milady, for the first time, I think you just might be seeing the way things are and not the way you want them to be."

Makenna openly studied the man. Not many would question the laird's new lady in an open forum, and even fewer would be so harsh. This medium-height, thin-framed man had expanded her perception, giving a larger sense of reason and reality. In a way, he had done for her what she had tried to do for Deirdre. Be honest, despite station or circumstance.

"What is your name?" Makenna's voice became soft and melodious. Accompanying it was a smile that the men in the yard would talk about for days.

"Dugan, milady," he answered with quiet emphasis.

"And I take it you are the baker."

He coughed, suddenly feeling the weight of everyone's stares. "There was one other, but he left."

The man looked tired, and now she knew why. He was doing the work of two men. With so few in the yard, Dugan's situation would no doubt be indicative of those surrounding him. Before she could help Dugan or any of the remaining staff, she would first have to understand just how bad things were and receive advice on what to do about it.

"Where is Gannon?" she asked loud enough for all to hear.

"I am here, Lady Makenna," came a strong, steady answer as a balding, thickset man with hawklike eyes stepped forward.

When Makenna was a child, the steward had seemed unapproachable and harshly demanding. Now he was the one man who could save her from the deep pit she had spent many years digging for herself. Gannon had been Lochlen's steward since before she was born. He knew everything that went on at the castle and in the surrounding estates. Skilled at accounting and legal matters as well as personnel management, the old steward was her one hope of fulfilling Colin's request.

Gannon had watched as Makenna fumbled with the baker and realized her mistake. It seemed she was finally ready to be lady of this grand castle. Of all the Dunstan daughters, she had been the one who had the heart, stamina, and backbone required to lead her people. Ula and Rona were self-centered and vain, Edna was too quiet and introspective, and Deirdre had been led through persuasion, focusing only on personal comforts and not what was best for the clan.

Unfortunately, like her sister, Makenna had foolishly married the arrogant Highlander. Their new laird spoke about rebuilding the Dunstan army and ensuring the clan's safety, but there was very little evidence he would ever be able to do so. Without the clan's support, Gannon had no doubt Colin McTiernay would be forced to leave Lochlen. Hopefully, Makenna would realize her folly and stay.

Before he could ask what she wanted from him, her voice rang out, her tone apologetic. "Ah . . . thank you very much for coming. I apologize for never before showing my appreciation, but I do, as does my husband. I promise to learn and assist you as I should have since my sister passed away. Please go back to your duties. Soon I hope to meet with each of you in a more convenient manner. Good day."

Makenna watched for a moment as the crowd dwindled back to the various places from which they originated. Seeing the backs of Doreen and Gannon, she called out asking them to wait. "I truly meant what I said, but as you are both keenly aware, I don't know how."

"Milady, I am but a lady's maid, why would you want my help?"

"Because you want what is best for this clan and its castle. I need someone both kind and honest to teach me how to work and converse with women. Will you help me with this?"

Doreen gave her a quizzical look. *Her Ladyship wants help on how to be a woman.* Lady Makenna had changed, even as recently as the previous evening. Whatever the reason, it was something worth supporting and nurturing. Lady Deirdre had been kind, but she had her faults and though no one said so, Lochlen had suffered for them. She had been unwilling to listen to her people's needs. Maybe, just maybe, Lady Makenna was the mistress they had longed for.

Doreen shrugged one shoulder and replied, "Aye, I will do my best."

Makenna turned toward Gannon and met his eyes. She saw hesitation and doubt in their rich brown depths. "Will you assist me? Teach me what I must know to help you and Colin?"

"Aye, where I can, milady." His reply was short, but it gave Makenna hope.

"Where do you wish to begin?" Gannon asked.

Makenna indicated for Doreen and Gannon to follow her to the great hall. "First I must understand how much our staff has been depleted. I saw perhaps three dozen people. Is this not terribly low?"

Gannon nodded. "Including the armorers, sword smiths, and stable hands, the laird usually employs between seventy and eighty-odd hands to support the castle. Currently, we are staffed at somewhere between forty and fifty, depending on the number of people who left this morning."

The number was even lower than she thought. Just over half of the people needed. Makenna looked toward a nodding Doreen. "Aye, milady, Gannon tells it correctly."

Makenna folded her hands together. "Did all those people leave because of me? Because I am now Lady of Lochlen?"

Doreen grimaced. If her lady wanted honesty, then she would receive it. "Many left because of your husband; others chose to go because you willingly accepted him."

Makenna rose from her seat and then stood motionless. Her insides clenched with fury. How myopic her people were, how limited their insight was to their situation. She might have much to learn from them, but the Dunstans had a great deal to learn from her as well. "Thank you for your honesty, Doreen. Where do you suggest we begin?"

Consolidation and efficiency. That was how they were going to weather being shorthanded. Hopefully, it would not last long. Meanwhile, by finding ways to strip unnecessary chores and activities, they could reduce the workload and thus lower the number of people needed to run a castle of Lochlen's size.

"Excluding the outer wall towers, do you know how many chambers are within Lochlen?" Gannon asked.

"I would assume almost twenty," Makenna surmised.

"There are indeed twenty, over two dozen if you include the tower basements. They are a lot of work to maintain."

"And a lot of privies to clean," Doreen added.

"Aye," Gannon replied, nodding. "Cleaning privies is a hapless job, but one that could be accomplished by the young and ill-experienced. We should consider hiring one or two lads as replacements for such a responsibility."

"Please do so immediately," Makenna said, tapping her lips absentmindedly with the tip of her finger. "What rooms are we using now?"

"Um, several," Doreen answered.

"Before Colin returns, I want his things removed and placed into the laird's solar in Canmore Tower. It is appropriate. He is now the Dunstan laird."

Shock and resistance invaded Gannon's expression for a moment followed by resignation and acceptance. "Aye, milady. It will be done."

"I will also be moving my things into the solar, but would like to maintain my current room for day use. It could also serve as an extra chamber for visiting ladies to converse in when the halls are occupied by men or soldiers." Seeing Gannon and Doreen nod affirmatively, she continued. "And where are you staying, Gannon? Is there room for you to meet with staff and pay them?"

"For some time now I have been working and staying in one of the outer gate towers."

Makenna bit her inner lip. The outer gate towers

were designed for defense and security. They were cold, damp, and uncomfortable to live in with arrow slits for windows and a narrow staircase only one person could traverse at a time. Those who slept in them were usually soldiers staying only for a rotation before they went back to the training fields or home. "But why? Did Father know this? I know he would not have approved."

Touched by Makenna's incredulity, Gannon suddenly didn't want her to realize why he had been forced to leave the comforts of the Black Tower. Though the order had come from Lady Deirdre, he was positive the Highlander had commanded it. "I suggest that as we examine castle activities and situations, we do not delve too much into why they have come to be as they are."

Makenna looked into the old man's eyes and saw the pain there. Instantly, she knew why Gannon lived in one of the outer gate towers. Deirdre had asked him to move so that Colin had a place to stay, away from Forfar and her chambers. It was hard to conceive that her sister had made such a request, yet she knew deep down Deirdre had done just that.

Sighing, Makenna replied, "I think that is an excellent idea, Gannon. Our time is best spent on finding ways to help our people as things are now, not dwelling on the past."

Relief flowed through Gannon's face, and he visibly relaxed.

Witnessing Makenna's sensitivity, Doreen felt hope for the first time. After a long time waiting, the Dunstan clan finally had a lady to lead them.

Makenna cleared her throat and continued as if nothing was amiss. "Gannon, please reside in the Black Tower. You need the room for your duties. As for the rest of the staff, how many require chambers at Lochlen, Doreen?"

"I, uh, for all positions? Or just the staff that we currently have?"

"Let's focus on current staff. Once others decide to return to their positions, Gannon can find them housing in the outer gate towers. Those who have elected to support the laird and me in our time of need will stay within the main castle." Makenna's voice was firm, steady, and left no room for compromise. On this, she was not asking for opinion or getting approval. She was a making a decision. She was also making an insertion that people *would* be returning.

Doreen swallowed. "Many have families in the village and therefore sleep in their own cottages. The armsmen, stable workers, and armorers have accommodations where they work. This leaves about a half dozen men and a dozen women who would like to have quarters."

Would *like* to have quarters, Doreen had said. Meaning some of them currently did not. "Right now part the Black Tower basement is already configured for sleeping quarters, but it is cramped. Gannon, would it be possible to move the items being stored there elsewhere? It seems to be a random mix of supplies, from food to armory."

"The weapons were supposed to have been removed some time ago. We were short of hands to do so. The food items can be moved to the rear tower, which I am sure the cook and the baker would appreciate." Situated in the middle of the rear inner wall, the kitchen was set to the rear tower's left and the bake house was located on the tower's right.

"Excellent. I will have Dunlop send us a handful of men to help us move Colin's chambers and the items from the basement. This should provide plenty of room for the men. Now for the women who need accommodations . . ."

"Most of them prefer to stay in the Pinnacle."

The Pinnacle. Makenna hated that tower. Situated at an

odd angle on a small hill, it distorted the square look of the inner yard and appeared to be taller than the other towers. Consequently Makenna's great-grandmother called it the Pinnacle, and the name stuck. Makenna preferred her name—the Rooms of Doom and Gloom. For that was what they contained. The whole tower was filled with chambers designated for spinning, weaving, tapestry, embroidery, candle making, cobblers, even the laundry was done near, in, or about the Pinnacle. All things she didn't understand and hated. Why anyone would *want* to stay there was a mystery.

"Then that is where they shall stay. I am assuming there is room. Am I correct?"

"Aye, milady. There is."

Makenna stood and began to pace. "Now for moderation. We'll start with the chambermaids and the—"

Hesitantly holding her hand up, Doreen interrupted, "Uh, besides me, there are none, milady. The one supporting the laird quit this morning."

Makenna stopped in midstride and looked at the woman. Gannon and Doreen didn't know what to say and remained silent in their chairs.

"None?" Makenna's voice was barely audible. "What other positions are now vacant, and by how many?"

Gannon prided himself on his ability to remain calm in any situation, manage any problem, and address any person whether a noble or a farmer. Yet right now, answering a simple question had never been harder. "As of this morning, the ladies in waiting, chambermaid, and embroiderer positions have been completely vacated. Totally staffed, their numbers reach nineteen."

Makenna licked her lips. The news explained much. "Then it is fortunate that we have no guests, nor are there any planned. However, until our chambermaids return, all of us will have to continue cleaning and maintaining our own chambers. I will see to Colin's and my own."

Doreen gasped. "No, milady!"

Makenna gave the woman a challenging smile. "It shall be no different from what I have been doing for near a year now, Doreen. Or were you unaware that I, Lady McTiernay, daughter of Alexander Dunstan, wife of your new laird, have not been attended to since the day after my sister passed?"

The blood drained out of Gannon's face, and he turned to look at Doreen. "Is this true?" His simple question was laced with insinuation and displeasure. Doreen opened and closed her mouth several times before letting her face fall into her hands.

"My deepest apologies, milady. I will do your room."

Gathering the soft, worn fingers in her own, Makenna leaned over and whispered in her ear, "What I most need is not a chambermaid, but your wisdom and feminine guidance. I am completely at a loss on any of those duties performed in the Pinnacle."

"Aye, milady, I will help where I can," Doreen cried, gathering Makenna in her arms, relieved there would be no residual enmity.

Pulling herself free, Makenna wiped a stray tear and said, "Now, then, let us go, and, Gannon, you can begin my long-awaited training on what it means to be Lady of Lochlen."

Two days later, Makenna stood speechless inside the bake house. It was the same here as it was at every station she had been to. At first, she had thought it was her ignorance. She assumed things could not truly be as inefficient and mismanaged as they appeared. Yet her inquisitive nature would not let her mind rest.

She discovered the truth by accident while meeting Lochlen's one remaining candle maker. "Are you terribly overworked, chandler?"

He stared at Makenna completely perplexed for several moments before answering. Despite his years of service to the Dunstans, he had only seen Lady Makenna at a distance and not very often at that.

A ruddy-faced man with a gray and brown beard, Amos permanently stooped regardless of whether he sat or stood. He narrowed his eyes at her. "You look like your father," came his answer. "'Tis good that you do. I like women who have color in their hair and face, reminds me of my sweet Bessie."

Gannon leaned over and whispered that Bessie was his late wife. Alexander had hired Amos upon her death ten years ago. Makenna squared her shoulders and replied, "Why, thank you, chandler. I have just recently begun to enjoy the features I inherited."

"Call me Amos."

"All right, Amos. How do you fare? Are you overworked since you are now alone?"

"Are you here to play a trick on me?"

"No . . ."

"Then I'm not sure what you're asking. The others left over a year ago because there is not enough work here for one chandler, let alone three. *That* is why I work alone, milady."

Makenna could feel her jaw slacken. "But not one candelabra in the castle has a full set of tapers. Most only have one or two." Turning she looked directly at Doreen. "What about the villagers, do they have candles?"

"Aye, milady, the chandlers that used to work for Lochlen now labor in their cottages making tallow candles. Their wives are most unhappy. The smell and the hours they put in are long and hard."

"Why are they not making the candles *here*? Gannon says this room was *built* for the craft. I am getting the same impression I did when we were speaking with the hoppers, the weavers, and the spinners. First, I hear the laundresses must wash on one side of the keep and carry the wet items to another to hang because someone didn't like the unsightly view of the clothes drying. Only time-absorbing tapestries with elaborate designs are to be created, and now there are *too* many candle makers when there are not enough candles? What is going on?"

Gannon shifted and Doreen wrung her hands. Neither spoke.

Amos grunted. "I will tell you, milady. Compared with beeswax candles, tallow candles smell. They do not burn as long, and soot accumulates on the stones and tapestries around them. Your sister hated the odor and the residue, and wanted them out of the keep. Beeswax candles are not harder to make, milady, but finding the beeswax is. It is only because your father was a comparatively wealthy laird that we even had candles lighting Lochlen these two years. Lady Deirdre asked me to stay because I have a trick for smoothing the wax as it's poured over the rushes so that the candles were all the same width and length. Such things were important to the poor lass."

Makenna found a seat and sank down on its hard wooden surface. *Poor lass, my foot.* She knew Deirdre could sometimes be self-indulgent, but she was not mean-spirited. Yet Makenna did not doubt the truth of the chandler's words. There had to be a better explanation that would clarify all of these decisions and demands.

And yet, with each new stop, Makenna heard a similar description of Deirdre's interference at almost every station at Lochlen. The castle normally employed two bakers, and three during festivals and four when guests arrived. Now only a lead baker and an assistant remained. However, they were both close to quitting. For two years, they worked extraordinary hours to meet their quotas, but what Makenna was shocked to discover—it was so very unnecessary. Deirdre had enjoyed the view walking along the curtain walls above the bake house, but she had not enjoyed the smoke associated with bakery brick ovens. Consequently, she had ordered only one of the three hearths to be used at a time.

Makenna had always believed her beautiful frail older sister to be this great lady of the castle taking over seamlessly when her mother had passed. But, in reality, everyone— or at least those actually running the keep—knew Deirdre was a poor mistress. Her kind nature, whimsical smile, and fragile features had allowed her to perpetuate the illusion of order and peace.

"Fire all the hearths you need to, Dugan. And if you need more help, and know someone willing to work here at Lochlen, hire them. The people need their bread, but you must also be allowed the time to raise your sons. Gannon will see that you have what you need," Makenna directed, and then turned to leave.

Caught off guard, the round baker stood in bewilderment as the fiery redhead exited. Just days ago, he was confronting a naïve woman who was unaware of how her actions—or lack of them—affected those around her. Though she still had much to learn, he knew that she could, and more important, would. Was it possible the old laird had been correct? Maybe the Highlander and Makenna *were* the right ones to restore the strength and prosperity the clan once knew.

Chapter Eight

Colin weaved his way through the rocky hills moving as quickly as possible. He personally needed to see the destruction before too much time passed. His men did not have the experience and skill needed to examine such a brutal attack. He could not take the chance they would overlook critical clues that could identify the perpetrators. Even if he did have such men, he might have ridden out anyway to let the families know they had his support.

"You have been quiet," Drake observed once he and Colin were out of earshot from the rest of the men in their small group.

"I'm always quiet."

"Aye, you are, but rarely do you brood, Laird."

Colin briefly glanced at Drake out of the corner of his eye. He had a gift for detecting a man's disposition. That and his skill with a multitude of weapons made him an excellent commander and a natural trainer of men. "My mind is on discovering the particulars of what we are to encounter. I thought your mind would be occupied on the same."

Drake heaved a great sigh. "Alas, it is not. My thoughts

have been on a sweet lass with golden freckles and hair the color of winter grass."

"And who is this lucky woman?"

"Her name is Ceridwin. Not only is she bonnie, but she was most understanding when I told her that I might be gone for an unknown amount of time. She made me promise to be careful and she pledged to wait for me. You are looking at a man in love, Laird."

Colin found Drake's pleased look irritating. His commander was well known to the ladies and well liked. He never slept alone when he desired company. Dunlop once accused Drake of using tricks to convince women to do his bidding and warm his bed. Drake's reply had been, "You just have to know how they think. And I do, thank the good Lord, I do."

It was hard to tell if Drake was truly smitten or having fun. "Be careful, friend. Love can mock even the truest of hearts." As the words tumbled out, Colin knew he had spoken more than he should have.

"Nay, you cannot mean our Lady Makenna," Drake countered in disbelief. "I do not think she is capable of that particular crime. The woman confronts, challenges, and argues, aye, but she would not scorn love. At least, not in the way you mean."

Colin decided to change the subject. "I'm surprised you told your lady love of your intentions."

Drake shrugged nonchalantly, and again it rankled Colin. "And why should you be surprised? Did you not relay the same to your wife before we departed?"

"I did not," Colin replied.

Drake let out a low whistle. The crisp manner Colin spoke those three words explained much. Drake sensed he should be quiet and let it be, but his instincts told him to counter the mental reenactment Colin was having of his departure. "I expect, knowing Lady Makenna, that your choice to keep her in the dark was not well received."

Colin tightened his grip on the reins. "I chose not to encumber my wife with burdens she could take no action to resolve." Colin paused and then uncharacteristically added further explanation. "I was trying to be kind to her female sensibilities. No woman wishes to hear of gruesome attacks. I chose to spare her that."

Colin had not spoken Deirdre's name aloud, but she was in the air. Drake knew Colin had wisely avoided subjects such as war, attacks, and battles concerning his late wife. She had despised such topics. Whenever Colin was away from Lochlen, she had told herself and others that he was out for a long ride or visiting friends. Deirdre was a lovely woman, but her intentional naiveté was one of her more aggravating traits.

Drake cleared his throat and decided to take a risk. "I agree some women do not take well to hearing such reports as were delivered last night. And for *those* women, it is a kind service to hold close information they find distasteful or bothersome. But I am surprised to learn Lady Makenna is one of them. She does not buckle at the sight of blood or at the receipt of ill news. Instead of faltering, her courage rises. It is one of the predominant reasons we Dunstan soldiers love her and enjoy training with her in combat."

Colin's face hardened as a ripple of possessiveness coursed through him. He had not known so many men *adored* his wife. "Makenna is indeed a strong woman, but she is still a woman and needs to be protected."

"From what? The truth? Do you truly believe word has not already spread throughout the village, and that she remains ignorant of the attack? Nay, I would wager our fair lady is completely aware of where we head and why. And while I would not be so presumptuous to speak for

Lady Makenna, *my* lady love would be quite hurt and possibly even angry with me if she learned the truth from another's lips and not my own. Come to think of it, if I knew I had caused Ceridwin such pain, I would probably choose to ride in quiet solace and reflection brooding about how I could make it up to her upon my return."

"Drake?"

"Aye?"

"You talk too much," Colin admonished and prompted his horse forward to rejoin the other men.

The attack had been merciless and cruel. This was not a mere thieving raid for cattle or horses. Evidence of deep hatred was everywhere. Fences were irreparable and had to be rebuilt from new. Two families had stables burned with the livestock still in them. One young boy had been seriously injured in an attempt to save his favorite mare. Other families, whose animals were allowed to graze at night, awoke to a nightmare of mutilation. Such acts were unheard of. The *capture* of livestock was the goal of raids, not slaughter.

Whoever did this wanted Colin gone. They also knew he would seek retribution.

"What do you think, Laird?" Drake asked in hushed tones laced with fury. His cheerful disposition had been replaced by one filled with vengeance.

Colin ignored the question and aimed his horse toward the broken portion of the nearby fence. He could feel the animal's reaction to what was around it. The big black knew murder of its kind had taken place. "Who lives here?"

"Calvin and his wife, Loreen. They have one infant daughter. They used to live near the village, but Calvin wanted more land to farm. Alexander offered him this out here."

"Their house?"

"Intact. Like the others. The focus appears to be killing the livestock that supported these people's livelihood."

"Ensure that Calvin and his wife receive the same as the others and have the men remove the carcasses before the family see their land again."

"Aye, it will be done," Drake said wearily. It was hard to see so much willful, cruel inflictions on innocent animals. Colin could do very little to restore these people's lives. He could give a cow and a horse to help soften their losses, but what he could not do was restore their peace of mind. At least not yet.

Colin halted his huge obsidian mount and swung off its back. Rocks were scattered everywhere. He walked down to a weakened but still intact portion of the fence and forcefully kicked it so that it toppled onto the ground. Then he stood back and gazed intently upon the result. He looked back at the pebbled ground.

Whistling he called his black and remounted. "There's more here than what we've seen, Drake. Search every morsel of this farm. Bring me what you find."

Several hours later, Colin sat on a makeshift bench composed of a dead log. The fire crackled and lit up the night sky. His men were gathered in silent reflection. Each soldier's palpable anger fed the man next to him. Last night, there had been much discussion. Angry words about payback had been bandied about casually and often. But then, yesterday, they had only seen a fraction of the horror bestowed upon these quiet farmers.

Colin knew it would take very little to unleash the rage warring in his men. Earlier, they had found very consistent and plentiful evidence of the attacking clan. The Donovans.

For those who knew them, the evidence fit. Donovan land bordered the Dunstan's eastern hills and stretched far both east and south. Mahon Donovan was a hard, unforgiving man, who had fought and lost men in the battles against Edward I. The Scottish laird was well known to be ruthless in combat, killing all enemies— even their animals—in battle. He disliked visitors and warned trespassers only once to make their travels via another route. He had publicly declined to support Colin and left Lochlen Castle shortly after MacCuaig.

Finding torn bloody pieces of the Donovan plaid hidden between rocks and underneath carcasses was more than enough evidence for his men to convict their eastern neighbor.

Colin was not persuaded. There was too much proof, and all of it was pointing to the wrong person. He would give his clansmen their vengeance, but first, he needed to meet with Mahon, just as the real murderer intended.

"Sean, tomorrow you are to ride back to Lochlen and tell Lady Makenna that we may be several more days. Then join Dunlop on the training fields."

Colin rose to lay his plaid down somewhat apart from the others and then disappeared into the dark. He needed quiet surroundings to plan how he would approach his quick-tempered neighbor.

Silence fell upon the group as each man watched Colin retreat into the woods. It would be some time before their laird returned.

"Does this mean war?" The question came from Sean, the youngest and most inexperienced of the group.

Drake sighed and straightened his shoulders as he stood to survey the small gathering. "Still to be seen, but we will be seeing Donovan. We'll know more then."

Drake left them to assimilate the information and moved to lie down on his plaid and think. Colin had not acted like a laird who had found proof of his prey. In fact, he seemed quietly suspicious. More than once Colin had performed odd and even repulsive acts including ripping some of his own plaid, laying it on the ground, and throwing the head of a dead horse on it. Drake had no idea how Colin intended to approach Donovan, but he doubted it would turn out as the men expected.

A light breeze came with the morning. Sean prepared and left for Lochlen. Colin went to visit Calvin and his wife. He did so alone and returned midmorning. Drake waited for Colin's order dispatching a soldier to go and return with more men, but the word was not given.

Drake asked the question on everyone's mind, "Do we ride east?"

"Aye. I want to meet with Mahon by nightfall tomorrow." Colin's answer meant they would be riding hard and possibly into the night.

When they stopped, it had been dark for some time and they were well into Donovan territory. Colin had caught more than one sentry make note of their entrance and their direction. Making camp, Colin located almost a half dozen men lurking about the darkness. And those he could not see, he could hear. Mahon had relaxed his training since Edward I died and Robert the Bruce took the Scottish throne. Maybe too much.

Laughter erupted from his men around the campfire. Trying to ease their nerves from what they had seen and the potential fight to come, they concentrated on happier times, moments, and people. Mostly they talked about their wives or loved ones.

When he was younger, Colin often wondered why his older brother Conor kept himself apart, never joining in on the conversation on nights such as this. Now he understood. Men you lead cannot see you as a friend. Friends can be questioned, even overruled. As laird and leader, he could not risk blurring the lines even a little bit. Hesitation, doubt, uncertainty—these were dangerous things on a battlefield. And they were cultivated during times like these.

Colin stood and moved his plaid farther away from the others. The bushes were swaying with semi-concealed onlookers. There would be no walk tonight. Lying down on the soft woolen blanket, Colin put his arm underneath his head and stared up at the stars.

By tomorrow morning, Donovan would receive word of Colin's impending arrival, but he wouldn't know why. Colin gambled Mahon's curiosity would be enough to receive him.

If they left at dawn, it would take nearly the whole day to reach Lonchlilar, the heart of the Donovan clan. Nestled in the northeastern hills adjacent to the cliffs of the North Sea, Lonchlilar Castle was well protected with typical walls, barbicans, and portcullises, but it had a secret weapon against those who were unwelcome. Behind the shadows of the simple valley surrounding it were hidden pockets of cleared land where dozens if not hundreds of men could lie hidden and attack without warning. Colin had never personally visited the stronghold, but he had heard much about it.

Colin switched arms, bracing his head, and tried to keep his thoughts on how tomorrow would enfold. But again they drifted to one person, just as they had every night since he left Lochlen. *Makenna.* He wondered how she was faring, if Brodie and Gorten were keeping her safe, if she was still angry, but most of all, he wondered if she missed him as much as he missed her.

He had not thought it possible to crave a woman the

way he ached for her each night. They had been married
for nearly three weeks, and for fourteen of those days,
she had shared his bed. Each night before retiring, they
would discuss both important and minor details of their
day and talk about events of the morrow. During which
one or both would get mad, argue, or just as often, go
into fits of laughter over some odd comment or incident.
He did not believe it possible to laugh so much with a
woman, but his wife had a way of relating a story that
made him feel as if he were right there witnessing or experiencing the humorous event himself. Regardless of
how the nights started, they had always ended the same.
In shared ecstasy.

Colin rolled over on his side and fingered the empty
spot beside him. "I miss you, Makenna McTiernay. God
help me, I do," he whispered.

The next morning, the small group rode across the
eastern countryside of the Scottish Border region. They
could not see the North Sea, but they could feel its cool
humid wind blow over the rocks and grass to greet them.
Much less friendly were Donovan's men. No longer lin-
gering in the shadows, sentries followed the group as
they made their way east.

Drake watched Colin carefully ready to respond to his
command but detected no concern from his laird. By
now it was clear an audience with their neighbor would
be allowed. It was yet to be seen if leaving would also
be on the agenda. Colin obviously had a plan, but what
it was, Drake had not a clue.

Midafternoon, Colin halted by a small stream to rest
their mounts and replenish their water pouches. He ordered the men to tie the horses and follow him. Colin
cut across the stream and broke through the bushes on

the other side. The scene was calm and peaceful and deadly.

"This, men, is the valley of Lonchlilar, home of Mahon Donovan. Beyond that hill in the distance is where we're headed. Before you remount, you will secure your sword and axe so that they are visible and nonthreatening, for there will be men watching, whether you see them or not. I do not expect war with Mahon, but we are not allies, and our company was not planned. I know not how we will be received, but unless provoked, Mahon will see me."

Mahon Donovan drummed his fingers on the thick-planked table in front of him. At his back was a roaring fire pumping welcomed heat into the room. His bones were no longer young, and they hated the cold. In his youth, men had called him the Lion because of his size, wild yellow hair, brown beard, and his deafening roar when charging the enemy on the battlefield. He was not tall, but wide and thick, and when people left his company they remembered him being much bigger than he actually was.

"Laird?" came a voice from behind.

"Aye, Ross, come in," Donovan replied without turning around. Every hour he was given updates to the location of McTiernay and his expected time of arrival.

Mahon had ordered his men to allow Colin's small band safe passage, but he had not forbidden intimidating them. He wished he could witness his men's attempt to frighten the Highlander. No doubt his soldiers would learn a well-needed lesson. The Donovan army itched for battle and had grown overconfident in their abilities.

"The . . . the Dunstan laird, Colin McTiernay, has entered the valley. Word has it that he and his men are armed, but their weapons are secured behind them where they cannot be easily reached."

Mahon nodded. Colin had never been to Lonchlilar before, but the man was obviously acquainted with the secrets of the valley. "Anything else?"

Ross swallowed. "Uh . . . just that . . . well, one of the men shot an arrow . . . "

Mahon turned around at the news. "My man or Mc-Tiernay's?"

"Uh . . . ours. The arrow was not meant to hit, only to scare, but McTiernay supposedly went and got the soldier who shot it and tied his hands to the tree he was perched upon. One of the men who spied the incident used the back trail to ride back and warn you."

"When is McTiernay to arrive?"

"Any moment, Laird."

Mahon swiveled back in his chair to a more comfortable position. "Until I tell you otherwise, the soldier is to remain tied to that tree until Laird McTiernay has departed from this valley. We would not want another accident to start a war."

"Uh . . . no," came a hesitant reply.

Donovan picked up the pewter quaich and swallowed the remaining contents. "For if we did go to war, we would fight, and we would kill many, but just so there is no doubt, in the end, we would lose. McTiernay knows this, and I know this."

Ross walked around the table and looked at his laird with a steady, but questioning gaze. "Lose? To McTiernay? His numbers are small, few, and I hear they are untrained."

Mahon eyed the slight man. "Are they, now? I say no one knows. The tricks he uses to hide his numbers are not unknown to me. My valley is riddled with them. But even if you were right, and we vanquish Colin McTiernay and all his loyal men, we would then have to deal with his allies. And even if those allies decided that avenging a dead Highlander is not of value to them, there is his brother. You have not fought alongside a horde of Highlanders, but I have. It is an awesome sight when they are beside you, and I imagine a terrifying one if they're in front of you. This is not what I want. This is not what I am about. Scots killing Scots is a waste. I will have no more. Leave me now and do not return until McTiernay has arrived."

"Aye, Laird," Ross quickly replied.

"That will be unnecessary, Mahon Donovan. I am already here."

Mahon rose, walked over, and grabbed Colin's large forearm with a firm grip. "McTiernay, welcome."

Colin tilted his thumb toward Drake. "If you agree, I would like my commander to be in attendance during our discussions. My other men have been instructed to wait just beyond the outer walls."

Mahon nodded. "Your commander is welcome, and my servants will see that your men outside are well fed."

"Your generosity is appreciated."

Mahon pointed at the padded armchairs at the head table and retook his own seat. "As you can see I have restructured the room to fit the needs of an older man. If I were having this room built now, the hearth would not be situated in the middle of the room with the entrance door to the side. The only way to keep my backside warm is to have my table situated most awkwardly, which in turn results in my back being to the door much of the time. Damn nuisance."

"It is a grand hall all the same, Mahon."

The old man nodded at a servant and swirled his finger in the air, indicating for him to bring drinks for his guests. Mahon propped his elbows on the table and looked Colin in the eye. "Enough with the pleasantries. It is a long ride to Lonchlilar. One does not make the journey uninvited and without purpose."

"If you wanted to kill me or my men, your sentries would have done so the moment we set upon your land."

"You saw them, then?"

"I had not realized that you intended them otherwise," Colin lied.

Mahon eyed the young laird. The Highlander's size would daunt many men, but it was the man's cunning that caught Mahon's attention. In an unthreatening way, Colin had cleverly warned Mahon that his men were clumsy and needed further training. It also affirmed Mahon's guess that Colin's visit was not to start a war between their two clans, but to avert one.

"You have ridden hard for a reason, McTiernay, and I expect I will not like the answer."

Colin reached into his leine and pulled out several torn bloody pieces of Donovan plaid and laid them down on the table in front of Mahon. "These were carefully placed throughout the remnants of an attack on my land."

"A raid?" Mahon asked, picking up one of the still wet pieces. It was without a doubt the Donovan tartan.

"Nay, raids are for livestock. These attacks were senseless slaughters of horses and stock animals."

"Attacks? More than one?"

"Nine all together, in the span of two nights."

"No sane Scot would do such a thing. You say *these* were found on the scene?"

"Those are but a handful of the pieces, aye."

"No Donovan committed such a crime," Mahon vowed with conviction.

"I never believed you or your clansmen did. There are too many pieces and their cuts are too similar. As you can see, all are the same size and shape. They were easily found, and in chosen locations. Some of the mayhem was designed just so that I would find proof of a Donovan attack."

The old laird leaned back into his chair and sat quietly for several minutes before standing up. "Do you know the reason why I did not support you along with Crawford, Boyd, and the others?" he asked, walking toward the impressive stone fireplace.

Colin looked at the man without expression. "I suspected you had had enough."

The accuracy of the answer startled Mahon. "I must admit I am surprised you ascertained as much, but I am glad you did. I have seen too much war these past ten years. Edward II is being manipulated by his barons, and chaos runs rampant in the English lands. During this time, we must replenish our forces and rebuild our strength. I do not want to see it squandered on battles against our own. Scots should not be killing Scots. It's a waste and disgrace."

"I agree."

"Edward's son is a fool, but he is not completely stupid. Eventually it will occur to him that attacking Scotland might unite his quarreling nobles."

"Robert knows this and will soon be mustering forces to attack England while it's vulnerable. It is a sprint to see who will attack first. Regardless, though, war is imminent. The decision I have now is whether to wait and fight a battle against my own at the same time I fight the English or to fight now." Colin watched the old laird wrestle with his thoughts.

Mahon took a deep breath and exhaled. "Turning potential enemies into actual ones is dangerous and costly."

"I can ignore a *potential* enemy, Donovan, but I will not ignore one that tries to humiliate me and cause suffering to my clansmen. When enemies make themselves known whether English, Irish, or Scot, one has two choices, fight now or fight later."

"And what are you inclined to do, McTiernay?"

"It depends on your decision. Someone intends for us to fight, no doubt to diminish your force and possibly eliminate mine, leaving Lochlen undefended for those who desire it. We can ignore what they did or we can band together against the one man who foolishly thought to pit us against each other."

"MacCuaig."

"There is no proof. No one saw any of the attackers, and unlike your tartan, I cannot link him or his clan to the attacks."

"You know it was MacCuaig, just as I. The man has a black and greedy heart, but he wants more than just Lochlen. If you had spent your youth in the Borders, you would know the obsession he has with your wife."

"He will never have Makenna, Donovan. I will leave the Dunstan clan and take her and my men to the Highlands before I would allow MacCuaig to touch one hair of my wife's."

Mahon swung around and marched back to his chair. He sank down into the worn cushions and locked eyes with Colin. "No man has ever dared to use me or my men before. If MacCuaig wants a battle, he'll have one."

"I am glad we are in agreement. But I came this way not just to show you MacCuaig's misdeeds, but to ask for your favor. I have two battles looming in front of me, and with your assistance, I can end them both definitively and perhaps simultaneously."

"And if I choose not to support you or your plan?"

"Then I leave here and devise another; however, I doubt my second plan will consider the state of the Lowland Scots to be a priority."

* * *

A week later, Colin left Lonchlilar. His mood was dark and ominous. All who saw him knew the talks with Donovan had ended, and a war between the two clans was brewing.

Mahon watched secretly from his private chambers as the fierce Highlander rode at a gallop out of Lonchlilar's gates.

The plan had begun.

It had taken a week to resolve all the specifics, and during that time, Mahon learned the fame surrounding the McTiernay strategic abilities was well earned. It all came down to timing and perception. Only one part of the elegant plan had caused Colin to hesitate.

"Your plan requires absolute secrecy of your numbers. Before MacCuaig makes his move, he will scour the hills to verify the size of your army. You have a month, maybe two at best," Mahon had advised.

"Aye, a problem, but not an insurmountable one. To keep my numbers hidden, I will need to relocate them in stages. What concerns me is the one element I don't control—MacCuaig. I cannot be certain how long my men's stay will be. It is too much to ask," Colin replied somberly.

"What is too long of a stay? Two, three months? Perhaps four? Where better than Lonchlilar Valley can you hide your men? And you know I am right. Your pride is preventing you from accepting this offer. Only under a cloak of mutual animosity will your plan be successful. You said yourself you suspect MacCuaig has already dispatched spies to Crawford, Moncreiffe, and Boyd to watch for any dispatches. He may even decide to send one or two men to my lands, but they will not dare enter the valley. *Here* is where your men must come."

"I cannot deny the truth of your words, Mahon. Your sacrifice is appreciated. My men will hunt their own food and bring supplies."

"I should be thanking you, McTiernay. Your plan allows me to save my own pride and keep my convictions. When this is done, everyone will know that I am your friend and ally," Mahon pledged, rising to stand. He extended his arm, and Colin clasped it. Mahon squeezed and let go before offering last words of caution. "Beware of Mac-Cuaig. He is crazed, but he is young and strong. And while no leader, he is gifted with the sword in one-on-one combat. None to my knowledge has ever beaten him."

Colin downed the last bit of ale in his quaich. "Again I thank you, Mahon. Shall we call for Ross? He will want to determine how and where to handle the invasion of my soldiers."

"Aye, Ross will handle the particulars for now, and though a good lad, he has much to learn. My previous commander is now in Fife. His time with me was recently completed, and he chose, understandably, to help his ailing uncle, a laird of a small MacDuff clan just north of the River Forth. He will soon be named their chief, and I wish him well. I have not chosen a replacement. My junior commanders have the talent to lead and do well with new recruits, but they lack the maturity needed to hone and lead my battle-experienced men."

"My commander Drake shall report to you directly then and do your bidding. He will be in charge of relocating and then overseeing my men."

"If it is not too much to ask, I would like to stage some sport, and if my men's skills have diminished as I fear, I would ask that they join your training. Your commander of course would treat them no different and conduct the practices as he chose."

Colin sheathed his sword and prepared to leave.

"Drake is your man and will see to what you wish. It is the least I can do for this burden you undertake."

"These are burdensome times, and we all must do what we can to preserve what is ours."

"Aye, that we must," Colin replied, following Mahon to the door. "Let us say good-bye now, for in a moment we must depart as enemies."

Chapter Nine

Colin clapped his commander farewell on the back and mounted his black. After days with minimal riding, the animal was restless and ready for a hard ride. Colin gestured once more to his men and then left the secret encampment. They were heading home. He was riding north alone. Several hard months lay ahead. Dunlop would be his sole commander while Drake secretly sharpened the battle skills of his men at Lonchlilar.

Colin sensed Drake's eagerness to be trusted with the assignment, but he also knew the young man was disappointed to be away from the freckled beauty who had so thoroughly captured his attention. Yet if all went to plan, his commander would enjoy her attentions this winter in peace.

Riding along the edge of Crawford territory, Colin confirmed his hunch. MacCuaig's spies were ill-hid, but numerous. Colin suspected several were camped out at every allied clan, ordered to remain there until activity was seen or MacCuaig was ready to make his move. After two days of combing the Lothian hills, Colin learned what he needed to know and headed south.

The ride to Lochlen from Crawford's should have

taken almost three days. Colin made it in less than two. He reached down and stroked the neck of the big black. He had camped late and rested sparingly. Rarely did he ever push a steed this hard, but never had he been so eager to return home. "Come on, boy. I know it's been rough, and it's late, but think how good it will feel to be home."

He urged his mount forward realizing that, for the first time since he moved to the Borders, he considered Lochlen to be his home. He had mouthed the words numerous times. But only recently did his heart no longer seek the Highlands. It reached to Lochlen. To Makenna. He was going home.

The last fleeting rays of sunlight disappeared behind the hills as night invaded the sky. He was almost there. At this pace, he would be in Makenna's arms before she fell asleep. Even the prospect of facing a cantankerous, feisty Makenna still mad over his departure could not curb the excitement racing through him. He needed to see her again, hear her news, and feel her in his arms. He would even be happy to continue their quarrel. The feeling of anticipation was unfamiliar; one he had never sensed upon returning to Lochlen after a lengthy trip.

In the past, each mile closer to home increased a phantom weight that pressed down upon his shoulders. The second he would pass through the outer gate, news of events that had transpired while he was away would be delivered. Rarely was it ever good. The guilt of not being there to relieve Deirdre of a burden or be by her side when she fell sick had become so heavy he had dared not ever leave.

In the moonlight, Lochlen stretched in the distance. Colin waited for the pressure, the guilt, the fear of learning what happened while he was away. It never came.

Fighting his desire and need to hold Makenna, Colin

altered his course and urged the black toward the loch. First a dive to wash off the dirt of travel; then he would find his wife and delve into her secret treasures she divulged only to him.

Washed and dressed again, Colin decided to use the night to cloak his assessment of the work done on the unfinished town wall during his absence. His jaw clenched as he passed through. Indeed, there had been progress. To the distant eye, the wall was near completion.

Colin quelled his anger and proceeded through the village to the heart of Lochlen. The enemy had tipped his hand. The wait would not be as long as he or Donovan presumed.

As he approached the outer gate, soldiers on watch caught sight of Colin. They waved in acknowledgment, and then signaled the guards to open the gate.

Colin rode to the stables, dismounted, and handed the reins over to the stable master. He turned and headed toward the inner gate. Desiring to see only Makenna, he did not stop when Dunlop rushed to his side.

"Laird! My apologies for not arriving sooner. I just received news that you were within the castle walls and came immediately. It is fortunate I was not in the fields tonight with the men, otherwise it might have been morning before I learned of your arrival," Dunlop explained, hoping to deflect some of his laird's frustration from landing on him. Those who knew Colin and had traveled with him on lengthy trips were very familiar with the Highlander's dark mood that came with his return.

"I'm glad to see you, Dunlop. I assume all is well with Lochlen and its people?" Colin replied jovially, not slowing his gait.

Stunned, Dunlop stammered, "Aye, Laird. All is well." Trying to keep up with Colin's fast, long stride as they neared the inner gatehouse, Dunlop asked, "Laird?"

"Aye?"

"Where's Drake? The others? Have they not returned with you?"

Colin paused and waited for Dunlop to come closer before replying softly, "There is much to discuss and do, and unfortunately it will require significant sacrifice on us all. Don't speak of Drake or the missing men. I will explain all tomorrow morning."

Before Dunlop could respond affirmatively, Colin resumed his rapid pace once again, practically sprinting inside the gate. Dunlop gave up his pursuit and grinned at the disappearing figure. "If you had waited but two more seconds, Laird, I would have told you she is no longer in the Black Tower," he said to the empty night air.

Dunlop pivoted to return to his bunk in the outer gatehouse wondering if Colin realized how much he had changed since his marriage. Deirdre had been a gentle person and beautiful lady, but never had she caused the look of peace and joy from the sheer expectation of seeing her that he had just witnessed on his laird's face.

Colin bounded up the stairs to the floor of his chambers. Sprinting down the short hallway, he opened the door and immediately knew something was wrong . . . or at least very different.

A mock cough erupted from behind him. "Uh, Laird McTiernay, it is good to see you home again. I know Lady Makenna, *who is waiting for you in your solar,* will be very glad to see you as well. Is there something you needed to discuss? I assure you all has been well with the keep and the castle in general. You would be proud of Her Ladyship."

Colin blinked and then blinked again. The old steward was trying to save either his own pride, Colin's, or maybe even Makenna's by lacing his statements with innuendo and hints. What Gannon failed to recognize was that nothing could alter Colin's good mood.

Colin laughed out loud and clapped the man on his back. "So I have been moved, eh?"

Realizing Colin was neither annoyed nor angered, Gannon relaxed and replied, "Aye, Laird. Your wife insisted upon it."

Your wife. Colin enjoyed hearing the sound of it. "I see you have moved back to the main castle. Never knew why you left, but it is good Makenna convinced you to return. It is late, Steward. Perhaps I should let you retire. I should probably retire myself," Colin said in an effort to be casual, all the while backing out of the room and into the narrow passageway toward the staircase.

Gannon stood speechless as Colin vanished down the stairwell. Had he been wrong all this time? Had Colin been unaware that he was staying in *his* old chambers? Never once had Gannon considered the possibility that it was Lady Deirdre's idea to remove him from his home. Perhaps he had misjudged the Highlander. Maybe a lot of people had. Lela's small group of discontents was growing, but starting tomorrow, he would no longer be one of them.

Colin climbed the Canmore stairs to the top floor and noticed the hallway sconces were lit. The door to the solar was open and the tapestries covering the small exterior window were pulled aside. Another step and he felt the light cross breeze between the windows on the opposite wall of the room.

Hearing movement, Brodie moved into Colin's view. The guard looked both relieved and pleased to see his laird and was about to say so when Colin motioned for silence. He briefly clasped the man's arm and then indicated for him to leave.

Moving down the curved hallway, Colin could hear

Makenna talking aloud. He paused at the entrance not at all surprised to discover she was addressing no one. Colin tried making out the words, but it almost sounded as if she were speaking in a foreign language.

She was sitting on a thick braided rug in front of the roaring hearth with her feet tucked underneath her brushing her hair dry. The fire crackled and caught the rich highlights of the long tresses.

Colin leaned against the archway. He had waited so long for the chance to pull her in his arms and kiss her long, deep. And now that he was here, he just wanted to drink her in visually, knowing that while he was gone, Makenna had been in his bed waiting for him. The most feisty, willful, and tenacious of the Dunstans was his *wife*, and nothing could make him happier.

Makenna felt one of her legs begin to tingle and shifted. She rubbed her calf trying to diminish the painful sensation. The stinging was indicative of her life these days. Irritating, but manageable.

Trouble had erupted again that morning. Like the other times, it was something small and innocuous, but it fit a pattern of events that could no longer be dismissed as "accidents." Worst, whoever was causing the problems was making things harder not just on her, but on everyone.

She had convinced Doreen to introduce her to the villagers and learn if they required any assistance. Visiting in person, Makenna needed no one to explain their needs. They were apparent. Blankets, roof repair, and wood for their hearths. Living close to the castle was supposed to be of mutual benefit. The laird and his keep received food and support, and in return gave protection and aid. Last year, she had not thought to ensure that her people were prepared for the winter, and they had paid for it. She vowed not to repeat her mistakes. Every villager would be protected from the winter's cold.

Today she had found newly weaved blankets in a fireplace just as they turned to ashes.

Her leg once again feeling normal, Makenna began to brush her hair, mumbling, "How will it all get done? Damn those that would hurt their own. Don't they realize they are not just insulting me, but the ones who spent the hours making the items they so callously destroy? I might have been irresponsible, but I was never cruel. What I would give to meet just one of these traitors with my sword. They'd never cross me or my own again."

Frustrated, Makenna tossed the brush onto the chair, pulled her knees up, and rested her cheek upon them. Harvest was coming soon and so many preparations had to get done. The weather this year had been especially good. Consequently, every available hand was needed to gather the food from the overly bountiful crops and prepare it for winter. Once the fields were picked, the farmers would immediately thresh and plow the land to plant the fall crops of rye and wheat. And only when the prepping and stocking of the harvest was complete could the roofs and cottages be repaired for winter. No matter how she looked at it, there were not enough people to get it done. At least not enough *willing* people. And because of her past shortsightedness and her clansmen's current stubbornness, everyone would suffer.

Makenna closed her eyes and stretched. She wished Colin was back at Lochlen. He would know what to do. Yet, deep down, Makenna knew she would not burden Colin with her troubles. This was her responsibility. She was Lady of Lochlen. Colin had his own worries with the raids. Rumors of the viciousness of the attacks still echoed in the halls. He had tried to spare her this worry when he left. Pride dictated she do the same and protect him.

"Never will he think I am not up to the task," she promised aloud.

When she leaned back, Colin saw the strain in Makenna's face as she spoke, again not loud enough to make out. She looked serious, as if she were working out a very complex problem. Suddenly, he wanted to let her know she wasn't alone. That he, too, had worries and concerns, and desired to share them with her.

Colin inwardly berated himself for even considering the idea. How could his instinct be to relate a horror with which even his own men had trouble coping? These were his burdens, not hers. No, instead of encumbering her with troubles, he should be relieving her of them. Colin walked in, determined to solve whatever was concerning her.

Makenna heard a scuffle and craned her head to see if Brodie was approaching. Since she had stopped trying to dislodge her two guards from her presence, they had been good about providing space, especially within the castle's inner walls. However, at night, they had been adamant that at least one of them stand watch outside her door. Makenna had tried to convince them otherwise, saying it was dishonorable for them to sleep where a chambermaid should. Both refused to capitulate. It mattered little if she begged, pleaded, shouted, or even threatened to fight them.

Seeing Colin, Makenna let go a soft shriek. She barely had time to stand when Colin pulled her to his side. Makenna melted into his arms, and Colin knew he had not been alone in longing for his return.

He ran his fingers through her hair, glorying in its red velvet softness. He looked down. Her smile was soft and inviting. She could not hide what she was feeling.

Her expressions were an honest reflection of her state of mind, and her brilliant green eyes were shimmering with unshed tears of joy of his return.

Being here, holding Makenna felt incredibly right. He felt a sense of certainty he could not put into words. "I take it you are no longer angry with me for leaving," he both stated and asked simultaneously.

Makenna grinned. "I was mightily sore at you, but I am now satisfied knowing that I was right, and you were wrong."

"*You* were right?"

"Aye, you should have told me what you knew before you left. As an incredibly intelligent laird, I'm sure you realized your error by now." Her smile grew at his shocked expression. "See, I knew you were well aware of your offense."

Colin was more shocked at his own reaction to her words than the words themselves. He had been prepared for anger, reprisal, and a good argument before kissing her into capitulation. His plan to calm her was suddenly unnecessary, and he felt robbed. "And what if I think I was right?"

Makenna playfully toyed with the loose strings at the opening of his shirt. "I am sure that you have been correct about a great many things, but I am hard pressed to think of the one you are referring to," she replied coyly.

"How about you missing me?"

Makenna could hear the pride in his voice, and it quelled her need to deny him the truth. Instead, she laid her head on his chest and hugged him. It wasn't a verbal affirmation, but she could feel Colin nod his head in satisfaction.

"I cannot tell you how glad I am to be home." His voice was deep, husky, caressing.

Makenna expected him to tease her further, but his admission completely disarmed her. Her throat constricted. It was followed by a familiar and comfortable sense of physical awareness rippling through her. She lifted her head and gazed into his eyes. There was no mistaking their intense look. Every nerve ending in her body responded to his unspoken message of need sparkling in those cobalt depths. And then Colin kissed her, his touch so tender she could barely find her breath.

Colin felt Makenna shiver in his arms, and deepened the embrace. Their lips moved hungrily against each other. He tried to slow down, but she wouldn't let him. Tongues teased, tasted, tantalized.

When it finally ended, he was burning with a near-uncontrollable need to bury himself in her. Lord, how she affected him.

No, he silently vowed. First, he would discover what or who had been troubling his wife while he was away. They had the whole night to satisfy his needs.

Colin kissed her forehead and whispered, "Never have I been better welcomed home, and before you tell me what was bothering you before I interrupted, let me get more comfortable."

Makenna watched, slightly stunned as Colin walked across the room. He undid his belt, throwing both it and his sword on the chest. She had half hoped, half expected him to throw her on the bed and remind her once again of the pleasures of being married. Maybe his feelings for her had changed.

Feeling foolish, Makenna tried to halt her own desires of the flesh. If he could so easily dismiss their kiss, then so could she. But the second he turned around and came back to her side, she knew it would not be possible. His legs were now bare and the only piece of clothing he wore was a cream-colored leine partially opened, exposing his broad chest. The light cloth could not hide the strength of his muscles. She needed to fill the awkward silence before she threw herself at him begging him to take her.

"Rumors came a few days after you left that the attack was no ordinary raid. Descriptions of horrors trickled in for days. When Sean returned with your message, I realized it had been much worse than what we heard. Sean would only say our people had survived, but the animals . . . how are you faring after witnessing such cruelty?"

Colin blinked. "Sean spoke out of turn. He should not have told you such things." The idea of his wife exposed to such hatred was not acceptable.

Makenna saw his neck muscles tense. "It was not Sean's fault. As I said, there were rumors. It was actually kinder knowing the truth. I won't ask you particulars, but were you . . . were you able to do what you needed?"

The question startled Colin. He knew what Makenna meant. Had he found the culprits and exacted revenge? But the concept of someone concerned and interested about his trip was unexpected. Previously, whenever he had returned from being away, it had been to a litany of mishaps and lectures of how he should never have left Lochlen. Never once had Deirdre asked about his trips. Colin almost gave in to the urge to tell Makenna all that had happened, his suspicions, and his plans with Donovan.

Instead, he refrained. Makenna was strong, but the burden he carried was one of *his* making, and he would not ask her to share it. "Aye, I was able to do what must be done . . . for now."

"Then you will have to return."

"Aye, possibly, but I cannot say when at this time."

Makenna nodded. "I understand."

Her voice was low and sad. Wanting to comfort her, he scooped Makenna in his arms and settled down in the middle chair. Makenna curled up in his lap and laid her cheek against his chest.

Her sigh reminded him of her previous strained expression. "Makenna, when I entered you looked as if you were working through a problem. What happened while I was away?" He forced his voice to be light and casual while he waged war with his instincts to demand the name and action of whoever upset her.

Colin heard her quick intake of breath. "Nothing really. Just little things. I'm Lady of Lochlen now. I'm a wife, and it's all still new to me." She forced a smile and added, "I just hate not knowing how or what to do. I have much to learn, and I am impatient."

Her answer had the ring of truth, but Colin suspected something more serious was behind her earlier murmurs and looks. Seeing the state of the town walls, he reasoned many still were unhappy at her for marrying him, an outsider . . . a Highlander. The division between the clan was growing, not shrinking, and Makenna had been alone to deal with the aftermath of their marriage. If he pressed any further, Makenna would withdraw. Patience was the quickest path to gain her trust and learn the full truth.

He shifted her so that he could hold her more comfortably while stretching his legs toward the fire. It was such a simple thing, to hold one's wife. Simple, but pleasing in a way he had never dreamed possible. "I saw Gannon on my way to you. He affirmed what I saw. Lochlen could not have been in better hands."

The sincerity of his voice completely disarmed Makenna. How she had needed to hear those words. Tears formed and began to spill. She struggled to stop them, but the more she tried, the faster they fell.

Colin held Makenna as her sobs grew to where they shook her body. Concern flooded him. So much had taken place in the past six weeks, and Makenna had internalized it all. Their marriage, her father, the raids, his absence . . . she needed to release what she had been keeping buried.

After a while, Makenna calmed but did not move from his lap. The sleeve of her chemise was gathered near her shoulder, and Colin began to stroke the exposed skin. It was like caressing the finest silk. Every few inches his fingertips encountered another small scar. Lightly he touched each one wondering how her skin could be so soft and perfect, yet be riddled with so many old wounds. Her body was covered with them—her sides, her legs, and a large one across her knee that must have been very painful. What crazy foolish hobby did she have as a child—climbing trees? Did she have a bad fall on the stairs? Someday he would ask, but not now. Tonight was about the present and the future, not the past.

Makenna felt like a terrible weight had been partially lifted. It was still there, but it seemed manageable again. Not one for crying, she had never realized how therapeutic it could be. She snuggled closer and felt the proof of Colin's physical need.

A surge of deep, feminine desire reawakened. She slowly uncurled her legs, enjoying the feel of his arousal. She didn't resist as Colin's hand moved across her stomach to the curve of her hip and pulled her even closer.

A surge of euphoria hit Colin. Makenna was making it very clear that she wanted him to change the type of comfort he was providing. He was more than willing to oblige.

She tipped her head back and let her hair tumble over her shoulders. He leaned down and trailed soft kisses along her exposed nape until he reached her earlobe. Suckling the soft flesh, he felt her tremble. Before moving to her mouth, he searched her face, noticing how pretty her eyes looked. They were like two sparkling peridots, green and wide. Her strong features no longer struck him as bold, but beautiful. Never was there a woman more physically desirable. He wondered if she understood her feminine power over him.

"I thought I'd never get home," he muttered as he covered her mouth with his own. A renewed sense of urgency filled him. He needed to reclaim Makenna as his wife in every way.

Colin's tongue plunged into her mouth, making his intent unmistakable. She inhaled his musky scent and slipped her hands around his neck.

He eased the kiss and felt her smile across his lips. In response, he captured her lower lip between his teeth. He tugged and heard her laugh in delight. Colin heard himself groan. She was both torment and salvation.

He would not be alone in this agony and slowly began to make love to her with his tongue. He delved again into the sweetness of her mouth. She tasted of life, vibrant and exciting and so very good.

Makenna couldn't help but respond to the powerful, passionate kiss. As his caress increased in intensity, her laughter morphed into a soft continuous moan. Her fingers plunged into his hair, pulling him even closer. She needed more and tried to advance the unhurried, torturous embrace into one of wild passion.

Colin's pulse pounded in his ears. After weeks of deprivation, needing her, dreaming of this moment, he found it near impossible to go slow—especially with her encouraging him to do otherwise. He grabbed Makenna's face between his palms. Colin knew he was in jeopardy of losing the last of his control. Her aggression was incredibly arousing. He had half a mind to raise her chemise and settle her on top of him in the chair. Just the idea of her riding him made him so hot he started trembling.

Makenna stroked his shoulders down to the base of his spine, and Colin caved to his primitive cravings. Emitting a low growl, he slanted his mouth over Makenna's again and again, his tongue giving and taking with wild, ravenous need. He couldn't get enough of her. If he didn't move now, their first coupling upon his return would be in a chair.

Makenna was barely aware of being lifted and carried across the room.

Colin laid her down on the soft mattress and settled himself between her legs. How he had ever thought Makenna to be unyielding and tough he never knew. She was fiery and passionate, but feminine as well. Tendrils of auburn-colored hair floated across her cheeks. Colin brushed them aside and kissed the faint freckles on her nose.

"You are so lovely," he declared, his voice strained.

Makenna frowned remembering the conversation she had overheard just a few weeks ago. Nothing had changed. She was still too muscular for her slender frame. The sun had forever darkened and speckled her skin most unbecomingly. Her hair remained wild and untamed, and her body was unnaturally flawed with scars. "Not I. I'm riddled with faults," she countered defiantly.

He brushed a soft kiss on her cheek and then moved to her temple. "I see not a one," he whispered.

"Then you are blind," Makenna said, struggling to free herself of the large man. She could endure most anything. Anything but dishonesty framed in kindness.

Colin cupped the sides of her face and trapped her squirming body, holding her still. "I admit I once was blind where you were concerned, but I thank God I no longer am. If I had not married you, Makenna, I would never have known . . ." His voice became choked at the end.

Makenna opened her mouth to ask what he now knew, but his lips settled on hers with a kiss that dismissed further conversation. All he had to do was touch her, and she could no longer think about anything except him and what he was causing her to feel.

Passion and need radiated from him. A soft whimper came from deep in her throat as he thrust his tongue back into her warm, welcoming mouth.

Her struggles ceased. Instead, she became wild, clutching his back, kissing him feverishly.

Her mouth was hot, open, and so very responsive. His control over his body was nearing his threshold, but before he could no longer restrain his desire, he wanted her crying with need along with him.

Makenna's heart quickened as Colin released her lips and removed the last remaining bits of clothing between them. Colin was watching her. His expression was unguarded, warm, and tender. She reached up to pull him down to her.

He shook his head and edged down her body to begin a new assault. Colin lowered his head until he was just a scant breath away from one perfect pink bud. Makenna arched her back, yearning for his touch. He smiled and then lowered his mouth to roam the valley between her breasts.

His fingers found one bosom and then the other. His thumbs brushed across her nipples, hardening them into taut nubs. His heart pounded as his lips moved to where his hands had been. He feasted on her, using his tongue to taste the sweet mound she so willingly offered.

With each flick of his tongue over the sensitive flesh, Makenna felt a surge of exquisite passion ripple through her. Her body was on fire, and the blaze only grew as he began to suckle. The added stimulus was almost too much, and Makenna squirmed beneath his heavy frame. She wanted him to both stop and continue the sensual torture.

Hearing her whimpers, Colin moved to let her feel the hardened hunger in him. His heart was pounding and he was going out of his mind with the twisting sensation building inside him.

Everything about his touch was erotic. With each movement, his pelvis rubbed against the junction of her legs. Between his mouth and his hardness, nestled so intimately against her, her senses were swirling out of control.

She parted her thighs to him, urging him to touch her where the throbbing for him was almost painful with unfulfilled need. "Please, Colin, please," she begged.

"Please what?" he asked, barely able to utter the teasing question.

"Touch me, like you did before. Please, I don't think I can bear any more," she cried, her body writhing as he began to stroke her inner thigh, coming close but never entering the hot, damp core of her.

"Oh, I will, Makenna. I will drive you as wild and crazed with need as I," he finished, burying his face against her throat with a soft groan of desire. At the same time, his hand closed possessively over her soft mound. He slid one finger between the warm folds and penetrated her liquid heat.

Makenna fought for breath. Her heart was racing; her body was ablaze. She dug her nails into Colin's back. Rhythmically, she flexed and arched her hips against his palm, urging him to stroke her and give her what she so desperately needed.

Colin moved in her most intimate of places, glorying in her passion. He was seconds away from diving in and seeking the comfort he sought, but was determined to drive her to the insane place of need he had been living in for the past two weeks. He introduced another finger and began slowly separating them, stretching her, preparing her for what was to come.

Makenna cried out as he slipped another finger inside her before going lower still to caress the sensitive flesh just below her warm, wet channel. He stroked and caressed until her body was overrun with uncontrollable shudders. She was going mad, and then the world exploded.

At that moment, Colin drove deep, seeking the release and reassurance only she could provide.

His entry brought Makenna back to earth only to drive her wild once again. She wrapped her legs around his waist and joined him in passionate rhythm, meeting each of his thrusts. A force even more powerful than before was building within her, becoming more fervent, more intense with each plunge.

Colin eased himself partway out of her channel and then pressed forward again. She lifted herself against him, silently demanding that he move more quickly. He complied. He thought he had remembered what it was like to be with Makenna, but he had been wrong. The sensations moving through him were so intense, it was impossible to breathe.

He tried to slow down. She looked so small, and he didn't want to hurt her, but his desire had become painful, a torture Colin could no longer deny release. Again and again he plunged back into her with long, sure movements. Each time she stretched and then closed around him.

The world had disappeared and all that remained was Makenna. He heard her cry out and then felt her small convulsions as she surrendered to the wonder of their lovemaking. Colin clung to Makenna as he erupted inside her, barely aware that the exultant shout echoing in the room was his own.

For long moments, Colin didn't think he would ever be able to move again. He wasn't even sure he wanted to. He felt magnificent, all-conquering, and all-powerful. More so than he ever felt on the battlefield. He longed to tell her so, to tell her how much she meant to him, but his throat was so constricted with emotion, it disabled him from saying anything.

Makenna lay in Colin's arms, truly happy for the first time since he had left her side. His head was upon her chest, his breath ragged. She reached up and stroked his hair lovingly.

There was no denying that the man had invaded her soul. Never would she want another.

Makenna had always wanted to fall in love, but never had she dreamed it would be with Colin. She had thought his love for her sister would protect her from such a foolish, vulnerable feeling. When he had left two weeks ago, she stayed up each night waiting for him, wishing for his return. She had talked herself into believing that it was their lovemaking, not Colin, she missed.

How wrong she had been. Every time they had joined, she had given a piece of herself to him. Tonight, she had given him her heart, completely, wholly, and without doubts.

Now she understood. Love was forever. It would not disappear with the body. Not when it consumed the soul. While Colin would always love her sister, she would always love him.

Colin rolled to his side and pulled Makenna's backside against him. He kissed her hair. "What are you thinking?"

She squeezed her eyes shut and lied, "I was just wishing

my clan would open themselves up and learn how wonderful you are."

"Right now I only care what you believe. Now hush, and go to sleep, for I doubt I will last the night before needing you again," he whispered into her hair.

Makenna nestled closer to him. His voice resonated contentment. He was happy, and it was because of her, not her sister. Her love would be enough for the both of them. She would make it be enough.

Chapter Ten

Makenna inhaled the fresh morning air as she walked across the courtyard to the Black Tower. The air was fresh and clear. It felt warm, but the color of the grass was starting to change, as well as the leaves on the village trees. Fall was on the wind and winter would soon follow.

Colin left early that morning with Dunlop, but only after he had brought them both to satisfaction yet again. Makenna smiled to herself remembering his good-bye kiss. It had taken some time and only ended with Dunlop asking if there was something wrong.

A door opened from the Black Tower, and Gannon emerged. Makenna waved to him to get his attention. He met her halfway and arched his brows knowingly. "I see your husband found you last night."

"And why would you think that, Gannon?" Makenna countered with just a hint of challenge.

Gannon gestured for her to turn and walk with him toward Canmore Tower. "Because if he had not, I have no doubt that your husband would have returned to my quarters and not in the good mood I had first encountered him in."

Everyone knew Colin was especially foul upon returning from a trip. Maybe he really had been pleased with her efforts. "He *was* in a good mood, wasn't he?" Makenna asked merrily.

Gannon nodded. "Oh, aye. Quite unexpected, his reaction was." Gannon had been even more surprised at his own reaction to last night's events. He had been the Lochlen steward for over two decades and loyal to the Dunstans his whole life. Having a Highlander as his laird seemed so wrong, especially with the overly indulged Lady Makenna as his wife. But life had been taking unexpected turns the past few weeks and with each new corner, his confidence in Alexander's decision grew.

Makenna patted the wrinkled skin of the old man and beamed him a grin. "I told you moving Colin into the solar was a smart decision. It demonstrated allegiance."

"If you say so, milady."

"I do."

"Well, as your steward, I have an announcement for you. As of this morning, you now have a chambermaid. She will tend to your room, see it cleaned every morning, and ensure that there is fresh water in the decanter. Vanora is too young to be sleeping outside your chambers. Consequently, she cannot tend to you as a lady's maid, but—"

Relieved that Colin and she would still be alone at night, Makenna hugged his wide body and kissed his cheek. Gannon blushed profusely. "I, uh, I sent Vanora to the solar. You must have just missed her."

Makenna knew she had embarrassed the hardened steward but didn't care. "Shall we go meet her, then?"

"Aye, but you go alone. I have work that must be tended to."

"Should I come as well? I can meet with Vanora and

then join you in the Pinnacle Tower, or will you be in the kitchens?"

Gannon waved his hand. "No, no. Meet with Vanora, but then *take the day off*." He raised a finger and gave her a direct look. "Now, milady, I believe you encouraged . . . no, forced is the better word . . . everyone—including myself, the cook, and the baker—to take most of the day off yesterday."

"If this is about the soldiers again, Gannon, I told you, if they can fend for themselves while at the training camps or when they travel, they can fend for themselves one or two days a month to allow those who support this keep a well-deserved break. I warn you now that I will order such rest again. Aye, I know winter is coming, but if we do not take time to enjoy life every once in a while, then—"

"Milady!" Gannon shouted. "You have convinced me!"

Makenna's brows furrowed. "Then what is your argument?"

"You! I discovered *you* did not partake in the same break. Doreen told me this morning that she caught you trying to weave something."

"You shouldn't believe everything Doreen says, Gannon."

"I don't, but I know it was true."

"They were blankets. And no, they were not pretty, but they will keep someone warm . . . or warmer."

"I am sure they will. But it is your turn for a respite, milady. And don't bother arguing with me. I've known you since you were a wee thing, and you cannot intimidate me as you do so many others. Tomorrow you may run this castle as you are so quickly becoming accustomed to doing, but not today. And if I find you sneaking into the keep and lifting a finger to do anything that does not bring you pleasure, then I shall tell the laird in detail exactly how you have been acting as auxiliary staff to keep this place running. I am beginning to wonder if I should tell him anyway."

Makenna halted and grabbed the steward's arm. "No, Gannon. Colin does not need to be burdened with my trials. He just needs to know that his keep is not falling apart while he focuses on the security of his people. He does not need to know how, just that it is."

"Well, I'm not eager to receive the scolding he would give me for letting you work the way you do."

"Bah, you *let* me do nothing. *This* lady of the castle goes where she is needed, Gannon. Pride keeps a lady from her hands and knees when that is where she is needed most." Makenna paused and looked the steward straight in the eye. "You promised me your silence on this."

"Aye, and now I'm telling you to rest. You have been running yourself too hard. My promise will matter little if you pass out from exhaustion."

The old steward was impossible to bargain with in this mood. "This isn't advice. It's blackmail," Makenna accused.

He smiled, knowing he had won the argument. "Call it what you wish, milady. Vanora and then relaxation. I mean it," he replied solemnly as he turned toward the kitchens.

Gannon hoped Makenna would go riding, which would take her away from Lochlen for several hours. That would give him enough time to meet with Lela and the others and give them his decision. While he still had doubts concerning the wisdom of a Highland laird, he would not actively work against the man. It would be up to McTiernay to prove himself, and if Lela and her associates wanted to plan and work to his destruction, the laird best watch his own back.

Makenna stood for a second in disbelief watching

Gannon retreat. Had she changed that much? Two months ago, she would have argued with Gannon until she had no more breath before caving into his or anyone else's will. Now she practically fell over at the mere push.

Marriage was making her soft. She wondered if Colin was also experiencing changes to his personality. "Probably not," she huffed and headed toward Canmore and the new maid. "The man is like his sword, hard and . . ."

Makenna stopped, her eyes huge with inspiration. She knew of a way for people to see Colin as their laird *and* a Highlander at the same time. She had the solution all along. With Gannon not expecting help, today provided the perfect opportunity to begin.

Picking up her skirts, Makenna rushed to her old room in Forfar Tower and sprinted up the stairs, completely forgetting about Vanora.

Dashing into the room, she rushed over to the unlit hearth and lifted a small board in the flooring. Picking up the key, she moved to the huge floor-standing chest and unlocked it. Using both hands, she shoved the heavy teak lid open. The chest was not an elaborate piece of art like Colin's, but it was sturdy, and it contained the one thing that would prove to all that Colin belonged at Lochlen.

Makenna reached in and pulled free the velvet bag. Clutching it, she dashed back down the stairs and out the outer gate, completely unaware she had been followed.

"Can you do it? Can you, Camus?" Makenna beseeched, careful to keep her voice down low.

Camus pushed his once red, now silver hair back and retucked it behind his ear. Makenna could never find someone to tell her Camus's age. He had lived at Lochlen since she could remember and had always looked the same. Withered, but strong. He was wiry and his bronzed skin had become loose and wrinkled, but he still somehow managed to appear quite appealing to the opposite sex. More than once over the years, Makenna had interrupted a visiting widow supposedly stopping by his shop to learn about swords and their value. She could not remember half the excuses she had heard, but not one had been believable.

"Well?" Makenna asked again.

"What you ask is not a light thing, *laochag*," Camus cautioned. He knew she was now the Lady of Lochlen, but to him, she would always be the daughter he never had.

"I know it is not," she replied brusquely. "I remember all you taught me of the importance about swords and their owners."

Camus sighed and walked to the small bench laden with tools and materials used for sword making. "Aye, and Colin already has a sword. A good sword, I might add. It will be hard to make its equal." He knew, because he had forged it.

Makenna walked over and placed her hand on Camus's arm. "But you can. You made my Secret. You have the skill and knowledge to make such a sword. I just know it."

"My arms guild is very busy these days. The laird has been adding men faster than I can arm them. I have two new apprentices, and they require much oversight. I don't believe it possible."

Makenna would not be deterred. "It is possible! Or at least it could be if you tried. I will not seek this task from another. Too many don't know this trade. It would be like asking the . . . the blacksmith to make such a piece."

Camus was fully aware that she was goading him, but her words still sparked his ire. "Blacksmith! Makenna, I taught you better. It is not just a matter of my time, but the sword itself. Just because I spent hours building a piece will not ensure the laird's willingness to take it. It is a personal area we invade here, Makenna. Men like to commission their own weapons, detailing their specifications. No man would just accept such a thing. He would consider it an insult."

Makenna dug into her gown and pulled the velvet bag free. "Not if you made it using these. I know they will make all the difference. Not only to Colin, but to my people."

Camus drew his brows together and took the offered bag. Loosening the strings, he peered inside. His jaw slackened. "Are these . . . ?"

"Aye, they are."

"And no one knows?"

"Not a single a soul. I took them just in case our clan needed them. They can do my father no good in heaven. I didn't tell anyone . . . well, because I couldn't risk Ula or Rona learning of it."

"Aye, you were right to do that. And the laird?" Camus asked.

Makenna shifted awkwardly. "Honestly, I forgot about them until this morning. I would have told Colin, but things were so chaotic with my father's funeral, and—"

"And so your answer is no."

"He will know if you agree to my request."

Camus stood and began to stroke his chin. He had fashioned Colin his last sword and knew exactly what the man preferred in size and weight. If he made a similar, maybe even better sword adorned with the Dunstan colors, it could be just the symbol to rally the clan. It certainly was worth a try.

"Aye, you just may be right at that, *laochag*. I hope the

laird knows what a treasure he received the day he married you."

"It was I who got lucky, Camus."

Camus shook his head. Makenna never did understand her full value as a woman. He didn't know when his gangly, awkward little warrior had changed into a beautiful lady, but she had. It was clear Makenna still had yet to make the realization. In time, with Colin's help, she would.

"The Dunstan clan is fortunate the old laird was so wise and obstinate in putting you two together. I'll accept your offer. I believe Alexander would have wanted it."

Makenna pointed to the bag. "Can you keep that safe?"

Camus chuckled. If a man had asked that question, he would have lost an arm or at least a hand. Makenna was the only one who could insult his abilities and leave standing. "Aye, your bag will be safe with me."

Makenna beamed and planted a kiss on Camus's cheek for the second time that day. "Thank you!"

Camus waved for her to go. The open affection she gave him was a bit overwhelming, and he knew he was in fear of tearing. "Now get out of here and stop bothering an old man. I have work to do. See me in about a month."

Makenna blew him another kiss and then glided out the door on a wave of happiness. She hadn't progressed two steps before colliding with Gorten.

Makenna stumbled and looked up into the stern face of her guard. His light brown hair was pulled tightly back, which only accentuated his angular features. His deep-set hazel eyes had chips of gold that sparkled with irritation. That alone might have alerted her to his mood, if it were not his most common expression.

"Gorten! Good grief, I did not see you. How are you this fabulous morn?"

He wanted to say fabulously annoyed, but seeing the level of delight in her face, he realized his carefully prepared lecture would have little effect. "I am well, milady, though somewhat troubled that you left the keep without letting Brodie or me know."

Makenna blushed at the light censure. "My apologies. It was not at all intentional, I assure you. I had a matter of some import with Camus this morning, and I totally forgot to let you know where I was going. However, I would like to make it up to you."

Gorten snorted and crossed his arms. She was playing her bewitching games again, and this time with full force. He had half a mind to order her back to the solar and have Brodie fetch the laird. The other half of his mind was curious to know her proposal.

His mouth moved only slightly, but it was enough for Makenna to know she had some room to influence the stern guardsman. "Let me go fetch my Secret, and I shall meet you at the stables. How would you like to spar with me on this fine and glorious day!"

Gorten hated to admit it, and would never do so aloud, but he had missed training with Makenna. She was not a strong opponent, but she was skilled and sneaky with a sword. Sparring with her improved his speed and his ability to think and predict movements. "I shall escort you to the tower and then to the stables," Gorten answered gruffly.

Makenna did not mind; she knew Gorten was as eager as she was to partake in her version of a relaxing and fulfilling day.

* * *

"You missed!" Makenna teased as she dodged yet another strike of his sword.

At first Gorten had decided to engage her lightly, believing time might have slowed her reflexes and ability to fight. He had been wrong. They both knew he was the stronger of the two, but Makenna's ability to think and outstrategize made her a tough opponent.

Colin watched from afar as the two circled around each other fighting for supremacy. He had never actually observed Makenna spar with anyone before. Soon after he arrived at Lochlen, he had heard of her peculiar interest and her purported talent and immediately ordered his men to end all activity involving Makenna and any lethal object. It seemed she had secretly recruited a few to continue her training, and now he could see why. Never did he dream his wife could wield a claymore with such dexterity. Most women could not even lift one let alone hold and battle with it for long periods.

Gorten was an excellent soldier. One of Colin's best. Not only was he skilled at riding and fighting, but he was not easily swayed. Once Gorten made a decision, he never deterred from it. It was for those reasons he had been selected to protect Makenna from harm.

Makenna's laughter drifted to the lone cluster of trees hiding Colin from her view. The sound haunted him; filling him with a physical hunger he thought to have assuaged that morning.

Swords clanked. Makenna turned, easily maintaining her balance where larger men might have fallen. She was self-assured in her abilities, but not overconfident. Her verbal banter was partially a ploy to throw off her opponent and catch him unawares. This was obviously not the first time Gorten had clashed swords with his wife, for he seemed to understand her tactics and countered them. Gorten was also tiring faster than Makenna.

Colin watched his guard advance, deflect, attack, and then retreat. Protecting Makenna had actually improved Gorten's cunning, but it had seriously reduced his stamina for swordplay. Gorten most likely could still outfight most of his men, but that fact would not remain true if he didn't have the opportunity to rebuild his strength. Makenna could keep Gorten's agility alive, but she could not improve his power.

Another crash of metal echoed throughout the hills. Makenna deflected a strike and then spun around, sending dust flying into the air as she aimed for Gorten's side. He jumped out of the way, slicing her sword down and kicking up further dirt. Then she did something unexpected. Instead of stepping back to ensure that she remained steady, she moved forward, twisting her arms back up. It threw Gorten off balance. Somehow, their limbs hooked together, and Makenna came crashing down with Gorten falling full length on top of her. Dust flew up into the air and took its time settling back to the ground.

Colin could see nothing but a cloud of dirt for a moment, but he heard their laughter. They were practically in hysterics. Makenna sounded so happy, so at ease. And though he knew it to be irrational, *he* wanted to be the cause behind her free, jubilant laugh.

Colin moved toward them, deciding the one-on-one session was over. When he was halfway across the clearing, the dust had settled enough to reveal their positions. Raw fury exploded.

Jealousy, hot and dark, pumped through him, racing over his nerve endings. Makenna was his. No man was ever to know what it felt like to have her beneath him. They belonged to each other and no one else.

Makenna's eyes widened in surprise upon seeing Colin. She was about to shout a greeting when her eyes

locked with his. Fear rushed through her. Colin looked
ready to kill.

"Gorten, I think you better get up," she murmured,
never taking her eyes off of Colin. His expression was
dark and stone-hard.

Gorten smiled, still recovering from his fit of laughter. "I suppose you are right. This new move of yours still
needs work."

Gorten was still talking when he felt someone grab
him by the shoulders and throw him aside as if he
weighed nothing. Reaching for his sword to attack the
unknown assailant, Gorten felt a sheathed foot slam
down hard on his hand. He looked up and realized who
and why he had been assaulted.

"Laird, I did not hear you approach," he managed to
say, trying hard to keep his voice level. He had disgraced
himself enough already this day. He would not show
pain to his laird.

"I believe you were too busy rolling on the ground
with my wife." There was no mistaking the wrath about
to be unleashed on Gorten.

Makenna quickly stood and tried to deflect Colin's attention off her guard, who feared to move or even
stand. "Take your anger out on me, Colin McTiernay.
Gorten has been a loyal soldier to you. We were only
sparring. Nothing more."

He knew she spoke the truth. He had witnessed it.
But he could not erase the vision of Gorten lying on top
of her . . . laughing. "I saw how he has been loyal to me."

Gorten remained motionless. One word spoken out
of place, and his life would end. Makenna must have
sensed that as well.

"How dare you!" Makenna admonished through her
teeth. She struggled for composure. Adrenaline pumped
through her, and she began to tremble violently.

Colin took a step back. Blue pools of fury shifted from Gorten back to her. "How dare I?"

Gorten took the chance to stand.

Without even looking in his direction, Makenna ordered, "Leave now, Gorten. I am about to fight with my husband and would like to do so in private. Please make sure no one comes within hearing distance of this clearing." Makenna's chin came up angrily, her green eyes sparkling with equal intensity, daring him to counter her order.

"Gorten!" Colin yelled without removing his eyes from Makenna. Very carefully, fully aware of his tightly leashed anger and its absurdity, he called out, "Leave, and do your lady's bidding." Then much more quietly Colin added, "For she is right. We *are* about to fight," he growled through compressed lips.

With Gorten gone, Makenna hoped Colin would calm and become more rational. He looked both menacing—and thoroughly male. She wanted the chance to explain her innocence and then throw herself into his arms and kiss all his doubts away.

Her hope died a quick death.

Gorten might be gone, but their quarrel was not over. Colin's pride had been injured just as deeply as a sword could do to the flesh. It would not be mended with the mere disappearance of one man.

"So this is what you have been doing while I was away. I am surprised you had the energy for me upon my return. Or maybe I should consider myself fortunate to have a wife with such stamina."

Makenna cringed at the coldness in his voice. She wanted to shake him into admitting that he knew she would never, ever even look at another man.

"Are you so insecure as to believe I would do that to you? Do you think that I have such a low sense of self-worth? Or maybe I do at that. I did marry you." Pride spoke now for both of them, slicing through newly built layers of trust.

Colin brought his face very close to Makenna's so that she had no trouble seeing just how blazingly furious he was. Makenna returned his stare. His eyes were brilliant and frighteningly bright. She saw his anger, but she also recognized possessiveness, pain, and fear. This man, who needed no one, who could stand impassively at a crowd openly hating him, who could ignore taunts delivered by his enemies, needed her.

Makenna pulled at his leine until he leaned down. She could feel the strength radiating through the soft fabric. Lord, he was as inflexible as his stubborn nature. "Listen to me now, Colin McTiernay, for I would never say this if it were not the utter truth. I didn't want to marry you."

She could feel him pull away, but she kept him near. "Aye, but I will be forever happy that I did. Never did I dream that I could love a domineering giant, but I do." Hot tears burned her eyes. She could feel them fall, but she continued. "Do you hear me, Colin? I love you. I would never bear the touch of any man but you. I will never, ever dishonor you or what I feel for you. You complete me in ways I never thought possible. It is because *of you* I was able to laugh today. It is because *of you* I feel safe enough, loved enough, to *be myself.* Do you know how much that means to me? How much *you* mean to me?"

She let him go and felt him rise, but his gaze did not leave hers. The heat rose in Makenna's cheeks as she saw the cool possessiveness fill his eyes as he realized what she was saying. It took him several seconds to regain his ability to breathe, and even when he was sure he had himself in hand again, he still did not dare to touch her.

Makenna reached up and cupped his cheek. Colin closed his eyes and felt his hot anger dissipate under the light touch. When it was gone, his eyes sprang open. Two tumultuous green pools shimmered into his. He spread his hands wide against the sides of her face, his fingers tangling in her glorious red mane.

Makenna needed him more than ever before. She had opened her heart to him, told him what she felt. "I love you, Colin," she pledged again.

The anguished whisper tore at Colin's heart. He wanted to say the words back, but fear stopped him. He had loved before and barely survived its loss. Loving and losing Makenna would cause a pain he would not be able to endure.

Colin looked down intently into her now serene and confident eyes. He needed some of that serenity, some of that assurance. "Never leave me," he said roughly, barely able to speak. "Vow it."

She nodded within his grasp. "I belong to you," she said, making the same promise she had the night before he left.

"And I to you, Makenna," Colin whispered just before his mouth closed roughly over hers, searing her lips with his own.

Makenna moaned softly and gripped his neck as he picked her up and moved to the soft grass near the trees where he had been hiding. He lay down and pulled her on top of him. Cupping his hand behind her neck, he gathered her close and brushed his mouth lightly, but possessively across hers.

Makenna wanted him, needed him, but this time she intended to sweep him away in passion. Never again would Colin doubt what she felt for him.

Makenna parted his lips and boldly stroked the inside of his mouth. Her tongue dove in, then withdrew, then plunged again, mimicking the rhythm of lovemaking. She kissed with wild abandon, tasting, teasing, drinking in everything about him.

Colin knew he should do something to gain control of this passionate assault upon his senses, but he couldn't muster the will to stop her. Not yet. It was the most incredible kiss he had ever experienced.

He moaned and moved his arms slowly around her waist. He felt her warm skin and realized her gown had ridden up, giving him access to inside. His hands stroked her round buttock, enjoying the soft skin before moving down her leg. The blood in his veins turned molten, and his male member rose hot and hard.

Makenna could feel Colin's fingers caress her, teasing her body into a fever. She decided it was time to issue the same exquisite torment. She felt him, hard and impatient against her thigh, and slid her hand down his body. She removed his belt and plaid and finally found what she sought. It was tight, hot, and hard.

Colin felt her fingers close around him and thought his heart might stop. "God, Makenna, what you do to me," he groaned softly, deeply.

Makenna smiled and leaned down to capture his lips in a kiss. Her hand never stopped moving up and down his hard shaft, leisurely massaging its tip with her thumb.

Colin could take no more and grabbed her wrist. Before she could argue, he shifted so that she straddled his thighs. Her eyes grew large on her face as she realized what he wanted her to do. "Colin, I—"

"Shhh," he commanded softly. He reached out and touched her between her thighs. She was hot and moist, and already wild with need for him. Picking her up, she naturally parted her thighs. Then Colin positioned her so that she was astride him, engulfing him with one long, sure movement.

Makenna gasped. She didn't think it was possible, but Colin felt even more enormous. At first, she expected to burst, but after a moment, her body adjusted, and sudden wild abandon filled her.

Slowly she began the primitive rhythm, moving up, down, and around, taking delight in his bold, aggressive hardness. Makenna gazed down at Colin, looking thoroughly satisfied. Her lips were dewy and swollen, and the sparkle in her eyes drove him into a new, frenzied level of need.

Colin could stand no more. Makenna didn't even have time to gasp before she found herself on her back with Colin driving himself into her. He pulled her close and showered her face and shoulders with hungry kisses, groaning with intense yearning as he removed clothing frantically, seeking new places to caress.

He was there at the core of her body, pushing into her with each thrust. His mouth was savoring and claiming every morsel of her, branding her as his own.

Her fingers sank into his shoulders. She tipped back, and a small cry caught in her throat. A sweet, hot flame scorched through her.

Makenna climaxed with a shock of immense pleasure that shook her whole body. Colin felt it all just before the wave of sweet bliss claimed him.

Minutes later, he could still feel her trembling with the aftermath of their lovemaking. He had rolled to his back and moved her onto him once again. She was limp, but he knew she was happy. His arms stole protectively around her and he kissed the top of her head.

Colin was glad Makenna could not see him. He was wearing a huge grin and all because Makenna loved him. It sent a wave of elation through him that couldn't be equaled by any other kind of knowledge.

If anyone had told him that passion and the need for

a woman could rule his head, his heart, even his life, he would have thought they were mad. He had needs as any man, but they were well within his control. That was until he had experienced passion with Makenna. Each time, whether hot and wild or slow and exploring, she had brought him to levels of physical want beyond the imagination. And each time, he floated down to earth filled with indescribable happiness.

With her, he felt complete.

Makenna swatted Colin's hand away for the umpteenth time. "Colin, stop that! You're making it very difficult for me to get dressed."

"I hoped to make it impossible," he said, tugging on her bliaut so that she fell against him.

Makenna surrendered to another kiss, and then tried once again to finish dressing. "You must let me finish, Colin. Someone might approach, and I would forever be shamed."

Colin let her go. "No one will come. Remember? Gorten is ensuring that none come near."

Makenna stopped and stared at him. "Lord, I had forgotten. Do you suppose he thinks we are still fighting?"

Colin laughed and stood up, helping her adjust the bliaut. "I highly doubt it." Colin knew Gorten genuinely liked Makenna and would have interceded on her behalf by now if he believed Colin still to be angry with her. It was both good and bad to have someone as loyal and devoted as her guard.

"There," Colin said, wiping off the last blades of grass from her sleeve. "No one will ever know how you seduced your husband after defeating one of his men in combat."

Makenna's jaw dropped. "*I* seduced you?" she squeaked.

"Aye, and you can do it again tonight if you wish," he replied, his voice both arrogant and lighthearted.

"Nay, husband. Tonight it is you who shall be doing the seducing."

Colin grabbed the reins to his black mount and walked with Makenna to where hers remained tethered to a tree and eating grass. She smoothed the chestnut-colored mane. Adjusting her sword, she sheathed her Secret into the specially made scabbard. She then spoke kindly into the mare's ear and mounted.

"Would you like to join me and ride to the training fields?" Even as the words left his mouth, Colin couldn't believe what he was asking. But even as he mentally explored the request, he knew that he would not take it back. "Just this once."

Excitement bubbled inside Makenna. *The training fields.* The place Colin prepared his men. She would finally get to see the size of his army and watch them display their skill with a sword. "Aye, Colin, I would like it very much."

"Come on, then. Let us tell Gorten that he no longer needs to fear for his life before we find Dunlop. Today, he is working with new recruits who think they already know all there is about sword fighting."

Makenna smiled and joined Colin in the brisk ride to find Gorten and then to the grounds where men learned to be Scottish warriors.

As they approached the wide expanse of land a few miles north of the Lochlen, Makenna could hear shouts and the clinking of metal swordplay. Dunlop rode out to greet them. "Ho, Laird! My lady! It is good to see you riding once again."

Colin caught the implication. "Have you not been riding, Makenna?"

"Nay, not once while you were gone," Dunlop interjected, knowing Makenna would somehow evade answering the question.

Makenna shot the commander a scathing look. "I thought it best not to since we did not know exactly what had happened to the farmers or by whom," she quickly explained and focused on the men practicing.

Colin stared at his wife as she intently avoided his gaze. Her answer was too full of logic, and much too safe to be true. No, there were other reasons that kept Makenna from partaking in one of her favorite pastimes.

Before Colin could ask, a shouting match exploded between several men, and he moved to intercede. Makenna persuaded her mount to move beside Dunlop's. She studied the fields, estimating over one hundred head practiced here. "Dunlop, how is it possible to train so many men at one time?"

"Colin has grouped them by skill and by weapon. Those you see in the distance practice the longbow. Over there, down the hill and to your right, those men are focused on the mace."

Makenna watched in fascination. Most were training on the battle-axe, the mace, and the claymore, but some were training on the small ballock knife. The men were quite good. They lacked originality, but they were quick and deadly accurate.

"I'm surprised Colin has so many men training with knives."

"'Tis a common mistake some leaders make to train only with swords. One does not fight just in war, and most men cannot afford swords. But everyone carries a knife. Why, even you carry a small version in your hilt, do you not?" Makenna nodded. "A man does as well. And it can be deadly if a soldier does not know how to fight, deflect, and disarm an attacker with a smaller weapon. Additionally, a man who is knowledgeable with a knife can defend, wound, and kill—important skills to have in battle."

Makenna pointed to where Colin was standing. "And what group are they?" Colin was surrounded by boys of varying ages, some very young, approximately thirteen or fourteen, but a few looked nearer to twenty summers.

Dunlop grimaced. "Beginners. They heard about our laird's leadership and his ability to train younger men and recently joined. They are inexperienced and young, but eager to learn. At least most of them are."

"Most of them?" Makenna inquired.

"Aye, most, but not all. There are some who feel learning the basics of fighting is beneath them," he answered, pointing to the obviously much older boys in the group.

They were training with single ash sticks, just as Camus had started his instruction with her. Makenna moved forward and was surprised to hear Colin declare that a truly skilled soldier could discern when to defend himself and avoid killing and when it was absolutely necessary.

One of the bigger boys leaning disrespectfully against the tree threw down his stick. "And I keep telling you that I am ready. I have no need to practice with sticks. I want to fight with real weapons and train with the men."

Again, Makenna was surprised. She expected her husband to lose his temper at the boy's insolence, but Colin remained calm, even patient, as the young man droned about how he had never been so underappreciated in his father's army.

Dunlop leaned over and whispered, "Most lads are eager to listen and learn, but the dozen or so that have been sent to us from Crawford deem they are already great fighters. They want to be moved over to the more advanced groups and begin working with the *claidheamh mor*."

Makenna gasped. The little she had seen was evidence enough they were not ready. "But they would be slaughtered."

"Aye, but at least they'd stop complaining," Dunlop returned, grinning.

Makenna couldn't help herself and smiled back, swallowing laughter. She watched as the group recommenced their training. They were too eager, consistently forecasting their intentions. Much practice would be needed before they would be ready for the *claidheamh mor*, the great sword, her weapon of choice.

A few years ago, Camus had specially made her a two-handed broadsword close to the size of a normal claymore, yet much lighter. She doubted if there was another man in all of lower Scotland who could equal Camus's knowledge on the properties of metals, how they reacted to heat and which combinations made them stronger. His skill and knowledge had created her Secret, a claymore she could wield much faster than her opponent expected.

Colin felt himself getting frustrated. Dunlop had not exaggerated when he told him about the new Crawford recruits, especially Jaimie's sons. They truly judged their skills to be the same or even superior to those of his men. Each time they lost, they claimed it was because they had competed against Laird McTiernay's finest.

An impulsive idea took hold. Hooking his sword in his belt, Colin crossed his arms and ordered the protesters to gather around him close enough for Makenna to hear.

"Do you see that woman over there?" Colin asked, pointing at Makenna but not looking in her direction. "She is my wife, Lady McTiernay. What you may not know is that she enjoys sparring with the *claidheamh mor*." He could see the disbelief in their eyes and continued.

"Aye, she carries her sword upon her even now." He paused as some of them craned their heads to look.

"You believe you are good enough right now to spar with the more experienced men and that I treat you differently because you are sworn to Laird Crawford, not to me. I say you are not ready because you lack basic skills. But I am willing to give you the opportunity to prove me wrong. Select one of your men, and I suggest that you pick your quickest and most skilled. If Lady Mc-Tiernay is willing to spar, and you win, then I shall move your entire group forward. If not, never again shall a complaint spew from your mouths."

One older boy scoffed. Makenna eyed the young soldier. He was of average height with bright brown eyes, short scrubby hair, and an expression on his face he thought made him look intimidating and fearsome. He had the body of a man, but he was not one yet. Misplaced pride and lack of humility stood in his way. "It would be unfair. I would not be able to truly fight in fear of hurting her," the boy complained.

At this comment, Makenna jumped down and unsheathed her Secret. Colin looked unsurprised. He considered warning her that these were the sons of an ally, but decided against it.

Makenna unpinned the bulky plaid from her shoulder. "Colin, I would not mind the least in offering a few of the lessons I learned during my singlestick tutelage. I request only that you not interfere for any reason unless I ask you to."

Upon Colin's nod in agreement, Makenna turned back toward the smirking boy who had been joined by someone who looked to be his brother. "What are your names?"

The more polite of the two similar-looking young men

stepped forward. "I am Auburn, and he is my brother Korbin."

"I was watching you, Auburn, and you as well, Korbin, and in many ways I agree with you, I think you have the promise of being great swordsmen. I also admit to never being in battle or a true one-on-one fight for my life. However, I enjoy the art of swordplay immensely and some even consider me quite good. Do you, Korbin, think that I could ever, even at my very best, defeat a Scottish warrior? Even a marginal one?"

Korbin looked at the healthy, but definitely much smaller woman and shook his head. "I do not."

"Thank you for being honest. I absolutely agree."

Makenna twirled her Secret and then moved to the middle of the clearing field. She pointed its tip to Korbin and then Auburn. "I shall fight you both simultaneously. And I warn you now that you both will receive scars to remember that no matter how good you are, there is always somebody better, and oftentimes it is the person you least expect. Now fetch your swords."

Colin was still mentally debating on whether he should stop her challenge. He had meant for her to fight *one* man, not two. But before he could make up his mind, they had both returned and the fight had begun.

Korbin made the first move and lunged at her with the idea of scaring her. Makenna easily sidestepped his attack. At the same time, she shifted her weight and angle so her sword cut the air in a powerful, fast arc, easily disarming her opponent when it came down. Without stopping the graceful and unexpected move, Makenna twisted and this time with an upward thrust neutralized Auburn, sending his claymore flying several yards away.

"Lesson one. Never underestimate your opponent," Makenna stated calmly.

Korbin looked at his brother. Auburn fetched his sword and returned, looking both embarrassed and mad. "I am afraid that I will hurt you, milady, if I truly try to fight."

A whipping sound sliced the air as Makenna moved with precision. She disarmed the young man, and at the same time carved a future scar into Auburn's upper chest.

Upon seeing Makenna's blade draw his friend's blood, Korbin raised his sword and came down where Makenna was standing with all his might. Yet when he arrived, she was not there. Somehow, she had been able to move behind him and with a speed Korbin had not thought possible when wielding such a large and heavy weapon. The shock of finding her gone was immediately replaced with a fiery pain of a sharp edge cutting his upper fighting arm.

"Lesson two. An emotional enemy can be your greatest asset in combat. Your own emotions, however, are your greatest weakness."

Colin wondered what Jaimie Crawford would think about his methods of training upon hearing who gave his sons scars during training. No doubt Trista would be even less pleased that Makenna hurt her boys. Then again, he doubted anyone could teach Korbin and Auburn the lesson in humility they desperately needed better than Makenna. This moment, while embarrassing, would someday save their lives.

Colin decided not to intervene.

Korbin and Auburn were now angry enough to fight, woman or no woman, lady or no lady. The wounds she issued were minor. They probably stung like hell, and Colin had no doubt that Makenna had fully controlled the size and placement of each slit.

Korbin began dancing around Makenna. Auburn fol-

lowed his lead. Makenna looked bored. Both began
twirling the swords and slicing the air in hopes of intimidating her with the sounds. Makenna let them continue
their exhausting dance for several minutes, easily sidestepping their jabs and thrusts.

"Engage!" Auburn yelled in frustration.

Makenna arched a single eyebrow and then pivoted on
one foot, bringing herself unexpectedly close to her opponent. Auburn shifted his weight back and at the same
time, she brought her sword down at precisely the right
time to ensure that Auburn lost his balance and fell.

"You won't find it so easy to do the same to me,"
Korbin taunted, continuing to dance around her.

Makenna didn't even aim for Korbin's sword. Instead,
she thrust her blade between his constantly moving legs
so that they twisted, causing him to fall. She kicked his
sword away. Then with two hands, she brought her sword
up and aimed it toward his heart in a mock display of
what it would be like if someone caused you to fall.

"Lesson three. Maintain balance or fall and die," she
said, completely devoid of emotion.

Korbin gulped, sought his sword, and then prepared
again for Makenna. He had thought sheer strength and
size were all that was needed to fight and win. Lady Mc-
Tiernay had neither, yet she found it not in the least bit
difficult to disarm him even when he had faith he was
completely prepared for her attack.

Auburn looked even less sure about continuing the
lesson and wanted to say so.

Korbin moved over to his comrade. Perhaps if they
fought together, not on opposite sides, they would have
the advantage.

Makenna recognized the ploy at once. She moved forward, slicing the air. As expected, the two jumped
slightly apart and then moved to attack her. This time,

instead of sidestepping or twirling her body out of the way, she easily stepped through the two men. In their efforts to land a blow, Korbin and Auburn reacted. By the time they realized how close they were to each other, or that they were facing one another, it was too late. Both received a nasty lash from the other on their arms.

Makenna twirled to face the men who were now clutching their wounds. "Last Lesson. Train, train, and when you become very good, train some more. There are ideas, strategies, and techniques your opponent will use against you. Through training, you will discover ways to turn even the most unfavorable situation to your advantage."

Makenna walked back to her horse, wiped her blade on the end of her bliaut, and then resheathed the sword. Once done, she turned around, beaming. It was clear she found the match to be exciting and exhilarating.

Colin was still shocked as was most of the crowd who had gathered to watch, including her guards Brodie and Gorten. Makenna was exceptionally skilled with the sword. If she had the strength and the size of a man, she would be one of the clan's best soldiers. She could think quickly on her feet and was always aware of her surroundings. It appeared as if she could sense what her attackers were about to do and prepare a counterstrike. It was incredible.

Watching her so quickly and easily defeat the two men, Colin worried Makenna had wounded their pride to a degree it could not be recovered. Then suddenly, as if she were privy to his thoughts, Makenna addressed the small group.

"I cannot thank you two men for sparring with me. It has been some time that someone has tested what took me so many years to learn. You both should be commended. And while Colin and Dunlop can best discern whether your skills should be honed with more stick training, I can attest of your strength and talent. If you train hard and listen, you will be able to avoid my attacks in less than half the time it took me to learn them."

Auburn and Korbin stared at her in open disbelief.

Makenna perceived their soundless expression, but she noticed that along with their skepticism, a little of their dignity was repaired. "We are fortunate to have such talent protecting our clan. I must go now, and I doubt I will be able to return any time soon. But I hope to see you again, perhaps during the evening meal in the hall."

Makenna smiled, waved at the small group, and grabbed the reins to her horse quite pleased with herself. Every man in sight was flabbergasted into silence. She swung onto her horse, and asked Brodie to see her back to Lochlen, knowing that her husband would want to stay.

Colin watched his wife leave with grace and dignity. Never had he felt such pride in a clanswoman, and she was his wife.

Dunlop ordered Auburn and Korbin to go see the midwife to stitch their wounds. The minor cuts Makenna had given them would have healed on their own, but ones they inflicted upon each other were much worse. It would be at least two weeks, maybe longer before they were healed enough to practice again with their group.

Turning around, Dunlop saw an ashen Colin. "Laird? Is something wrong?"

Colin shook his head no, not daring to speak. It wasn't until Dunlop said the word "midwife" that Colin realized what he had done.

Makenna could be carrying their child unknowingly even now. Since his arrival, he had carried on about how she was wild and reckless with her life. Today, out of pride in wanting to show all her skill, he had needlessly put her and the potential life of his unborn son in danger. How could he have been so senseless?

Never again, Colin vowed. Never again would he allow possible harm to fall upon her.

Chapter Eleven

Makenna leaned against the cool stones framing her chamber window and stared down at the busy people below. Part of her felt obligated to join them; but a larger part knew her health and mind needed this break. Almost two months had passed since that July morning she had sparred with Gorten, and in that time, she had not taken another full day off.

Colin was working equally as hard. Every morning he was in the village handling immediate clansmen's needs before riding to the training fields for the remainder of the day. Some nights he fell into bed exhausted, too tired to mutter a word, much less summon the energy to make love to her. Makenna would lie down and hug him to her side, content just to have him home and in their bed. His arm would curl around her possessively, reminding her there was more to their relationship than passion.

Today would be her third try at a day off; she and Gannon had established a rotating schedule that gave them both a chance to rest. Guilt had persuaded her to forgo her first break and offer assistance where she knew she could be of help. The second time, an accident in the

kitchen with the new baker required her medical attention. Benny was young, but everyone had taken to him immediately. A natural comic, the boy made Makenna laugh
whenever she was near him. He was one of the new staff
she hoped would stay for years to come.

Makenna let the tapestry fall back into place partially
covering the window. She knew exactly what she wanted
to do to relax. She donned one of her warmer bliauts
and set out to find Brodie to let him know she was ready
to leave.

Within the half hour, Makenna and her guard
breached Lochlen's outer walls and cantered toward the
River Dye Water. Feeling the air whip through her hair
was both invigorating and cathartic.

Makenna knew that much of the strain and stress associated with her position as Lady McTiernay stemmed
from Lochlen being so short-staffed and the frequent,
intentional sabotages to progress. Despite these set-
backs, she was becoming more adept at managing all
the work and the people at Lochlen Castle. Though her
confidence had grown, she could never see herself truly
enjoying the burden of responsibility.

Makenna urged her mount to move into a full gallop
and thought about her biggest conundrum of late. Colin.

Although he denied it, Makenna was positive Colin
regretted his decision to let her spar with his men. Immediately following her match with the two boys, Colin
had seemed happy, almost proud of her abilities. Yet
later that night when he returned to Lochlen, his happiness and satisfaction had morphed into something
difficult to name. Whatever it was, it continued to haunt
his demeanor toward her.

Colin was not angry. He was not disappointed, nor
did he exhibit shame. The nights he came home early,
he was an amazing lover and willingly conversed about

his day. It was when she spoke of *her* duties and activities that his mood darkened. It mattered not the topic. The crops, the canning, the preparation for winter—each would alter his disposition and result in moody silence. She could not discern what was so alarming about helping Gannon run the keep or manage the harvest.

Feeling the large sorrel-colored steed run at a steady pace, Makenna let go of the reins and spread her arms open, sensing the wind on her face. It felt like years, not months, had zoomed by since she had ridden in this carefree way. Makenna had forgotten how wonderful the sensation was.

She had just closed her eyes when she felt someone yank her off her mount in one powerful swoop.

Landing most uncomfortably, Makenna exclaimed, "Brodie, what the hell!" while twisting to address the man who almost killed them both with such a stupid move.

Colin pulled back his reins and slowed his mount to a slow gait.

"Colin!" Makenna shouted, recognizing her husband. She quickly looked around to see if Brodie was nearby and spied the guard riding opposite their direction to capture her horse. She tried adjusting to a more comfortable position, but Colin's arm would not budge. "You could have just told me that you wished to talk. There was no need for such dramatics," she scolded.

Colin refused to speak. He was fully aware that his tightly leashed anger had been spawned from abject fear. But the vision of her riding full-out across the fields with her arms opened wide would haunt his dreams forever. In his vision, the horse stumbled or she became unbalanced. Whatever the cause, the result was always the same—Makenna fell to her death. The idea of her being ripped away from him was unbearable. He would never survive such a loss.

Colin knew he was falling in love, and it frightened him.

Loving Makenna made him vulnerable, in many more ways than he had ever been with Deirdre. Over the past few weeks, he had grown to enjoy their discussions about various clan happenings. She had a different perspective; one he had quickly learned to respect. It was reassuring knowing that even when he was not there, Makenna supported him in both speech and action. And the nights . . . he never understood what a comfort it could be just to hold someone close as they slept.

Life was good. Love would only disrupt the solitude and peace he had found.

Colin kept silent as he turned the black toward Lochlen.

Makenna watched him in fulminating silence. Colin's chest and back rippled with tension as he worked the reins of his horse. The one time he did look down at her, the expression in his sapphire eyes was almost unreadable. It seemed to fluctuate between fear and fury. The muscle in the side of his cheek was flexed, accentuating his clenched jaw.

Makenna had no idea why Colin was so angry, but one thing was for certain, when he did finally speak, it would be loud and explosive.

Impatient to discover what had him so mad, Makenna slanted him a questioning glance. "I cannot imagine what has set off this latest crazed action of yours, Colin, but I would like to understand."

He told himself it was *not* love that had caused his heart to thump wildly at seeing her so close to potential death. "You're my wife. I take care of what belongs to me."

Makenna tried twice more to discover the root of his anger, but Colin refused to speak again. Instead, he rode directly into the inner ward, slid off his black, and then proceeded to carry her up and into her personal room within Forfar Tower. Once there, he let her go and without any explanation for his mood or action, he moved to leave.

She felt empty, angry, and cold.

Her first day of relaxation in months was turning into the worst day of her marriage.

Makenna ran to block the doorway. "Oh, no, you don't. Do not think for one moment that you can deposit me in my old chambers as if I were a child and then leave. I have done nothing that warrants this treatment."

"Nothing? You call nearly killing yourself riding arms wide open at a full gallop nothing?"

Makenna listened in bewilderment. "This was all because of how I was *riding*? You will have to do better than that, Colin McTiernay."

Colin caught Makenna by the shoulders, forcing her to look up and face him. "Do you want me to do better? Then how about this? You are never to ride in any fashion I would deem unsafe, and that includes dashing about the countryside as fast you can ride. It is dangerous, and I won't allow it. I'm considering switching your mount with one that is older and unable to move at such speeds just to ensure that my orders are followed. And another matter, I don't want you sparring with the men again, and that includes Gorten. I'm not sure I even want you carrying around your sword."

Makenna crossed her arms. The man was indeed crazed if he truly thought she would agree to any of his nonsense. She didn't care what reasons spawned this dramatic change in attitude, but Colin was just going to have to get over them. "No."

Her simple, but emphatic reply startled him. He let go of her shoulders and stalked across the room. "You cannot say no. I am the laird of this clan and its people and that includes you," Colin stated, using his most authoritative voice.

Makenna was unmoved. "Aye, you are laird, but I will bow to no man's unjust request, laird or not, husband or not."

Colin had been in countless rows with Makenna, but never had he heard icy brittleness in her voice before. "Unjust? I have every right to protect what is mine from harm. Had it ever occurred to you that you might fall? Or what would happen if you were not quick enough when sparring and was speared by my man's sword?"

Makenna boldly met his gaze. "Do you think I have never been injured? Colin, surely you jest! I have both fallen and have been cut a great many times. You have seen my body. It is riddled with scars as reminders to each mistake. I have no doubt that I will fall and be hurt again, but that is no reason for me to give up the things I love. What you ask is impossible. Even for you, I will not stop being who I am."

Colin grabbed the stone-carved mantel above the unlit hearth and took a firm grip on his resolve. He had to stay calm and rational if he was going to win this war. "If not for me, then do it for the sake of our child."

Makenna frowned. "Our child? Colin, again you make no sense."

"Makenna," he began, "you understand how babies are made."

She tossed her hair behind her shoulders and went to sit down. "Don't be silly. I know as well as you. And I also know that we have not been married long enough for me to be with child. Why, we married only three months ago."

"Aye, three months in which practically every night you sleep in my arms."

Makenna's hand went to her stomach. She had felt no differently in the mornings, but not all women reacted badly in their first months of the babe's growth. Could she be? Her monthlies were inconsistent, and she never paid much heed to when they came.

She calmed her racing thoughts. She was *not* pregnant. It would be impossible. "So? You were married to my sister for over a year, and she never conceived."

Colin snorted. "Makenna, couples usually have to make love more than a handful of times to conceive. You and I are together more in one night than Deirdre allowed in six months."

"But you . . . and she . . . I thought . . ." The halting words stumbled and disappeared without completion.

Colin sighed and raked his hair. He turned and moved by the window and looked down to the inner ward. "Deirdre didn't . . . enjoy the physical part of our marriage. She tried a few times. Maybe she was too frail. I loved her and wanted to protect her, not hurt her."

It explained so much of her sister, and her strange decisions, the reasons behind which she never divulged. "Is that why she kept her old room?" Makenna asked, her voice full of hesitation.

"Aye. Deirdre stepped in my bedroom only once when we were married. Maybe out of guilt, maybe out of fear. After our last coupling, I decided to wait and let her come to me when she was ready. She never came."

Makenna blinked and then stared down at her hands in her lap. So, just as Deirdre had not been the model lady of the castle, she had not been the ideal wife. Still, Colin had loved her. He even freely admitted it just now. Words he had never spoken to Makenna. Until now, the pain of their absence had been manageable.

If Deirdre had not been the ideal wife or the ideal lady, why had Colin loved her so? The only answer that made any sense was her grace, how she made those around her feel, but most of all her delicate beauty unmarred by masculine hobbies. All qualities Makenna would never possess.

Makenna could feel her fingers being pulled into his strong hands. She glanced up and saw Colin squatting in front of her, his blue eyes large and compelling. "Now do you understand? Do you believe that you could be carrying our child? Do you understand that I cannot have another life taken from me? I will do anything and everything to protect you and our child from harm, including taking away those things that you love."

Colin stood and sank into a chair next to hers. He stared at the cold ashes. "It is not pleasant to speak of such things. I will do so only this once. I loved Deirdre . . . I loved her very much," he began softly. "But our marriage was different from the one you and I share. Maybe it would have grown better, if she had not been taken from me. I will never know." Colin paused.

Makenna could feel her heart pounding. She wanted to scream and tell him it was too painful hearing about his love for her sister. It was cruel for him to speak with such reverence about his late wife. Instead, she sat in pained silence, listening.

Colin squeezed his eyes shut. Remembering. "I used to wish that I had died with her that night."

"You don't anymore?" Makenna asked, her voice barely capable of being heard.

"No."

Makenna waited for him to continue, to give her some verbal balm for her heart. That he was glad to be alive, because of her, of what they shared . . . something. Instead, he briefly gave her an artificial smile and then looked away again.

"I know giving up some of the things you love will be

hard, but just to be fair, I want to give you something as well. I have not been pleased with the amount of work you've been doing while managing the keep. Your load is too much. I want you to have Gannon assign your duties to someone else. Now, won't this make you happy?"

Makenna nodded stiffly. She would curb her sparring and riding, but she would not inflict more work on the few people she had supporting Lochlen. But, rather than argue, she whispered, "I understand, Colin." *Much more than I want to*, she added only to herself.

Colin pulled her into a tender embrace. Makenna complied but felt oddly separated from herself. The piece of her heart that enabled her to feel completely free and safe with Colin, the piece that gave her hope that someday he would feel for her some of what she felt for him, had died. She felt like running away and crying.

A shadow quietly crept down the tower staircase and exited unseen. It had been a close call. Makenna was supposed to have been out of the castle for several more hours, allowing plenty of time to search Her Ladyship's room. Lela had no idea for what, but Leon seemed sure Makenna was hiding something of value. Something she would recognize as important as soon as she spied it.

Lela had been waiting for weeks for today's opportunity. When Makenna was working in the keep, it was impossible to sneak into the tower. There was too much activity, and Her Ladyship had a habit of meeting with servants in her room. Nights were not an option, since the blasted lady encouraged several of the women to sleep in her old chambers, stating it was warmer and much more comfortable than the small beds in the Pinnacle Tower.

So Lela had waited until Makenna's scheduled day of

rest, knowing she would leave the castle walls. Lela first attempted her search several weeks ago, but Makenna had inexplicably stayed within the castle walls to help. The second time, the clumsy cook burned himself. Today, Makenna had indeed left as planned, but returned early. Lela had barely enough time to hide in the nook just beyond the door before the despicable Highlander marched up the stairs carrying his traitorous bride.

In fear of being imminently caught, Lela hid in the shadows. Hearing the two bicker, Lela felt her dread slowly transform into excitement. Leon would be pleased to hear of what she had learned.

Exiting the tower, Lela headed straight toward the gatehouse and into the village. The timing was perfect. Many of the villagers were breaking and relaxing around the Commune Tree for a few moments before they resumed their work.

"Mona! Bidelia! Gillian! Come listen to what I have just learned. You, too, Angus. Bring David and Keith with you."

Lela waited until a small crowd had gathered around her. "I have just come from Forfar where I overheard the laird and his wife arguing quite loudly."

Gillian, a short, rotund woman with very curly gray hair and thick eyebrows, shrugged her shoulders dismissively. "*That* is your news, Lela? Husbands and wives fight all the time."

Another woman elbowed Gillian and answered, "How would she know? Her husband was too afraid and too weak to stand up to her!"

Lela clenched her jaw. This was not going as planned at all. "*My* husband never had to explain that I might be pregnant. And *my* husband never slept in another bedroom because he was too afraid to bed me!"

"Wherever you are getting your stories, you best look again. I doubt the laird's slept one night away from his wife since he's been home. Common knowledge," one of the men replied, turning to walk away.

"Not his current wife, I'm talking about Lady Deirdre! Did you ever wonder why his first wife never became with child?"

"As it is not my business, no, I didn't. And truth be telling, I don't care now either. It does make me wonder why you do," came a muffled reply from a gentleman enjoying a piece of bread.

"Well, you should, David, and you will. Even now the laird speaks of reducing her workload and enabling her lazy ways. Not once did he mention or praise the support of the people tending his manor, just on ways of burdening you and your sons and daughters more."

"Why do you care?" one of the more respected men asked. "The way my middle daughter tells it, Lady Makenna works more than her share, and most of the women would like her to unload some of her burden onto them. My youngest daughter is even considering helping out a few days a week. I have encouraged her to do so."

Lela's jaw slacked. "Did you say *encouraged*? Have you forgotten that McTiernay is a *Highlander*? He is not one of us! He has no right to lead the Dunstan clan. Lady Makenna forfeited her right to be one of us the day she married that man."

A middle-aged woman of medium height with shoulder-length brown hair and dark blue eyes stepped forward. "I once thought as you, Lela. I did not like the idea of an outsider in our midst, and certainly not as our leader. I resented Lady Makenna for making it possible for the Highlander to become our laird. My husband and I both made our feelings well known." She paused to stand back and get the attention of the crowd. "But my opinion changed the day that my son, Rory, injured himself in the fields. The laird personally carried him home and stopped by every day to see if he was getting better. He even had one of his men help work the fields until Rory recovered."

Gillian walked over and placed a hand on Lela's arm. Lela shook it off. "You have let yourself become blind to the truth, Lela. Your petty jealousies have always been unbecoming, but stop whatever vengeance you seek. It will do you no good."

Lela glowered at the friendly-looking woman. *Never will I stop*, she vowed to herself. *And neither will Leon. But he'd better act soon, if he wants the clan to support his attack.*

Moving to leave, Lela took a last look around for the faces who still advocated removing the Highlander. Most were not there. She smiled in satisfaction. They were completing the wall, just as MacCuaig had asked.

Chapter Twelve

"Ready?" Colin asked Dunlop, who had just entered the stables. It was dark outside. The sun was not due to rise for at least two more hours. Besides the night guardsmen, everyone was asleep.

Dunlop nodded, wary of Colin's strange mood the past week. For the last three nights, Colin had slept with the men in the training fields, something he had not done since he married. Only once did the men inquire as to their laird's behavior. Dunlop swiftly ended speculations that something was wrong.

But something was wrong.

Colin was pensive and uneasy. Anger would be much easier to dismiss or even understand. Never, since Dunlop had known the Highlander, had Colin acted this way. It was very odd and very disturbing.

Colin ignored his black, grabbed the stable torch, and left on foot for the outer gate. Dunlop followed. They moved quietly until Colin reached the portion of the town wall that was recently completed. The wall, just like his marriage, seemed to be solid and good. In reality, it was not.

Makenna was not happy. She was unusually quiet and

aggravatingly agreeable. Her smiles never filled her face. Bold green eyes, once luminescent and vibrant, had lost their mischievous twinkle. Her newly submissive nature was driving him mad.

He hated it, and he wanted it to stop.

Never did he realize how much Makenna's spirit made everyone, including him, come alive. He needed her passion and fire; he depended upon it. And he was at a loss as to why it was gone.

Thinking her to be angry over some unknown slight, he had tried to be more loving and attentive. It only seemed to make her even more distant and withdrawn. Even their lovemaking was affected. He became aroused by her slightest movement but was reluctant to touch her. The spark, the passion, the wild honesty had suddenly disappeared. Without it, their coupling felt hollow, reminding him that he once had something fragile and precious, and now it was gone.

The loss only doubled when he learned Makenna was not pregnant. But the fact did not explain why she had been withdrawn before her monthly flux had come.

Desperate, he had asked her directly if she was angry with him. Did she want to ride, desire to train, need more help, or wish he would remain at Lochlen more? Each time her answer was no.

He was losing her, and it was killing him inside.

Colin moved to the wall and pointed to a place where the rocks were joined. He pushed on it, and the pieces moved very easily. Then he went to where the wall had been completed just two months ago. Dunlop pushed on it. It was solid.

Silently, they continued to examine the wall, identifying exactly where it was weak and where it was secure. Only two feeble sections were found, both located in areas the wall remained dark, even when the sun was high. The largest, once broken, would let between six and eight men in simultaneously. The second weak spot was farther down, but much smaller. It would allow a single man to sneak into the castle while all the attention was on the swarm of attackers coming through the larger break.

Colin had first spied the sabotage upon his return from the raids. A few days later, the wall was once again being built correctly. Then a month ago, the builders started again to build and conceal weak spots, but on a much greater scale. Once more, Colin chose not to mention or correct the faulty work.

Together the two sections could be a lethal combination without being a fully destructive one. Whoever was orchestrating this treachery obviously needed to break through the wall, but did not desire having to rebuild large parts of it once in control.

Colin estimated the time till the wall's completion was approximately a month. Timing would be critical if he were going to unite this clan under his lead. If his estimations were off, there was a chance he could be driven from the Borders and back to the Highlands.

Oddly, the idea did not appeal to him. In the past, the vast mountains that jutted into the sea beckoned him to return. The Highlands were the place of his birth, his heritage, but the day he kissed Makenna, Lochlen had suddenly become home.

Retreating into the inner ward, Colin and Dunlop met in the shadows near the chapel tower. Colin verified no one was close enough to see or overhear them.

"Do you know who is behind this?" Dunlop whispered.

"Aye, but I cannot prove such an allegation."

"Do you wish for the wall to be dismantled and rebuilt, this time by your own men?"

"I'd rather not announce what we know just yet. I am confident the rest of the wall is and will be quite solid. I doubt MacCuaig wants to spend any more than he has to once he takes over."

"You suspect MacCuaig, then?"

"I have no evidence, but I also have no doubts it is him," Colin replied evenly. "Starting tomorrow night, I want two guards posted between the two areas of entry, and two more at the end where there is still construction."

"Aye, Laird. Would you have them inside or outside the town wall?"

"Inside. We will not openly reveal our knowledge of the traitors, but it should make the clan as a whole quite nervous."

"You suspect the whole clan?" Dunlop asked, appalled.

"Nay, only a handful of people are actively behind this plot, but there are many more who know of it."

Dunlop was about to ask another question, when Colin shook his head indicating his unwillingness to explain. "I want the guards posted from sundown to sunup."

Dunlop looked quizzical for a moment, balancing his desire to know more and his duty to obey. Choosing, he replied, "It will be done as you ask."

Both departed, going separate ways, avoiding the moonlight. Colin headed toward Canmore, hoping Makenna would still be sleeping in the solar. She was.

Askew in their bed, she had kicked off most of the covers and was lying on her side. The diaphanous linen chemise Makenna was wearing clung to her gentle curves featured in the golden hue of the firelight. She was slim and delicate, and her fiery red hair was fanned out on the white pillow, giving Colin a view of her soft, vulnerable nape.

He could feel himself becoming aroused by the sheer

sight. Stripping off his sword, belt, and leine, he got into bed, pulling his plaid over them both.

Instinctively Makenna snuggled up to him, wiggling her backside against him to get more comfortable. The pain of her touch was excruciating, but worth it to feel her again in his arms.

So much of him wanted to kiss her awake and make love to her, but even more, he wanted the feeling that things were as before.

He fell asleep vowing to be gone before she awoke.

Shouts from outside woke Makenna. The room was dark with only hazy shadows dancing on the walls from the dying embers. She knew Colin must have also heard the noise, but neither moved. Colin was on his back and Makenna's head lay comfortably on his chest. Her legs were intertwined with his. She did not want to give this up.

Colin had been visiting her every night for almost two weeks after she had retired and pretended to fall asleep. He would lie holding on to her and leave her side in the morning just before the sun rose.

Makenna squeezed her eyes tight. If the noise continued, Colin would be forced to rise, and when he did, she could no longer pretend she was unaware that he came to her when she slept.

The noise was getting louder. Fear enveloped Makenna. These precious nights where he just held her were all that was keeping her sane. Without them, she would break down in tears and never be able to stop. At any moment, Colin would leave and this time, he wouldn't come back.

Colin lay awake, torn between his need for Makenna and rising to end the commotion. The time was late, but it was not yet morning. He guessed it to be two or three hours before sunrise—much too early for all the activity he was hearing.

A loud pounding came from the door. Colin grimaced. The choice between Makenna and duty was no longer his to make. Carefully, he slipped off the bed and rose to see who killed the last semblance of his dream life.

Colin opened the door to a young soldier covered in blood. Behind him, he heard Makenna exclaim, "Good Lord!" before she rushed to his side to help the man.

"Colin, carry him in! Where are you hurt?" Makenna asked, searching his body for the wound that caused such loss of blood.

"I am unhurt, milady. It's Sean. Dunlop has him in the lower hall. He sent me to fetch you, Laird." The man's voice was shaking severely as he spoke.

Colin nodded and moved to get dressed when he heard Makenna order the soldier to enter as she was throwing on her own wrap. "Come in here and sit by the fire. Colin and I will take care of Sean. I will have someone bring you some drink."

Makenna followed Colin out the door. He hesitated. "Sean had to have lost a lot of blood to cover him like that. You should stay here," he suggested more than commanded.

Makenna shook her head. "The midwife has gone north to help deliver a baby, and even then, I am better skilled with sword and axe wounds. Let me tend to Sean. You find out who did this, why, and how it happened."

Colin waved for her to proceed down the tower stairs and followed her into the cold night air. When they reached the lower hall, several people had already congregated. Two more men were covered in blood, and a third was on the table.

Makenna moved quickly to the man's side. Dunlop

looked up, surprised that Colin allowed Makenna to be there.

"Tell me exactly what you know of his wounds," she directed, her voice calm but full of command.

Dunlop instinctively responded, "There's a good gash on his left upper arm and one somewhere on his face. But he was severely stabbed here."

Makenna followed Dunlop's finger to Sean's right side. Someone had already fetched water and some cloths and laid them at the end of the table. Picking one up, she put it on the side wound and instructed Dunlop to hold it in place.

Then she dipped a second cloth into the water and began cleaning the young man's face. The soldier resisted. She moved closer, and as if she were comforting a small child, she crooned, "Sean, I need to get a better look at these wounds. I know you are in pain, but you are going to be just fine. I have worked on many knife wounds, and I know just what to do. Do you trust me?"

Sean nodded his head.

Makenna ordered someone to fetch Camus and bring his stitching bag.

Makenna quickly wiped Sean's face and located the arc-shaped gash on the side of his forehead. As she suspected, a lot of the blood was coming from that. Next, she stole a brief glance at his arm, confirming Dunlop's description. It was quite deep and would need to be tended, but not until after she addressed his side wound.

Carefully, Makenna took the cloth from Dunlop and inspected the serious injury. Camus arrived and placed a large bag on the table. "What do you need first?" he asked.

Makenna kept her attention on the deep gash. "I'm going to need a compress made of ground ivy for his arm and head. I'll need a needle, thread, and a candle to stitch his side."

Camus began digging in his bag, removing the items. "What else?"

Makenna turned, swiftly looked around, and plucked the dagger sheathed in Colin's belt. Colin saw her intentions and moved to help. Carefully, they cut away most of Sean's clothing, trying not to cause him any more pain. By the time they were done, Camus had threaded the needle and was burning the tip in the candle's flame.

Makenna took the needle and pierced the skin. She heaved a sigh of relief when Sean passed out from the pain. Realizing the soldier was no longer conscious, Colin gathered the men in the room into a huddle.

Quickly Mackenna made small stitches along the long gash and gave Camus further instructions. "When I'm done here, I'll want to keep a poultice of marigold and John's Wort over the incision. And include henbane, if you have any more. I'll need one of your men, Colin, to bring in a bed and a more comfortable chair. It will be easier to take care of him here. Once he's on the bed, Sean should not be moved again. I don't want anything reopening that wound. Hopefully the poultice will keep down the pain and bleeding." Out of her peripheral vision, Makenna saw heads nod as people began to execute her instructions.

"Will he be all right?"

The question came from one of the soldiers who had obviously carried his friend in by the amount of blood on him.

Makenna made the last stitch and tied it off. She stood up and looked the young man in the eye. "The wound is deep, and Sean is very weak. But he was strong and healthy prior to this. If we can avoid fever, he should make it."

Colin ordered the man to help the others with the bed. Then he pulled her aside. For the moment, with the exception of Camus and Dunlop, who remained with Sean, they were alone.

"Tell me the truth. How does he fare?"

Makenna sighed and looked at the unconscious body. "I spoke in earnest before, though I might have given more hope than I should have concerning the fever. When it comes, I'll give him a hot broth mixed with elder, yarrow, and peppermint." She paused and looked up at Colin.

"How did it happen?" she asked, positive Colin had discovered how and why Sean had been injured.

"I assigned a few men to watch over the wall until it was complete for security. Bored, they began sparring. Sean heard a noise, was distracted, and did not deflect the dagger coming at him in the dark."

Colin hated the dishonesty, but after what he just heard, he had no choice. Four men had tried to sneak through the incomplete portion of the wall. Sean was the first to attack, killing the initial invader. The other guards joined and the battle quickly ended. One attacker, in his last gurgles of breath, had laughed and let them know that MacCuaig was coming and he was after Makenna.

Makenna knew Colin was lying. She had witnessed Colin fighting to control his fury when speaking with his men. All three of the undamaged soldiers still had their daggers with them, and all the blades had been bloody. None of the men apologized either; something she would have expected if Sean's wound had been caused by a friend. No, whoever did this was an enemy, but whose enemy—Colin's or the clan's?

She thought about calling Colin on his lie, but decided against it. For some reason, he did not want to tell her the truth, and she sensed it was not to be condescending or to be in control, but from a need to protect.

"Will you have to go? To check out that noise?" she asked, giving him a way to perpetuate his lie.

Colin's brows shot up in surprise. "Aye, I . . . will," he answered. Blue eyes searched hers for a moment, seeking an indication of whether she believed him or not.

The men returned and began assembling a bed, tightening the ropes before laying the mattress down. Warily, under Makenna's watchful eye, they lifted Sean and placed him on the bedding. She quickly inspected the poultice bandage on his side and applied the ground ivy compress to his arm and forehead. The wounds were clean and the bleeding had stopped, at least for now.

"Camus, I need to go to my chambers and dress. I will return directly."

Makenna headed toward the archway to exit the hall and entered the night air. Colin caught up with her and pulled her into his arms. Needing his strength, Makenna gave in to her desire to be held by him.

Things had been so tense between them, and Colin knew this embrace had not resolved whatever was wrong, but it felt good to hold her once more. After a long moment, he kissed her head and whispered into her hair, "Dunlop and I need to leave now. Gorten and Brodie will remain here and protect you. It should not take me more than a few days."

Makenna nodded against his chest, soaking up his warmth. "Just you and Dunlop?"

"Aye, we should not be gone long. Few days at the most."

Makenna wanted to say, "Take care. I love you," but

the words would not come out. She felt vulnerable and exposed enough just by his holding her heart.

After a while, Colin slipped Makenna out of his arms in preparation to leave. He looked down and was temporarily frozen. Her eyes had turned a deep forest green. Without thought, he closed his hand around the back of her head and brought her lips up close to his. "Oh, how I will miss you, Makenna." Then Colin cupped her chin with his hands and kissed her.

His mouth came down on hers before Makenna could even think of moving. She wanted to fight the passionate onslaught, but she didn't have the strength. A shudder passed through her, and she knew the ragged moan that had escaped was her own.

Colin meant only to give her a gentle kiss. Aye, he meant to say good-bye and remind her of what they once shared, but when Makenna's arms went around his neck and her mouth opened to him, inviting him in, he found himself kissing her with a hunger akin to pain. Gathering her in his arms, he gave her a hot, searing kiss that held nothing back. Finally, he reluctantly eased himself away from her and disappeared through the gatehouse calling for his horse.

Makenna leaned back and released a joyful sigh. Sean was going to live.

The morning following the attack Sean had started running a fever. During the next twenty-four hours, it continued to grow. He fought drinking the tea and tried to hit anyone who came near him. More than once, Makenna was glad that she had learned to dodge and weave so well, though she never imagined applying the skill in such a way.

Camus came in and relieved her for short bursts, but

his knowledge of medicines was only limited to what Makenna had taught him.

The summer he had first started teaching Makenna the ways of swordplay, she had gotten scraped a few times. Fortunately, a visiting nun had taught Makenna the healing properties of some herbs and how to apply them. Afraid that her father would discover her injuries, Makenna had begged Camus to keep the bag of herbs with him lest her father inquire why she would need such items. Camus had held them ever since.

The next two days Sean's fever raged. He seemed to go through bouts of insanity either attempting to hit Makenna for trying to bury him under burning covers of flame, or lunging at her seeking a kiss while calling Makenna by a female's name she had never heard before.

Near midnight of the fourth night following the attack, Sean's head began to cool. He no longer burned her fingers to the touch. She stood and stretched and went to shake Camus, who was sleeping in a chair with his head propped up on the table. "Camus," Makenna whispered, nudging her friend.

"Huh? What? He worse?"

"No, better. I think our soldier is going to live to fight another battle. He should wake soon. Try to make him drink, but don't—under any circumstances—let him move. I need a bath. No." She wagged a finger at him. "I already know I stink and don't need to be teased about it."

Camus grinned, glad to see Makenna in better spirits. She had taken only spots of sleep the past few nights and had done very little for herself as she deemed it would keep her away for too long. "I was only going to ask if you wanted me to wake the staff and have them heat some water."

Camus knew her staff wouldn't mind. The past few days had shown everyone, even the most hardened,

Makenna's true character. There was a good chance they would argue over who should be the one to serve their mistress.

Makenna yawned and then shook her head left to right once. While she was watching over Sean, the staff had taken the load of her work onto themselves. They had done it without complaint, but she would not burden them further by lessening their sleep. "No, I think I need the cool waters of the loch."

"When you return, go to bed. Do not come back here until you have slept. If you do, I'll carry you to your chambers myself."

"Ah, Camus, you remind me so much of my father."

"That is the highest of compliments, milady. But it won't change what will happen if you come back without a good night's sleep."

Makenna waved at him and left. She was too tired to argue. She desperately wanted sleep but knew it would not come until she felt clean once again.

Colin arrived at Lochlen and hastily handed his black to the sleepy stable master. He went directly to the solar to check on Makenna. The bed had not been slept in. Assuming she was with Sean, he headed to the lower hall, finding only Sean and Camus awake by the hearth. Sean was taking some broth offered by the old sword smith.

At the noise, Camus looked up and waved Colin over. "Laird, it is good to have you back."

Sean glanced over his shoulder. "Lady Makenna was like a beautiful angel. She saved my life."

"Glad to see you are doing better," Colin managed to get out. It was hard to be civil to another man so open with his affection for Makenna. She was his, and since the distance had erupted between them, he had grown only more possessive of her.

"Aye, she did," Camus added. "Your wife stayed in here day and night. Only when Sean's fever broke did she acquiesce to a swim and some sleep. I believe she left for the loch less than a half hour ago with both Gorten and Brodie in tow."

Makenna stared out at the water glistening in the moonlight. There was a slight breeze causing the surface to ripple and her exposed skin to bristle. She looked around searching the shadows once again. When she had arrived, she thought she heard footsteps and felt the weight of eyes upon her. But when she had gone to investigate, nothing had been there.

Makenna approached the water's edge and dipped in her toe. The always cold water had taken on a frigid temperature. Fall had started in earnest and she could see her breath in the early morning air.

She took a few steps, braced herself, and then plunged into the icy depths. Her body immediately shunned the cold. Small bumps rippled along her flesh as she stroked the water trying to build heat within her veins. It was not working.

Swimming over to the rock where she had placed her bathing items, she took the soap and began to scrub vigorously at her flesh. It had been only four days since her last bath, but it felt more like thirty. Slowly, she felt the layers of grime wash away and began to massage her hair. She submerged, twisting her head back and forth under the water, rinsing all the soap out, feeling at last somewhat normal again.

Colin saw her emerge out of the water like a siren calling to her next victim. He had no intention in fighting the pull. Immediately he began to strip off his clothes.

Makenna rubbed her eyes to free the attached droplets and felt her jaw drop. Colin was there. And he was removing his belt. "What are you doing?" she snapped, appalled that he just might come in and join her. After their last kiss, she had sworn not to let him catch her in a vulnerable position again.

Colin smiled. It was the first feisty comment she had made in weeks. "Now, I remember a time when you greeted me quite differently when I returned from a trip."

Makenna pointed at his plaid he was throwing next to hers. "Well, that is not now. Put those clothes right back on!"

Chuckling, he responded, "Then they would get wet." He sat down on a smooth knee-high rock and proceeded to unlace one of his leggings.

A large sense of unease enveloped Makenna. She would not be able to withstand both her emotional need and physical need for him. She was too tired, and her desire for him was too great. Pride rallied one last time. "Colin, I forbid you to come in here. I am bathing. I was here first, and I want to be alone. Come back when I am done." Her voice had started out strong but had evolved into a desperate plea.

Colin silently removed his second legging. He knew she was serious in wishing him away, but he also knew that this was the first real conversation they had shared since things had started going terribly wrong. A full battalion of men couldn't drag him away now. This might be his one chance to discover exactly what had caused her to change so dramatically toward him.

Colin stripped off his leine and then dove into the dark waters. Makenna nervously searched the surface, dreading where he would appear.

Colin emerged right by where she was standing. She took two steps back. He let her.

"Please, Colin, please leave. I am so tired, and I cannot verbally banter with you tonight. I am not up to the task."

Colin lowered himself into the water until just his shoulders were above the rippling surface. He moved in close and gently cupped her face in his hands. Her scent filled him. "Bantering is not what I had in mind," he murmured, lowering his head to brush his mouth against hers.

Makenna was startled into temporary submission. Colin persisted in making it impossible to talk by touching her, his big hands smoothing over her shoulders, her back. So much of her yearned to let him continue, to make her feel loved and wanted. But, later, when it was over, she would only feel worse, even hollower than she already did.

Makenna pulled back. Colin released her lips but refused to let her go. "Makenna, speak to me. What's wrong? I know that you want me as much as I want you. I can feel it. You want to respond to me, but you won't let yourself."

Makenna balled her hands on his chest into fists. "I cannot be her. I tried, I really wanted to, for both our sakes. But I cannot do it. I loved my sister, but I am not her. And I cannot be her for you."

Colin did let go then. "Is that what you have been doing?" he asked, raking his hand through his wet hair. "God, Makenna, that's the last thing I want. I thought you knew that. I need you, just the way you are!"

"You still love her."

"She's dead, Makenna. I have buried her and moved on. You are the only one I want, and I promise you it is *not* as a replacement for your sister."

"And what if I were to die?"

The thought of Makenna dying was so repulsive Colin could only stare at her for a moment. "I won't let you."

"Won't let me? Die, you mean? Women do all the time, they become ill, die in childbirth, and what will happen then? Will you mourn me as you do Deirdre? Will you speak fondly about me to your next wife along with your words of undying love for my sister?"

Colin forcefully grabbed her shoulders, splashing the water around them. "*I won't let you die.* I will have no other but you, do you understand me?" His voice choked on the words.

"Say no more," she pleaded softly, looking at his chest, unable to meet his gaze. "It hurts when you say such things. You make me think you care."

Colin felt like he was caught in a whirlpool, losing control of everything by trying to hang on to it all. He forced Makenna's chin up. She caught her breath when she saw the fear in his eyes.

Colin saw misery and dejection shimmering back in her green pools; he could no longer deny the truth. "Care? Makenna, I care so damn much it terrifies me." He let go of her and moved to the large boulder nearby for support. "What I feel for you is . . . stronger, deeper than what I have felt for anyone. Do you understand what I am saying? For *anyone.* Every time I kiss you, touch you, God, even just *talk* with you, I betray Deirdre. Never once did I wish you were like her, but you don't know how often I wished she had been more like you. I loved her, but *you* complete me in ways she never could. And every time I thank God that I have you, I feel like I am saying I am glad she is gone."

Makenna moved then and put her fingers against his lips. Tears streaked down her face and splashed silently into the water. "Shhh, say no more. I love you, Colin. Deirdre warned me that I would. She said I could make you happier than she did, but I didn't believe her. Not even when I lost my heart to you did I think you could feel anything for me. But she was right. She was beautiful and kind and much wiser than we thought, Colin. She would want us to protect what we share."

"Aye, she would," he said softly.

Makenna held his face between her hands, searching his eyes. She could see it now. He loved her and was deeply afraid of saying it aloud. He had loved and lost before.

Colin pulled her roughly into his arms. Makenna melted into him. "God, Makenna, never leave me," he whispered into her hair. "You are my very breath. I didn't know how much until these past few weeks."

Makenna's fingers maneuvered up the broad expanse of his chest, twining in his curly dark hair. "I've been so lonely. You are my best friend. The nights only became bearable when you started sneaking to our bed."

She could feel his lips curve into a smile. "So you *were* awake. I thought you might be, especially when you all of a sudden started retiring much earlier than normal, but I didn't want to say anything. I didn't want it to end. It was the only thing holding me together."

Gently his fingers curled into her red mane and pulled her head back. He leaned down and kissed her again. The sweet, sensual caress went on and on, suffusing her body with an aching need for more. She leaned into him moaning, stroking his tongue with her own.

Colin's heart pounded so furiously against the walls of his chest, he felt light-headed. He kissed her again, softer this time, consuming, with so much tenderness it nearly choked her.

Makenna felt her body being raised out of the water and carried to shore. She laid her head on his shoulder, periodically kissing his neck and ear. He smelled good, like leather and male. Her breath fanned his cheek. "Everything I am is yours. I love you."

Her words and kisses were like a healing balm to his soul. They also aroused a hunger for her that was all-consuming. He almost stepped wrong on the rocky pebbles. His concentration was strained; all he could think about was touching her.

His Makenna had returned. She was once again the spirited, spontaneous, and passionate woman that set his body ablaze. He knew he would not be able to wait until they returned to Lochlen to have her. He would barely be able to lay his plaid down.

Finally, they reached the grass. Colin put her down. "Don't move," he ordered. His voice was deep and affected, husky with desire.

Within seconds, he was back spreading his thick plaid on the soft clearing. Before she could take a step, he was at her side lifting her up into his arms. Makenna closed her eyes, luxuriating in Colin's strength as he carried her to the soft awaiting blanket.

"I thought I'd lost you," he muttered as he covered her mouth with his own. The sense of urgency that was driving his emotions tonight had created an aching hunger in him that only Makenna could assuage.

"Never," she vowed softly as his lips took hers again in another slow, seductive, mind-numbing kiss.

Colin could barely control his need for her. He cupped her buttocks and pulled her up against his hardness, discovering she was already moist and hot with need. Makenna shivered at his touch and leaned into his smoldering heat. Her hands moved to his shoulders, stroking him. Her legs entwined with his.

Colin glided his fingers from her hip to her breast. As he took the freed soft mounds in his palms, his body began to shake. "God, you are so beautiful, so very, very beautiful. What you do to me," he groaned with ragged need. He lowered his mouth to her breast and encompassed a pink bud.

He gently held the bloom between his lips and began to suck.

Makenna instinctively arched upward, thinking that she would die of pleasure. She twisted and moaned while her hands clung to his shoulders. Someone was shouting Colin's name, and Makenna knew that it was her.

Overwhelming passion took over. It was like a dam had exploded, enabling an emotional connection between them that intensified every touch, every sensation, every emotion. Colin released the tasty nub and he kissed her soft, pink, bewitching lips until she clung to him again. His muscled leg was hard and hairy and enticing, sliding up along the delicate skin of her inner thigh.

Colin pulled her roughly against him, letting her feel all of him. He began to move his hips, rubbing his arousal against her. When Colin shifted to allow his hand access to her hot core, Makenna dug her nails into his backside to keep him firmly against her, refusing to let him move.

He lifted his head to look at her. Colin thought he was going to drown in the green depths of Makenna's eyes. "Please let me touch you. I want to feel your need for me."

Unable to form a coherent thought, Makenna released her hold. Part of her felt so excruciatingly sensitized that she didn't think she could endure his deliciously erotic caress.

He slid one finger across the small, swelling button of desire hidden in the soft hair and heard her quick intake of breath.

Then he eased his finger into her snug passage, coaxing forth a honeyed flood that dampened his hand. She felt warm and liquid and sweet, like thick nectar. He didn't ever want to stop touching her.

Colin eased his finger back out and explored Makenna with a deliberate possessiveness that made her tremble. He repeated the action slowly and deliberately, easing into her and then teasing the small nubbin of female flesh. He did it again. And again.

Makenna was growing wild beneath him, writhing in his powerful grasp, as he continued to touch her in ways he knew would drive her to climax. Her pleasure heightened his own.

She cried out softly as deep tremors shook her.

Colin's blood pounded in his veins. His male appendage was hot and hard. He knew that he could wait no longer.

"Tell me you belong to me, that you need me, that you want me inside you. Now. Say it, Makenna," he muttered, his voice strained and husky with passion.

"I need you. Please, Colin, love me now." It was half plea, half demand.

He came down on top of her, burying his hands in her hair, twisting his fingers in the silken tresses, hugging her to him. His body was incredibly tight and hard with arousal. He kissed her again and tried to calm his own tumultuous need, then reached down and opened her to his first thrust.

Makenna closed around him, hot and wet and clinging. Nothing had ever been this good.

His fingers crushed hers in a grip that spoke volumes about the fierce emotion coursing through him. Colin thought he was in both heaven and hell being tortured with pleasure and devilish fire. And then he started to move and could no longer think at all.

Makenna opened her thighs wider and wrapped her

legs around him. Together they began to move in a primitive rhythm all of their own.

The climax hit him, and he surrendered to the hot whirlwind of spasms. Simultaneously he felt Makenna convulse beneath him, her entire body trembling with erotic release.

Nothing in his life had ever felt so right.

Long minutes passed before either was capable of moving. Knowing that he must be crushing her, Colin propped himself on his elbows and looked down for a second before moving to lie down beside her.

Makenna swallowed. She had seen a steady glow of love and happiness in his eyes and knew the same expression mirrored in her own gaze. Makenna nestled against her husband. She felt both lovely and loved. It was the most incredible feeling she had ever known.

Makenna could feel the cold wind begin to rise and nip at her exposed skin.

Colin felt her quiver. "God, Makenna, you're freezing."

She chuckled and snuggled closer. "Pretty understandable when you are forced to bathe in a cold loch in the middle of the night."

Colin pulled the loose edges of the plaid around her. "Why didn't you wake your lady's maid and tell her you desired a bath?"

Makenna laughed and pushed against his chest to get free. She walked toward her clothes and started dressing. "Wake my lady's maid? Colin, when have you seen me with a lady's maid?"

Colin shrugged, and then stood, following her lead by pulling on his leine. "I never paid much attention. I thought you just used them when I was not around."

She scoffed. "The reason you have never seen me with a lady's maid is that there are none. There is but a single chambermaid, and I am careful not to overuse her lest she want to leave."

"Then go to the village and hire some help. We have the funds," he said, holding the reins to her horse.

Makenna shook her head and took the leather strips. "You say it so casually, as if that was all it took. I want help and then suddenly help will appear. The truth is that if I were to do something so foolish like you suggest, the staff I currently *do* have will disappear. We are incredibly shorthanded and the people who are now supporting Lochlen are overworked. I have learned the hard way that soliciting more help only gets you the kind you don't want. Too many times, new blankets, tapestries, and rushes mysteriously ended up in one of the hearths. Food went missing, and candles destroyed. Only when I released 'my new help' did such activities ease. So, you see, forcing people to my aid causes resentment, and they take it out not only on me, but also on my staff. And when I do find someone *willing*, I immediately assign them to a position where their help is more needed by the clan, not just me." She exhaled, realizing that she had just made quite a speech. Still, she couldn't help but add, "*Now* do you understand?"

Makenna didn't expect an answer, and she didn't receive one. Yet she knew Colin had heard and comprehended every word she had said.

Colin helped her mount and then swung onto his large black. It was time. He would send Dunlop to the Highlands tomorrow.

Chapter Thirteen

Conor watched his son spy the wooden cup his twin sister was chewing. Casually, the toddler waddled over to his father and then slyly snatched it out of her hands. Brenna looked dainty and sweet, but she was nobody's victim. Instead of yelling or crying, she squinted her eyes and pushed her twin brother, hard. He fell back but held on to his prize with a tight grip. Both met each other's gaze and smiled triumphantly, each believing they had won.

"Brenna!" Laurel lightly admonished. "How many times have I told you not to push your brother? And, Braeden, you have to know it is your own fault. Why is it that you always think your sister has the better toy?"

Conor shifted his gaze to his wife sitting by the hearth. She was intently working on something for her friend Aileen, who recently discovered she was again with child. Pale ringlets curling around his daughter's face proved she inherited his wife's wavy gold hair. And though Brenna was barely a year old, he could see much more of his wife in their feisty daughter. She never backed down from a fight and usually won them. And of course, she had her father completely under her spell.

His son tickled him, and though he would never admit it to Laurel, he was proud Braeden had the instinct to know what he wanted and the fight to get it. But the small boy never went too far with his sister. Braeden intuitively knew that he was much bigger than Brenna and always sought nonphysical means to procure her toys. However, when it came to playing with his uncles, he loved to get rough. Conor's son was only a year old, but he was a McTiernay through and through.

Conor stood and stretched his long legs. Spying Laurel out of the corner of his eye, he asked offhandedly, "They should go down for a nap soon, aye?"

Laurel put down her needle and cloth and stared at her husband. Dark and huge with twinkling silver eyes, he was the most handsome man she had ever met. He was also pigheaded, stubborn, and prideful, but he was all hers.

She looked back down and resumed her work, trying to hide her smile. "Yes, Brighid agreed to look after them while I try to finish this for Aileen," she answered in her strongest English accent, knowing how it would rile him.

"If you keep speaking like that, woman, I might order only Gaelic to be spoken on my lands. There's no way you can create that awful sound with Scottish words on your tongue," Conor growled.

"*Chan eil mi sgìth. Tha mi ag obair,*" Laurel repeated in Gaelic.

"*Agus chan eil mi sgìth. Tha mi teth, shonuachar,*" Conor replied thickly, his voice husky and deep, emphasizing the desire he spoke of.

Laurel smiled. She loved being called his soul mate, and they both knew she was going to agree to his suggestion.

Conor wandered around her chair and stopped just behind her to enjoy the view. Just the thought of having Laurel alone made him ache for her. She had just moved the babes to real food and her delectable breasts were once again completely his. The day was beautiful, and with only a little more coaching, she would be convinced to leave with him for a few hours this afternoon.

The door of the great hall swung open and heavy footsteps entered. It was definitely not one of the servants.

Startled, Laurel looked up wondering who was coming to visit. Conor swiveled to glare openly at the intruder. Recognition set in as he watched his brother's commander walk the length of the hall toward them. Conor knew instantly that there would be no midday tryst.

Conor turned back to Laurel and whispered, "*Annochd*," promising that his plans were not canceled, just postponed until later.

Dunlop approached the young family and realized he was interrupting their private time. "I am sorry, Laird McTiernay. Your commander, Finn, told me you were here and that I could enter. Good day, Lady McTiernay, it is nice to see you again."

Laurel stood and greeted him with one of her more dazzling smiles. Dunlop was temporarily transfixed. He had forgotten how beautiful Lady McTiernay was. Slender with gold hair and sea-blue eyes, her physical appearance reminded him of Lady Deirdre.

Conor saw Dunlop's transparent appreciation of his wife's beauty. It was a common reaction, far from unusual when guests arrived, but he still didn't like it. Laurel never flirted. She did something far worse. She was kind and welcoming. Two things Conor knew to be almost as powerful as any spell a woman could weave on a man, especially an unmarried soldier like Dunlop.

Laurel sensed Conor's possessive bristle. "It is truly lovely to see you as well, Dunlop. We heard of Colin's recent marriage. Tell me, is it a good one?"

"Aye, milady. A very good one. I believe you would

approve of my laird's choice. Her character is similar to yours."

Laurel laughed, and it filled the room. "Then she must drive poor Colin in circles. I hope to meet her soon."

"I am certain she feels the same."

Conor coughed. Laurel stroked his arm, trying to ease the tension. "Unfortunately, Dunlop, I must leave and see these two little ones have their afternoon nap, but I hope to see you at dinner. Promise me you will tell all about Colin's new bride and how she has turned our staid Colin into a man of adventure."

Dunlop's brows flew up in surprise. He wouldn't describe Colin as an adventurous man, but there was no doubt that Makenna had definitely changed him. "Aye, milady. I look forward to this evening."

Laurel smiled and then reached up and grabbed Conor by the neck to get his attention. He had been preoccupied with glaring at their visitor and had not noticed she was preparing to leave. Yielding to her pressure, he turned his head and captured her lips in a brief but searing good-bye kiss, reminding everyone whom Laurel belonged to.

Just as he released her, Laurel whispered into his ear, "Do you think Dunlop hopes you might share me, or should you kiss me again? I vote for the latter, *a ghrà mo chroì.*"

Her light tease and reminder that he had her love and her heart brought him somewhat out of his dark mood. He swatted her lightly as she broke away, taking the twins out of the room.

Conor motioned for a servant to bring some drink and then leave. He waited for Dunlop to reveal his purpose and explain why he was traveling alone.

Dunlop took the quaich offered and drained its

contents. "I am sorry for interrupting your family time, but I assure you it is not without cause. Your brother sends you a message."

Laurel plopped down in front of her best friend's hearth and crossed her arms watching Brenna and Braeden play with Aileen's two-year-old son on the bed across the room. Dark-haired, Gideon looked nothing like his mother, who though not a petite woman, had small feminine features and light coloring. The cottage was comfortable, warm, and inviting . . . and Laurel's typical destination whenever she needed advice or just someone to hear her frustrations.

Brenna, a daredevil and performer, stood up on the soft, wobbly surface. Aileen congratulated the small girl on her feat, and Brenna's two misty gray eyes beamed with pride.

Braeden, seeing all the attention being lavished upon his sister, then tried to stand. Pleased with his success, he clapped his hands together in onē swooping movement and immediately fell over. Seeing Brenna still standing, he reached over and pulled her down beside him. Just as she was about to get mad and retaliate, Gideon, seven months older, began to jump up and down on the spongy mattress, completely mesmerizing the twins.

Aileen handed Laurel a cup of mead and moved to join her friend in the adjacent chair. "I would tell Gideon to stop, but I am afraid without his entertainment, Brenna will remember her brother's behavior. It is amazing at the young age men begin to protect their pride."

Laurel drank the sweet beverage, enjoying the strong honey flavor. "It is not just boys. Brenna will have to learn to manage her own pride as she grows, lest it get her into trouble."

"It has been a while now since you have visited with that look upon your face. Has our good laird been foolish enough to quarrel with you again?"

Laurel let a long sigh escape. "Not yet, but a row is brewing in the air, Aileen. It has been some time since I have crossed words with Conor, but I fear we will battle tonight."

Aileen almost choked on her drink. "Some time? Wasn't it just last week that you two argued about having too many visitors? Or was it you giving Fiona a week off without asking him?"

Laurel waved her hand. "Those disagreements occurred two weeks ago. Last week, Conor tried to postpone my monthly trip north to Hagatha's *again*, and you made your point. Conor and I butt heads . . . often. We always have and in truth, I think we like it."

"You like making up," Aileen chided her playfully.

"'Tis part of the fighting," Laurel replied, joining in Aileen's laughter.

Laurel took another drink and then sighed. "Tonight, I fear, will not end like the others. You should have been there at dinner. Never have I been so embarrassed in front of a guest. Conor behaved atrociously, and Dunlop was not blameless. All throughout the meal, the commander found ways to poke and incite Conor's anger. Both of them were unbelievable."

"Was it really that bad?" Aileen asked, trying not to be too skeptical.

Laurel curled her feet underneath her and faced her friend. "From the very beginning, it was clear the two men had crossed words since I left them earlier that afternoon. At first, I tried to learn what was wrong and see if I could defuse the hostilities. What I tell you now is an accurate accounting, Aileen. I do not exaggerate."

Laurel began to disclose the night's events, reliving them as she spoke.

"You're not eating, Dunlop. Does the food not please you?" Laurel asked, hoping he would divulge the reason behind his cold mood rather than insult her.

"Your cook is excellent, milady," Dunlop responded without inflection. He took a bite and then openly glowered at Conor.

Laurel gulped. Very few men ever had the nerve to look annoyed at her husband, let alone palpably angry. "Then perhaps it is the company that causes you to frown so?" Laurel asked, undaunted.

Dunlop's normally cheerful face tightened further. "Perhaps you are correct, milady."

Laurel ate a bite of potato and watched her husband out of the corner of her eye as she chewed. He was tense, quiet, and dangerously reserved. The air was almost tangible with male aggression. Whatever had transpired between them had taken several hours and had not ended well.

"Then let us talk of your new mistress," Laurel offered, attempting to move the conversation to a more receptive topic. "I understand Lochlen Castle to be something of a fortress and the lands quite beautiful."

"Aye, it is. I am confident Lady Makenna would enjoy showing it to you," Dunlop remarked.

Before Laurel could reply, Conor slammed his quaich on the table. Its contents sloshed over the sides of the lip and onto the plate of food. He leveled a stare at Dunlop, who returned it unflinching.

Laurel bit her lip to keep from asking why Conor was acting so rude. She agreed long ago to refrain from disrespecting him in public, but that did not mean she would remain passively quiet once they were alone.

Laurel finished her mead and put the empty cup on the small table nearby. "I quickly tried to change the conversation to any number of subjects. Edward I's death, Robert the Bruce's recent success at Urquhart and Balvenie. Nothing. No one would engage. I finally could stand no more of my lone voice bouncing off the walls and left. I could actually feel them hurrying me out of the room so they could resume their argument. It was then I decided to visit you. The only thing going my way this evening is Finn's absence."

Aileen widened her eyes and then exhaled. "You may not think so later. I believe my husband is right now with Conor, no doubt supporting our laird in whatever discussion was taking place when you left."

"It was no discussion, Aileen. It was a silent battle of wills. There is only one reason Dunlop would visit Conor without Colin by his side. Colin wants his brother's help and could not personally leave to request it."

"And you are guessing that Conor said no."

"What else explains Dunlop's disrespectful and belligerent behavior?"

"If what you think is true, then I must admit that I, too, am stunned, Laurel. The laird must have a strong reason not to come to his brother's aid when asked. It makes no sense."

"It does if you factor *me* into the reason that Conor said no."

Aileen let go a low whistle. "It's possible."

"Possible and true," Laurel said definitively. "Conor would never deny help to any of his brothers."

"Unless it involved you or the children," Aileen said, finishing Laurel's thought. It was common knowledge how the laird felt about his wife. When he almost lost her the previous year to a jealous and deceitful man, he became a man possessed. Even with the threat gone, Laird McTiernay was very conscious of keeping his wife safe.

"I have no doubt that Conor's reasons have something to do with me. My husband has not left my side for more than two weeks at a time since last year. He's afraid I will disappear while he is gone or do something worse such as visit a friend and leave the protection of this place," Laurel grumbled, twirling her hand around before laying it back down on the armchair.

Aileen watched Laurel unconsciously drum her fingers on the wood. A clear sign Laurel was strategizing and preparing for a confrontation. "And just what is your devious mind planning now?"

Laurel smiled as an idea came to her. "Goodness, Aileen, I, devious? I would never use underhanded tricks to get my way. Not my style."

Aileen shrugged her right shoulder as she leaned over to place her empty cup beside Laurel's. "I stand corrected. You are more like a . . . aye, that's it, like an immovable boulder when you are in the frame of mind."

Laurel arched her eyebrows briefly in protestation. "Not flattering, but quite an apt description. But with Conor as a husband, I must be or I would find myself doing only his bidding. First, I'll confirm my suspicions."

"And if they are right?"

"Then I may be over here more often during the next few weeks in need of your company. Conor will have to trust that I will be fine without him here to oversee my every move, for tomorrow he will head south toward Lochlen."

Conor made his way up the multiple stories of the Star Tower to his solar. He had seen Laurel return from

Aileen's earlier and knew she was there waiting for him. With each step, the memory of their afternoon kiss filled his mind, and he felt himself harden in anticipation. Despite the afternoon's events, he hadn't forgotten the promise he made earlier that day.

His insatiable need for his wife used to scare him. Now he took peace knowing she loved him as much as he loved her.

Conor walked along the stone corridor that shielded the cold winter wind from the inner chamber. The door was ajar. Laurel was sitting cross-legged in front of the firelight brushing her hair. No one in the world was lovelier. She was his heart and soul. He would never allow the possibility of anyone or anything to hurt her.

"I'm sorry, Colin, I just cannot do what you ask. Not even for you," he whispered to himself.

Laurel gave one last vigorous stroke and then stood to put the brush on the carved bench. She saw Conor just before she turned back toward the hearth. He was leaning casually at the room's opening, his stance calm, his arms relaxed and crossed. But he didn't fool her.

Desire swam in his gray eyes . . . along with fear. If he could, Conor would keep her locked within the McTiernay Castle walls forever.

Laurel leveled her eyes at him. They were dark like a North Sea storm. When she reached for her wrap and put it on, Conor knew his plans for the night had just been placed on hold.

They were both strong-willed, and arguments were inevitable. And while their quarrels were numerous, rarely were they truly heated as long as two simple rules were followed. Laurel hid her displeasure until they were alone, and Conor promised to hear her side before exploding. A clear signal for him to prepare and control his temper was the wrapper.

Conor walked in and unhooked his belt to hang it over the never-used arch chair against the wall. He did so patiently, not saying a word. It had been a hard lesson to learn to keep quiet when Laurel was angry. And any attempt to soften her mood with sweet words made things worse, not better. And questions like "What's wrong?" or "What did I do?" only excited her anger by many levels.

Laurel watched him unwrap his plaid, fold it, and lay the cloth beside her brush on the bench. "Dunlop seemed to be fairly prickly this evening at dinner."

Uh-oh, Conor thought, remembering his momentary loss of control at the table. He knew then that Laurel would call him on it later, and later was now.

"Aye," Conor replied, continuing to undress.

Laurel took in a deep breath and committed herself. "I think you should help Colin," she stated, waiting for the explosion.

Conor scowled but did not reply.

Laurel knew instantly her assumptions had been right. The man had multiple types of scowls, ranging from irritation to frustration. Tonight, his face resembled a stone surface, utterly unbending. Conor wore it every time their argument was about her safety.

"You don't know what he is asking, Laurel," Conor eventually countered.

"You are correct, I don't know. But I do know that your brother has been through much this past year after the death of his wife. I expect his marriage to Makenna Dunstan was not exactly what he wanted, but what was needed. Colin is a prideful man. He would only come to you if it was important."

Laurel could tell her arguments had not swayed her husband in the slightest. She rallied her resolve and continued. "Colin is family, Conor, and I know how protective you are of what's yours. I also know the reason why you are so stubbornly refusing your brother and infuriating Dunlop is because of me. And I won't have it. I lost my family. I will not let you lose yours. Not because of your incurable need to protect me from nothing."

Conor made a low, growling sound deep in his throat, venting his frustration. "Your brother was a fool to disown you, and you have a family now. *I* am your family. My brothers and the twins are your family. And my 'incurable need' to keep you safe, as you put it, is something you will just have to live with. For not a day goes by that I forget how close I came to losing you. And I will not ever come that close to hell again."

Laurel gave him a challenging smile. "You are changing the topic, Conor. You will not win this battle under the guise of 'I will not lose you.' How is it that you can rationalize helping our neighbor, Laird Schellden, but you will not leave to aid your brother?"

Conor came to a sudden halt and rounded on her, his expression grave and serious. "If it were just me Colin sent for, there wouldn't be a problem."

Laurel stared, not comprehending. "What do you mean, if it were just you? Why else would Dunlop be here if it were not for you?"

Conor remained silent and looked intently into her eyes, watching them widen in surprise and trepidation. He knew the instant she understood what he had meant.

"Colin wants m . . . me? But why me? How can I help him?" Laurel stammered as understanding dawned on her. Conor was not afraid to leave her alone, but to take her with him.

Conor let go of her shoulders and moved to sit on the bed, burying his face in his hands. "He thinks you can help his new wife. Colin is certain you and Makenna are much alike and enjoy the same things."

"If I remember right, he was quite vocal against some of my habits," Laurel interjected.

"You remember right. It seems he has had to adjust his position some since his last visit."

"I must admit I am surprised. Lady Makenna must be a remarkable woman to bring about such a change."

"Dunlop believes Colin is in love with her."

"But what can I do?" Laurel asked, sitting down beside him on the soft mattress.

"You were right in that Colin was not eager to marry again. Makenna was also disinclined, but agreed for the sake of her clan. Unfortunately, her people have strong feelings about a Highlander as their laird. Some are openly hostile. Colin has a plan to unite them under his rule as well as solidify alliances with neighboring lairds."

"But that does not explain why he wants me."

"It seems as though Colin's new wife has had very little support and is new to managing staff. From what Dunlop tells me, Lady Makenna is more accustomed to training with men than running a keep."

"Training with the *soldiers*?"

"Aye, that's my sentiments. He also related that she has made admirable progress in learning her duties as a lady and providing for her clan. What she lacks is another female's perspective on her accomplishments, someone who can provide insight on how to handle a few rebellious incidents and reinforce her overall confidence. And as I have told Dunlop over and over again, that is not enough reason to risk my family traveling into a hostile environment."

"Then why is Dunlop forcing the issue?"

"Because Colin told him to. My brother knew exactly what my reaction would be. But what he failed to realize was that on this matter I will not relent. Colin will just have to fare on his own."

With the whole story finally revealed, Laurel sat for several moments thinking. The solution was obvious, but she would have to use some of those devious ploys she had just told Aileen were not her style. *Only for my family*, she rationalized to herself.

Clapping her hands on her legs, Laurel rose and walked over to the basin to wash her face. "Well, you are certainly right about the twins," she began offhandedly. "They are not leaving the safety of their home. I will have to see if Brighid is available to look after them while we are gone."

Conor felt his temper start to slip again. "No, Laurel, I won't discuss it. You are not going. I forbid it."

Laurel visibly bristled. She patted her face dry and gave him her most withering stare as she returned to his side. "It would be wise not to dictate what I can and cannot do. If I recall, this approach has not worked well for you in the past."

Conor found himself mesmerized by her swirling deep blue and gray eyes, flashing with indignation. Lord, he loved her. "Threatening me has not worked in your favor either, love," he lightly countered.

Laurel exhaled and let him maneuver her between his legs. "You're insufferable when you are right," she retorted, gently slapping his shoulder.

Conor smiled. She had called him insufferable. Her strange pet endearment indicated she was not going to fight him about staying in the Highlands. He had won.

Laurel took a step back and slowly unlaced her wrap, throwing it on the chair nearest to her. Her thin chemise did little to shield her body from his view. The scooped neck hinted at the pale skin it covered, her hidden breasts rising up and down with each breath.

Conor moved to stretch out on the feather mattress

as he felt himself harden. Just looking at her gave him intense pleasure.

Laurel moved slowly to the edge of the bed. Conor watched her chemise fall to her waist and then to the floor. She threw her hair back over her shoulder, revealing the soft, vulnerable curve of her neck. God help him, she was driving him to distraction.

Laurel slipped underneath the covers and moved to his side. "Conor, it will be very hard leaving the twins. I don't think we should be gone for more than a few weeks. Four at the most."

Conor pulled back from the soul-searing kiss he was about to plant on her lips. "You are not going, Laurel."

Reaching up, she stroked her fingers lightly through his dark hair. Then turned to fluff the pillow and snuggle closer to him. "I'm too tired to pack this evening. Glynis can help me get ready in the morning. Oh, and I will need some time to discuss the twins with Brighid. I think I can probably be ready after the noon meal," she finished, reaching up to place small kisses along his chin and lips.

"Laurel . . ." Conor began, pulling her shoulder so that she faced him once again.

Undaunted, Laurel asked, "Is it possible for Finn to stay behind? Since you will be with me, I would like him as well as your brothers to remain here with the twins until we return."

"I told you—"

Laurel put a finger against his lips. "And I was thinking, if there is time, I would like to stop by your favorite spot—remember the one you showed me near Stirling Castle?"

Conor did remember. He remembered everything about the trip where he rescued and fell in love with her on his journey home. Part of which included a quick stop at one of his favorite respites. They had not made love there, but he had mentally vowed never to miss the opportunity ever again.

All he could do was nod as the mental vision of her naked on the private cliff danced in his mind.

Laurel beamed him a mischievous smile. "And I thought this time, we can do more than just look at the view. . . ."

Conor swore to convince her to stay home in the morning as he rolled her beneath him and began to press hot kisses down the column of her neck. Reaching her ear, he described in erotic detail what he intended to do to her. Laurel moaned and moved closer, and Conor knew that at last the conversation was over and his original plans for the evening had begun.

Chapter Fourteen

Conor waited patiently for Laurel to join him. Riding on the gray stallion he had acquired for her two years ago, she approached him still smiling the same grin he had put on her face the day before.

They had stopped at the vista he had found as a guardsman many years ago. One could sit forever and stare at the sky caressing the earth and sea. Two days ago, they had enjoyed it in sensual and fulfilling ways that made Conor contemplate turning their unexpected trip into an annual occurrence.

"Is that Lochlen?" Laurel asked, arriving at Conor's side.

They were on a small crest, but it provided a good view of the castle, its walls, and the gently sloping land stretching around it.

"Aye," Conor replied. "We've been on Colin's land for over two hours."

Laurel nodded, glad they were close. The small group had moved slowly, and Conor was showing no signs of being in a hurry to see his brother. Laurel, however, was more than ready to arrive at their destination. She didn't mind sleeping outside for a day or two, but after a week, she was ready to enjoy a bath and a real bed.

Seamus, one of Conor's elite guards, guided his horse next to Conor's and pointed. "Someone approaches. And they ride hard."

Conor recognized Colin along with two dozen men. Dunlop must also have seen his laird and ridden out to greet him. Signaling for Laurel to follow, Conor moved to meet his brother at an unhurried pace. He could see both the joy and relief in Colin's expression when he saw Laurel.

"Conor! Laurel! You came! I am both surprised and comforted. I gave Dunlop orders to be persistent, but I must admit I was prepared for your refusal."

Conor pinched his brows together and beamed an icy look at his brother. "I did not agree. In fact, I am completely against the idea. And as soon as you and I are alone, you will learn exactly how displeased I am that you would even *ask* Laurel to put herself in danger."

Laurel nudged her mount forward, interrupting Conor's glare. "Lord, Conor, the way you are talking right now your brother would never believe me if I told him that only yesterday you were thinking we should come and visit every year."

Conor opened and then closed his mouth, shifting his heated gaze from Colin to Laurel. She shrugged, completely unconcerned.

Colin watched the interchange, appreciating the chemistry and friendship Conor and Laurel shared. Last summer, he had traveled to see the first of the next generation of McTiernays. He had not been around such affectionate banter since their parents had been alive and he found his brother's lighthearted and often passionate exchanges with his wife very uncomfortable. He had not admitted it at the time, but he had been desirous of what they shared. Deep inside he knew that only relationships built with honesty, passion, and trust could endure. Friendship and admiration were not enough.

Laurel ignored Conor's open rudeness and addressed Colin. "I am so pleased you invited me. It has been some time since I have been in the Borders. Magnificent country."

Colin gave one of his rare smiles to his sister-in-law. "I, too, am grateful and glad that you have come. I forgot for a moment that Laird MacInnes is your grandfather."

"Indeed. He's a Highlander destined to live in the Lowlands. Though I know many men, including present company," she said waving her thumb toward Conor, "who cannot imagine living out their days so far south, I know my grandfather is happiest here. And I can see the same applies to you."

Colin quickly assessed Laurel. She possessed many of the same outward features as his dead wife, and though no one could deny her beauty, he was no longer lured to women with pale features. A wild redhead with bewitching green eyes held much more appeal. "Will you be visiting your grandfather before your return?" Colin inquired.

Before Laurel could answer, Conor found his voice. "No. MacInnes lands lie too far to the west to visit. Laurel does not want to be away from Brenna and Braeden for that long a period."

Laurel narrowed her eyes. Conor was right, her grandfather lived near the River Nith by the Lowther Hills, a significant journey from here, but he didn't need to be so abrupt. She was about to say so when Conor asked, "Is that not what you told me yesterday, love?"

Conor did nothing to hide his glee at seeing her flounder in a manner similar to what she had just minutes ago caused him.

Knowing exactly what Conor was doing, Laurel replied in her most prim and proper voice, "If you do not think we should visit my grandfather while so close to his home, that is, of course, your decision, Conor." She paused and cleared her throat. "Just as it will be *your* responsibility to explain it to him when he learns of our whereabouts," she added, changing to a singsong manner in both voice and behavior.

Dunlop, who had been watching the interchange beside his laird's side, elbowed Colin and cackled, "Can you see what I have been through, Laird? They are worse than you and Makenna ever dreamed of being!"

Laurel tried to look offended, but failed.

Colin just produced a sideways grin.

Conor faked a grimace and pointed at Dunlop. "You might want to counsel your commander, brother, lest you find yourself suddenly shorthanded."

Colin ignored the warning. "And just where is *your* faithful and ever-perfect commander?"

"Exactly where I told Finn to be. Overseeing the safety of the twins."

Laurel knew the polite conversation would continue until she left. "Before you ask, Colin, they are fine. Both spirited, growing, and mischievous. If you want to know more, I will gab on about them profusely during the evening meal. Meanwhile, I would love to ride ahead and meet Makenna before you and Conor begin to discuss things I have little interest in."

Colin nodded and moved his horse out of her way. "Dunlop, remain with us. Tavis, escort Lady McTiernay to the castle."

Laurel waited patiently as Conor selected four additional men to ride with her toward the stone structure.

Conor watched Laurel leave until he was positive she was out of earshot before speaking.

"*Aireamh na h-Aoine ort,* Colin!" Conor growled, suppressing the true rage coursing through him.

Colin moved his head back as if he were avoiding a physical strike. "*Pòg mo thòin,* you didn't have to bring her. Dunlop is stubborn, but you could have said no."

"Don't even think about telling me you didn't know what would happen. You knew Laurel and how she would react, and you wagered she would figure it out and conceive of a way to come."

"You *still* could have said no," Colin countered, understanding exactly why Conor was so angry. If it had been Makenna, his reaction would have been the same.

Conor stared at his brother, gripping his reins firmly. "Then you were lucky, Colin, that much of your plan depended upon Laurel. You have no idea how persistent she is."

"There will be activity, Conor, but Makenna and Laurel will be well protected and away from Lochlen when it arrives. On this, I give you my word. I would not risk either of our wives."

Conor looked his brother directly in the eye. Colin met his gaze, and Conor knew that his brother spoke the truth. Conor gestured toward the group of men riding with Colin, wearing McTiernay colors. "And the twenty men?"

Colin shrugged. "I could not just assume it was you. On the chance you were someone else, I thought I would bring a small reminder of who I am and just who my family is."

Conor grinned and raised his sword high into the air. "Aye. It is good to be a McTiernay." Conor lowered his sword and looked back. "I thought that might be your intention. So I brought just a few more of us so that there would be no confusion."

Colin watched as a hundred or more men came into

view over the ridge. Conor might say it was for his brother's benefit, but Colin knew otherwise. He slapped Conor on the back. "Aye, trust that I understand, and I do not condemn you, brother. If positions were reversed, I, too, would have brought an army."

Conor sighed. He could deny his real reason for bringing so many men, but it would be pointless. "Laurel remains unaware that I brought any other men than the few she saw."

Colin grunted. "That must have been difficult."

"Aye, more than you know. At home, she reluctantly agrees to a single escort. If she knew how many men I actually have ensuring her safety, I would never hear the end."

Colin nodded in understanding. "I, too, have the joy of a willful and infuriatingly independent wife. Only recently did Makenna agree to stop evading her escorts when she leaves the town walls."

"Creative, is she?" Conor asked, grinning out the side of his mouth.

Colin snorted. "You have no idea. I waver between wanting to throttle the woman and applauding her ingenuity."

"Prepare yourself. It is a never-ending battle in which you are engaged."

Colin's mouth tightened and then he shook his head realizing Conor was telling him of his future. A future he wanted very badly. "Who else knows of the force you bring?"

"If you mean the spies we spotted about an hour north of your boundary, they are aware only of the handful I wanted them to see."

"Excellent. Your main guards can stay at Lochlen or join my men in the training fields. The rest can stay behind the Lammermuir Hills. Come, the path is well hidden. Passersby avoid the area believing it to be impassable. This will do until MacCuaig makes his move."

Conor lifted his brows appreciatively and followed Colin as he headed toward the moderately tall and deceptive hills. It was a rare asset to have a natural place in which to hide and train men. "So you have a plan?"

"Of course I have a plan," Colin said with a confident grin. "I may have moved south, but I am still a McTiernay. Dunlop, send your best men to our allies and then ride to Donovan's and tell Drake to come home."

Laurel passed through the last of the stone gate barriers remembering the first time she entered the McTiernay Castle. This experience was significantly different. Instead of friendly and welcoming, the Dunstans were cautious and removed. It was obvious they did not like or want outsiders, especially those that came from the north.

As the last of her escorts crossed the final portcullis, Tavis swung off his horse and ordered someone to inform Lady Makenna her husband's family had arrived.

Laurel remained seated on Borrail absently stroking his gray mane as she looked about. The inner ward of the castle was odd-shaped, made of four long walls, each unique in length. There was no standard tower keep; instead three great towers appeared to serve as living quarters for the laird, his family, and guests. Thick walls connected the gatehouse to the massive corner towers. From the tower on the left, the curtain wall traveled only a short distance before ending in what looked to be a sizeable chapel. The long wall on the right angled toward a tower somewhat higher than the rest. Between it and the chapel tower were two battle towers that served as hubs, bowing the extended wall to match the small river behind it.

Between the battle towers was a sizeable building Laurel guessed to be the great hall. Farther down was a smaller but similarly shaped structure that could only be the lower hall. Sandwiched between the two buildings were the kitchens and the bailey.

But none of these were as fascinating as the round mammoth to her right. Although only three stories tall, the large black tower rivaled the others.

"Tavis," Laurel prompted, getting the attention of Colin's guard. "That tower. It is most unusual."

"We call it *tòrr-dubh*."

"The Black Tower," Laurel whispered. "Most fitting, and most curiously different. I have never seen or even heard of a tower made of such a dark stone."

"Aye, I doubt you ever will again. For the past three hundred years, different lairds have expanded Lochlen for various purposes. The laird who commissioned that structure ordered its rocks to be retrieved from the mountains of Skye."

"The Cuillin Mountains!" Laurel exclaimed. The Black Cuillin Mountains were nestled in the Highlands off the Isle of Skye. She had never seen the hard dark hills that straddled the isle, but she had heard of them and how the hill's black jagged and twisting rocks touched the heavens.

"Aye, you heard correctly. Laird Ranald was one of the first to build onto Lochlen. His intentions were to create a keep using the hard rock of Skye, believing it would make his castle impenetrable to enemies."

"How did he ever get the stones all the way down here?" Laurel asked, taking in the black structure with new appreciation.

"By ship. For several years, as soon as winter passed,

he would send ships north to bring the rock through the Sea of Hebrides and up the River Clyde where his men would then carry or oftentimes drag it here by land. Only after they began constructing the tower did the laird discover that while the rock was indeed hard, it was near impossible to cut and shape. Stories are that the laird's wisdom caused him to order the inner walls and other towers be built out of local limestone, but pride made him finish the tower's exterior out of the wicked rock."

"It is unique and quite powerful on the eye. Is that the laird's tower?"

"Alas, no. Laird Ranald lived just barely long enough to see it finished. Until that time he kept his solar in the Canmore Tower," Tavis answered, pointing at the immense tower on her right, "which still holds the laird's sleeping chambers."

Laurel was just about to ask another question, when she spied a woman with deep red hair escaping its braid walking rapidly toward them from the far tower situated higher than the rest. Laurel dismounted and moved to meet Makenna halfway.

Makenna watched the beautiful woman coming toward her. Graceful, tall, and slender, Laurel was everything Makenna feared. The woman exuded a regal elegance that only complemented her beauty. A beauty startlingly similar to her dead sister's.

Makenna had no doubt Colin would be reminded of Deirdre each time he looked at Laurel. Blond and blue-eyed, her sister-in-law reeked of femininity just as Deirdre had.

"Remain calm and for God's sake smile," Makenna ordered herself as Laurel approached opening her arms wide. Makenna stepped into them and felt a genuine embrace. Instinct caused her to give one in return.

"My apologies for not greeting you properly. I had not been told that you had arrived or that Colin had left to meet you," Makenna said apprehensively, wondering what Laurel must think of her and her abilities to be lady of a castle.

"Nonsense. I just arrived and the few minutes I was waiting let me view your home. I must say I am awed. I can never just walk across my courtyard without fear of running into someone or getting stabbed."

"Stabbed?" Makenna asked, horrified.

"Exactly my sentiments," Laurel answered, hoping to ease the fear and unease she saw in Makenna's vivid green eyes. It was obvious Dunlop had spoken correctly. The young woman had a lot of pride in her keep, but also a lot of self-doubt. Laurel hooked her arm in Makenna's and prompted them toward the great hall, continuing with her explanation. "Conor refuses to conduct all of his training with his men outside the castle walls. We finally agreed that most of his men would train elsewhere, but he still insists on 'not wasting the space' and allows contests to take place where 'everyone can enjoy them.' Now, I enjoy a good spar as well as the next woman—"

"You do?" Makenna interrupted.

"Of course, but not every day, and certainly not in a place that makes it difficult for people to do their work." Laurel waited as Makenna ascended the steps to the great hall and opened the doors.

As Makenna stepped through the entrance, a shot of fear ripped through her. It subsided. The hearth was roaring and the rushes were still fresh. Incidents of sabotage had significantly diminished in the past few weeks, but they still occurred and usually where she least expected them.

Forcing her voice to remain steady, Makenna waved

Laurel to one of the chairs situated by the main fireplace. "Can I offer you a drink or some food, milady?"

"No, thank you, and please call me Laurel. I really hate the title, and I doubt I will ever become accustomed to it."

Makenna reassessed her sister-in-law. The woman might have many of Deirdre's features, but her sensibility was vastly different. Based on her few short comments, Makenna wondered whether the woman's nature was more like hers.

Laurel sank gracefully into the padded high-back chair reserved for family and special guests. "Your hall is splendid. Warm and inviting." She pointed to the sunlight. "You must have a love-hate relationship with those enormous windows."

Makenna's eyes popped opened wide, for that was exactly how she felt about them. At that moment, Makenna decided to relax and be herself. She knew she would not be able to keep up the pretense of a lady fully in control of her castle and those around her for long, so she might as well stop now and conserve her energy for the next catastrophe. "Aye, I often think they mock me," she replied, slipping into a cushioned chair beside her sister-in-law.

Laurel inhaled the scent of the new rushes and pointed at the rainbow of colors hitting the tapestries hanging across from the arched stained glass windows. "Those are lovely and complement the room well."

Makenna sucked in her breath and decided to plunge forward with the truth. It would be best to divulge now her limitations. "They have been there my entire life, just as most of the castle's decorations," she commented quietly.

Laurel smiled. "Blessed are those that come before us, for they do make our lives easier, do they not? Can you imagine preparing for winter *and* having to adorn our homes? I do not think it possible."

Makenna twisted in her chair and openly appraised Laurel once again. This time she decided to say exactly what was on her mind. "You don't know me, and yet you speak as if we are old friends."

Laurel sighed, but instead of conveying irritation with Makenna's bluntness, she exuded relief. "I'll have to remember to thank God in my prayers this evening for giving Colin a wife like you. I have a tendency to be unbearably forward and honest, and I made a promise to myself not to be that way with you. I was going to try to be everything a proper lady should be. Complimentary, friendly, and talkative about nothing. I can't believe I failed so miserably so quickly."

Makenna tried to swallow her laughter, but could not. "You didn't fail, I did! If my sisters were here, you would be stuck here hours and hours learning about those damned tapestries, how the colors were chosen, and the difficulty and skill needed to complete each and every stitch. Trust me, I know."

"Oh, what a pair we make. If Conor came in right now, he would probably hang his head down and sigh with defeat," Laurel said haltingly as she joined Makenna in fits of ill-repressed giggles.

"Oh, it feels good to laugh. I never thought I would say this, but I am glad you came."

Laurel sat forward and smiled, no longer wondering why Colin asked her to come. Makenna needed an understanding female friend. "Do you know what I would love to do right now?"

"What?" Makenna asked, very curious to know what Laurel was thinking.

"I know this sounds completely crazy as I have been on a horse for days now, but you have no idea the infuriatingly slow pace we were going. It was maddening. For the past two days, I have wanted to ride like wind. Will you join me?"

Makenna hesitated and then nodded. "I'll have to find Brodie or Gorten first. I promised Colin that I would no longer leave the castle walls without my guards."

"You, too? I think Conor would be happiest if I were surrounded everywhere I went. He's getting better, but the man practically defines overprotection."

"Ha! Has your husband ever snatched you off a horse you were riding perfectly safe upon because of an irrational idea that you might fall off?" Makenna asked, snaking her way through the great hall to the large wooden doors.

Laurel followed Makenna outside. "That is bad, but wait until Colin orders a hundred men as escort when you come to visit us in the Highlands. Then you will see what I mean."

Makenna swung around and shielded her eyes from the afternoon sun. "Good Lord, is that true?"

Laurel followed Makenna inside the stable. "Unfortunately, yes. And I love Conor so much that I pretended not to notice."

Makenna sent two of the stabled lads for their guards and moved to prepare her brown mare. Laurel's gray stallion was still bridled and enjoying some fresh hay in a stall.

"Come on, boy," Laurel said, encouraging Borrail back out into the open. "This time I promise you we will run until we tire."

Makenna helped the stable master bridle her horse and then waited with Laurel in the outer yard for her guard.

"Makenna!" came a gravelly voice behind her. Immediately, she knew who it was.

"Camus! How are you?"

Camus drew her in his arms and whispered quickly in her ear, "The item you requested is nearly finished. Give me a few more days for polishing, and it will be complete."

"Thank you," Makenna returned and then pulled back. "Laurel, please let me introduce to you the finest sword smith in Scotland. Camus, this is Lady McTiernay, Conor's wife."

Laurel beamed him a smile that showed true interest and appreciation for such a skill. "Please call me Laurel."

"Aye, Laurel, I think I will. That is a fine dirk you are wearing, and my guess is that you are quite proficient with it."

Laurel shrugged. "Some would say I have skill, others would say I need more practice."

Laughing, Camus waved good-bye just as Gorten and Brodie and two other men under Conor's command approached. Soon all six of them were free of the castle, the town, and its walls.

For an hour, they rode along the river and across the hills. Sensing each other's readiness to stop, Makenna and Laurel slowed down near a brook so that the horses could drink.

Gorten met with Laurel's guards, who agreed to stay back and give the two women privacy. Then he moved beside Brodie, whose brown eyes were filled with concern. "Was it just me, or was Lady Makenna riding with more restraint than normal?"

Gorten nodded brusquely. "Aye, and with much more care. At first, I thought her companion was slowing their gait. Now I am not so sure."

"Maybe she's afraid the laird will snatch her off her horse again."

"Possible," Gorten murmured, full of skepticism.

Laurel stroked the gray neck of her large friend. "There now, Borrail, was that not fun?"

Makenna slid off her mare and allowed the animal to drink and move about freely. She looked back and wrinkled her nose in disgust. No longer were there just four soldiers overseeing their safety but almost two dozen. Picking up a rock, she threw it into the brook and then sat down on the yellowing but still thick grass. Makenna arched her back and took in a deep breath. "It is so good to get out of those depressing walls. When I leave, I feel like an enormous weight has been taken off of me."

Laurel joined her on the ground. She picked some nearby fall wildflowers and spun them in her fingers. "And when you return?"

"I just want to leave again. Is that not awful? Those are my people, my clan, and yet they seem so foreign to me. I both love and loathe them at the same time." Makenna lay down and stared at the sky. "You probably think I am being ridiculous."

Laurel didn't know what to say. Lochlen was so very different from McTiernay Castle. The McTiernays were a loud, welcoming bunch that greeted guests with smiles. On the other hand, she was very familiar with the push, pull feeling Makenna was experiencing. "On the contrary, I quite understand."

Makenna angled her head to see if Laurel was serious. "You mean . . ."

"No, no. McTiernay Castle is, well, very different from Lochlen, just as it is very different from the home I grew up in."

"Colin says that you are English, yet you speak Scot very well."

Laurel threw her flower into the breeze and watched it float away. "I'm half English and grew up not far from here in the Cheviot Hills of Northumberland. Most of the people speak Scot or something very similar. You have to go much farther south toward London to hear pure English."

"Your English home, was it very bad?"

Laurel studied the folds in her gown. "Not when my mother was alive. Then it was warm and welcoming."

"Isn't it odd how one person can both add life to a home and take it away?"

Laurel nodded and picked another flower. "When she passed away, my father grieved terribly and kept himself distant from my stepbrother and me. I think my father mourned my mother until he died. It was like his grief permeated the walls, affecting all who walked them."

Makenna searched Laurel's face. "Is that why you left?"

"If things hadn't changed, I don't think I would have stayed. However, it was my brother, Ainsley, who actually initiated my leaving. He decided to marry the eldest daughter of our wealthy neighbor. I was clearly unwanted, and his attempts to marry me off were quite unsuccessful."

Makenna considered that briefly. "I cannot imagine it would be hard to arrange a marriage to you. You are very beautiful."

"Ah, well, Ainsley had little inclination to put down a dowry, and let's just say I had little inclination to be ladylike when being introduced to prospective husbands," Laurel answered, her voice laced with false innocence.

Makenna giggled at the thought and hugged her knees. "What did you do?"

"I left," Laurel said softly, her mirth disappearing as she remembered her brother's words of disownership the day she departed.

Makenna recognized the sadness in Laurel's voice. "So you do understand about not being wanted by your own people."

Laurel let go the blossom and wiped her hands on her bliaut. "In a way, but your situation is different. Only my brother made me feel unwelcome, and secondly, I am not at all positive that your people want you gone. On the contrary, I think the majority of them think very highly of you. Lochlen is well run and organized. You should have seen McTiernay Castle when I first came upon it. Nightmare is a soft way to describe such mayhem. And when I tried to help . . . well, you should have heard the rows Conor and I had. The man is very touchy about my making decisions he feels are only his to make."

Makenna gave Laurel a challenging look. "Ha! I have met your Conor, and he was most agreeable and forthcoming compared to Colin. Sometimes I wonder if my husband actually *works* at making the most simple of conversations difficult. And his *pride*, his infuriating pride! It drives everything he does and says!"

"I know someone else with a significant dose of pride," Laurel squealed as she threw some wildflowers at Makenna and then quickly moved to avoid the revenge attack.

Gorten and Brodie stared at the two women rolling in the grass laughing and throwing weeds and plants on each other whenever they got the chance. "Whatever are they doing?" Brodie asked incredulously.

"I don't know," Gorten replied. "But it is good to hear our lady laugh and be herself again. I didn't know if another Highlander staying at Lochlen was a good decision, but I am beginning to realize just how shrewd our laird is in all things, including his wife."

Laurel blew stray pieces of grass off her mouth and sat up. "If Conor could see me now, he'd think the southern air has addled my brains."

Makenna stood up and started brushing off the evi-

dence of their momentary lapse in decorum. "Just tell
him it was all Colin's fault."

"Colin's fault?" Laurel questioned as she rose fluidly
and began to remove loose grass from Makenna's back.

"Aye, I am sure it was talk of his pride that led you to
attack me."

"No, it was talk of *your* pride," Laurel argued, turning
around so that Makenna could brush away any remnants of their merriment. "I saw your face when you entered the great hall and all was in order."

"Good Lord, it will take a year to pluck this stuff out
of your hair," Makenna murmured. "That wasn't pride.
That was sheer relief. I didn't want your first sight of
Lochlen to be of the truth. Things are bad, Laurel. Very
bad. I have less than half the staff needed to maintain a
home of Lochlen's size. My efforts to maintain the castle
and prepare for winter are continually being sabotaged
by my own clan."

"But that doesn't make sense," Laurel said, loosening
Makenna's tight braid to remove the embedded branches.

"Oh, that feels better. And it would make sense if you
understood just how much they resent me for marrying
Colin and making a Highlander their laird."

"What does Colin say about this?"

"I have only told him a little of what has been happening. I know it angers him a great deal when the attacks
involve me, but when they are aimed directly at him, his
attitude is almost dismissive. When someone says something rude, he acts as if he didn't hear it. I haven't the
heart to tell him that his approach isn't working. I don't
know if anyone can turn a person's heart, let alone a
whole clan. I fear that he will do as you did and leave.
Then Colin will lose his chance of being a laird."

"I wouldn't worry too much about that. If Colin
didn't want to leave Lochlen, then he wouldn't. And if

Colin's plan allows for leaving the Lowlands, then he is not upset at the loss. My guess is that he has found something far greater than being laird of a clan."

Makenna turned and gave Laurel a doubtful look. "Did you say Colin's plan? I don't think he has one. He has more hope than a plan."

Laurel chuckled and walked toward their horses, grabbing the reins to Makenna's mare as she retrieved Borrail's. "I forget you have only been married to Colin for a few months. In a couple of years, I'll remind you about this conversation."

"Aye, we have been *married* only a short time, but I have known him for over two years," Makenna countered.

Laurel swung onto Borrail's back and watched in curiosity as Makenna carefully mounted. "And how much time did you actually spend getting to know him?"

Makenna adjusted her skirts and gave Laurel a semiscathing look. "So I avoided him most of the time. Still, there were two very aggravating years in which I saw very little of this great ability to strategize."

"Get ready," Laurel said, smiling as if she were just about to divulge a juicy secret. "You married a McTiernay, Makenna, and they are the masters of strategy. And to them, the very best plans are ones that don't reveal themselves until *they* want them to be seen. Trust me, Colin is about to teach your people a hard lesson, and it will be your responsibility to help him when the time comes."

Makenna scowled at Laurel. "But if he doesn't tell me anything, how can I help?"

Laurel lifted one shoulder in an elegant shrug. "All he needs is your trust and your love. To know that regardless of the situation, you will support him . . . even if it means turning against your clan."

Makenna grimaced and kicked her brown mare into

a canter. She hoped it would not come to that, but if Colin were to leave, she would go with him.

Laurel watched in astonishment as Makenna rode proudly by her. Tears were springing up in her green eyes. Laurel suspected Colin had never told his wife how deep his feelings ran for her. She rode up and grabbed Makenna's hand to get her attention. "Does he know you love him?"

Makenna nodded. "Aye, I told him."

Laurel squeezed Makenna's fingers and let go. "Makenna, we have not known each other very long, but I need you to trust that what I am saying is not just for your benefit, but because it is true. Colin loves you very much."

"I know he cares for me, and sometimes when we are alone, I can see the love in his eyes, but then it is gone. He doesn't want to love again after Deirdre. I can understand that."

"He may not *want* to love you, but he does, even if he doesn't say so aloud. A man protects what he cherishes, and by the number and size of the soldiers watching over you . . ."

Makenna glanced at Brodie, Gorten, and the rest of the soldiers keeping just out of earshot. "That's not evidence of love, that's just . . . annoying."

Laurel shrugged. "Just wait until he learns that you are pregnant. You have only begun to see how annoying his hovering can be."

Makenna's hand jerked slightly at the comment. It was enough to confirm Laurel's suspicions. Makenna was with child, and Colin had no idea.

As Makenna and Laurel neared Lochlen the majority of soldiers following them swung back toward the training fields, leaving Gorten and Brodie and Laurel's two guards to see them safely back inside. Cresting the hill leading to the town gate, Makenna could see several figures hunched outside. One was unmistakably Colin.

Makenna pointed. Laurel nodded, seeing Conor crouched down on the other side. Makenna slid off her horse and moved quietly toward the group. Laurel followed.

Hearing someone approach, Colin turned and gave Makenna a quizzical look. He motioned for her and Laurel to come closer but remain silent. Then he made a strange gesture that Brodie and Gorten must have understood, for they immediately moved to the opposite side of the gate.

The second she was in arm's length, Colin grabbed Makenna and placed her behind him. A second later Laurel was behind Conor.

"Whatever are you doing out here? We thought you were inside," Colin growled.

"It was my fault. I wanted to see the countryside. No one told us that we were to remain confined," Laurel shot back.

Conor rolled his eyes, and Laurel knew that he was praying for patience.

Laurel ignored him. "What's happening, Conor? Is something wrong?"

"Not a thing," Conor answered. "It's all going exactly to Colin's plan."

Makenna's eyes widened in surprise. Laurel had been right. "Why do we have to remain hidden?"

Colin grinned and then leaned forward eagerly. "Because, it would interrupt the show Lela is giving. And it is quite an interesting one. Come here," he said, moving just enough for her to see.

Makenna looked through the small opening in the

wood planks and saw Lela pacing around the Commune Tree shouting something.

Laurel whispered, "What's that woman saying?"

"She's challenging everyone to turn against Colin and join MacCuaig, the laird of a neighboring clan," Conor whispered in explanation.

"*Striopach*," Makenna murmured, unaware she had just called Lela a harlot out loud.

"I actually think you might be right," Colin affirmed softly. "She's been meeting with MacCuaig regularly."

"How much longer are you going to stand by and watch as McTiernay destroys our way of life?" Lela shouted loud enough for all to hear.

"The only destruction and filth I've heard is from your own mouth, Lela Fraser. We might not like the Highlander, but MacCuaig is no better. We've heard rumors about how he mistreats his own people. Not a man I want to be shifting my allegiance to," said an older man with short scrubby hair and a wrinkled face.

Lela scoffed and gave him a placating smile. "Make your choice, then, but I would rather be led by a strong Lowland laird with an army who could protect me and my clan than a weak Highlander with a handful of untrained recruits and a vulnerable wall."

The small crowd became smaller as more turned away and resumed their duties. Still, Lela kept on. Only a few Makenna knew to be adamantly against Colin as their laird remained behind for a while before they, too, decided to leave.

Colin stood up and pulled Makenna up beside him. Conor assisted Laurel and said one word, "Interesting."

"Aye, 'tis that. It shouldn't be long now. As soon as Dunlop returns with Drake we'll be ready," Colin replied.

Makenna spun around in Colin's arm. "Returning? I thought you said Drake was out training the men."

"Aye, I did. I just didn't tell you where," Colin pointed out with a touch of self-satisfaction.

"The question you should be asking, Makenna, is what your husband is getting ready for," Laurel advised.

Makenna crossed her arms and looked directly into her giant's sparkling blue eyes. "I've no need to ask. I already know. He's about to teach my obstinate, short-sighted clan a well-deserved lesson."

Colin favored her with a blindingly bright smile. "Aye, wife, and I hope they are quick learners."

Colin opened his arms, and Makenna stepped into them and held him close. "I hope they are, too," she whispered against his chest. "For I am ready for this to be over."

Colin leaned down and kissed her hair. "And if things go wrong, and we leave?"

"Then we leave," she whispered back.

"Don't worry. I don't know if I ever told you this before, but we McTiernays are great planners. Things rarely go wrong."

Makenna hugged Colin tightly to her. Twice in one day, she was told about the McTiernays' ability to strategize and plan. Makenna didn't know if that was a good sign or an omen of bad things to come.

Chapter Fifteen

"Normally, I would agree. But tonight, we want to be late. Let the festivities be well along before we arrive," Laurel said to Makenna as she plucked furiously at Ceridwin's dark gold hair. The intricate weave had taken almost an hour to complete, but the end effect was worth the effort. The past two weeks had been extremely illuminating, and Laurel was just starting to feel like she was making real progress.

Her hardest goal had been easily achieved upon meeting Ceridwin. The young woman had come running into the courtyard the day Drake returned, throwing herself quite unladylike into his arms.

She had a heart-shaped face, a sweet disposition, and a mischievous twinkle in her hazel eyes. She openly kissed Drake full on the mouth and cared very little if anyone admonished her for it. She was just as open with her displeasure when she found out Drake had been ordered to continue overseeing the soldiers in the fields. Ceridwin calmed only after he promised to come back and see her every few days.

When Makenna asked Ceridwin to participate in the planning of a semilarge feast celebrating Drake's return and Conor's visit, Laurel knew her new sister was going to be fine. Aileen's friendship gave her a safe, honest place to turn to for questions and support, and she wanted Makenna to have the same.

The two women were like halves of the same loaf, destined to be friends. Ceridwin's father had raised her alone, and she had often felt out of place knowing more about how to be a man and planting crops than she did about being a lady. A few months ago, her father had passed, and Ceridwin's aunts had offered her shelter within the village. There she had met Drake, but everyone else she encountered thought her odd and uncultured for a woman of her age. As Makenna shared similar situations and feelings, the two had become fast confidantes.

"There," Laurel said, looking at Makenna, who was standing over her shoulder, "did you see how I did that? It isn't hard at all, just a little time-consuming. You just need to remember that trick of how to cross the pins holding the braids so that they don't come down when you are dancing."

Ceridwin looked in the polished silver and admired the end effect. "I don't know if I can go looking like this. I look like a . . . a real lady," she said softly.

Makenna nudged her new friend lightly in the shoulder. "You absolutely must. I cannot wait until Drake sees you."

Ceridwin stood and turned around admiring how the gold velvet of her new gown swirled complementarily around her ankles. Never had she felt more beautiful. Her heart was pounding heavily. Drake had been away for over a week and had returned just that morning, but she had yet to see him.

Laurel waited until Makenna donned her dark green silk bliaut over her cream-colored chainse. Makenna looped her gold embroidered belt matching the stitching around the gown's collar and sleeves twice around her abdomen, placing a decorative knot in front so that it hung flatteringly with the ends nearly touching the floor. Being careful not to crush the silk, she descended carefully onto the wooden stool and waited as Laurel placed intermittent gold threads throughout her hair. Makenna then loosely pinned back the sides of her thick red hair, leaving the rest to flow freely down her back.

Ceridwin came up beside her and sighed. "Your hair is so beautiful, Makenna. You should always leave it loose like it is now. Until tonight I think I have only seen it braided."

Makenna reached up and touched the softened strands. She never thought so little effort could achieve this effect. Laurel had showed her how to combine certain plants and then rub minute amounts of the mixture into her hair as it dried. The effect was amazing. No longer was her hair so voluminous and frizzy it drowned out the rest of her face when left unbound. The rich red waves almost reached her waist and smelled of rosemary and lavender.

Laurel pinned the last thread into Makenna's hair and smiled at the effect. "Yes, I believe our men will be quite pleased with their choices in women this evening," she said, smoothing out the royal-blue gown she knew to be Conor's favorite. "I think they have waited for us long enough."

Laurel grinned and walked toward the door with Ceridwin close behind. Makenna stood and fought her tendency to fidget when apprehensive.

It had been her suggestion to celebrate the harvest, Conor's arrival, and Drake's homecoming. But it had been Colin who had requested that she invite the entire clan. She knew then he was going to use the event to carry out some part of his grand scheme. Yet no amount of coaching had persuaded him to tell her in what way. All he would say was "Wait and see." He promised there would be no fighting and that it would be a relaxing and enjoyable time.

Makenna watched Laurel and Ceridwin disappear down the stairs. "Why do I think you will be the only one relaxed and having fun, Colin?" Makenna sighed aloud.

"Makenna!" Laurel shouted from below.

"Coming!" Makenna returned and quickly descended to join her friends.

As soon as they exited into the cool night air, several soldiers flanked them as they made their way through the mass of people gathered in the inner yard. Makenna had asked Doreen to spread the word that all were invited, but never did she think so many Dunstans would come. Even the feast following her father's death did not draw so many out of their homes.

There was a large bonfire in the center of the courtyard, and Makenna could see the smoke rising from two others in the outer yard just beyond the curtain wall. Music was erupting from everywhere.

Slowly they made their way into the great hall that was even more crowded than the inner yard. Seated at one end were Conor and Colin engaged in a lively debate about something. Both paused in midsentence upon seeing their wives.

Makenna was barely aware of Ceridwin being pulled away by Drake. Her eyes were locked on to Colin. For a brief moment, the world disappeared. Colin looked at her with so much glittering emotion that Makenna wanted to weep and cry out with joy at the same time. No longer did she see just hot sexual desire blazing in his eyes, but something deeper and far more powerful.

It had been two weeks since Laurel had arrived, and in

that time she had given Makenna something she had not realized she was missing—a sense of worth as a woman. Never before did she think she was beautiful, or enticing, or capable of turning a man's eye. But with Laurel's and Ceridwin's help, Makenna had slowly gained the confidence to accept what Colin felt for her, and not diminish or belittle it.

Makenna smiled as Colin skimmed appreciatively over her before locking his eyes once again on to hers. She belonged to him completely and knew, beyond a shadow of a doubt, that Colin belonged only to her.

She would tell him tonight.

Colin watched as Makenna approached, unable to look anywhere else. A surge of pride and possessiveness flowed through his veins. It struck him that he had finally found with Makenna the elusive and special bond his parents had shared.

When he had been very young, he had asked his father what made his mother the most beautiful woman in the entire world. His father's answer had been "love."

There in the midst of a boisterous crowd, Colin looked at Makenna and accepted what had happened. He had fallen in love. He waited for the guilt to fill him, but it never came. He gazed into her green eyes and knew she truly loved him as well.

"You're finally here, and so very beautiful," he whispered just before he brushed his mouth across hers in an incredibly gentle, almost reverent kiss.

Tingles went down Makenna's spine. With a soft, low groan, Colin released her lips and pressed his mouth to her ear. "Tonight, love, I shall make love to you in ways that will let you know exactly what you mean to me. You are my heart. I need you, Makenna."

And then he maneuvered her to the chair next to his, praying he could control his growing desire long enough to commence the next phase of his plan. Tonight provided just the right setting. He would not get such an ideal chance again.

Makenna complied and sank down in shock, wondering if she had just imagined it or if Colin really had called her "love." It was a little name most men called their wives, but Colin had never once used it with her.

The night continued merrily, and Makenna forgot all about her apprehensions about the McTiernays and their plans. She and Colin had danced until her feet could take no more. More than once Laurel grabbed her to go visit with clusters of women around the room and outside the hall. And for the first time, she felt welcomed into their enclave, able to participate in their conversations about homes, husbands. Even the topic of children didn't frighten her.

Ceridwin and Drake had disappeared soon into the festivities and had yet to reappear. Makenna had no doubt a wedding was imminent and could not be happier for them both.

Colin moved by the roaring hearth, adjusted the chair so that he could see across the room, and then sat down.

"Come here, *m'eudail*, I want to kiss you," Colin beckoned.

Makenna blushed, as she knew that many had heard his endearment, and went quickly to his side lest he became even more vocal.

As soon as she came near, Colin pulled her into his lap and uttered a thick, husky groan as his body responded to the sensual weight of her. Makenna gasped at the feel of his hard, fiercely aroused body. She stirred against him in an effort to get up.

"Stay right where you are, lest I leave here to do what has been on my mind since the second I saw you."

Feeling emboldened, Makenna turned and nipped playfully at his lower lip. "And would that be so bad?" she asked, twining her arms around his neck.

Colin buried his face in her hair and inhaled the scent of her, part lavender and rosemary and part feminine arousal. He knew she was already moist and ready for him. "Just a little bit longer, love. I promise you I will make the wait worth it for us both."

Makenna leaned into him and tilted her head back for his kiss. Colin knew Conor was waiting for him, but he couldn't resist the temptation and took her mouth hungrily. Begrudgingly, he ended the kiss.

"Do you trust me?" he asked, his voice thick with need and shades of uncertainty.

Makenna pulled back and held his blue eyes with her own. "Aye. I will always trust you."

"Then, trust me now, love."

Colin shifted her slightly so that she remained on his lap without impeding his view of his brother seated on the other side of the room. Makenna glanced around the room to see how many people had been staring at them. She was relieved to see most couples were engaged in conversations or activities of their own and were either oblivious of or indifferent to her and Colin's passionate embrace. Laurel was situated very similarly across Conor's lap looking like she, too, had been thoroughly kissed.

Out of the blue, Colin's voice rang out loudly, cutting through the multiple conversations around the room. "Conor, how does Olave fare?"

"Very well. He has done much to unify the roaming clans in the north. He says they soon will be ready for a leader. He has hinted that they are hoping for a

McTiernay," Conor replied, his voice casual but loud enough for everyone to hear.

"I thought Olave would be seeking the title. Banded together, they will be quite fearsome."

Conor shrugged his shoulders, somewhat exaggerating the gesture. "I told him he should be chief, but he doesn't want it. He believes only someone from one of the nearby larger families can truly bind the sparse nomadic tribes and keep them together."

Colin angled his head slightly and leaned forward to pick up his quaich. "There may be some truth behind his sentiments. The tribes would be more likely to unite if they knew their leader had the support of nearby clans." Colin swallowed a gulp of ale. "But Olave has our support. This should not be a reason for his refusal."

"It's not," Conor said in agreement while tapping Laurel possessively on the knee. "The man's in love. Hazel finally convinced him to marry her."

Colin finished off his ale and put the cup back on the table for it to be refilled. "Quite a determined woman, Hazel. Not many like her."

Laurel gave her husband a sidelong glance and tried unsuccessfully to get up. "You are being quite loud, Conor, and seriously out of character. Since when do you talk of love, yell across rooms, and keep me planted on your lap in front of company?" she asked in hushed tones.

"Since now," Conor whispered, hoping the tight squeeze of his hand on her abdomen would encourage her silence. It didn't work.

"And is it a coincidence that Colin seems to be suffering the same bizarre inflection that has come over you?"

"What do you think?" Conor asked rhetorically before continuing. "Olave is a lucky man, very lucky indeed. How many women would spend five years of their life with a man who vowed himself against the evils of marriage?"

"Most people thought Hazel was a fool waiting for him," Colin returned.

"Aye, but a dedicated fool. And it paid off. You know what he told me when last we met? That he had finally found where he belonged."

Colin raised his eyebrows appreciatively and again held firm as Makenna tried to pry his fingers free from her waist. Frustrated, she gave up and crossed her arms. She looked over at Laurel, who shrugged her shoulders as if to say, "I think we are here until they decide otherwise."

Colin eased his grip, satisfied to see more and more of the hall's crowd paying attention to their conversation. "I think of Olave often these days."

"Though I have been at Lochlen but a fortnight, it is clear why," Conor remarked critically.

This statement cut through even more of the crowd, leaving only a handful of people still pursuing personal conversations. Makenna waited for Colin to speak, but he said nothing. The majority of the room was waiting for Colin to respond, but he showed no intention of doing so.

Exasperated, Makenna waved her hand and asked the question on everyone's mind. "Who is Olave? And what makes you think of him?"

Colin picked up the refilled quaich and twirled it so that the metal glinted from the firelight. "Olave is probably the greatest skilled fighter I have ever known, and as to why I think of him? You would have to know his story and why his loving and marrying Hazel is so extraordinary."

Colin took a deep breath as if he were about to continue. Then he hesitated.

This time Laurel pushed him to resume the story. "Is it a secret?"

Colin shook his head. "Olave's story is no secret. It is

about a Highland soldier who meets a beautiful woman from the Lowlands." Again, he paused and gazed thoughtfully at Makenna and then the crowd. "I warn you now the tale does not end well. It is a tale of intolerance and pride. Do you still wish to hear it?"

Makenna bit her bottom lip and looked at Colin. His expression dared her to say yes. She knew he had been waiting for this moment all evening. An interested audience listening to him tell this particular story.

"Indeed I do. How about you, Laurel? Do you know the story of Olave the Highlander?"

Laurel shook her head, coming to the same realization that Makenna had. "No, I do not, but I am exceedingly curious."

A triumphant grin grew on Colin's face. "Then I will tell you."

Colin rose from the large hearth chair at the same time lifting Makenna in his arms. He placed her back on the soft cushions and moved to stand by the hearth's mantel in a position seemingly casual but perfect to be clearly heard and understood by all in the room.

"As you just learned, Olave is a Highlander who lives in the northern lands adjacent to Conor's. You might have assumed he was a McTiernay clansman, but in truth he has never claimed to be part of any clan except that of William Wallace," Colin began.

"But Wallace had no clan," a young boy interrupted, already completely captivated.

Makenna glanced at the quiet portion of the crowd recognizing that they, too, were seeing a new side to him. She had seen so many facets of Colin's personality. Hard, stubborn, passionate, commanding, but tonight she was witnessing the man who was to be the father of their child.

Colin cocked his head to the side and clicked his

tongue. "True, but then again you'd have to understand Wallace when he first began to fight the English. I fought with him at Stirling and Falkirk, but Olave knew him from the beginning.

"Many years ago, when Wallace began his crusade to free Scotland, he banded together a group of men who supported his cause. Olave was one of William Wallace's original rebels. It was he who helped Wallace launch his campaign against the English and free the towns of Aberdeen, Perth, and the lands north of the Forth."

"So Olave was a hero?" asked an older boy who had moved closer to hear Colin speak.

"Olave, a hero? I don't know, to some he might be, but he certainly wasn't one when Wallace started his crusade. Wallace liked Olave's height and strength and crazed approach to fighting the English, but his inexperience nearly got him killed. During one action, Olave became badly injured."

"Did William Wallace save him?" came a question from an unknown face in the back of the crowd.

Colin shook his head. "No. He would have if he had known, but it was another of Wallace's men, a Lowlander, who found him and nursed him back to health. As Olave grew stronger, he wanted to go out and fight. Quickly the Lowlander recognized Olave's lack of skill with any type of weapon."

One of the boys held his hand up in protest. "I thought you said he was the greatest swordsman you have ever met."

"He is the greatest," Colin affirmed.

"Better than you?" another lad asked.

"Aye, better than me, but he wasn't back then. It was the Lowlander who taught Olave how to use the sword, battle-axe, and spear."

Conor spoke up from across the room. "I would have

liked to meet the Lowlander who trained Olave, for there is no one better with a spear."

Laurel shifted in Conor's lap and stared at him quizzically. "Why didn't you?"

Conor's answer was low and deep and full of reverence. "Because the man died at Loudoun Hill over ten years ago."

Completely engrossed in the story, Makenna urged Colin to continue. "What happened next?"

"Now, as all of you know, Wallace's battle at Loudoun Hill was one of his first major successes in driving the English from Scotland, but not all of Wallace's band survived. Many died, including the Lowlander who had befriended Olave."

"As was most of Wallace's men, the Lowlander had been from Ayrshire. So when his friend died, Olave felt honor-bound to find his daughter and tell her what happened. He had planned to return quickly to Wallace and fight again, but the moment he met Lisbet, his plans changed."

Makenna widened her eyes at the unexpected turn in the story. "She must have been remarkable to keep him away."

Colin smiled. "Aye, she was. Olave described her as the bonniest of what Scotland had to offer with dark brown hair and golden eyes that could melt the hardest of men's hearts."

"I thought you said this tale ended sadly," came a female voice from the back of the room. "Did Lisbet spurn him?"

"Unfortunately, no. Lisbet welcomed Olave's attention, and soon they handfasted. They lived just south of the lands of Sorn, and Olave joined the small group of locals helping them build fortifications on the newly commissioned keep. All that summer and winter Olave and Lisbet were happy."

"What happened?" This time the question came from Makenna. Like everyone else listening, she wanted to know the fate of Olave and Lisbet. Suddenly she thought of Deirdre. "Did she . . ."

Colin knew what she was going to ask and shook his head before she could finish. "Then in the spring, Lisbet's family learned about the death of her father and arrived to assume control over his home and land. When they discovered Lisbet was handfasted to a Highlander, they made their displeasure known. Nothing he did or could do would please them."

Suddenly the remaining activity in the room ceased. People laughing swallowed their mirth as Colin's words lingered in the air. Though they had been pretending not to care about Colin's tale, it became obvious they had been listening the entire time.

Colin prolonged his silence for several more seconds before continuing. "Despite all of the work Olave had done restoring her home, regardless of what he did for his neighbors on the Sorn keep, Lisbet's family harassed him mercilessly. It was not long before they had the whole community acting hostile toward him."

A group of older boys mature enough to begin training moved to the other side of the hearth to better hear the tale. Colin stopped and looked at them intently before asking, "What would you do?"

Their eyes popped open and Colin asked again, "What would you do? How would you react if someone continually attacked you for the color of your hair? Your height? Your size?"

Colin watched the boys fidget as he waited for an answer. After a minute of silence, a skinny boy sitting in front of the crowd announced, "If it were a man, I would thrust a sword right through his heart." He followed the statement by slicing the air and then stabbing his friend next to him with a pretend claymore.

Colin pointed at him and said, "You, lad, just might, but Olave . . . well, he chose to do nothing. Instead, he hoped his actions would change their hearts. For during this entire time, the English were attacking in an attempt to reestablish the strongholds Wallace had freed. And each time, Olave would grab his sword and defend them."

"Did it work?" asked one of the older boys standing a few feet away. Colin recognized him. He was Ian, the one who had publicly ridiculed Colin's offer of training.

Colin took a deep breath and sighed. "A heart is the hardest thing to change, and unfortunately theirs was so hard against Highlanders, they could not see what Olave was doing for them until it was too late."

"Too late? Did he go mad and kill them all? Did he kill Lisbet?" asked a woman engrossed by the story.

"Ah, Lisbet. She never acted against Olave, but in many ways she did something just as vile."

"What?" shouted several voices simultaneously.

"She did nothing," Colin answered, his eyes level and unflinching as he scanned the people crammed close around him.

"Nothing? How is that worse than what her family was doing? What could she have done?" Ian demanded, his tone defiant.

Colin looked at him and said, "That question you must learn to answer for yourself." He returned his gaze to the crowd. "Then came the day after a year of handfasting, and do you know what he did?"

"I expect he left and never returned," one frizzy-haired woman retorted. Colin recognized her as one of the women who had once worked in the keep but no longer offered her services.

He looked her straight in the eye and replied, "Aye, that is *exactly* what Olave chose to do. Scottish pride, regardless of whether Highland or Lowland, can only be beaten and assaulted for so long.

"On the morning of the second day after their handfast, Olave dressed and waited for Lisbet and her family to rise for their morning meal. Once they had eaten, he walked over to the door and reached up for his sword that hung above the frame. Then he went and retrieved his axe and his ballock knife. And while Lisbet and her family were still watching, he went out, retrieved his horse, and mounted. And just before Olave left, he said, 'I leave you, Lisbet, to find someone that will make you happy, but I take my sword with me.'

"Now Lisbet began to panic as she realized Olave was leaving them defenseless. When the English attacked again, they would be unprotected and very vulnerable. She ran after him and begged him to stay."

"What did he say?"

"He told her that all Scotsmen should know where they belong and accept the price that comes with it."

"What does that mean?" Ian spoke up, confused by Olave's departing comment.

"I, myself, didn't understand what he meant when Olave related his story."

"But you do now?" Ian asked.

"Aye, I do."

The woman with frizzy hair stepped forward. "But what happened to Lisbet? Her family? The village?"

"They are all gone, including the Sorn keep. Murdered by English soon after Olave left." He shrugged his shoulders. "I told you the tale ended poorly."

Colin clapped his hands, indicating the tale was done.

He slyly studied the room. Many were openly nervous; others tried to hide their unease. It was just as he had hoped. He looked at Conor, who lifted his quaich silently to him and nodded. Soon the tale would be repeated over and over again throughout the clan.

It was the Dunstans' last chance.

Colin closed the door to the solar and watched as Makenna carefully removed the gold threads intertwined in her hair. It had been a long night ending in quiet retrospection. As clan members headed toward their homes, Makenna had taken Colin's hand and led him back to their room. There she had let go and begun to prepare for bed.

He had expected her to question his story, his motives, what he hoped to accomplish, yet she said not a word. Makenna glided about the room as she prepared for bed. Nothing she did was out of the ordinary. Still, every graceful movement was far more sensual, far more feminine than he could ever remember.

Makenna pulled at the long lace to free her gown and slithered out of it. Lifting a hand to push an errant tendril of auburn hair back behind her ear, she could feel Colin's blue eyes riveted to every move she made. Pleasure derived from feminine power washed over her.

Colin watched her smile light the deep emerald windows to her soul. He knew that look very well. Makenna wanted him, and she had invented a new version of foreplay. Never did he realize how incredibly arousing it could be just to watch her prepare for bed. He forced himself to enjoy the gift until he could no longer contain his restraint.

Only a single piece of her clothing remained to be shed—her chemise. One side of the semidiaphanous garment slipped off her shoulder as she moved to sit on the edge of the hearth chair. As she brushed her hair back over her shoulder, Makenna's chest thrust outward, emphasizing the tempting outline of her full breasts and the pink, erect nipples barely hidden beneath the thin cloth.

Slowly she edged her leg out to balance herself as she moved to brush the other side. In doing so, the chemise rose above her knee and with each stroke edged farther up her thigh. She was exquisite.

Colin remembered the first time he kissed her by the loch and how alive she had made him feel. He had been unprepared for Makenna. The first time they had made love, he discovered how lonely he had been, how much he needed what she gave him. Then she had told him she loved him.

He hoped she loved him enough.

Makenna heard his belt rattle on the chest, and then the sound of a thick cloth falling on the floor. She hesitated for a moment and then continued her brush-strokes again.

Colin sank into the chair beside her and stretched out his limbs, hoping that the rest would calm his arousal enough for him to hear the words that would set his heart free or doom him to loneliness. "What did you think about tonight?"

Makenna stopped brushing and turned to look at him. The masculine hunger in him was palpable. She knew that she had stirred his desire and yet he wanted to talk . . . no, he *needed* to talk. Maybe he knew . . .

Makenna swallowed and replied nervously, "You mean the story about Olave?"

"Aye, I mean Olave."

Relief surged through her. "I thought I would like to

meet your Olave and his Hazel someday. Although it has taken him a while, I am glad he has her."

"Do you not feel for Lisbet?"

Understanding crept into Makenna's eyes. This strong man, so secure and sure of himself, needed reassurance he wasn't going to lose her. "Aye, but she was a fool. I understand the desire to listen to one's family, but to ignore your heart is unwise." Their eyes locked. "I would never be so foolish, Colin," she promised in a quiet, but firm voice. "If I had been Lisbet, I would have followed Olave to the ends of the earth."

"And if those ends were in the Highlands?"

"I love Lochlen and these lands, Colin, but I love you even more. Wherever you decide to live, I and our children shall reside there as well," Makenna vowed, hinting of their impending family.

Choked with emotion, Colin sat still, absorbing what she said and what it meant. He would never be lonely again. "God, Makenna, I need you so very much."

"I know. I need you, too," she whispered back.

He shook his head. He knew he needed to say the words, have her understand. Never before had they been hard to say, but then never before had they meant so very much. "That's not what I meant. I love you, Makenna."

The three words she had longed to hear, but never thought she would. Makenna pressed the back of her hand to her mouth and bit down on her knuckle. She watched the flames bounce against the blackened stone walls. Colin was waiting for her to speak, wanting her to acknowledge him in some way, but this was not something she could just accept. Those words had the power to destroy her.

Makenna lowered her hand and spoke. "Colin, please

don't. Don't say it if you don't mean it. What we have is good enough, but it won't be if you lie to me."

Her voice was hollow and filled with pain, and Colin knew then the agony he had inadvertently inflicted upon her. He reached over and clasped her hand, pulling them both up out of their chairs. Colin folded her tightly against him for several minutes before framing her face in his hands, forcing her to look at him. No one had ever looked at him the way Makenna did. The love in her eyes was so bright and clear, he knew it would never waver, regardless of what was to happen.

"If I lost you, it would destroy me. You are the most important thing in my world. I have never felt for anyone what I feel for you. It's so strong it terrifies me. I can deny it no longer, to you or to me. I never thought it was possible to love someone as much as I love you."

Colin loved her.

Without saying a word, she lifted her face and kissed him, slowly, deeply. Powerful emotions raged through him. Wild, desperate hunger flooded him.

He shrugged off his leine and turned her around, leaning her back against him. The heaviness of his arousal pressed into her buttocks, reminding her of the heat and strength of his body. Makenna could feel his breathing. It matched her own—excited, uncontrolled, ragged with need.

Makenna felt his fingertips slowly maneuver the chemise off her shoulders. The sensual movement captivated all her senses.

His hands shook as he drew his palm down between her breasts and over the small curve of her stomach and then lower. Makenna grabbed his thighs and felt his muscles flexing beneath her hands.

The full, heavy heat of his erection rubbed against her backside as she squirmed beneath his touch. "I need to touch you, love, so very much." It was half plea, half demand.

She arched herself against him as his fingers cupped the heat of her, pushing aside the tight curls of her red hair. Slowly, at an almost torturous pace, he edged a finger inside the already slick, hot channel.

Makenna cried out softly and closed her eyes. He was driving her wild with need of him. She wanted to order him to throw her on the bed and bury himself in her, but she just trembled, losing her ability to speak or stand. Colin held her upright and continued to tease her senses with his fingers. She writhed within his grip, grabbing his neck, pleading for more. She was so incredibly hot.

Makenna shuddered beneath the sensual onslaught. She thought she was going to die from pleasure, but did not pull back from it.

"God, Makenna, I don't think I am going to live through this if I wait any longer," Colin groaned as he drew her back toward the bed.

Makenna moaned a soft whimper mirroring his own need. The primitive erotic sound nearly drove Colin mad. He came down on top of her and pulled her into his arms. She didn't resist. Colin growled and sought the intimate connection with her body.

Makenna's need for him was beyond urgent. Her body took control. She parted her thighs wide for him, and he lowered himself over her. He gripped her hips, and Makenna felt Colin's broad shaft brush against her, probing gently. Unwilling to wait, Makenna met his exploration with an upward thrust of her hips and they were one.

Colin pulled out and drove slowly into her again, feeling her close around him, clinging to him. She was incredibly hot, wet, and so very tight. She was more than ready for him.

Makenna captured his lips and dove into his warm mouth, kissing him with an almost violent need. She crushed her body against him, rocking, taking him deeper and deeper inside her with each thrust.

Suddenly, Makenna arched against his aggressive hardness and cried out. Colin answered her with an explosive climax so overwhelming he shouted out her name again and again. He was out of control. He was safe. He was loved.

Their bodies were damp with perspiration, and the scent of their love filled the air. Colin didn't think he had the strength left in him to roll away from her and decided to kiss her instead. First, he kissed her brow, then the tip of her nose. Then he captured her lips, kissing her slowly, taking his time, letting her feel the endless need and love inside him.

"You are so beautiful," he muttered, awed.

"I'm a complete mess," she countered, her voice still husky with passion.

"I'm the luckiest man in the world," Colin sighed with a sense of peace deeper than he had ever known.

Makenna put her arms around him and stroked the sleek, muscled contours of his back. "Why do you say that?"

Her deep green eyes were dark with passion and love. He had never known such contentment. "With the exception of my parents, and to a degree my brothers, I have never felt completely accepted by another soul. I didn't realize how lonely I had been until that night at the loch when you first told me you loved me. The depth of your confession shook me deeply. I couldn't sort out my emotions. The only thing I knew was that I wanted you more than ever, and that I had to protect you."

"People say they love each other every day. You heard it many times from Deirdre. Why should my declaration be so different?"

"People fall in love every day, and their love *is* real. But it is a rare thing for a man to be completely loved by another. To be accepted without question. To be trusted with blind faith. My parents had such a bond. They would fight, sometimes furiously, but oh, how they loved. Visiting Conor last year, I realized that he had found it with Laurel. You've seen them. It is as if they are each parts of the other. Watching them reminded me how rare it was to find someone to share your life with that loves you in that way. I knew then that I would never know the solace it brings. The day I married you I asked you to trust me, and you did, more than anyone had ever done before."

"Many men have trusted you with their lives."

Colin rolled onto his back and tucked his arm beneath his head. "Not like that. It is one thing to rely on someone to save your life, but it's another to trust someone with the *quality* of your life. The latter takes a far greater leap of faith. You gave that to me, almost from the very beginning. Without it, I don't know if I would ever have had the courage to love again." Colin turned to his side and captured her gaze with his own. "And that is why I am so lucky."

"You are luckier than you think." Makenna sighed as Colin pushed the heavy weight of her hair aside and started a trail of kisses down her throat.

"Aye, I sure am," he murmured against her skin, ready to show her again just how much he loved her.

"If being completely loved by one Dunstan is enough to make you lucky, how about being loved by two?"

Colin craned his head back and propped himself up on his elbows. He furrowed his brows questioningly. "By two?" he asked, not understanding.

"Aye, by two. Me and our child, whom I have no doubt will love you and think you are the most wonderful father in the world, just as you are a husband," she clarified while scattering small kisses along his chin and neck.

"A baby?" he croaked. "We're going to have a baby?"

"Aye, in the late spring. Are you sure that you are fine with the idea? I know it is soon. We have not been married long, and you have so much on your mind with the—"

Colin lightly pressed his finger on her lips and then slowly released them. His eyes were alight with pleasure. "It is not too soon, though you may think so tomorrow when I assign a hundred men to follow you about and see to your safety." He bent his head and again started kissing the sensitive areas of her neck before moving lower.

Makenna swatted playfully at his shoulder. "A hundred men! Gorten and Brodie are more than enough and listen to me—nothing is going to change. I will be more careful, but I am not going to sit about through the winter. I would go mad. Do you hear me, Colin? *Nothing* is going to change."

Colin stopped his foray, his eyes dancing. "*Nothing*, Makenna? Then, I guess we should continue with my most favorite time of the day." Just the thought of burying himself within her sent another rush of desire through his veins. Tonight he was going to indulge himself in a detailed exploration of her body. Every inch of her would be recommitted to his memory.

"And which time is that, husband?" Makenna asked,

trembling as he traced the lines of her jaw with his fingertips.

His smile broadened. "The times I get to ravish your body again and again throughout the night," he reminded her as he lowered his mouth to her breast. The taste of it sent a shudder of excitement through him.

"As I said, *nothing* is going to change," she affirmed between gasps as his mouth trailed down past her navel. Sexual tension seized her insides. She shuddered again as Colin tasted the very heart of her. Tonight she would remember for the rest of her life.

Chapter Sixteen

Late the next morning, Makenna met Laurel and Ceridwin in the great hall. Immediately, Laurel could tell the previous night's events had continued quite favorably for her friend after she had left the party.

"So you have finally arrived. I take it Colin knows about the expected expansion of the McTiernay clan?"

Ceridwin turned in the chair abruptly. "You are going to have a baby?"

Makenna's grin broadened even farther. "Indeed, I am."

"And Colin is happy." Laurel's statement was more a question than clarification.

"Colin is *more* than happy," Makenna confirmed, turning to face Ceridwin. "I have decided that you and Drake shall move into my sister's old room. I doubt Ula will be returning, and there is no reason it should collect dust from nonuse. Besides, she had the most wonderful view from her window."

Ceridwin sat in shocked silence, her hazel eyes wide with surprise. Drake didn't want to delay their marriage, but neither of them wanted to stay with her aunts, and as a soldier he had never had a need for his own cottage.

"Really? I mean, to live in the castle . . . it's such an honor."

"Nonsense. It's silly not to make use of those rooms, and I am feeling incredibly generous today."

"But what about the laird . . . ?"

"It just so happens Colin is feeling just as generous as I this morning," Makenna remarked. "Shall we go now and see what must be done?"

Nodding, Ceridwin leapt out of the chair and followed Makenna and Laurel into the inner yard. They made their way quickly to the tower that acted as a hub for the rear curtain wall.

Laurel was the first to enter the room. Makenna heard her sister-in-law's sharp intake of breath and knew instantly there was something wrong. Squeezing between the stone doorway and a frozen Laurel, Makenna walked into the room and felt her blood begin to boil. Ceridwin must have come in as well, for Makenna heard her squeak, "Oh my."

Tapestries were shredded and on the floor. What bedding was left was ripped and ruined. Hearth ashes were thrown everywhere. Worst of all was the McTiernay plaid. It hung over the hearth, burned, leaving only scraps and pieces to prove what it once was.

Laurel sensed the extreme tension winding in Makenna and knew she needed to get her out of the room immediately. With Ceridwin's help, Laurel managed to get Makenna out of the tower and back into the yard.

Once outside, Laurel began rubbing Makenna's arms now shaking with rage. "I don't think it was recent, Makenna. There was quite a bit of dust collected, so the steps you took to remove the staff you didn't trust probably worked."

"My home!" Makenna hissed through gritted teeth.

She shrugged Laurel's arms off her and bunched her fists. "How dare they!"

Ceridwin bit her bottom lip and fought back tears. "It may be only one person. Perhaps, Lela . . ."

"Aye, it was Lela, but there were others. Others who *knew* what she was planning and did nothing about it."

Laurel took a deep breath knowing that if this had occurred in her home, she would be just as furious. "You need to tell Colin, Makenna. It's time he knew the full extent of what has been happening. And while you have every right to be angry, you must calm down. You are too early into your pregnancy. I have seen more than one woman lose her babe under emotional stress."

Makenna took several deep breaths. "You are right. I will *not* let them take my child from me. And it is time I told Colin what is happening. He is planning something and should know."

Laurel let go the deep breath she was holding. "Ceridwin and I will check the other unused rooms and then meet you in the hall."

Makenna nodded in agreement and then left.

"Should we go with her?" Ceridwin asked, looking a little alarmed.

"What if it were you and Drake?" Laurel countered.

"Aye, I'd want to be alone."

"Just know that the next time you see Colin, his anger is not *at* Makenna, but *for* her. I hope the Dunstans are ready, because very soon, I doubt it will matter anymore to Colin if they are."

Makenna knocked and then opened the door to Colin's dayroom located on the second floor of Canmore Tower. With Colin were his brother, Drake,

Dunlop, and few other men she recognized from Conor's guard.

Colin was surprised to see her and waved her over. As Makenna neared, the expression on her face conveyed more than any words she could have uttered. "What's wrong?" he demanded softly.

Makenna shivered at the coldness in his voice. "There has been another incident. Someone wrecked Ula's room. The tapestries were ripped, most of the bedding was ruined, and what was of any value was stolen. Very little can be salvaged. Laurel is right now with Ceridwin investigating the other unused rooms of the castle."

Conor waved at Seamus. "Go find Laurel and do not leave her side until I say otherwise."

Makenna watched as the tall, thin, handsome man left the room. Horrified that she left her friend in harm, she asked, "My God, Colin, is Laurel in danger?"

"No, but it would ease Conor's mind to know that she is protected."

Makenna crumpled into the empty seat vacated by Seamus. "This is my fault. It was my decision not to maintain the vacant rooms. It was my decision not to tell you everything that has been happening."

"There is more?"

She nodded. "I've only been telling you some of the things that have occurred, but there have been many harrassments. Until today, they have been aggravating, but relatively minor. But Ula's room . . . it was a deliberate attack against you and me. I could rip Lela's hair out by the roots. I know it was her."

Colin moved in close and clasped her fingertips in his hands with gentle authority. She didn't realize how cold she was. "Listen to me, none of this is your fault. I will take care of this. You are not to do anything. I know you want to find Lela, but don't. I need you to trust me."

Before she could answer, Colin rose and leaned against his fists on the round table in the room. "Drake, you were about to tell me about last night. How many?"

Makenna stared at the muscles in Colin's back, tense underneath his leine. She was seeing the strategic Colin, the planner. Last night he had been father and husband, and she had seen him as laird in many circumstances, but this was the first time she had witnessed him as a warrior preparing for battle.

Drake sat across the table. His jaws were clenched together. "At least a hundred have moved in across the loch. They haven't budged since they arrived at daylight."

"They're waiting for a signal," Conor surmised.

Drake nodded in agreement. "Aye, we think so. We didn't want to risk being seen to find out."

Colin turned toward Dunlop. "And what did you discover?"

The guard stopped stroking his chin. It was clear that he, too, was very disturbed at the timing of Makenna's news. "Just as you suspected. He has help from at least two clans, but neither leader is going public with his support. We saw several changing into MacCuaig colors."

"How many men?"

"Two, possibly three hundred of his forces are waiting in plain view just outside the southern border of Dunstan lands, perhaps two hours out on horseback. No doubt there are many more hidden."

Colin bent his head and studied the grain on the table for a moment. When he spoke, his voice was full of authority and decision. "Drake, move the men along the ridge and wait for my signal."

"Today, then?"

"Aye," Colin answered solemnly. "It is time for the Dunstans to learn the might of my sword and the meaning of its absence. My wife and child will be with people of honor, and if the Dunstans cannot find their integrity, Lochlen is theirs; I want it no longer. Move all the men along the ridge."

"*All* the men?" Dunlop asked, somewhat surprised.

"Every last one of them. When it is time, I want only a sea of McTiernay soldiers to be in sight." Dunlop inclined his head and left with Drake.

Conor rose with easy confidence. "I'll order my men to remain hidden in the hills. I'll talk to Laurel and then will meet you at the stables. I'm sending Laurel to my forces when I leave. Do you want Makenna to go with her?"

Standing, Makenna reached out and grasped Colin's arm. "Colin, what is happening?"

Colin turned and said, "My hope is to mend this clan and bring them together, united under my leadership. I might have been willing to remain here until they were ready. Now I no longer care. Only you and the baby are important. I like Lochlen, I admire the Dunstan determination, but I will no longer stand by and wait while they persecute my family. Today, your clan will either prove they trust me, or you, my men, and I will leave." He brushed his mouth lightly across hers before adding, "I need you to prepare to leave immediately. Pack only what is necessary and meet Laurel and Ceridwin by the gatehouse. Four soldiers will be waiting to take you three to Lammermuir Hills, where Conor's force is waiting."

"But would it not be better, safer, to remain here?"

Colin chuckled, pulling her close. "There are over a hundred of Conor's men in those hills. You will be quite safe there."

Makenna shrugged within his embrace and rested her head against his chest. "Your force may be smaller, Colin, but I am quite sure I would be just as safe with your men as I would be with Conor's."

Colin gripped her head between his hands and kissed

her forehead with a surge of exasperation and pride. "My force is not smaller, love. Over a thousand of my men are lining up on that ridge. Men loyal to me, not the Dunstans. And if I pull out of Lochlen, I want you already safe and gone. Trust me."

Makenna gave him one last hug, praying that her people heard what he had tried to tell them last night. Heard and paid heed to the warning.

Makenna was packing her bag when she remembered Camus. She quickly dashed out of the tower and across the courtyard. There was one more thing she had to get. She refused to leave without it. And, if possible, give it to Colin before he faced her people.

Laurel saw Makenna heading toward the inner gatehouse and moved to intercept her. "Makenna, over here! I am waiting for Ceridwin to finish packing. She is coming with us."

Makenna gave a curt nod of gratitude for taking care of her new friend. "I must get to the armory before Colin leaves."

Laurel put out a hand to stall her. "The armory? I don't think . . ."

Makenna's smile was without humor. "You don't understand, but you will. I have to hurry if I am going to catch up with Colin. He was going to the stables when I went to pack."

"Makenna, Conor said that you were to come with us. He was very clear."

"Once I leave the armory, I am going to try one last time to convince Colin to let me ride with him."

"But . . ."

Makenna's eyes were the color of jade, firm, resolute and unbending. "I ask you, Laurel, truthfully. Would you not try to be with Conor, show him loyalty, visibly support his decision, if you could? You told me once I might have to choose between Colin and my people. I have chosen. I will always love this land, Lochlen, and my clan, but my loyalties lie first and foremost with my husband. Please say you understand."

Laurel blinked away tears welling up in her eyes. "Yes, if it were Conor, I would want to be there."

Makenna clasped Laurel's hands, thanking her. "I promise to return immediately to the stables if Colin says no. I won't argue, I promise. Ten minutes is all I need. If I do not meet you there, then you will know that I have persuaded him to let me come."

Laurel embraced Makenna, fighting a growing sense of unease. "Hurry, Makenna," she whispered. "Ceridwin and I will wait for you."

Makenna gave one last squeeze before letting go. "I will and take care, my newest sister."

Laurel watched as Makenna disappeared through the last portcullis hurrying toward the right. Moments later Ceridwin and she headed toward the stables and waited.

Colin marched across the outer yard heading for the stables. Dunlop met him halfway and handed him the reins of his horse. He had seen Colin in many moods, but the cold anger that had flared to life that morning would chill anyone who looked upon him, even his own men.

Retrieving the leather strips held out for him, Colin looked up. The dark sky was overcast, but it was not yet raining. Most likely, it would not break loose until night-fall, and then it would rain heavily. One way or another, this matter would be closed by then.

Seeing Camus across the yard, Colin signaled him. The sword smith raised a bronzed, wizened hand and then disappeared inside his shop. Heavy pounding of a horse approached from behind. His brother was ready.

"Shall we ride?" Conor asked, pulling his dark stallion to a stop beside Colin.

"Almost," Colin answered. "I am waiting on Camus and then we will go."

As if on cue, Camus appeared again carrying a very large clublike weapon reinforced on the end with a thick metal used in armor and battle-axes. "Per your specifications, I believe, Laird," he said curiously as he handed over the heavy object.

Colin took the macelike club in one hand and examined it. "Aye, this is exactly what I need. If you are ready, get a horse and ride to the *Lammermuir Hills.*"

"I'm ready," Camus replied, patting a bag he had swung over his shoulder.

Colin threw the heavy object at Conor and mounted his horse. Grabbing it, Conor grunted at the weight and then turned it over appreciatively. Lifting his brows in approval, he silently praised Camus's workmanship. "Fine instrument. It should do quite nicely."

Colin reclaimed the weapon and faced Dunlop. "Are they expecting me?"

Dunlop nodded and replied through stiff lips, "They are. Word was sent you were coming. They are gathering by the Commune Tree near the wall. No doubt more will come at the moment of your arrival."

Colin's face hardened, his expression ominous. "Then let us ride."

Seconds later the group headed toward the outer gate and proceeded directly to the town wall. Colin rode out front, keeping the gait slow and steady as he rode deliberately alongside the wall. Conor and Dunlop remained a safe distance back knowing what was about to happen.

Colin could feel the crowd growing and following

him. He felt no pity. Mercy now would hurt them more than compassion.

The moment Colin reached the first and widest sabotaged section of the wall he swung the large club and let it crash into the weakened stones. They crumbled instantly upon the collision.

Moving forward, Colin swung again and then again. Each time the wall caved under the assault. Arriving at the second intentionally weakened section, he swung the club one last time and the stones shattered all around him.

He threw the club at the crowd, causing several to jump back or be hit. He exited through the broken wall. Conor and Dunlop joined him.

Colin stopped and sat still for several moments staring at the fidgeting assemblage, the expression in his eyes unreadable. The gathering continued to swell. Many moved outside the broken pieces of evidence that proved their disloyalty. They waited in silence, unnerved by their laird's cold and distant behavior.

Finally, Colin spoke. "The Dunstans are a proud clan, one weakened by wars. You needed an army to protect you, and I started building one. I had hoped to see the Dunstans grow again into a powerful family of Scotland."

Colin looked out, capturing the twitching eyes of several village clan leaders one by one. His face remained a stony mask, his normally bright blue eyes dangerously dark. "My wife wanted the same for you. Her love for her people was so great that she married this Highlander and learned how to be the Lady of Lochlen, a position she never aspired to have. Makenna wanted to make you proud. She hoped you would accept her and allow her to help you make your lives better." His rapier glance passed over the masses, chilling them with its coldness. "But you chose to reject the kindness offered by her generous heart."

Colin pointed to the portion of the wall no longer standing. "You do not want the safety being offered to you by a Highlander. You would rather help would-be attackers and have enemies raid your home than live under a McTiernay's rule."

Reaching down, he pulled out his sword. Colin held the crowd still, his eyes now burning with raw hurt and pained acknowledgment of what he must do. "I accept your decree. Return to your castle. Give your wall as a gift to a new laird that will make you happy. For while I will lose this castle and the lands to which I have lost blood and lives, I will leave with my pride, my self-respect, and my family," he said smoothly. "But I will also be *taking my sword.*"

The crowd watched in half shock, half horror as Colin raised his claymore up in the air. Over a thousand soldiers appeared on the ridge.

Turning to face his men, he punched his sword higher into the air. "With whom do you stand?" he roared, his voice full of command.

Every one of them including Dunlop, who had been watching in silence alongside Conor, raised his sword and yelled, "McTiernay!" The echoes of their definitive loyalty could be heard for miles.

Colin pulled the right rein and rotated back toward the sea of visibly shaken faces. His blue eyes were flat, hard, and remote even as understanding flooded into their expressions. McTiernay was not as weak as they had been led to believe. He had amassed an army loyal to him that could defeat any enemy. They were not stronger or better off under MacCuaig. They had made a terrible mistake and were about to pay the price.

Colin was just about to direct his black toward his men and ride away, when a voice rang out in the crowd. "It was not all of us! Not even most of us betrayed you!

Do not leave us defenseless for what only a few did!" the voice cried. It was Gannon's.

Colin stopped abruptly. His stern-faced expression leveled onto the steward's. The muscle in the side of Colin's jaw flexed, indicating how deep his anger ran. "Did you not?" Colin challenged, his voice filled with condemnation. "Can one of you tell me that you were innocent of knowing about the treachery taking place around you? Can you give me your word that you knew nothing, Gannon? Can you swear an oath that you had no knowledge of who acted against my wife? *Your own lady*?"

Colin slowly surveyed the rest of them and demanded, "Can any of you claim you knew not of the town wall's weakened state or who caused it? Betrayal comes in many forms, but those cowards who know of treachery and do nothing hold even less value to me than those who actively support my enemy's cause."

His voice was laced with dark accusations, ones none of them could refute. Any hope that he would change his mind vanished when Colin spurred his horse and rode away with Conor and Dunlop. Upon joining his men, he led them north, away from Lochlen toward the Highlands. He never once looked back.

Chapter Seventeen

Three hours after leaving Lochlen, Colin amassed his men on the western side of the Lammermuir Hills. The clouds had thickened, causing the sky to hint of dusk versus early afternoon. Rain was imminent.

Colin roamed clasping arms and greeting men he had not seen for months. Expressions of eagerness and respect stared back at him. Dunlop squeezed his shoulder to get his attention and pointed to a group of men apart from the crowd. "Drake's leaders are assembled and waiting for us. Conor has already joined them."

Colin nodded and approached the small gathering. He supported Drake's decision to divide the men into ten mixed-skilled groups, each with its own leader that reported to him. Now they reported to Colin. "It is good to see you again. I shared your frustration these past several weeks at being forced to remain hidden until today. But your patience has paid off. Drake has told me why he selected you, and I stand behind his decision. You ten will now form my elite guard with Dunlop and Drake as your commanders." Colin scanned the group, finding his brother there for support, but not interfering. "Conor, is Seamus here?"

"I just sent him to the hills to prepare my men. I plan to follow once we are done here."

"Then I will ride with you. I want to make sure Makenna is well before we return."

"Are we going back?" asked one of the guards.

"Aye, we are going back. MacCuaig is most likely invading as we speak, looking for us and finding us gone. He will be sloppy, seeking ways to relieve his frustration. I expect a villager or two to arrive any moment and ask for our help. Each of you, rally your men and prepare for battle."

Immediately the small cluster of leaders disassembled to carry out their orders. Excitement buzzed all around them. For too long they had been away from Lochlen waiting for a chance to rid their home of threats and deceit.

"Dunlop, ensure that the men are ready to move upon my return. Drake, if you want to see that lass of yours, you best ride with Conor and me to the hills."

Colin was moving toward his black tied with several other horses when he saw three riders coming from the south. He mounted and rode partway to meet them, his face expressionless. Conor and Drake followed.

The three riders slowed, each in various states of nervousness and fright. One of them was Ian. The defiance had left his eyes; his posture no longer carried the rebellious attitude. It was he who spoke. "Laird?"

Colin eyed him with a calculating expression. "I am no longer your laird. Go back to your home."

Overwhelming panic invaded the young man's face. His brave countenance wavered. "We've come to ask you to return. We know now how wrong we were. What you said was true. Though we never saw ourselves as such, we were the cowards you claimed us to be."

"Your needs and fears are no longer my concern," Colin said flatly.

Hot, furious tears burned in Ian's eyes. "They *are* your concern. You are our laird, and right now enemy soldiers are entering our lands and occupying Lochlen!" Panic filled his voice. The clan's only chance was Colin's return.

"Then you must be happy to have a Lowland laird so amenable to your customs, ways, and values," Colin replied, his voice remote.

A skinny redheaded boy approximately fifteen years old spoke up. "You misunderstand. *MacCuaig* has invaded Lochlen with several hundred men. The clan leaders have told him that we will not accept him. *You* are our laird, and we will fight until you return to our side."

"He threatened to kill us, Laird," added the youngest of the three boys. "Our father told us to ride and find you. That you are honorable and would come back to defend us. That you would not let MacCuaig kill loyal Dunstans."

"Is he right? Are you going to return?" Ian asked directly. A thin flicker of hope burned in his eyes.

Colin's blue gaze studied Ian. He knew the boy was frightened and ashamed for his previous behavior. Still, he came. "Aye," Colin said gently, followed by a very firm "Follow us." He kicked his horse into a gallop toward Lammermuir Hills. The three boys didn't have a chance to ask why they were heading away from the battle and toward the rocky mounds everyone knew better than to try and cross. A half hour later, their questions were answered without ever being asked.

Ian looked down at the mass of men below as they descended the sloping path toward the hidden army. Armed with bows, broadswords, battle-axes, and halberds, they clearly were soldiers preparing for battle.

"Those are Laird Moncreiffe's men!" gasped Ian, taking in the huge numbers. In addition, there were plaids from Boyd and Crawford. "Are those *Donovan* colors I see? Aren't they with MacCuaig?"

Colin smiled and clapped the young man on the back. "All part of the plan," he said and then rode on ahead, leaving the young man gaping.

Conor came up beside the stunned lad. "He knew," Ian stammered. "The laird knew all along what was going to happen. Probably even knew we'd come after him."

Conor let go a loud snort. "Of course my brother knew! Colin is your laird, and lucky for you he is a Highland McTiernay. Nobody better at planning battles."

"Did he *ever* plan on leaving?"

"Not that I am aware of. Colin needed to expose two enemies simultaneously, MacCuaig and those Dunstans truly disloyal to him." Conor leaned over and whispered, "If you had joined Colin when he asked, you would have been in on the plan."

Ian's eyes popped open wide with realization. "Was there ever an Olave?"

"Aye, Olave lives and is happily married to Hazel. Not an aspect of the story was embellished. It all happened as Colin related."

"But if it were true, then why didn't the laird leave, like Olave?"

"Ah, you forgot the end of the story, young Dunstan. What did Olave say when Lisbet asked him to stay?"

"He said something about knowing where he belongs."

"Aye, and accepting the price that comes with it. Your laird knows where he should be, here at Lochlen, leading and supporting the Dunstan clan. If Colin had any doubts, he never would have married Lady Makenna."

"Was she the price he paid?"

"No, his foolish pride was the price. And know this,

Ian, when a man finally abandons his youthful ideas of how things should be and embraces people as they are, he gains something more powerful in return, something a man can take true pride in."

"What does he get?"

"For your laird? It was his wife. For you? I don't know. Each man has to discover that on his own," Conor answered. Laughing gently, he pushed the young man on the shoulder and edged his horse into a lope to join Colin. It had been a relaxing couple of weeks watching his baby brother run a clan and formulate plans, but he was itching for action. Any more leisure and he would slowly go mad.

"I'm going to find Laurel. I want her to start planning our trip home," Conor hinted as soon as he reached Colin.

Deftly, Colin maneuvered his black through the thick crowd of men. "I'll go with you. I have a need to tell my wife that her people are with us, and we will not be leaving Lochlen." Colin threw a speculative, sidelong glance at Conor. "I am not surprised you are ready to leave. If positions were reversed, I might not have made it so long. Your sacrifice is appreciated. Sending Seamus along made a good show when enticing the other lairds to join us. It is one thing to say you have the support of the McTiernays, it is another to show it."

Conor was about to reply when Seamus appeared with Drake beside him. Colin swung off his horse and clasped his commander around the shoulders. "Ceridwin here?" Colin asked, knowing how Drake felt about his future bride.

"Aye, she is with Laurel and Lairds Moncreiffe and Crawford."

"And Makenna?" Colin asked, looking in the direction Drake had pointed.

"I have not seen her, but I did not think to ask."

Conor clasped his brother's shoulder. "Come, she rode with Laurel. My wife will know where she is. No doubt off sparring with one of your soldiers teaching them a couple of maneuvers right before they go to battle."

The tease in Conor's voice received him a sharp elbow to the ribs. "So my wife spars with men. I admit that I am not fond of the idea, but I am man enough to admit that she is damn good. If she had the strength, Makenna could lay any man out. Possibly even me."

"Such praise! Come on, brother, and let's find our wives. It's going to be a long afternoon and if the clouds tell true, a wet one. I shall need a quick reminder of what awaits me when this skirmish is done."

The crowd parted as Colin and Conor neared the small group of leaders. Seeing Conor, Laurel smiled and rushed to his side. Then she tried to look around Colin's large frame for her friend. "Colin! Wherever are you hiding Makenna?"

Colin looked at Laurel quizzically. "Why would I be hiding Makenna? Is she not here with you?"

The blood drained out of Laurel's face, leaving her ashen white. "No," she murmured, grabbing Conor's arm for support. "She's with you."

Fear gripped Colin's heart. He had to have heard wrong, misunderstood. "What do you mean she's with me?"

Laurel licked her lips, panic filling her green-blue eyes. "Makenna said she had to get something from the armory and join *you*. She promised that it would be all right because she would be with *you* if she did not return. Makenna told us if she did not meet us at the stables, then she had gotten your approval to ride with you and show her clan that you had her complete support. I swear, Colin, that we waited twice the time Makenna told us to before we left. But if you are here, where is she?"

Colin stood transfixed. Icy fear seized his heart. If Makenna had not found him and she had not returned as promised, only one explanation remained. She was in the hands of MacCuaig.

Conor moved his distraught wife to a nearby makeshift bench and made her sit down. Returning, he said evenly, "How do you wish to proceed? MacCuaig might have ordered her to leave."

"No," Colin choked. "What you don't understand, what even I didn't understand until recently was why MacCuaig was even interested in the Dunstans. He already had a clan, money, and an army. What he wanted was Makenna, and God, Conor, he now has her."

"We will get her back," Conor promised, trying to evoke a feeling of hope rather than the fear coursing through him.

"No, you lead the attack as planned in the village. I will go after my wife, and God help MacCuaig when I find him."

Makenna watched as the elongated shadow moved down the small staircase and into the room where she was held bound. The dim light coming in from the door indicated it was mid to late afternoon. The mounting humidity in the already damp storage room promised rain.

Leon MacCuaig entered and stared at his captive with a sick look of satisfaction.

Makenna glared back wishing she had been just a little faster at Camus's this morning. She had searched almost everywhere in the small shop before finding the claymore carefully wrapped and hidden behind several crates. It must have been during those precious moments that Colin had left.

Exiting the shop, Makenna heard the thunderous pounds Colin was generating against the town walls. She had been too late.

Immediately, she ran back to the solar to grab her bag when she heard footsteps ascending the staircase. The thudding echoes were followed by a low questioning hiss, "Makenna? Where are you? I know that you are here. I saw you enter. Now don't make me chase after you, especially after all I have done just to have you be mine. Come out and show me how appreciative you are."

Knowing there was no escape, Makenna hid the sword underneath the mattress and exited the solar. That had been five hours ago.

Leon stared at his bound captive. When Makenna had met him willingly on the staircase, he hoped she would be reasonable. He had been disappointed. Her greeting had been filled with acid, not the appreciation due to him.

He should have expected the reaction, he told himself. The woman had endured a Highlander for nearly five months. It was bound to addle her mind temporarily. And while he was not a patient man, Leon knew Makenna would see reason eventually. As soon as she realized the Highlander had left her as well as her clan, she would know Leon was the man for her.

Leon circled around Makenna, stopping when he got in front of her, caressing her cheek with his knuckles. He reached behind and removed her gag. "Have we calmed down a bit? I somewhat regretted having to restrain you like that, my dear, but then I couldn't risk you calling for help. Now, as you might have surmised, you can yell all you want and no one will hear you. No one but my men. Your famed Highlander has left the Borders and you with them." His rich-timbred voice was oozing with poisonous charm.

Makenna stared at the madman in silence. There was no point warning the crazed man that Colin would never leave without her.

"What do you want, Leon?" Makenna asked, wincing as she struggled against the ropes binding her wrists to the chair. Her flesh ripped again, and new blood dripped down her hands.

Leon motioned for one of his guards to release her. "That is simple. I want you and only you. I, of course, will take Lochlen as my main residence for your benefit."

Makenna rotated her freed wrists. They burned. Placing her hands on her lap, she examined her captor, twisting her lips into a cynical smile. "Leon, you are ten times the fool I thought you were. You must know that you will soon die by my husband's hands." Makenna paused, lancing him with her vivid emerald eyes. "I just hope he lets me watch," she said, full of sincerity.

Leon's growl grew into a scream. He marched over, grabbed her hair, and pulled her against him. Eyes of golden rage stared obliviously into Makenna's green pools of revulsion. He was too consumed with his own hate to recognize the full extent of hers.

"Your Highlander is soon going to be dead," Leon hissed. "And the moment he exists no longer, you will be free to fulfill your true destiny and become my wife."

"Never," Makenna spat, waiting unflinchingly for him to retaliate.

Leon threw her violently away from him, causing her to fall out of the chair and onto the dirt floor. About to grab her again, he came to a sudden halt, his eyes coldly furious as an evil smile slinked across his lips. Maybe the redheaded viper just needed some persuasion, and he had just the perfect influencers locked across the yard in the great hall.

"Bring her," he ordered his men and then exited into the courtyard.

Chapter Eighteen

Colin maneuvered down the castle allure, slithering below the walkway on the top of the curtain wall. He glanced back. Dunlop, Drake, and three of his ten commanders were following his lead.

Reentering the castle without alerting anyone to their presence had been fairly simple. Once Conor began the main attack, most of MacCuaig's men had focused on the battle. Those who had not left the outer gate were easily silenced. Ignoring the sizeable number of soldiers guarding the inner gate, Colin headed toward Forfar Tower. Finding the murder hole cleverly nestled at its base, Colin went inside knowing very few were aware of the steep, narrow staircase leading straight to the tower's battlements. On top of the tower, Colin encountered two more MacCuaig soldiers and disposed of them quietly.

Crouching low, Colin scooted down the allure until he reached a secret opening to the hidden passageway leading to the Chapel Tower and slipped in.

Hunching down, Colin led his men down the small corridor leading straight to the confessional chambers. For decades, the postern and passageway served as a discreet way for women to visit the Lochlen's chamberlain.

When Alexander's grandfather dismissed the position and converted the tower to a chapel, the passageway had ceased being used. As far as Colin knew, most clansmen, including the priest, had not even known of its existence. Colin only found out about it after he arrived at Lochlen and spied an odd pattern to the floor of the curtain wall. Colin had asked Alexander about it and agreed to keep it a secret.

About thirty feet from the chamber entrance, Colin stopped cold. A bellow roared from across the courtyard. It was MacCuaig, and he was furious. The little hope Colin was clinging to died. Makenna had not eluded MacCuaig's capture. Only one person could infuriate Leon that much on his perceived hour of victory—Makenna.

Moving quickly, Colin advanced to the small door and freed the latch frozen from years of nonuse. He looked through the peephole, motioning for his men to wait as he pried the heavy wood slats open and stepped through the doorway. He verified the sanctuary was empty and signaled for his men to follow.

Colin held up a clenched fist and immediately all movement ceased. Something was wrong. Very wrong. Besides the distant clanks of metal from Conor's attack, Lochlen was eerily quiet. Had it been abandoned?

Colin moved to the chapel's spiral staircase and descended, indicating for his men to follow but make no sound. Carefully, they emerged out of the tower and crept into the inner yard. Hiding behind a nearby cart of hay, Colin peeked around the tilted box to survey the courtyard. Standing outside Canmore Tower was Leon. Behind him was a fuming Makenna. Surrounding them both were at least a dozen men, maybe more.

One of MacCuaig's men pushed Makenna forcefully,

causing her to lose her step and tumble to the ground. Colin gripped his sword and fought his mounting rage.

He flexed his fingers in an effort to remain coldly detached and methodical as he trained his men to be. It proved to be impossible. Separating oneself from fear to save one's own life was infinitely different from trying to do so when it was someone you loved who was in danger. The only thing restraining him was knowing that if he attacked now, Makenna would most likely be hurt, possibly be killed. He had no choice but to sit silently and wait for an opportunity to present itself.

Dunlop sat huddled beside Colin with his back against the cart and felt his laird tremble with rage. Twisting carefully, Dunlop peered underneath the cart and into the yard. The blood drained out of his face as he witnessed the source of Colin's anger.

Dunlop nudged Drake and was about to gesture for him to look when Makenna's voice rang out clear across the courtyard.

"What about my people?" Makenna demanded, moving to stand up. She brushed the dirt off her gown with the air of a regal queen. Her voice and demeanor were full of calm, but one had only to look into her flashing green eyes to realize the fury within her.

Leon spun around. "*Your* people? You mean *my* people. They will swear allegiance to me, wear my plaid, and pay me the homage I require. If they don't, they die. I will not bandy about with your prideful clan as your dead Highlander did. I will not tolerate disobedience or disloyalty."

Makenna gave him a challenging smile. "My Colin is not dead."

Leon's face turned a blotchy red. "No, but he soon will be. As we speak, my best men are advancing on him. They will wait until he is vulnerable, and then they will strike. No matter how long it takes, I will see you free to fulfill your true destiny."

Makenna narrowed her eyes. "And just what do you see my destiny to be?" she asked through gritted teeth.

Leon advanced until she was just inside his arm's reach. "Why, to *become my wife*," he announced. Before she could back away, his hand sneaked out, gripped her chin, and held it still while he brutally pressed his mouth against her lips.

Colin's heart felt as though it were being ripped from his chest. All he could think of was getting to Makenna. He clutched his sword and was about to attack regardless of the dangers when two MacCuaig guards dragged a dead body through the inner gatehouse and into the courtyard. Leon wrenched free and turned away from the sight.

Makenna wiped her mouth off with her sleeve and stared at the dead young baker. The boy had made her laugh with his smile and quick wit. He would never do so again. He had been badly beaten before someone had sliced his throat. Something inside her went cold. "What's wrong, Leon? The sight of Benny's blood bother you? Or was it his mangled body that made you blanch like an old woman?"

Leon swung around and came within inches of her face, but spoke loud enough to be heard by everyone in the courtyard. "He deserved it! The fool actually tried to stop me from coming after you."

"He was just a boy!" Makenna screamed.

"A boy who was fool enough to defend you!"

"Is that why you brought him here? So I can see what you will do to anyone loyal enough to protect me?"

"I thought he might prove the lengths I will go to have you. Several people in the great hall will suffer the same fate as your *Benny* if you or your people continue to fight me."

Makenna stood wide-eyed realizing MacCuaig was

insane. With anyone else, that would be an empty threat, but MacCuaig was ready to act on his promise. She looked about her. The keep was vacant. The only people in sight were MacCuaig and a dozen of his soldiers. She pushed one out of the way so that she could see the doors of the great hall. Several more men were blocking both the main and kitchen exits.

"What did you do?" she asked, her voice hollow at the promised horror of his answer.

"What any self-respecting laird would do. I am not a fool like McTiernay thinking that I can change the hearts of men loyal to another."

"Loyal to Colin."

"Not just to him. It seems my pretty little Scottish bride has done what many thought impossible. You learned to run a keep and gained the devotion of all who serve you."

"What are you going to do with them?"

"That is up to you, my sweet. You see, they are loyal to you. If you agree to renounce your husband and join me, there is a good chance they will follow your lead, and I will let them live."

Makenna glared at him. What she would give for any kind of weapon. She would die, but so would he. Hope suddenly invaded her thoughts. She did have a weapon. She just needed to get to it.

Makenna eyed him cautiously. For her plan to work, she needed to lead without being obvious. "What about *my* loyalty? Just how do you expect to gain my allegiance, Leon?"

"Mayhap by oppression at first, but I had your heart once before and I will have it again."

Makenna gaped at MacCuaig incredulously. "Do you truly believe I will reject my love for Colin and accept yours?"

"You are many things, Makenna Dunstan, but you are not obtuse. Your Highlander has left, retaining the one thing I admired about the man—his pride. And while his army is considerably bigger than I was led to believe, he would not be foolish enough to attack my considerably larger forces, especially not for a clan who betrayed him."

Makenna arched her brows in disbelief. Leon's eyes glinted like black beetles as his mouth crinkled into a smile. "I can see the surprise and doubt in your eyes. Over two thousand of my men are converging on your stronghold as we speak."

The blood drained out of Makenna's face. "But there is no one here but women, old men, and children!"

Leon clucked his tongue. "Left to defend themselves by your Highlander. Would you like to renounce him now? The man you agreed to marry has left you and your clan vulnerable. I assure you, I protect what I value."

Makenna took a deep breath. Leon MacCuaig was filled with hate and greed, but he was not unintelligent. She would not have multiple chances to make her move. "Colin does as well. I would never renounce him, not even if you forced me in the very bed we share."

Colin felt Dunlop lurch at her words and grabbed the angry commander pulling him back. Dunlop look confused at his laird's unnatural calmness. "Why, Colin? Why would Makenna—"

Colin motioned for him to be quiet. He knew his wife was loyal to him. Makenna must have a reason to goad MacCuaig to their solar. Something was there. Something that would give her an advantage.

"You *will* renounce him, *and* in that very room. Do you think the Highlander will come back for you? A wild Lowlander so incredibly different from his beloved first wife?"

At the mention of her sister, Makenna recoiled. Leon

pounced. "Ah, forgot about her, did you? Do you honestly think that a man who would love Deirdre, could love you? She was everything you are not. Meek, fair, mild, and soft-spoken. I ask you. Do you believe him when he says he loves you? The man was devoted to her. Never left her side, but with you it seems he leaps at the chance. He is gone for weeks at a time, leaving you to deal alone with your troublesome clan. And now, he vanishes for the Highlands without you. How could he promise his heart to you when he had already given it away?"

MacCuaig was speaking the questions aloud she had so often asked to herself. She forced herself to ignore his sharp barbs. Colin did love her.

Leon saw the pain swim in Makenna's eyes and knew that he had guessed correctly. "I have always loved you, and yet you spurned my requests for your hand. I have decided to forgive you for marrying McTiernay. I am here now, and you will never have to see him again. You will be with me. You will be *my* wife."

Makenna jutted her chin into the air and looked at him with mute defiance.

Her silence infuriated him. "I will have you, Makenna," he whispered, yanking her to his side, gripping her so that his fingers bit into her flesh. "I will have you, and you will beg for my forgiveness before this night is over." He thrust her away from him. Makenna stumbled again but remained upright and silent praying that God would grant her last wish. "Lock her in the solar. Search it first. I will be there soon to collect what she will give me."

As she was being dragged away, Makenna finally found her voice and cried out, "And what is that?"

MacCuaig turned back and smirked, "Why, legitimacy, my sweet."

* * *

Outside the town wall, Conor moved his men forward
as Crawford and Donovan flanked the enemy from opposite sides. They had met and ended the majority of
MacCuaig's army by the loch and now moved toward
Lochlen. MacCuaig's men watched in horror as the
coming army grew in size. The Highlander had not left
as MacCuaig had promised. And he brought allies.

Screaming they moved to barricade the town wall
gate and block the broken sections of the wall. Their
only hope was to keep McTiernay's army outside the
town walls until support arrived. Runners had been sent
to find other MacCuaig soldiers, but most of the men
had scattered throughout the town or were looting
within Lochlen's outer walls.

Dunstan clansmen and women recognized the fear
on the MacCuaig soldiers' faces and began anew in their
fight. Their laird had returned.

Gannon glanced around. A blood-spattered battle-axe
was on the ground. Grabbing it, he pumped it in the air.
"Dunstans! Open that gate! Show our laird that we *are*
men of honor. That we know where he belongs. With
us!" A roar of renewed purpose erupted just before a
loud crack filled the air.

MacCuaig's men gathered near the gate heard the Dunstan cry followed by a thunderous sound they assumed to
be a lightning bolt. Moments later crazed Dunstan men
and women came from nowhere attacking with a wild
vengeance. Anything that could stab, puncture, or slice was
being used. Realizing their numbers would not hold the
gate, MacCuaig soldiers attempted to retreat, only to discover that Conor and his men had already breached the
troops securing the broken portions of the wall.

Within minutes, Dunstans freed the gate and pulled the
portcullises open. Riders from allied Lowland clans crossed
the threshold. As understanding of their circumstances

crept into their awareness, MacCuaig soldiers tried to flee or surrender. Those who decided to fight the impossible odds died quickly.

Ending the last skirmish, Conor looked around. No more MacCuaigs were in sight. He joined the other lairds to discuss the next move.

"MacCuaig's men have vanished," Boyd said, stating the obvious.

"They are here," Moncreiffe countered with conviction. "And they are numerous."

"Aye," agreed Conor. "I saw masses of them pour out of the outer gate as I was fighting."

Crawford took a deep breath and exhaled in disgust. "They must have seen our numbers and are hiding. They are just biding their time to attack or flee."

Conor smiled and said, "Then I suggest we change our style from fighting to hunting. Just remember the inner walls of Lochlen are to be untouched until Colin says it is time."

Boyd moved his men to skirt the western town wall, Crawford did the same for the east, and Moncreiffe guarded the openings so that Conor and Donovan could skirt the northern and southern portions of the town wall. Once all were in place, Conor gave the battle cry and they moved forward investigating every house, every recess, every hiding possibility. The MacCuaigs had a choice—immediate surrender or death.

Leon was at the Pinnacle Tower about to appraise his new wealth in goods when he heard the battle scream. That was no thunderbolt.

He had assumed the distant ongoing clanking of metal swords to be a few Dunstan clansmen fighting for their lives. He glanced up as lightning streaked across the darkened sky, followed by an icy wind. The battlements on two of the towers were empty of men. Instinct told him they had not retreated because of the impending storm. Not a drop of rain had yet fallen, but soon it would be pouring from the sky.

Leon headed toward Canmore Tower. So the Highlander had not left the Lowlands as he had led everyone to believe. It mattered little. Leon still possessed what he had come for. He had Makenna.

"You!" Leon screamed at one of the guards standing in front of the main entrance to the great hall. "Go tell those not standing watch to close and bar the main gate!"

The man scurried away, and Leon continued toward his destination. He was just passing the Black Tower when the wind kicked up and his senses came alive. He stopped cold and his heart began to pound. He was too late. McTiernay was already inside. MacCuaig turned and disappeared.

Conor surveyed the last group of MacCuaigs captured and ordered them to be brought outside the town wall and held with the others. The men obviously had not supported their laird's decision to attack their neighbor. Too many of them had surrendered rather than fight to their death.

Hearing a rider approach, Conor turned around, whipping his claymore into position. Immediately, his arm slackened at his seeing Drake.

Drake swung off his horse. "Colin sent me to find you."

Following Conor's lead, the other lairds dismounted and circled around the young commander as he used a stick to outline Colin's plan.

Easing back to a standing position, Conor rubbed his

chin and then nodded. "Seamus, go tell the men we advance on Lochlen. Colin is ready."

Makenna wiggled her numb fingers, feeling the coarse rope of her bindings against her wrists. She drew a lungful of air and exhaled. Her breath was briefly visible before it disappeared. She thought about shouting at the guards stationed just outside the door to light the hearth but decided she would rather wait for MacCuaig. Having him delay his intentions until the room was warm might give her the time she needed.

A shout filled the air, then another. Then came the screams. The battle being fought was clearly one-sided and coming from the great hall. Something had changed MacCuaig's mind about keeping her people alive to be used against her as leverage. They were dying.

Makenna resumed her struggle against her bindings. Tricking MacCuaig into sending her to the solar seemed like a brilliant plan. She could retrieve the sword Camus made for Colin, and with some luck, use it to kill MacCuaig.

Luck, however, had different plans.

First, MacCuaig had not brought her to the solar, but a huge nameless brute. Luck continued to desert her when the soldier conducted an infuriatingly good search of the room. Upon finding a hidden halbert in Colin's chest, he decided to bind her to a chair rather than leave her free until MacCuaig arrived. After ensuring that the rope could not be untied, he left her to freeze.

She still had hope. The guard had not found the true reason behind her desire to be brought to the solar. Colin's sword was still hidden. But, unless she could find a way to loosen her bonds, there would be no way for her to retrieve the heavy weapon and attack an unprepared MacCuaig.

Pain shot through Makenna's arm as more skin ripped against the ropes. She knew her efforts were in vain. Her struggles seemed only to tighten the knots binding her.

Approaching footsteps caught Makenna's attention. She stilled and prepared her mind for what was about to come. She could hear the door behind her swing open and refused to turn around.

"You are a monster, and Colin will send your soul to hell for what you are about to do," she promised.

Heavy footsteps approached, and Makenna felt her bindings loosen. A rich-timbred voice vowed softly in her ear, "Aye, he will."

Suddenly, she was free and in Colin's arms, his mouth covering hers. Makenna clung to him as he crushed her to him with a savage intensity, seeking proof she was alive, and still his. He moved his mouth over hers, devouring her softness.

Finally, Colin eased his lips from hers. His love for her was abundantly clear in the depths of his blue gaze. She was safe and loved. Colin had come for her, just as she knew he would.

Lifting her hand, she brushed a dark lock freed from its leather bonds and tucked it behind Colin's ear. There were tears in his eyes. "Colin?"

He planted a gentle kiss across her forehead. "Forgive me. I never knew such terror as I have known these past hours. I love you more than I ever thought it possible to love another. When I saw MacCuaig . . . with you . . . I . . ."

Makenna held his head between her palms. "I wasn't afraid. I knew you would save me. *And you did*, Colin. You did save me."

Colin's eyes swam with doubt. "The baby?" he barely choked.

"Fine. We are fine." She kissed him briefly, reassuring him that what she said was true.

As she pulled her hands away, Colin was reminded of her bloody wrists. He grabbed her forearm firmly and examined the damage. Suddenly his face contorted into a cold nightmare. Makenna remembered him telling her that she had never seen him angry. He had been correct. For never before had she seen him thus.

"Are you hurt anywhere else?" he asked, his voice low and strained.

Makenna pulled free and took a step back. "I did this, Colin. I was struggling against the ropes to get free and I . . ." Makenna stopped talking. Her explanation was not mollifying Colin, but only inflaming his anger. It suddenly occurred to her that it sounded as if she were defending MacCuaig. "He bound me, but only my wrists were injured. We need to save Doreen and the others. I heard them screaming . . ."

Colin's gaze shifted from her wrists to her face and eased a little. Then he took her hand and headed to the solar door. "That was not our clan you heard, that was MacCuaig's men."

Makenna stopped short. "Not *our* clan? I thought you . . ."

"Left them defenseless?"

"No, not exactly. But . . ."

"But what, love? When I agreed to be the Dunstan laird, it was a decision for life. It was not I who doubted if I should or even could handle the responsibility. The clan needed a reason to join me unconditionally, and I needed a decisive way to determine who had aligned themselves with MacCuaig. If I had not left, it might have taken years for the Dunstans to unite behind my leadership."

Makenna's lips parted in surprise. "Why, that is . . ."

Colin smiled and kissed the tip of her nose. "Fiendishly clever?"

"Aye."

Colin took her hand again and pulled her toward the exit. "Come, we must go. MacCuaig no doubt will be searching for a way to come and retrieve you before he flees."

Just before they got to the door, Makenna turned and ran to the bed. "Wait! Your sword!"

His brows drew together questioningly as he looked down. His sword was hooked in his belt. Curious to see what she meant, he watched as Makenna ran to their bed and pushed the mattress to the side. The effort revealed a gold basket-hilted broadsword embedded with the same jewels he thought had been buried with Alexander. Makenna must have removed them. From the beginning, she had seen him as the Dunstan laird.

Colin picked up the blade and knew instantly Camus had fashioned it specifically for him. It was perfectly balanced and weighted. The intricate pattern on the hilt was a detailed combination of Lowland and Highland symbols placed in such a way that showed unity rather than opposition or conflict. He knew without asking that Makenna had conceived the unique design.

A booming voice interrupted his awe over the unexpected gift. "Colin!" It was Dunlop.

Clutching the new sword in one hand and Makenna's fingers in his other, Colin headed toward the door. They rounded the stairwell quickly and soon exited the tower into the frigid night air. Flames from the lit torches around the courtyard flickered wildly in the wind. Drops of rain were beginning to fall, warning of the impending cold, wet weather.

Dunlop was the first to spot Colin entering the court-yard. Seeing Makenna beside him, Dunlop smiled in relief. "Glad to see you, milady." Then he turned to Colin and spoke. "Lochlen's men and women remain in the great hall, but they are now being protected by your men. Conor just sent a runner saying the fight is com-plete and he, Crawford, Boyd and the others should be arriving any moment."

"What about MacCuaig?"

Dunlop shook his head without attempting to hide his frustration. "We have not found him, Laird, but every entrance has been sealed. There have been sol-diers surrounding the castle capturing all who try to flee. He must have left before then."

Colin briefly glanced at Makenna and gave his com-mander a speaking glance. "He is still here."

Dunlop didn't argue. "Then, there is no way he can leave." Pointing to the inner gatehouse, Dunlop an-nounced, "Your brother just arrived, and he brought friends . . . and a woman."

Colin walked over to meet his allies, grasping the arms of each man in gratitude. He pointed toward the lower hall and asked everyone to assemble in the warm shelter.

Makenna ignored Colin when he indicated for her to follow. Her eyes watched as Conor semidragged Lela Fraser by the arm and into the inner yard. Her hands were bound and a nasty gash cut through her gown had bloodied her upper arm. Seeing the way she favored it, Makenna guessed it hurt.

Conor stopped in front of Colin holding Lela to his side. "This one got a nice reminder of what happens when you betray your own people. Said she was MacCuaig's woman."

Lela scowled and stared directly at Makenna. "I am. Leon will protect me, and I will see you dead."

Makenna raked her eyes over the hateful woman. She felt nothing. Not hate, not pity, not even the desire to engage her verbally. Turning, Makenna reached up and touched Colin's shoulder. "Don't bother. She wouldn't understand anything you said."

Lela snapped, "You think I am alone, Makenna *Mc-Tiernay*! Even your own sister, Ula, hates what you have done. She wanted to know everything! She even wanted to know how she could help me get rid of you."

Colin looked down at Makenna as Lela continued shouting. He was surprised to find a quiet serenity staring back at him. "Seamus, take her away," he ordered quietly and linked his arm with Makenna's before heading to the lower hall.

Upon entering, Makenna immediately sought the warmth of the hearth. Colin joined the men assembled around one of the larger tables. "How's the battle outside?"

Conor gave a relaxed shrug. "As expected. Most of the noise has been the capture of MacCuaig soldiers. We are holding them until you have decided what to do. Only a few chose to fight."

"The Dunstans?"

"Very few deaths. The men are separating those who died fighting against the MacCuaigs from those who fought with them. Have you found the vermin?"

"He is still here, cowering."

"What do you suggest?" Moncreiffe asked.

Colin was about to reply when Makenna stepped forward and offered, "I know one way to get Leon to come out."

"How is that, Lady Makenna?" Donovan inquired as he stroked his thick gray and yellow beard.

Makenna smiled at the older man known as the Lion. "Appeal to his pride. His warped sense of pride."

Colin eyed his wife for several seconds and then exited the hall without a word. Everyone followed despite the worsening weather.

Minutes later, Colin reappeared in the courtyard with Lela in tow. "MacCuaig!" Colin bellowed, his voice cutting through the whipping rain. "Show yourself! I give you a chance to fight me, only me, and determine who is the better swordsman."

Seconds later, MacCuaig stepped out from the chapel enclosure and advanced toward Colin. "And if I win?" His confident swagger was of a man who knew the unmatched level of his skills.

"Then you go free."

"And what if I want more?"

Makenna watched as Lela smiled triumphantly.

"If you want Lela, you can have her, for if I see her again, I'll have no qualms returning her to you dead."

The wind caught Leon's laughter and distorted the evil sound. "Why would I want her?"

Lela spun around. "Because I helped you! I gave you everything you asked for! Spies, people to weaken the wall, even me."

MacCuaig spun his sword around in his hand so that the metal blade blinked in the torchlight. "Ah, lovely Lela. You were fun . . . for a while, but of late you have been burdensome and how can I put it . . . boring. My tastes have always been for more fiery women," he finished, staring lustfully at Makenna.

"Her! You told me you wanted to see her dead!"

Leon's eyes shifted from Makenna to Lela and back

again. "I intend to have so much more than just my freedom. I want Makenna."

MacCuaig paused waiting for Colin's reaction, knowing that emotion—especially rage—was most debilitating to swordplay. Colin never flinched. MacCuaig narrowed his eyes wondering if he had been correct all along. Colin never did care for Makenna or the Dunstans. Only pride had brought him back to help them fight. "Then again," MacCuaig continued, "with you gone, I assume there would be nothing in my way of me staying here with my prize."

"Then you accept."

"I do."

Colin turned to his commanders and then to Conor. "You heard the terms. Abide by them. MacCuaig returns to his lands unharmed, and Lela is of no consequence. Regardless of what happens, she is to be banished."

Conor grimaced and nodded in affirmation. He had heard the terms. Not one MacCuaig soldier had been negotiated and neither was permanent peace part of the package. If by some accident MacCuaig lived tonight, he would return to his lands, but he would not live to see the next day. Conor would invade and exact revenge.

Colin glanced up at the stormy sky as he shrugged out of his leine. The rain was spitting and lightning continued to light the sky. At any moment, it would begin to pour. Colin welcomed the slippery distraction. Battles were fought in all types of weather, and he doubted MacCuaig had spent much time on the battlefield acclimating himself to the elements.

MacCuaig followed Colin's lead and removed his shirt.

Colin grabbed the sword Makenna had made for him

and surveyed his opponent. Despite his preference to fight indoors, MacCuaig looked surprisingly calm and unaffected by the weather.

Makenna clutched her arms as the two men prepared for battle. They faced each other in nothing but their tartans secured by leather belts. Colin's dark hair was tied back with a piece of leather, but MacCuaig chose to leave his sandy locks loose in the rising breeze.

A muscle in the side of Colin's jaw jumped. The approaching storm could not compare to the one swirling in the depthless waves of Colin's sapphire eyes.

Slowly they began to circle each other as if walking on opposite sides of an invisible ring only the pair of them could see. MacCuaig suddenly lunged forward with his body weight, thrusting his blade into the space where Colin had been standing. Stunned by Colin's unexpected celerity, MacCuaig almost did not move in time to deflect Colin's following stroke.

Both had tested the other and found neither without skill. Lightning streaked across the sky. Thunder followed, but both men remained oblivious of nature's show as they once again took a revolving stance.

MacCuaig began to taunt Colin. "You play yourself off as the trainer of men, not as a swordsman. But I see I have been deceived. Perhaps that is why my Makenna takes to you so. She always enjoyed playing with swords. Perhaps after she sees your defeat, she will move her affections to me."

Makenna wondered how much of MacCuaig's words were reaching their target. But when Colin glided around again so that she could see his expression, she realized her husband had become another man. It was MacCuaig, too consumed with his own arrogance, who did not realize the danger he was in.

Unused to a slow, methodical opponent, MacCuaig

lurched forward, spinning quickly to pull out a hidden dagger in an attempt to slice Colin as he twisted out of the way. Usually the move ended the life of his opponent, but Colin emerged on his right with just a superficial slice to his side, but no more.

MacCuaig glared at the nimble Highlander. Not only did Colin not appear to be in pain, but he looked calm, almost bored. Enraged, MacCuaig quickly slashed the air as a distraction before running with his broadsword determined to puncture it through the Highlander's heart.

Again, Colin easily deflected the attack.

Immediately, MacCuaig spun and executed a number of skilled thrusts, expecting one of them to find his target. Instead, the sound of metal echoed in the air as Colin thrust, pivoted, blocked, and thrust again.

Suddenly the rain began to fall.

MacCuaig fought a shiver and rallied. Colin might think he was an equal in swords, but very few were skillful enough to fight with equal facility with either hand. MacCuaig prepared his grip to make the switch. The unexpected stunt should leave Colin vulnerable for a few seconds—but that would be all MacCuaig needed.

Colin watched as MacCuaig performed the telltale signs of an imminent hand switch and quickly executed the maneuver himself. The unanticipated ability stunned MacCuaig. Colin seized the opportunity and sliced Mac-Cuaig across his chest. The wound was not deep, but very painful.

Blinded by rage and stinging rain, MacCuaig lunged forward right into Colin's sword. It pierced him straight through.

Colin pushed the man who dared to take his wife off his blade. He watched unremorsefully as MacCuaig fell into muddy pools of water.

Makenna rushed to Colin and buried her head into his chest. Colin stabbed his sword into the ground and pulled her close to him.

Makenna watched as the men led a screaming Lela out of the gate. Suddenly she was cold and Colin was the only one able to make her warm again. "Do you think Lela was right? Was Ula working with her? Does my own sister hate me that much?"

"No, I don't think it's true. I have been watching Mac-Cuaig for some time. Never did we see anyone indicating Ula or Rona continued their support of MacCuaig after they left. Most likely, Ula had only been a sympathetic ear. It's over, love. It's finally over."

Makenna kissed the wet skin of his chest, refusing to leave his arms. "No, *annsachd*, it is finally the beginning."

Chapter Nineteen

Makenna studied the crowded hall brimming with joy, laughter, and merriment. She knew similar scenes were taking place in the yards, the town, as well as the training fields now overflowing with soldiers. The last two feasts at Lochlen had been somber events that ended with men, women, and neighbors choosing sides. Tonight those neighbors and clansmen felt nothing but a bottomless peace and satisfaction.

The day after the attack, Makenna awoke in Colin's arms and took a deep breath of the fragrant air. The storm that had blown in had left as quickly, bringing in the last warm taste of fall. In a few weeks, the cold would return, and this time it would not leave until the spring.

Later that morning, Laurel and Ceridwin returned to Lochlen with nonstop questions. Finally, when they were satisfied, Laurel suggested that before everyone returned to their homes for the soldiers to stage some competitive games for all to come and enjoy. Meanwhile they would prepare a feast to celebrate the victors.

Makenna leaped on the idea knowing it would be at least a year before she and Colin would see Laurel again. Her only fear was there would not be enough help to prepare for such an event. Already she knew her staff would be stretched thin just cleaning rooms and seeing to the needs of the visiting lairds. Two hours after Colin and the other lairds agreed to host the tournament her concerns were no more.

Arriving in the village courtyard by the clan's request, Makenna and Colin surveyed the huge crowd. It was hard to believe that only yesterday Colin had made them aware how loyalty ran both ways. Their laird had returned, and it was now their turn to support him. They had identified knowledgeable people to rebuild the wall, and a mason to ensure that it was done correctly. No castle staff position remained emptied, and there were volunteers to help while the visitors stayed at Lochlen.

The result was an incredible success. For the past three days, games had been conducted followed by dancing and feasting. However, tonight's festivities outdid them all. Everyone knew that tomorrow brought good-byes, and everyone intended to make the night last as long as possible.

Alliances had been strengthened among the Moncreiffes, Crawfords, Boyds, and Donovans. One of Donovan's men had been proclaimed the grand champion, while several others representing each of the clans sported the title of champion for individual events. Dunlop had agreed to be Laird Donovan's commander and continue to train his army. Drake was going to oversee the MacCuaigs and ensure that there was no further uprisings until Robert the Bruce decided how matters should be settled, but the best announcement of all came from Colin, who declared he was soon going to be a father.

The pride and joy on his face as he spoke left no doubt how he felt about the idea of having a son or daughter. And if anyone wondered how much he loved his wife, he or she only had to look at him or see one of the many embraces he publicly pulled Makenna into to understand the depth of his feelings.

Makenna began to clap to the rhythm of the dance and felt Colin's arms sneak around her waist. Her heart sang with delight. She knew he was about to swing her back into another reel. Then suddenly his arms were gone and Laurel was yanking her toward one of the few vacated spots across the room. Makenna looked back and saw Conor leading Colin away.

Feeling Laurel tug again on the sleeve of her gown, Makenna turned toward her friend, who immediately began speaking. "Makenna, Conor tells me that we are to leave on the morrow."

The news had been expected, but still hard to hear. In the past few weeks, Laurel had given her so much—friendship, confidence, and a new female confidante, Ceridwin, with whom to share husbandly frustrations and dreams of the future. "Oh, I will miss you so, but I know that you will be glad to see Braedon and Brenna once again."

"Yes, while I admit that at the beginning I enjoyed the break knowing they were safe and well cared for, I yearn to see my babies."

"I wish you a safe journey. Hopefully I will be able to persuade Colin to travel north and visit soon."

Laurel waved her hand at the idea. "Well, not this spring—you will be too great with child. But do not worry. We will visit again, and I hope often. Until then, I wanted to give you a couple of wise words imparted to me when Conor and I were married."

Makenna almost reminded Laurel that she had been married for several months now, but did not have the heart to squelch the eager sparkle in Laurel's blue-green eyes. "And what were these juicy morsels of wisdom?" Makenna asked.

"You can never change a Highlander. I know it sounds obvious, but you will find yourself trying to do it nonetheless."

Makenna grinned and whispered back, "Just as long as Colin realizes he shouldn't try changing this Lowlander's odd ways either."

A slow infectious grin grew on Laurel's face before she erupted in laughter. Following Makenna's warm green gaze, she spied her husband looking lustfully her way. "That brings me to my last bit of wisdom. Remain your wild, unpredictable self. He will try to place all these rules on you . . . let him for his peace of mind. But when he . . ."

Conor picked up two quaiches filled with ale, handing one to Colin. "Enjoy the merriment, Colin, for you have married yourself a wild mare that will not leave you any relaxation."

Colin smiled and accepted the drink, keeping his gaze locked on clover-green eyes sparkling at him from across the room. "I would not have it any other way."

"Listen to my words, or you will suffer my fate."

Colin furrowed his brow and gave his older brother a brief sidelong glance infused with curiosity. Laurel was the love of Conor's life, a fate not suffered, but relished. "And what dire future do you see for me? For I can see only beauty and happiness in my path."

Laurel's laughter filled the hall, and Conor was temporarily transfixed by his wife as she tipped her head back, causing blond waves to tumble over her shoulders and shimmer in the firelight. He wondered whether he would ever become used to her beauty. Her laughter, even today, still entranced him.

Conor took a large swallow and then used his quaich

to point across the room. "The fate of a beautiful, strong-willed wife. Such a fate will give you no peace. You would be wise to lay down the rules now or you have no chance."

Colin almost choked on his ale when Conor spoke his last words. Had the man been blind? Did he not realize that Makenna thought rules were things to be broken, not followed?

Conor saw Colin's look of defeat and laughed. "Then again, it seems you are already lost to your fate. It can only be endured if you love the woman."

Colin grinned. "Then my fate is sealed, and it will be a happy one."

"Aye, but now I must warn you about wives when they become strong-willed mothers. . . ."

Colin barely heard his brother when Makenna captivated him with a private smile meant just for him. He knew he would hear an earful from Conor later as he left his brother's side knowing that Conor was still in the process of warning him about his future. Colin also knew that it would be worth it.

"And now about babies . . ." Makenna heard halfheartedly as she listened to her sister-in-law's well-intentioned advice. Most of her attention was on the huge Highlander coming toward her. His sapphire eyes were full of mischief and love and unabashed pride that Makenna was his. She would never get enough of this man, and he was all hers.

"Excuse me, Laurel, but I must steal my wife from your side for just a moment."

Laurel stood with her mouth open. "Again?" she asked in exasperation.

"Aye," Colin replied as he swept Makenna behind a nearby wooden partition hiding them from the others.

"Again and again," he added as his mouth came down possessively on hers.

Makenna giggled and asked between his teasing nibbles, "What did you want?"

Colin shrugged, still holding her close to him. "That's not a tough question. I want to be inside you. I want to feel you wrapped around me, shivering with your pleasure. I want to know exactly how much you need me."

Makenna playfully slapped his shoulder. "No, seriously!"

He raised his head and looked down, his expression both tender and sincere. "I am serious, but I also wondered whether my lovely sister-in-law was imparting some last words of marital wisdom."

"Aye, how did you know?" Makenna asked, wrinkling her brow in puzzlement.

Amusement flickered in his eyes. "I, myself, was a recipient of my brother's wealth of spousal knowledge. But what he failed to realize . . ." Colin said, pausing to nibble on her neck.

"What?" Makenna returned, arching her head back to give him better access.

Colin pulled himself back just far enough away and smiled down at the emerald gems sparkling with love. "That this Highlander knows where he belongs."

Put a Little Romance in Your Life With
Georgina Gentry

Cheyenne Song
0-8217-5844-6
$5.99US/$7.99CAN

Apache Tears
0-8217-6435-7
$5.99US/$7.99CAN

Warrior's Heart
0-8217-7076-4
$5.99US/$7.99CAN

To Tame a Savage
0-8217-7077-2
$5.99US/$7.99CAN

To Tame a Texan
0-8217-7402-6
$5.99US/$7.99CAN

To Tame a Rebel
0-8217-7403-4
$5.99US/$7.99CAN

To Tempt a Texan
0-8217-7705-X
$5.99US/$7.99CAN

Available Wherever Books Are Sold!

Visit our website at **www.kensingtonbooks.com**.